THE DARK ARCHIVE

Genevieve Cogman started on Tolkien and Sherlock Holmes at an early age, and has never looked back. But on a perhaps more prosaic note, she has an MSc in Statistics with Medical Applications and has wielded this in an assortment of jobs: clinical coder, data analyst and classifications specialist. She has also previously worked as a freelance roleplaying-game writer. Her hobbies include patchwork, beading, knitting and gaming, and she lives in the north of England. *The Dark Archive* is the seventh novel in her Invisible Library series.

By Genevieve Cogman

THE
DARK
ARCHIVE

GENEVIEVE COGMAN

PAN BOOKS

First published 2020 by Pan Books
an imprint of Pan Macmillan
The Smithson, 6 Briset Street, London EC1M 5NR
Associated companies throughout the world
www.panmacmillan.com

ISBN 978-1-5290-0060-3

1 3 5 7 9 8 6 4 2

A CIP catalogue record for this book is available from the British Library.

Typeset by Palimpsest Book Production Ltd, Falkirk, Stirlingshire
Printed and bound by CPI Group (UK) Ltd, Croydon, CR0 4YY

MIX
Paper from
responsible sources
FSC® C116313

Visit www.panmacmillan.com to read more about all our books
and to buy them. You will also find features, author interviews and
news of any author events, and you can sign up for e-newsletters
so that you're always first to hear about our new releases.

To all librarians, whatever sort of librarian you are and wherever you may be.

ACKNOWLEDGEMENTS

Sometimes characters come back – even if you killed them off five books earlier. Is it necromancy when an author brings them back to life?

Some of the events in this book had been planned all the way back in book one. Others are new – as Lois McMaster Bujold has said, the author always reserves the right to have a 'Better Idea'. (Of course, sometimes those ideas come part-way through the story and necessitate huge rewrites, but that's life – or at least, that's writing.)

Many thanks to my editor, Bella Pagan, whose questions and guidance turned this book into something which I could be pleased to have written. Thanks to Lucienne Diver, my agent, for her support, and to my beta-readers and friends, Beth and Jeanne and Phyllis and Anne, Aliette and Charlie and Stuart and Sarah, for your suggestions and comments. Thanks to my family for being there when I needed them – and thanks to Crystal for the names of certain dragons.

Thank you to everyone who helped in the creation of this story. Authors act on the world around them, and it acts on us; imagine, if you will, a whirlpool sucking up everything around it, physically and electronically and hypothetically, and feeding it all into the author's head, and a book eventually spooling out through the author's fingers. You may be somewhere in that universe that I borrow from, and that I use when writing – if so, thank you.

This book was written and edited in a world with problems ranging from climate change to COVID-19, and that's just within the letter C. Different people get different things from stories: it may be a moment of distraction from the present trouble, or a daydream for the future, or a thought which makes sense of the past, or something entirely different. If you enjoyed this book, then I'm glad. Thank you for letting me tell you a story.

PROLOGUE

My dear Irene,

What on earth is going on? You've reported kidnap and even assassination attempts? You've done your best to make them sound inconsequential, but having half a dozen werewolves try to snatch you out of your cab is not normal. Nor – whatever your friend the detective says – is an attempt to drug and abduct you over supper. His perspective on the subject is severely biased. I'm sure these things happen to him all the time. And while Prince Kai may also shrug at assassination attempts, his family would take a far more serious view.

Irene, you simply can't treat these things as normal. I realize the last year or so has been more than a little stressful. However, you're getting blasé and that's dangerous. I would suggest you take a vacation – but at the moment you're very close to being essential, and handling some very important problems on behalf of the Library. (Don't get smug. Nobody's totally essential.) If these attacks are due to criminal elements within Vale's homeworld, then get Vale to sort them out. Or if they're being organized by someone from outside your posting – by Fae or dragon – then get more information, and fast.

Speaking of very important problems, your request to take on a Fae apprentice has caused some controversy and has led to a great

1

deal of discussion. I know it was to get the Fae to commit fully to our peace treaty, but some Librarians still don't like it.

It won't surprise you to know that we have had previous attempts at this. They all failed. We have no record of a Fae ever managing to enter the Library – meaning that no Fae has ever managed to become a Librarian. In addition, we both know that the Fae aren't interested in the training you'd offer their candidate (researching, filing, subterfuge, theft et cetera). They want one of their kind to have access to the Library. (Despite the peace treaty between them, us and the dragons, everyone's still looking for advantages.) But equally, a Fae loyal to the Library and indisputably on our side would be an advantage for us.

As Melusine has pointed out repeatedly, as head of internal security, one of our greatest strengths is our privacy. Fae can't enter the Library at all. Dragons can only enter if brought in by a Librarian. This has helped keep us safe from invasion in the past. If you – somehow – manage to get a Fae in here, you'll be setting a precedent which will change our security protocols forever. And if Fae can enter the Library, then what about other creatures of chaos? What about Alberich? He was so chaos-contaminated that he might as well have been Fae.

By now you're wondering what we actually decided about your apprentice. It was nearly sent back to committee for another discussion, with a due date of this time next year. However, I'm glad to say that we do have an answer. Or at least a partial answer.

You may take this response back to the Fae: The elder Librarians have no record of any Fae entering the Library or taking oaths as a Librarian. However, the Librarian Irene can accept a Fae apprentice for a trial period if the apprentice sincerely wishes to become a Librarian. Irene shall then do her best to help this apprentice enter the Library. If this proves impossible after two years, then we will negotiate the situation further. *They'll probably want to push the 'two years'. You have permission to let yourself be argued up to five years if necessary. Do your best to stick to two, though.*

Unfortunately, we'll be thoroughly bound by this agreement, without wiggle room. We're going to have to get a Fae into the Library (posing a security risk to us), or provide unarguable reasons why we can't. And if we don't succeed, the Fae will believe we won't do it, rather than can't do it. It's what you call a lose–lose situation. I'm not saying this is treaty-breaking stuff, but it will tarnish their opinion of us and make negotiating future concessions that much more difficult. Blame yourself, Irene: you've acquired a reputation as the Librarian who can do anything!

I'll have someone bring you our research on the subject of Fae, Entering Library, Failure to. *It may give you some ideas of where to start, or at least what not to repeat. (Don't try to channel lightning from a thunderstorm. That always goes wrong. Yes, personal experience.)*

As when you took Kai as our first dragon apprentice, I need to warn you: absolutely no harm must come to our up-and-coming Fae apprentice. (Do give my regards to Kai, by the way. How's he doing?) If she gets damaged in any way, you'll have to answer for it. Keep us informed, especially if problems arise.

Looking back at this letter, I may seem overly negative. What you're about to try may be a great step forward, and I appreciate that. But progress can lead to danger too. Please be careful. I do worry about you, you know. (And do something about those kidnappings!)

With affection and concern,
Coppelia
Senior Librarian

PS – Yes, the cough is getting better. Stop asking about it.

CHAPTER ONE

The ether-lamps illuminated the wide tunnel with harsh brightness. Irene estimated that they were about two hundred and fifty feet beneath the English Channel at this point, close to the coast of Guernsey. Fans set at regular intervals in the walls churned the stale air with their burnished brass blades, providing a soft background purr of sound. This was comforting in the otherwise eerie silence. Irene Winters, Librarian and spy, found herself perversely wondering who kept this tunnel dusted. And who polished the brass? But letting herself be distracted was, she recognized, an indication of how nervous she was at being here. She was capable of many things, but she couldn't hold back the sea or save them from an earthquake.

There was a heavy brass airlock at the end of the passage, with overlapping petals of iron and glass set into its roughly circular frame. A control pad with a recessed wheel and two huge levers were embedded in the wall by its side. This Victorian technology was perfectly appropriate, though, given that Irene was on assignment in a Victorian-era world. Her companion, Vale – private detective and the person who'd requested her help down here – was a native inhabitant. But their dapper clothing had been designed for London society, rather than tunnels under the sea. Irene eyed Vale's top hat and suit wryly as she considered her own incongruous hat and veil.

'Is there some reason why this document's been sent through private diplomatic channels, rather than just in the mail? Why did we have to come *here* to collect it?' she asked, feeling suddenly claustrophobic. Vale had been silent for most of their walk down the tunnel – a brooding, thoughtful silence which didn't welcome conversation. But the time had come for more information. After all, she thought with some irritation, she was doing him a favour by accompanying him. The four of them – her, the dragon prince Kai, her new apprentice Catherine and Vale – had come here to Guernsey so that Irene could collect a very specific book for the Library. She'd also wanted to get them away from the recent rash of attacks targeting not only her, but her companions. After they'd arrived, Vale had asked Irene to come on this little subterranean excursion with him. She'd agreed, on condition that they'd get back in time for the book handover. She'd left Kai and Catherine together for some tea, cake and quality conversation. 'I didn't ask earlier in case anyone was listening, but surely down here . . .'

Vale tapped the paved floor thoughtfully with his cane – which, Irene knew, was an electrified swordstick. It was the sort of equipment that Vale, as the greatest detective in London, found useful. When dealing with criminals, werewolves, vampires, cultists and spies, a prudent man took what precautions he could. 'I know I was less than forthcoming earlier, Winters. Your new student places me in a difficult position. Catherine *is* your student and therefore loyal to your Library, one hopes. But she is also Fae, and the niece of Lord Silver. He might be the ambassador from Liechtenstein to the British Empire, but he's also its spymaster in London and highly untrustworthy besides. The risk of Catherine passing information to him, deliberately or otherwise, is far too high. I simply can't take chances on this job.'

'I see your point,' Irene admitted. 'But you must have noticed how much she dislikes her uncle.'

'Precisely the attitude I would cultivate if I were her and wanted to convince you I had no ulterior motives,' Vale replied. He spun the wheel like the tumblers of a safe.

Irene couldn't argue with that. 'Very well,' she said. 'So, since we're now completely alone, and unlikely to be overheard . . . What can you tell me? I should have known you had a motive for coming along, rather than just avoiding our mysterious antagonists.' She softened her words with a smile. Heaven knew she owed him a few favours.

'I'd appreciate your patience for just a little longer, as I would like you to approach the situation with an unbiased mind,' Vale answered. He pulled the nearby lever down with a clang, and the airlock irised open, metal and glass petals retracting into the wall. 'When I show you the document—'

They both fell silent. The air beyond smelled of disinfectant – but below that was the tang of fresh blood.

Immediately on the alert, Irene flattened herself against the tunnel wall, peering through the opening. Vale did the same, their conversation forgotten. The corridor beyond opened into a large room filled with mysterious machinery and radar equipment.

There was still no sound except for the slow turning of the fans.

Vale frowned. He stepped through the airlock, cane ready in his hand. Irene followed a couple of steps behind. She didn't have a weapon on her, apart from a small knife for emergencies. But she did have the Language, a Librarian's most powerful instrument. With it, she could command reality with a single word, and that was dangerous enough.

The chamber appeared to be some sort of control room. Heavy steel and brass switches and toggles were embedded in panels that stretched from floor to ceiling. She could also see lengths of cabling which vanished into ducts in the walls behind. On the primitive radar viewing screens, green circles fluoresced against dark backgrounds. But no targets had been identified – not that she knew what they were tracking. Two rickety metal chairs were positioned in front of the most important-looking controls, but both stood empty.

'Stand where you are, Winters,' Vale said. 'Don't disturb anything.' He began to search the room methodically, examining the equipment. He paid particular attention to the other two passageways out of the room – also sealed with airlocks, though without any security locks of the sort that had blocked their entrance.

'Were you expecting to meet your contact here?' Irene asked.

'Yes. This Guernsey monitoring station has a duty staff of six men. There should be two on duty here.' Vale went down on one knee to check something. 'And an additional five men somewhere within this complex. I happen to know a submarine is currently moored alongside, and the crew should have disembarked here.'

'And the only route in by land was the one we came through?'

'Indeed. And Dickson up on the surface, in the St Peter Port office, signalled them when we were about to come down. He received authorization for us to descend. That was only twenty minutes ago.'

A chill ran up Irene's spine. Someone had known she and Vale would be here – trapped underground. And they'd been met by the smell of blood and the absence of allies. She refused to believe this was a coincidence, given their past few weeks. 'This doesn't look good for us or the staff on this station. But who is the target here?' she wondered aloud.

'It is imperative that I find my contact – and the document I'm here to collect. But let us exercise extreme caution.' Vale rose to his feet. 'The airlock on the right goes to the submarine dock, and the other one leads to the living quarters. I can perceive nothing from the clues here, except that at least one man fell to the ground and suffered a minor injury. There are also some curious scratches, which might or might not be innocent . . . This floor is not conducive to the preservation of evidence.'

'Let's block off the living quarters then, just in case. The last thing we want is an inconvenient ambush from that direction. Or for an aggressor to make an escape.' Irene crossed to the airlock and placed her hand on the opening mechanism. **'Lever which I am touching, bend sideways and out of true.'**

The heavy brass lever warped until she was sure no one – no one human, anyway – would have the strength to straighten it, and another use of the Language would be needed to reopen it. She then listened at the airlock for a moment, but could hear nothing from the other side – no shouts from trapped enemies, no cries for help . . . no unspeakable slithering. She'd seen a lot in her line of work.

'Good work, Winters.' Vale paused at the other airlock. 'I'll open this one. Be ready for anything.'

He pulled the lever, the airlock opened – and three men came bursting through. After anticipating everything and nothing, Irene was almost relieved at this frontal assault. They were moving jerkily, but with unexpected speed and ferocity. Irene stuck her foot out, tripping the beefiest one of their number. He sprawled on the floor and writhed unnaturally, like a broken toy. But the other two turned to face them.

Their aggressors both wore naval uniform, as did the man on the floor. This close, Irene could see the ones facing them had smears of blood on their collars. Even more worryingly, silvery threads glittered in their irises and their faces displayed an inhuman slackness. Their mouths hung open and their heads were cocked oddly, like marionettes. One held a crowbar, and though the other was unarmed, his huge hands were clenched into fists, ready to attack.

In the distance, Irene could hear the sound of running feet. Reinforcements? Or more 'marionettes'? She had to assume the worst. She glimpsed Vale raising his cane, but her attention was on the man lunging at her. With surprising speed, his hands went for her throat. She dodged and let him collide with the wall – but it hardly slowed him. He rose and barrelled towards her again, still moving like a puppet with hands outstretched. As she backed away, she saw a glint of metal at his throat. Something that bulged under the concealing fabric of his collar . . . and *moved*.

Time to finish this. **'Uniform trousers, fall and hobble your wearers!'** she ordered.

The two men crashed to their knees, joining their companion on the floor. Irene noted that none of the three were reacting with the modesty one might expect at such an exposure. And Victorians did have a reputation for prudishness. They merely thrashed in an effort to regain their feet. Even the one who went in for purple silk underwear.

Vale's erstwhile opponent was already rising, so Vale tapped him with his cane. There was a flash of electricity and the man screamed in pain, his back arching, before finally collapsing to lie motionless. Something rippled around the back of his neck, wriggling under his collar like a snake. Irene took a hasty step back.

'What the devil is *that*? Can you do something about it?' Vale asked, as he delivered shocks to the other two men. Both had shed the handicap of their trousers and were jerking to their feet.

'Not without knowing what "it" is,' Irene answered. The Language was a powerful tool, but to use it she needed the correct words. 'Mysterious object wriggling under that man's clothing' was insufficiently precise, as her mentor Coppelia might have put it. Irene smothered a smile, feeling a little giddy as the adrenalin of the fight faded. 'But at least electricity seems to work.'

'Indeed.' Vale was standing over the writhing men. 'But my cane has a limited charge,' he noted, as the screaming died away.

'Airlocks, shut,' Irene ordered. As the remaining airlocks closed, blocking any further attacks, she leaned forward to look at the unconscious men. Curiosity was prompting her to unbutton their collars to investigate what she'd seen, but her imagination was painting a vivid picture of something horrific. Irene wasn't familiar with all the magical monstrosities that Vale's world might or might not contain. Vampires and werewolves she knew about, but what else might there be? She couldn't see enough . . .

'Uniform jacket on the grey-haired man, unbutton and open,' she ordered.

The jacket obeyed, peeling back like wrapping paper. The man's shirt was stained with fresh blood. The thing that moved underneath it was two feet long, writhing and twisting like a length of cable.

'Note the fresh wound on his neck,' Vale said quietly. 'He appears otherwise uninjured. I fear it will not emerge on its own, whatever *it* is. You will need to undress him further.'

11

Irene nodded. Such instructions from the upright Vale would be amusing – under other circumstances. **'Shirt on the grey-haired man, unbutton and open.'**

As the buttons slid from their holes and the shirt-front parted, there was a flash of gleaming metal. Something leapt at her, and Irene took in burning blue eyes and dripping blood. She threw herself backwards, dropping under the creature as it sailed over her head. Vale's cane flashed out to intercept, but missed. The creature curved through the air before landing on the floor, skittering across it. It moved, Irene thought, like a woodlouse rather than a snake – could there be claws or legs underneath it?

More to the point, how did she stop it with the Language? What should she call it – 'metal contraption'? But that would shut down all the equipment in the room. 'Vale!' she shouted. 'Do you know what that thing *is*?'

'No, but don't let it get into the air ducts!' Vale answered. He advanced on the creature, his cane ready.

'Keep it busy.' Irene edged sideways and picked up a nearby stool. She glanced back at the other two men; but no more creatures had emerged.

The creature scuttled along the floor, hugging the wall and trying but failing to writhe into the machinery. Fortunately the panels were all well-sealed. Then it darted at Vale in a horrifyingly fluid rush of speed.

Irene took advantage of the creature's focus on Vale to craft a swift sentence. **'Stool that I'm touching, pin down the moving mechanical creature,'** she ordered in the Language.

The stool tore itself out of Irene's hand, upended itself and slammed into the creature, holding it in place with the seat. Irene rubbed her forehead, wincing at a momentary pain. While it hadn't been a major use of the Language, it was imprecise and had drained her strength. The creature squirmed under the stool, metal legs scraping manically against the floor and leaving long scratches.

'All right,' she said. 'What do you make of it?'

Vale knelt down to inspect it, as thuds came from the blocked airlock door. Irene's earlier work was successfully blocking their entry – for now. 'Interesting,' he said, ignoring the noise. 'I believe I *do* know what this is. It's rather more advanced than reports I've read, though.'

'Is it a device that controls human victims by invading their nervous systems?' Irene 'guessed'.

Vale gave her a hard stare. 'Have you been reading my correspondence again, Winters?'

'Now why would I do that?' she dissembled.

Vale's eyes narrowed, but he eventually relented. 'Yes – this contraption appears to be derived from the work of Doctor Brabasmus. But it is self-propelled . . . and rather larger than the doctor's original designs for cerebral controllers. Those were barely the size of a scarab, and lodged at the back of the neck.'

'What happened to the doctor?'

'Murdered a couple of months ago, and his laboratory looted.' Vale frowned. 'Now, what did he call them?'

Out of the corner of her eye, Irene saw a second creature's head emerge from the neck of its host's jacket. 'Vale,' she said quietly, her eyes flicking towards the creature.

Vale's hand tightened on his cane. 'Brabasmiators, that was it,' he murmured.

Irene froze. That wasn't even good *English*. Why did scientists have to create their own words, rather than use perfectly good existing ones? Did nobody ever think of the poor translators? In desperation she grasped for Vale's earlier description. **'Cerebral controllers, deactivate!'**

The light vanished from the new creature's eyes, and it and the one beneath the stool went limp. A third one stopped its disquieting wriggling under its host's clothing. Irene gave a sigh of relief.

Vale checked for a pulse on the nearest man's neck, then the other two, and shook his head. He rose, dusting his hands off. 'We have no way of knowing how many of the other men on this station are similarly controlled. Inconvenient.'

'Just how important is this document?' Irene asked. 'What aren't you telling me?'

'Under the circumstances, my hopes of you viewing it without prior bias are somewhat pointless. I believe there is a master criminal at large in London, Winters, a manipulator and emperor of crime. I also believe that he is responsible for the recent kidnapping attempts on you, the bullet which nearly hit Strongrock, the stabbing of Madame Sterrington . . . Lord Silver isn't the only foreign spy in London. I was informed that the French Secret Service had obtained some valuable information on this mastermind: a letter which named very interesting names. Our agents had intercepted it and brought it here.' His eyes glittered almost feverishly. 'This is our chance at some proof, Winters, finally. This is my adversary as much as yours. He is striking at all my contacts, all my . . . friends. But I need *evidence*.'

'I see,' Irene said slowly. It made sense that Vale would be invested in this. She didn't voice her deeper concerns, though. In high-chaos worlds, stories and their tropes had a tendency to come true – for both good tales and bad ones. Now London's greatest detective had found a worthy adversary, a master criminal. If this were a story, the two of them would now be bound together – as closely as lovers – until one or the other was dead. She shivered. 'Did you know about this before or after you accepted my invitation to Guernsey?'

'Know about what?' Vale asked, scrutinizing the scratch marks on the floor.

'The evidence about the "emperor of crime".' Irene was deeply, *deeply* irritated that Vale hadn't mentioned these theories earlier, but unfortunately it was true to his character. He was the sort of person – the sort of *detective* – who wouldn't mention his theories until he had evidence to back them up. Vale had Fae blood somewhere in his family tree, and at times he strayed regrettably close to the archetype of the Great Detective – for worse as well as for better.

'Shortly after you planned to visit Guernsey and I agreed to accompany you.' He turned to give her the full focus of his attention. 'You believe it's a trap?'

'Either that, or our timing is extraordinarily unfortunate.' Irene nodded at the corpses. 'What are the odds that we'd walk in just at the moment when they've been controlled and are attempting to kill intruders?'

'If so, then we shouldn't remain here any longer than necessary.' He experimentally flicked a couple of switches and scrutinized one of the viewscreens. 'The submarine is still docked here. Be ready with that Language of yours, Winters. I have no desire to find out first-hand what it feels like to be controlled by one of those creatures. You'll have noticed the scratches on the floor come from the direction of the submarine airlock.'

Irene nodded and stepped back, willing to let Vale take the lead – he was the one with the electric swordstick, after all. She was an agent of the Library, an interdimensional organization that collected books to preserve the balance of worlds. As such, she could use the Language to force reality to her will. But only if she wasn't distracted by cerebral controllers.

However, her stomach remained knotted with tension. If this was a trap, every moment they were down here was a further risk. And they were under the sea here. Even if Kai – dragon prince, colleague, friend and lover – had a natural affinity for water and mastery over it, *she* didn't. Being unable to speak due to drowning could be a great drawback when attempting to use the Language. This all made it an excellent location for an ambush . . .

Of course. 'Wait,' she said. 'What aren't we noticing?'

'Clarify, Winters,' Vale said impatiently.

'We come down here. We're attacked. Our first impulse, so we could get out as quickly as possible, would be to go directly to the submarine to collect the letter. That's where you were supposed to meet your contact. If your reasons for being here have been discovered, are you sure we want to be that predictable?'

'Cogently argued, Winters. Unfortunately, I *need* that letter.'

'I know,' Irene countered. 'I'm just *trying* to think like a master criminal.'

'You hardly need to *try*, Winters.' But there was a certain affection to his words – he knew all about her frequent book thefts. 'Hmm. My logical next step would be to radio the surface and report the situation. Let us see . . .'

He indicated one of the consoles. 'This is the one radio link to the surface. So if I *were* to think like a master criminal, this is where I would place my trap. Can you use your Language to deactivate any such unpleasant surprises?'

Irene knew her mentor Coppelia would have approved. You only needed to be blasé once to be dead. **'All explosive devices or dangerous traps, deactivate,'** she ordered.

There was a tiny but satisfyingly audible click from behind a panel.

Irene and Vale shared a nod. He slid his fingers behind the edging on the right-hand side, pressed two buttons, and the panel swung open. Behind it was a narrow recess, carefully stacked with sticks of dynamite. A wire ran from the small stack, through a tiny hole drilled in the panel and snaked towards the lever that opened the airlock. Positioned on top was a phonograph, loaded with a record and ready to play.

Irene was disturbed. This was very elaborate. First the controlled men, now this dynamite – what next? 'Those men who attacked us – in their condition, there's no way they would have had the intellect to set this up.'

'I agree.' Vale switched on the phonograph. 'Let us see who is leaving us mysterious messages.'

A click. The record began to revolve, and the needle dipped to touch it. There was a noise of rustling paper. 'Good evening,' a male voice said. 'Or possibly afternoon. I'm not sure what time it is where you are. But since you are listening to this and not dead, my congratulations to you, Peregrine Vale.'

Irene's fingers bit into her palms hard enough to hurt and the colour drained from her cheeks. She knew that voice. She'd *killed* its owner. 'Lord Guantes . . .' she said in horror, staring at Vale. He was Fae – a manipulator and plotter who'd tried to touch off a war between the Fae and the dragons. That was why she'd killed him. Irene remembered, uncomfortably clearly, the feeling of the knife sliding between his ribs and the blood on her hands. There was no way she could have been mistaken as to his death.

'Of course,' the recording went on, 'like all things in this life, my congratulations are strictly temporary. You have caused me a great deal of inconvenience, and you are about to pay for it. Don't bother looking for that letter, Mr Vale. It has already left the premises. Which is more than you'll do.'

The blare of an alarm suddenly split the air. Irene spun round, trying to determine where the noise was coming from. Red glass shades slid over the ether-lamps, which flashed in a panic-inducing strobe.

'According to my arrangements, that noise will be the base's self-destruct signal,' Lord Guantes said helpfully. 'I imagine your friends back in the town will have an edifying view of any underwater explosions. Goodbye.' The record clicked off.

The alarm continued to shriek.

CHAPTER TWO

Vale strode to the control panels, flipping switches with the certainty of a man who knew which ones did what. Irene had to admire his thoroughness; very few men would memorize a subterranean base's self-destruct protocols before visiting.

Unfortunately, it didn't pay off.

Vale pressed his lips together in what Irene recognized as a sign of extreme bad temper. She decided it was time for her to attempt their salvation. **'Self-destruct system, deactivate!'** she ordered the air.

Sudden silence fell across the room like a benediction, and the lighting returned to normal.

Irene rubbed her forehead, not sure whether her incoming headache was due to her use of the Language or the alarm. It had been very shrill. *'Your friends back in town*, he said. Lord Guantes didn't expect me to be here.'

'Your presence is greatly appreciated,' Vale said. But there was an undertone to his gracious words, something which suggested he felt somehow . . . cheated?

I've stepped into his private duel with a master criminal, Irene realized. *It feels like an intrusion, however much common sense tells him otherwise, and however much he hates the suggestion he might be affected by Fae archetypes.*

19

'Do we need to do anything to make sure that the self-destruct doesn't, well, self-destruct again?' she asked.

'We must assume that the entire control system is compromised.' Vale eyed the panels of switches with irritation. 'And, as you've just demonstrated, Winters, you can deactivate a *trap* with the Language. But the normal functioning of equipment – such as the self-destruct switch – might not seem like a threat. You may not be able to turn it off fast enough next time.' He moved in closer, inspecting the phonograph. 'Yes. There's a wire behind here – once it finished playing, the stylus lifting off the disc triggered the signal to the self-destruct. He correctly assumed we'd play it to the end.'

'So far he's demonstrated an annoying ability to predict our moves,' Irene muttered.

Vale favoured her with a rare smile. 'He didn't predict that I'd ask you to accompany me, Winters, or that you'd agree.'

'Or that I'd leave Kai and Catherine behind,' Irene said, a cold hand closing round her heart. It had seemed safe enough to leave them alone for a short while, but now . . . 'Vale, we have to get back at once. If Lord Guantes *is* the one who has been attacking us over the last few weeks, you won't be his only target. And if he's to be believed, your letter isn't here anyway. Are we going to have to use that tunnel, or is there a quicker way out of here?'

Any sensible secret base should have an emergency exit, and Vale seemed to have studied its plans. She had to get back to the surface right *now*. If Lord Guantes *had* somehow returned from the grave, then Kai was in great danger. After all, Kai had been Lord Guantes' primary target – and saving him had been the goal of her Venice mission. It felt so long ago now.

Vale frowned. 'There is a quicker way out of here, yes.

But, Winters, we absolutely have to check for that letter. The British government is depending on me.'

'The British government can cope with one more would-be crime lord in London,' Irene retorted angrily. 'Besides, Lord Guantes said it was gone! And I need to protect Kai.'

'Strongrock's capable of looking after himself for five minutes,' Vale countered. 'And Lord Guantes may be lying. I simply can't take that chance.' His face was set and expressionless. She knew that he'd analysed how much danger Kai might be in, just as she had. 'I need your help, Winters.'

For a moment Irene couldn't believe what he was asking. Then practicality cut in, harsh and unwelcome. Vale had a responsibility to the British Empire, even if she didn't – and this wasn't her world, after all. She knew that if she were to say no, Vale would accept it and show her the emergency exit. Five minutes might make the difference between safety and danger for Kai – and Catherine, too. But Vale was her friend, and her help might make the difference between *his* life and death. She couldn't abandon him.

Irene clenched her hands and forced herself to decide. 'All right,' she said. 'But there's no time to waste.'

Prince Kai, the dragons' treaty representative, son of his majesty Ao Guang, King of the Eastern Ocean, once apprentice to Irene Winters and now her lover, but also – and most importantly – her friend, looked out of the teashop window. He wished he could somehow erase the street's heavy grey stone buildings so he could see the ocean beyond. Humans called it the English Channel – if they were English, of course. The French called it La Manche, 'the sleeve', and other nationalities called it something different again. But the sea had its own identity. He could *feel* its presence, its motion, its long heartbeat. The rolling waves and dragging tides sang in his

21

blood and hummed in his bones, soothing his current irritation until he could almost forget it.

Almost. It was very hard to ignore the irritation in question, as she was sitting directly opposite him.

Catherine scribbled in her notepad without looking up, the top of her pen jerking enthusiastically with every added underlining or exclamation mark. She'd bisected the table between them with a barricade composed of the teapot and cake-stand, an unofficial declaration that she wasn't interested in conversation. The harsh ether-lights drained the colour from her golden-brown skin and the red from her chestnut hair, and turned her navy coat dull and drab. She was smaller than he was, so the high back and arms of her chair rose around her like walls. She resembled nothing so much as a minor, but still intimidating, enemy force. And she was ensconced on the other side of his table.

There was no point checking his watch again. It had only been five minutes since the last time. He shook out the local newspaper and skimmed through its contents. Cattle-breeding. French politics. English politics. Radiation experiments in the local tomato greenhouses. Tide tables. He sighed inwardly.

The rain slapped against the window and rattled forcefully on the cobbled pavement outside with a noise like gravel. Men and women hurried past, bundled up in heavy knitted guernseys and shawls. The teashop itself was empty of customers except for the two of them; it was a Tuesday morning, so working men and women were at their jobs. And it was too early for elderly ladies, gossip being their main occupation, to turn up and crowd the tables with nodding bonnets and whispers.

The waitress caught his eye, giving him a smile. Kai gestured at the teapot and obtained a refill.

'Thank you,' Catherine said, putting down her notepad

for a moment. The sentiment wasn't particularly gracious, but Kai decided he'd take it as a victory. Light glinted off her bronze-rimmed glasses as she poured herself another cup, then – remembering after a moment – one for him. 'Anything interesting in the paper?'

'Not particularly.'

'Unsurprising. There's *nothing* of interest here,' Catherine muttered.

'That's not true,' Kai protested. 'There are . . . um . . . purebred cows, buildings left over from the Napoleonic Wars, even a thriving witch-cult. They're known as the Gens du Vendredi, or the Friday People . . .'

'Are they on the agenda for today?'

'Probably not,' Kai admitted.

Catherine planted her elbows on the table. 'This would have been a *quick* pickup job if Irene—'

'Miss Winters,' Kai corrected her.

'She told me to call her Irene,' Catherine said smugly. 'Anyhow. We could have collected our target book and left already if she hadn't gone off with Peregrine Vale. Which she shouldn't be doing.'

Kai was still rather bitter that he hadn't been asked along himself but had been left to take charge of Catherine instead. 'I'm sure he has reasons for asking her.'

'No, you don't get it. She's supposed to be politically neutral in this world, isn't she? Like you? Yet she's hanging out with someone whose sister is high up in the British government. Not only that, but they're visiting a top-secret submarine base together. How can that be neutral?'

That was actually the most politically astute comment Catherine had made since they'd met. Kai had had the dubious pleasure of making her acquaintance just a few weeks ago, and it felt as if she hadn't stopped glaring at him since. He disagreed with her, of course, on principle. 'Vale is a good friend,' he parried. 'She has every reason to spend time with him.'

Catherine rolled her eyes. 'Yes, and pigs fly, and my uncle's planning to take vows of celibacy. Come *on*. Also, I don't see why I had to come in the first place. I could have stayed in London.'

'Irene wanted you to get some first-hand experience of being a Librarian. And when we pick up the Merlin document, that's exactly what will happen.'

'By standing around while she hands over money? I could understand it if she wanted me to learn something cool. But if not, why not leave me behind to do something useful?'

Kai shrugged. 'Irene wanted to give you a thorough grounding in Librarianship. Besides, have you forgotten the recent little . . . unpleasantnesses?' He wasn't sure that Catherine was a target – nobody had tried to kidnap or kill *her*, after all – but he and Irene had both been victims of near misses or failed abductions in the last month. Vale had said he was looking into it, but he had yet to come up with an answer.

Catherine hunched down in her chair, drawing in her narrow shoulders until she seemed even smaller than before. Kai knew that she was in her early twenties, but when she acted like this she seemed no older than a teenager. 'This is so *stupid*. Can't we even go hang out in the local library – the Guille-Allès? I could read something and I wouldn't be getting on your nerves so much.'

'Your uncle doesn't take well to following instructions either.' Lord Silver, Catherine's uncle, was London's biggest libertine and the head of the Liechtenstein spy network. He was generally untrustworthy, devious and well dressed in equal measure.

'Just because my uncle's a miserable excuse for a . . .' Catherine picked through her options, and clearly couldn't find any that satisfied her. 'How can I convince you I don't like him – or trust him – any more than you do?'

Kai felt he should try to be honest. 'He's a Fae, like you. And he's your family, your blood. Of course you're going to be closer to him than you are to us.'

'And you think I'd betray you to him,' Catherine said tonelessly.

Kai had carefully avoided saying just that. To her, at least. He should know what it was like, after all. He lived with his lord father's expectations, and he'd always been aware of his duty. To his family. To his own kind. And to Irene, always.

'Have you been paying *any* attention to me? Any attention at all?' Catherine demanded, her tone rising. She glanced across at the waitress and lowered her voice to an angry hiss. 'Have you noticed what I actually *want*?'

'Well, to do a good job, obviously.' Kai backtracked, trying to work out what he'd said wrong. 'To be a Librarian like Irene, to help keep the truce . . .'

'What I *want*,' Catherine said quietly but emphatically, 'is access to the Library. I want to get in among those books. If Irene can do that for me, for all I care, my uncle can fornicate until syphilis makes his private parts drop off.'

Kai didn't *like* Lord Silver, but his own niece shouldn't be using that sort of language about family. Family was important. 'Control your tongue!' he ordered. 'That is not acceptable.'

'You aren't my boss,' Catherine flared back. 'Where do you get off acting like you're superior – just because you're in bed with her?'

Kai felt the bones grind in his hands as he curled them into fists, the prick of fingernails that yearned to become claws. Anger sang in him as the ocean had done earlier, pride and fury urging him to treat this child – his junior, his younger sister in apprenticeship, his *lesser* – with the proper discipline for such an insult.

She flinched.

Moment by moment, counting his heartbeats, he made himself relax. 'Could you pour me some more tea, please?' he asked.

Her hand shook a little as she poured. 'I'm not getting paid enough for this,' she muttered.

'I didn't know you were getting paid at all.'

'I have an allowance.' Her mouth twisted unpleasantly. 'From my uncle – which means nothing, before you judge me on that too. I thought you knew.'

'I know he and Irene had an argument about it, but I don't know the details.' Kai had sadly not been witness to that.

Catherine visibly perked up at the notion that he didn't know everything, then sighed. 'I don't *want* money, anyhow. I want books.'

'But money gets you books,' Kai pointed out.

'Not the sort of rare "one-per-world" books the Librarians hunt down. That takes connections. The sort you don't seem to want *me* to make, as I'm Fae and not a dragon . . . Whereas I suppose you're letting Irene run mad in your father's library?'

'You may infer what you wish from this, but I *have* invited Irene to visit my lord father's palace and library,' Kai said with dignity. 'But she refused. She said if my lord father hosted her, he'd have to host a Fae representative too – in the spirit of the treaty. That it could cause a diplomatic incident if he wasn't willing to do so.'

Catherine shook her head in wonder. 'I'm glad one of you has some sense. Though, as she's sleeping with the dragons' treaty representative, maybe I'll take that back. Unless to keep things fair, in the spirit of the treaty, she's also sleeping with the Fae representative . . .'

'What do you mean by *that*?' Kai snarled, leaning forward.

'Excuse me, sir, madam.' The waitress had approached while they were distracted.

Kai held up an admonitory hand. 'A moment, please. Catherine, I *demand* an apology.'

'Excuse me!' The waitress had raised her voice. As Kai and Catherine both turned to glare at her, she said, 'There's something you should know, sir, madam.'

'And what is that?' Kai snapped.

'You've both been poisoned.' She folded her hands primly in front of her. 'But please don't let me interrupt you. I can wait.'

CHAPTER THREE

Irene had not expected to walk through a door in a submarine base somewhere under Guernsey, and emerge somewhere entirely different.

She and Vale had managed a successful sweep through the remainder of the base. The other men they'd found had all been under the influence of cerebral controllers. They'd therefore lacked the intelligence to stage more than very basic ambushes, but they'd still fought savagely. As a result, Vale and Irene had had to deactivate all the controllers – which had proved fatal for their victims.

She'd seen Vale's face grow more tense with each new confirmed fatality, the leashed anger showing in his shoulders and the quick jerk of his head. He and Irene were being deliberately manipulated into killing these men – however necessary this was. They too were *victims*, being used as mere tools and then discarded.

You didn't have to be a Fae to be that amoral a manipulator, but Irene couldn't deny that it helped – especially if this was somehow Lord Guantes, returned to gleeful life.

In the criss-cross of passages, the route to the submarine dock wasn't obvious. And yet the longer they'd searched, the more certain Vale seemed that he'd find his letter on the submarine moored there. It was Vale who'd eventually halted and raised a hand for her to wait, then prodded at what looked like a cupboard door with the tip of his cane. The resulting shock knocked him across the room.

The cane lay to one side, smoking. Vale glanced at it regretfully, then back to the door, and his brows drew together in a frown. 'That door shouldn't be there.'

'It's in the wrong location?'

'In a way . . . That door is not on the base's plans. There should be nothing but solid rock at that point. And look – more of the cerebral controllers' scrapes on the floor, spreading out from this point.'

Irene carefully moved her hand towards the door, halting before touching it. The air around it prickled with chaos. As Irene approached, she could feel the Library brand on her back flare in response, rather like a guard recognizing an enemy. The door itself looked like any of the other cupboards on the base: metal, set into the wall and painted dark grey. There was nothing to mark it as significant – except for Vale's knowledge that it shouldn't have been there, his dramatic propulsion across the room and her own recognition of chaotic power.

'That gives us two problems,' she said. 'Finding the letter – and *this*. There's chaos behind it.' To leave this door uninvestigated would be an open invitation for someone to come through and shoot them from behind.

Irene glanced sideways at Vale, saw the uncertainty on his face and made a decision. 'You said we'd find eleven men here – and we've dealt with all of them. I'll check this out while you retrieve the letter.'

There was a flicker of relief in his eyes. 'I'll call if I need you, Winters.'

He ran down the corridor, leaving Irene to stare at the mysterious door. Objects infused with chaotic power often didn't react well to Librarians – and Vale's broken cane served as an additional warning. Fortunately, with the Language she didn't *need* to touch it. When she looked at it more closely, close enough to feel her nose prickle, she could see that there was something written on it *under* the grey paint, barely visible, totally illegible but indisputably there.

She picked her words carefully, not wanting to force open every locker and exit within the sound of her voice. If any others contained dynamite, that could see them both drowned. **'Any bombs within the sound of my voice, deactivate. Door in front of me, unlock and open!'**

It shuddered in its frame. Irene gritted her teeth at the drain on her strength, knotting her hands into fists as the tumblers in a lock audibly clicked open. The door opened towards her, but slowly, as if an invisible hand was dragging it open and it was fighting to resist. Irene peered through the gap.

A shadowed corridor lay beyond – formed of wood and stone, not slate and metal – and dimly lit by distant windows. It definitely wasn't beneath the sea. She had no idea where it was.

Did Vale think that I was just going to stand here and look at it? Well, too late now.

Irene rubbed her forehead with the back of her hand, forcing herself to ignore her growing headache, and stepped through. The door pulled itself shut behind her, closing with a muffled thud.

She sniffed the air. Dust. Paper. Old cigar smoke. The floor was white marble, but even in the dim light she could see the dust that had settled into the cracks. The walls and ceiling were panelled with dark wood; paler rectangles on the walls showed where paintings must have once hung.

But all this was secondary to the tingling which spread across her back like poison ivy, radiating from her Library brand. She felt a sense of dread, suddenly realizing that she'd left Guernsey far behind. And not for a moderate-chaos world like Vale's. This was definitely a high-chaos world, so she probably couldn't reach the Library from here. And if she couldn't retrace her steps, she'd be trapped here . . .

Beyond the window, a futuristic city sprawled out to the horizon, sown thickly with electronic lights under a shrouded twilight sky. The approaching darkness and glow from the lights obscured the buildings, reducing them to shadowy spikes or low shapeless masses. Some more distant structures seemed to curl gracefully upwards and outwards like living organisms, but they were too far away to see clearly. Tiny in the distance, Irene spotted the twinned lights of what might be vehicles – crawling at ground level, or drifting through the air.

Irene suppressed a curse. She'd hoped to identify the city, if not the world, by its architecture, but that was hopeless in the encroaching darkness. As for the climate and temperature, it was neither arctic nor tropical, but beyond that she couldn't guess – or deduce – anything.

At the other end of the corridor, a thin rim of light outlined another door. She listened, but could hear nothing. Either the room beyond was empty, or whoever was there was silent. Or perhaps someone was lying in wait for her . . .

This was no time to hesitate. She tried the door handle.

It opened.

The room beyond had once been a lounge, high-ceilinged and elegant; it had gone to seed just like the corridor behind her. Tall windows in the opposite wall were covered by tattered curtains. The marble fireplace held a radiator rather than logs, and the bare lightbulbs that hung from the ceiling glowed unevenly, as though they might burn out at any moment.

Close to the fireplace, a man huddled in a battered

armchair, a laptop resting on his knees. A cigar smouldered in one limp, gloved hand and the computer screen was blank. The man drooped forward, head nodding, on the edge of sleep.

It was unmistakably Lord Guantes.

She knew that man. She'd *killed* him. She'd put a knife into his heart, then watched his wife mourn over his corpse and promise vengeance.

She could accept alternate worlds, dragons, Fae, vampires, werewolves and magic. But now a part of her – the logical, rational part – urged her to run, to slam the door closed and escape back to the submarine base. Even if all the men there had been turned into lurching zombies by cerebral controllers, at least the threat was something she *understood*.

Lord Guantes had almost gained control over her, once. He'd nearly twisted her around his little finger and made her answer to his bidding. She would have been his pawn, his captive, his tool. Confronting him now was pure idiocy. She had no idea of his resources, how many guards he had or what snares might be waiting for her. Every instinct in her body screamed for her to get out of here. She'd learned what she needed to know. It really was him.

But if she ran, she would always be running from him. She might know enough . . . but there must be still more to learn.

Her mind somewhere on the scale between pure terror and stomach-curdling fear, she made herself say, 'Lord Guantes, I assume?'

His head jerked up and he twisted round in his chair, the laptop clattering to the ground. He still looked just as she remembered: dark grey hair and a small imperial beard, deep-set eyes with the power to compel. His business suit could have come from any decade and almost any world, and the gloves that sheathed his hands were plain black. The

32

left side of his face was concealed by a leather mask which started at his forehead and ended above his upper lip.

'You should be dead,' he said after a moment, his voice deep velvet, but with the old iron behind it. There was something in his eyes that took Irene a moment to recognize. It was . . . fear? He was afraid of her?

'I could say the same about you,' she said. 'Clearly someone has made a mistake.'

At the back of her mind a clock kept counting down. Just because Lord Guantes was here, didn't mean that Kai was safe. Lord Guantes could be working with – or for – anyone.

'Fresh from an imploding submarine base and not even damp.' He looked her up and down. It wasn't the measuring glance of a martial artist judging her competence, or the deliberately insulting appreciation of a libertine like Lord Silver. It wasn't even the cold stare of an assassin deciding how best to remove her. It was as if she was less than human – a paperclip, a crumpled newspaper, a disposable coffee cup – and he could either stand up to put it in the bin, or get away with simply throwing it to the floor. 'What *does* it take to dispose of you, Miss Winters?'

'A miracle,' Irene said promptly.

'According to Dante, thieves like you end up in the Eighth Circle of Hell.'

'Dante placed "evil counsellors" like *you* in the next ditch along,' Irene countered. 'So tell me, Lord Guantes, what precisely are you up to? Besides trying to kill us. You must have some far grander plan than that.'

She was hoping she could play on one of his archetypal weaknesses. Very few Fae who based their personalities on cunning masterminds could resist the urge to gloat. If she was really lucky, he might even go into detail about how very doomed she was . . .

To her surprise, he only laughed. It was a thin, hollow

sound compared with the full-blooded chuckle of their previous encounters. 'Kill *you*? My dear Miss Winters, you have no idea how much I enjoy hearing you say that. And such a brave attempt to learn my secrets, too. But I'm afraid . . .' He coughed, and his whole body shook with it. 'You're too late.'

Irene froze. Anyone who knew her would have known she'd try the mysterious door. Was this all some further elaborate trap?

Then common sense kicked in. He'd been genuinely surprised to see her. He'd been *afraid*.

'You're wasting your time taunting me,' she responded. 'As you can see, I'm still alive. Your *little* plot didn't work.'

As she'd hoped, the adjective stung. His hands trembled, clenching into fists. 'You have no idea . . .' he said, voice smooth again, the words both a promise and a threat. 'As usual, Miss Winters, you have come into the story partway through, and you'll be removed from the gameboard long before you can appreciate the grandeur of this particular plot. It's already too late for you, as I said. Before, you've always had other people to save you. Not any longer.'

'My friends and I keep each other alive. You didn't plan on my accompanying Vale into the submarine base, did you?'

'I admit I failed to make allowances for that – for whatever sentimentality caused you to accompany him rather than do your job. I thought better of you, Miss Winters.'

'Stop playing games,' Irene said flatly, suppressing a growing sense of dread. What if he was telling the truth, and it was 'already too late' for Kai and Vale as well? 'Get to the point – or I'm leaving.'

Lord Guantes frowned at having his gloating so cruelly cut short. 'Very well. It's true that I want revenge on my enemies, but there are others who have something even worse in mind for you. I cooperated with them – but I have been betrayed. I have been *used*.' A deep fury at this flared in his eyes. To a Fae of his archetype – mastermind and schemer – this was the ultimate violation. 'Since you have conveniently walked past my threshold and into my home, I will give you the tools for vengeance. If—'

He broke off, seeming confused for a moment, and raised one gloved hand in protest. 'So soon?' he asked the air.

'Lord Guantes,' Irene said, pitching her voice to get his attention. 'Why *are* you here? In this sordid place, with this old house falling to pieces around you? *Who* are these others you mention?'

His eyes focused on her again. Without answering, he thrust himself out of his chair towards her, tottering as he tried to stand upright.

Irene dodged. She'd been ready for any sort of attack – if this was an attack – but she hadn't expected something so . . . ordinary. Or, to be honest, so uncoordinated. He moved like an old man – or someone who'd been injured but hadn't realized it yet. This was all . . . *wrong*.

The Fae's motion turned into a stagger, then a collapse. He sank to his knees, then to the dirty marble floor. His gloved fists clenched and his whole body convulsed, breath coming in great heaving gasps.

It could all be a pretence. But it didn't feel like one. Lord Guantes enjoyed showing off his cunning. To him, watching his enemies scurry round trying to escape was the icing on the cake, the cream in the coffee, or the hand-rolled cigar and brandy that set the seal on a good evening. He wasn't the sort of Fae who would be taken by surprise in a dirty old house and go on to reveal his weaknesses.

Unwillingly and extremely carefully, Irene approached. 'Are you ill?' she asked.

Lord Guantes rolled to one side, looking up at her. She had never thought that she'd see vulnerability in his eyes.

Genevieve Cogman

'Under the cathedral . . . the dark archive . . .' he gasped, the last of his breath hissing between his teeth as he fought to get the words out. For a moment he managed to focus. 'Irene Winters, the man behind the Professor knows you, and he *wants* you . . .'

And then he stopped moving and his body went limp.

Irene hesitated, then reached out a hand to check the pulse in his neck. But as she touched him, his neck *crumpled* under her fingers. She snatched her hand back in revulsion. A bruise spread under his skin like ink, and as it grew, the flesh behind it collapsed into dust. She leaned back to avoid inhaling her erstwhile enemy. And she shivered. This was the second time she'd seen him die.

Shadows seemed to grow in the corners of the room, and the back of her neck prickled with the sensation of being watched. It felt as if she'd caught someone's attention – and they weren't amused.

Someone knocked on the door. 'Sir? May I come in?' It was a man's voice, speaking Spanish.

Damn. Irene had lost her best source of information, she couldn't fool Lord Guantes' servant by imitating his voice with any hope of success, and she'd run out of time. Kai and Vale – and Catherine – needed her. The body in front of her was nothing but an empty suit of clothing and a scattering of dust. Desperately she checked the suit's pockets, but there was nothing – no wallet, no conveniently revealing documents. Not even a note saying *Meet me next week at a helpfully specified location.*

Her eyes fell on Lord Guantes' laptop. Even if it contained nothing of interest, someone might be able to track where it came from. She scooped it up, then turned and ran. As she hurried down the corridor, she could hear Lord Guantes' remains being discovered – followed by yells for assistance.

Her sortie through the door hadn't answered her questions;

it had just given her a whole new set. For instance, who'd created that chaos-infused exit from Vale's world? It didn't match what she knew of Lord Guantes. He was a Machiavellian schemer, not an engineer – or whatever the appropriate term was for someone who could make a stable portal between alternate worlds. Fae could walk from world to world without doors, dragons flew in the space between them – but she'd only seen a permanent door between worlds once. And that had been in an ancient Fae prison, not a modern convenience. Who had that kind of capability, anyway? *The man behind the Professor . . .*

The way back loomed in front of her. Without breaking step, she ordered, **'Door, open!'**

Pain rammed itself into her temples like a blow to the head. Both the door before her and the one now far behind – to the room where Lord Guantes had died – flung themselves open. She ignored the sudden yells of pursuit, and the bullet that sang past her to hit the distant wall. She staggered through the exit, nearly collapsing. Someone caught her, and it took her a moment to recognize it was Vale.

The door slammed shut.

'And you complain that *I* am reckless,' Vale muttered. 'Winters, whatever you've done, I hope it was worth it . . .'

Then the station's alarm sounded again, and lights flashed red.

'The self-destruct . . . maybe they reactivated it?' Irene said with horror. 'Let's get out of here – then I'll tell you what I found.'

'What about that door?' he asked.

'With any luck, it'll be destroyed with this base. But I've found something that may help.' She tapped the laptop, still clasped under one arm. 'Come on!'

They rushed down another corridor, at a sprint this time. As the alarms continued, shrieking in time with the pounding in her head, Irene could only hope that the door *would* be destroyed.

Its existence was a huge unanswered question – and it worried her.

Kai actually *looked* at the waitress this time. She was now a threat, rather than a convenient provider of tea and cakes. She didn't look sinister, garbed in the long black dress, white apron and mob cap common to all the waitresses in this cafe . . .

However, he now realized, none of the other waitresses had been visible since this one had entered the room. He'd thought the privacy was convenient, allowing him and Catherine to have an unobserved chat. Now this signified something rather more dangerous. Her manner was also far less subservient than he'd expect from someone who waited on others and washed dishes for a living. While Kai lacked Vale's skill at deduction, he realized this woman probably wasn't a waitress, he and Catherine were compromised, and the whole mission was in danger.

'Please excuse me a moment,' he said, and sipped his tea.

'What are you doing?' Catherine hissed. 'She just said that was poisoned!'

'No, she just said that we *had been* poisoned. But as far as I can judge, there isn't any poison in this tea.'

Kai glanced sidelong at the so-called waitress from under his lashes; she seemed taken aback by his lack of panic. He'd managed to get her off-balance. Now to see if he could provoke her into talking.

Catherine looked as if she was about to boil over. 'We have been *poisoned*,' she said again. 'We're about to *die*! I'll never get at those books!'

'Now that's the right attitude,' Kai agreed, glad to see her demonstrating a proper sense of priorities. 'But from my personal experience, people don't inform you that you've been poisoned if you're about to die on the spot. It's usually to blackmail you by offering the antidote – or something like that.'

'Wait a second,' the waitress said. 'You've done this before?'

Kai put down his teacup and raised an eyebrow. She was still just out of arm's reach, but if he could persuade her to come closer . . . 'I was taught to recognize a large number of poisons as a child. Though unfortunately not this one.'

'Seriously?' Catherine said. 'I'd heard noble dragons were bad parents, but I'd thought that was rumour. Looks like I was wrong.'

Kai charitably forgave her this slander – she hadn't been raised as royalty, after all. 'So you see,' he said to the waitress, 'if you were serious, we'd be dead already. As it is, we have no reason to believe your threats.'

The woman pulled herself together, trying to regain control of the situation. 'What if I told you it wasn't in the tea?'

'The petits fours?' Catherine asked. 'I thought they tasted a little bit off.'

'No, not the petits fours either. It was . . .' She paused dramatically. 'It was in the gâche!'

Kai looked regretfully at the remains of the local fruit bread. 'Ah, raisins. My fatal weakness.'

As he spoke, he was thinking as fast as he could. He hadn't tasted anything unusual, though the mixed peel, raisins and sultanas could have masked a number of poisons. More to the point, he hadn't *felt* anything yet, and it had been at least a quarter of an hour since they'd eaten.

Dragons were harder to poison than ordinary humans, but if he'd eaten a dose sufficient for the poisoner to march up and boast about it now, it must be something with a delayed effect . . . Heavy metals? Black lotus?

'Or maybe you're bluffing.' He smiled at the so-called

waitress, but there was nothing pleasant about the curve of his lips. 'A cheap attempt at extortion, maybe. Why should we believe you?'

'Well, fine,' the woman declared, throwing her hands in the air. 'Sit there till you curl up and die. See if I care! I thought you'd appreciate a chance to bargain, but if you're going to be pig-headed about it . . .'

'What exactly are you *claiming* to have poisoned us with?' Catherine demanded.

'It's something you won't have heard of before – a new discovery,' she said smugly. 'But trust me when I tell you it's utterly fatal.' Her smirk blossomed. 'Did you know that it's possible to extract a lethal poison from castor oil plants?'

Ricin. Kai maintained his ruthless smile, but inwardly he sighed in relief. Ricin was toxic in food, but it wasn't as bad as if they'd inhaled it. Assuming they received proper medical treatment within six hours or so, they should be fine. 'Oh, that,' he said. 'Should I be worried? It's not as if I'm suffering from anything that would require a dose of castor oil.'

'Yes, you *should* be worried.' The woman could barely contain her irritation. 'And if you don't follow orders and come along with me now, your worry will be short-lived. Because you'll be dead. Painfully.'

'I can see you haven't had much experience at this sort of thing,' Kai said kindly. 'You should have told us that first. So who are you, and why do you want us to go with you?'

The woman tried to assume an air of menace. 'We know you're here to exchange money for a certain book. We know you're waiting here to make the exchange. You're both to accompany me now. Then we'll give you the antidote.'

Now Kai was worried. The woman's air of incompetence and the simplistic nature of her demand concerned him more than the demand itself. This was obviously linked to the earlier kidnap attempts on Irene: clearly whoever was behind the crimes had traced them here. But if that was the case, why send in such a pathetic agent to deliver threats? What if she was a pawn, delaying them while someone else made a move on them – or Irene? But all he said was: 'I see. Now I'll make you an offer in return.' Kai leaned forward, feeling his claws prick at the ends of his fingers as anger rose in him. 'Tell us who gave you this information, and I'll allow you to walk out of this cafe alive.'

His fury must have reached her, for she flinched before she could catch herself. 'Don't be ridiculous,' she attempted, her voice trembling. 'If you don't get the antidote, you'll die. I won't be bullied like this—'

Kai rose to his feet and casually picked her up by the neck. 'The poison you've given us won't take effect for hours yet,' he said, and watched her eyes dilate in terror. She hadn't known that. No more than an intermediary, then, and probably a sacrificial pawn. 'And believe me, I haven't even *begun* to bully you. Now. Who are you working for?'

She tried to say something, but was having difficulty breathing.

'I think you'd better let her down,' Catherine suggested. She didn't look well. Maybe the poison was acting faster on her metabolism than on Kai's. 'Before she, you know, chokes.'

Kai complied, but kept his hand on the woman's throat. 'Talk. If it's true that we've been poisoned, I'm not in the mood to waste time.'

Irene and Vale should have been back by now. And what if all this was an attempt to distract him from their absence? Their contact for the book purchase would be here in fifteen minutes, and Irene would *never* miss that. A combined twist of fear and fury knotted in his guts. If something had happened to them while he was babysitting Catherine . . .

The door creaked open, and an elderly woman shouldered her way in. She bore all the markers of Victorian widowhood:

a heavy black bonnet shadowed her face, a dark woollen shawl hugged her shoulders, and her black bombazine dress dragged on the floor as she walked. It left a damp trail like a slug's passage. Behind her followed a younger woman, modestly dressed, carrying a small suitcase in one hand and a hastily furled umbrella in the other. She was dripping miserably – clearly *she* hadn't been the one under the umbrella. If these were their contacts, they were early.

'Dear me,' the elderly woman said, leaning forward like a hungry stork. 'Have I interrupted something?'

Even as she spoke, Kai heard an explosion far out at sea. The island trembled in response, and Kai *felt* the waves mount in tumult, thundering in the aftermath of some cataclysm far below. He froze in shock.

CHAPTER FOUR

The explosion drew everyone's eyes seaward. Even though Kai could already feel the ocean's shuddering disquiet, he couldn't help turning to stare at the tossing waves outside.

But his affinity with water couldn't tell him what he most wanted to know. Where were Irene and Vale? Had they been trapped out there? Were they dead? Every impulse urged him to take on his natural dragon form and plunge down into the sea to find them.

'Oh, hello,' Catherine said faintly. Her eyes were fixed on Kai, begging him to do something, and she looked even paler now. 'You must be Madame Pipet.'

'What a clever young girl you are,' the old woman exclaimed. She sat down in the nearest chair, her attendant standing behind her. 'So are you the Miss Winters I'm supposed to meet?'

For a moment Kai was strongly tempted to say *Yes*, and leave it to Catherine to handle the situation while he went to find Irene. But he saw the sheer panic in Catherine's eyes, and his sense of honour forced him to stay.

'No, madame,' he said. 'Miss Winters has temporarily stepped out. But we are empowered to act on her behalf.'

It would only take a couple of minutes to exchange the

money for the book. Then he could be out of here and looking for Irene. Besides, if he prioritized saving *her* rather than collecting the book, she'd make him regret it.

'I'll take your word for it,' the old woman said, a mercenary glint in her eye. 'Assuming you have the money. And you still haven't told me why you have your hand around Julie's neck.'

At least it wasn't *Take your hands off that woman or I'll call the police!* 'She was trying to blackmail us by claiming she'd poisoned us.' A flash of inspiration made him add, 'She was trying to interfere with the deal for some reason of her own. I don't suppose you'd know anything about that?'

'Oh, was she now?' Madame Pipet spat something in the local Guernésiais, or Guernsey French. Kai couldn't understand the meaning, but it clearly frightened the woman in Kai's grip, who trembled under his hand.

Madame Pipet shifted to English. 'You, Julie Robilliard. You don't have the courage to challenge me up on Pleinmont or in front of La Gran' Mère, so instead you try to sneak round behind my back and steal what's mine. What game are you playing?'

Julie swallowed nervously. 'We, ah, that is I –' She looked round desperately at Kai. 'You'll protect me?'

'Well, *I* won't kill you on the spot,' Kai said. 'I make no promises for Madame Pipet.'

'I was given something to put in your food,' she babbled. 'I was told there would be three people, two women and a man, and your names, and that I was to give you the poison and then get you to come with me to the church. If I did that then I'd get to keep the money you'd brought with you. But the other woman wasn't with you, so I tried to go ahead with it, but then –' Her gesture took in the utter failure of the operation.

'And who made this deal with you?' Kai demanded.

'I don't know his name,' Julie said hastily. Her eyes flicked to Madame Pipet. 'He was from France . . . he was very polite, very upper class, he had a beard . . .' She trailed off, clearly aware her story wasn't very convincing.

But Madame Pipet nodded, as though she'd heard something she expected to hear. 'Another attempt to make me step down, hmm? Working with the smugglers, maybe? Well, I'll be generous, since you've spoken so freely. Get out of here and don't let me see you again in a month of Fridays, or I'll give you and your family reason to regret it.'

Julie Robilliard stammered something unintelligible, squirmed free of Kai's grip and fled the room. He considered following her to bring her back, but decided it wasn't worth it: she was a pawn with no useful information.

'You let her go? But she's poisoned us!' Catherine objected.

Madame Pipet shrugged. 'That's not my problem, little girl. Besides, you don't look very poisoned. Nice bright eyes, a flush to your cheeks, good strong voice. I'm sure she was lying.'

And if she was telling the truth, Kai thought, *you don't particularly care, as long as you get your money.* 'Very well,' he said. 'We've delayed long enough. Shall we go through with the exchange?'

At the side, Catherine was trying to catch his eye. 'Kai,' she said through gritted teeth, 'I want to become a Librarian. I don't want to die in agony!'

Kai wondered if he'd ever been that obstructive when Irene was trying to make a deal.

Madame Pipet ignored the byplay and gestured to her attendant. The younger woman put the suitcase she was carrying on a table and unlocked it, displaying a bundle of shawls. She unfolded them to reveal a heavy book bound in battered black leather, with a silver falcon stamped on the front.

'There you are,' she said. 'Malory's *La Vie de Merlin*. The companion to his *Morte d'Arthur*, from a print run by Caxton. *Very* limited, for a very exclusive clientele.'

The sight of the book distracted Catherine from her complaints. She leaned forward to peer at it, clearly itching to touch it. 'Authentic?' she asked.

'You're free to examine it, though I know you're in a hurry.' Madame Pipet shrugged. 'But don't let me make your decisions for you.'

Kai knew *exactly* what Irene would do under these circumstances. He restrained himself from looking out towards the ocean, where the waves still churned in furious disruption. 'Check it,' he told Catherine.

Fortunately Irene had left the payment with him. Kai reached into his jacket and brought out a heavy buff envelope. He opened it, extracting a signed bank draft with a satisfactory number of zeroes attached to the sum. 'I trust this will suffice?'

In the shadow of her bonnet, Madame Pipet grinned hungrily. A couple of lonely teeth gleamed briefly in the cafe lights. 'It will do.'

Kai's mind drifted as Catherine verified the book's authenticity. He urgently wanted to know how Julie Robilliard had found out about Irene's visit. The most obvious explanation was that Julie had spied on Madame Pipet . . . but that didn't explain the mysterious bearded man from France. And it certainly didn't cover whatever had happened to Vale and Irene.

If anything had happened to them, he would raze this island to the bare granite.

'Correct binding, correct printer's mark, correct chapter headings – I believe it's genuine.' Catherine folded the shawl back over the book and closed the case.

'Good,' Kai said with relief. 'In that case . . .' He offered Madame Pipet the envelope.

'Most generous,' she said, and tucked it into her bodice. Leaning on the arms of her chair, she levered herself to her feet. 'I don't suppose you'd like to buy a remedy for poison?'

'I thought we didn't look very poisoned,' Kai said.

'I could be wrong. Julie has a real fondness for her herb garden. Her henbane, her foxgloves, her castor oil plants . . .' Madame Pipet's gaze was bright and sharp; she kept one eye on Catherine, who flinched. 'I wouldn't ask you very much for a cure.'

'How much?' Kai asked, out of curiosity.

'A certain suitcase with a book in it, maybe?'

'But we just paid you thousands for it!' Catherine said.

'Quite right too. But they do say that nothing's more important than one's health.'

'No deal,' Kai said firmly.

Catherine glanced sidelong at him, then set her jaw, trying to look stern. 'No deal,' she echoed.

'Ah well,' Madame Pipet said. 'Adieu, my children. Enjoy your time on Guernsey. Whatever time you have left.'

Her attendant opened the door for her, juggling the umbrella to shield the older woman from the driving rain, then followed her out.

As the door shut behind them, Catherine turned to Kai. 'So it was all a bluff, then, and we aren't really poisoned?'

'Actually, we probably are,' Kai admitted. 'But we ate it rather than inhaling, which should give us sufficient time for treatment. First we need to find Irene—'

Suddenly they heard the rattle of gunfire outside, and screaming.

Both Kai and Catherine hit the ground, Kai snatching the suitcase as he went down. 'Keep an eye on that,' he instructed Catherine, as he crawled towards the window.

'I thought Guernsey was a nice quiet place, with cows,'

Catherine muttered bitterly. 'Since when did they have gangsters?'

'I think they're actually smugglers – they're notorious here,' Kai said, cautiously peering through the window. 'Four of them. Two have shotguns, two have pistols. Madame Pipet's down. So's her assistant. We'd better go out the back.'

'What makes you think they won't have people out there too?' Catherine demanded.

'They did,' Irene said, appearing in the doorway to the kitchens, a bundle under her arm. 'They don't now. Let's get out of here while we can.'

Given the rest of the mission had collapsed into desperate improvisation, Irene supposed she shouldn't be surprised to find this part was also chin deep and sinking. So much for a quiet journey to a pleasant holiday location, with some straightforward training for Catherine. And it was *still* raining.

'Situation report, Kai,' she said, since he seemed to be having trouble pulling himself together.

He blinked, then said, 'We have the book. We may have been poisoned. And our purchaser's just been shot down outside by a faction of local smugglers.'

Irene's heart clenched. She *knew* that she should have been faster, that she shouldn't have gone hunting Lord Guantes. 'What was the poison?' she asked.

'Ricin.' Kai didn't look as nervous as she'd expected.

'Inhaled or ingested?'

'Ingested, but we're not feeling anything yet.'

'Speak for yourself,' Catherine muttered. 'I feel *awful*.'

'That's just nerves,' Kai said reassuringly. 'We've at least six hours before we need to start worrying. What have *you* been up to, Irene? Why did something blow up out there under the sea? Where's Vale?'

'Long story,' Irene said, deciding the Lord Guantes update could wait till they were safely out of danger. The Fae had kidnapped Kai, tried to auction him off and had intended to start a war by selling him. So Kai wasn't going to be very happy when he heard Lord Guantes had been alive all this time. Or raised from the dead. Whatever. 'I'll tell you later. We'll leave through the back, this way.'

Kai snatched up the suitcase and followed. They hurried through the kitchen, and out to the side street.

From the main road there came the mournful hoot of a steam whistle. 'That's the steam tram!' Irene exclaimed. 'We can catch it to the zeppelin port – Vale's meeting us there, he went ahead to secure transport.'

Even poisoned and carrying the suitcase, Kai outpaced both Irene and Catherine. Irene caught the younger woman's arm, tugging her forward. The steam tram was just starting to pull away from its resting place; a plume of smoke trailed from the funnel that crowned the sleek maroon-painted engine. In the exposed carriages, hard-bitten travellers perched on the benches, stoically wrapped up against the elements.

Shouts came from behind them. Irene knew that symphony; it started with *There they are* and continued on to *Stop them*, with occasional gunshot obbligato.

'Get on!' she gasped.

Kai swung the hard-won suitcase up onto the open carriage, then vaulted over the side as the tram picked up steam. Irene forced herself to sprint. She grabbed Catherine under the elbow, and boosted her up into the carriage as Kai reached out to catch the Fae.

But then Irene stumbled. She frantically grabbed at one of the carriage rails, her skirts tangling around her ankles – and missed, clutching fistfuls of air instead. Lord Guantes' laptop was like a dead weight under her free arm, and it was taking everything she had just to keep pace with the tram. Desperately, she put on one last burst of speed. By some miracle, Kai grabbed her shoulders and dragged her safely inside.

The steam tram rattled its way through St Peter Port, the open sea on one side and shops on the other: grey granite and white-painted facades disappeared behind them, washed clean in the constant rain. The sound of pursuing feet and yells died away as the tram jolted towards the edge of town.

Irene tried to catch her breath. 'Thank you,' she said. She turned to Catherine. 'Are you all right?'

'This is not the serene life of reading and study I expected,' Catherine muttered. She hunched her shoulders defensively, looking thoroughly miserable. 'And I've been *poisoned*.'

The rattling of the open carriage drowned out their quiet conversation – though Irene suspected the local passengers were probably hanging onto every word they could hear. 'Yes,' she agreed. 'If I remember correctly, it takes about six hours for ricin to have a significant effect. It'll be easier to do something about it once we're on the zeppelin and out of public view.'

'Can't you just use the Language to order it out of my body?' Catherine asked.

'I might if it had gone in via a wound,' Irene said. 'But if you've eaten it, that's more difficult. And right now we can't stop for help.'

Then Irene looked at Catherine – *really* looked at her, for the first time that day. The young woman was genuinely shaken. Poisonings and gun battles weren't an everyday risk to her – and wasn't that a depressing reflection on her and Kai's lives, she reflected bitterly. No, this needed to be handled carefully, with empathy.

This was why Irene wasn't keen on students. She didn't like being empathetic. She would much rather be business-like. Lord Silver had assured her this was the life that Catherine wanted, and Catherine had agreed . . . but at this precise moment, her student seemed to be reconsidering her choices.

She sat down next to Catherine and put an arm round her shoulders. 'I'm sorry this happened to you,' she said. 'This was supposed to be an easy pickup job, getting us *away* from assassins and kidnappers. But right now, I need you to stay calm and keep things together.'

Catherine wriggled round to look up at Irene. She hadn't had a chance to adjust her hat and veil, and raindrops lay like mist on her bronze hair. 'This isn't just some sort of joke?' she said, not very hopefully.

'No. I'm afraid a trap was set, and we very nearly all walked into it.' Irene tried to think of something suitably encouraging to say – something to reassure the topaz-eyed young Fae who suddenly seemed so terribly fragile. 'If I had known this job would be dangerous, I'd have left you back in London. I'd have sent you to your uncle to keep you safe.'

'That wouldn't have been very safe.'

She had a point. But while Lord Silver wasn't the most reliable of people, he did have a lot of money, and money could buy a lot of guards. 'Well done on getting the book, anyhow,' she said. 'Now we wait. We'll be on our way home soon.'

Kai settled himself next to her, the firm strength of his body a comfort against the cold rain, and folded a hand around hers. She returned the grasp and watched the countryside go past. The occasional farms and houses were granite or whitewashed, and some had seats set round the chimneys – to stop the witches, other passengers informed Irene. Roadside stalls promised fresh vegetables, cows grazed in fields, and enormous greenhouses appeared in the middle distance. It all looked so safe . . . but Irene had no way of knowing who might be chasing them. She felt like a mouse scurrying across an open field, with birds of prey circling above. They had no allies here, and they were dangerously exposed.

And what if this whole affair had been *calculated* to make them run for the zeppelin port? Irene wouldn't put it past Lord Guantes . . . while he was alive, at least. She'd seen him die twice now, and she wouldn't put money on him staying that way.

'We're coming up to the port,' another passenger said, helpfully pointing to a couple of small airships tethered behind a metal fence. 'But not many will be flying today. The rain, you know.'

'I know,' Irene said with feeling. She disembarked with Catherine and Kai. A couple of locals clambered down from the carriage, but none headed for the zeppelin port, making their way towards the main road instead.

'Kai,' Irene said quietly, as they trudged towards the airfield entrance, 'can you do anything to clear up the weather? I've seen you cause a storm before.'

Kai was already rather pale, and the rain sleeked his hair, enhancing the bone structure of his face till he looked positively consumptive – though, as usual, in the most handsome way possible. 'It's easier to call a storm than stop one,' he admitted. 'My affinity with water makes it possible to invite the rain and turn it loose at a chosen moment, in the right conditions. But stopping the rain and wind . . . no, not really. Maybe when I'm older.'

'What a pity we don't have years to wait,' Catherine said, her temper not improved. 'Irene, why can't we just find a hotel and stay there till the weather's better, and deal with the poison there? Even if someone saw us get on the tram, they won't know where we got off. We can go cross-country and hide.'

Irene swallowed the objections that came to mind, such as the difficulty of going cross-country over winter fields on foot in the rain. Catherine was doing her best to make a helpful contribution, and Irene was sure she'd made similarly 'helpful' contributions during her own training. 'We have a problem.' She lowered her voice. 'Someone knows too much. Someone knew that Vale was going down into that submarine base. Someone knew we were planning to buy that book. We can't be sure how much *else* they know, or what other plans they may have in motion – which is why I want us off the island and well out of their reach. And I want you two to receive proper medical care as soon as possible.'

'What about Vale?' Kai asked.

'Already here,' said the man slouching next to the gates. To all appearances, Vale was a local engineer in canvas trousers and one of the island's heavy knitted sweaters, with heavy boots and flat cap, nursing a cigarette. 'Don't react. Just keep going, then turn right and head for the small zeppelin with two yellow stripes at the far end. I'll follow you.'

Irene jerked her head in a gesture that might have been shaking rain off her hat and veil – though Vale would understand it as acknowledgement – and kept on walking, as did Kai. Catherine hesitated, then hurried to join them.

The zeppelin with the double yellow stripes hung above them in the sky, pivoting in slow arcs but anchored by ropes and ladders to the ground. Irene felt her shoulder blades tense as they approached it, as if she had a target painted on her back. She suppressed the urge to look round in case someone was following them. At least in the open field, nobody could sneak up close . . .

'Stop right there!' someone shouted in French.

Irene cursed fate, timing, and everything that thwarted escapes by ten seconds. 'Help Catherine up there – I'll handle this,' she told Kai, shoving the laptop into his hands. Before he could stop her, she turned round, adopting an air of mild confusion.

Half a dozen men were running towards them, wearing the uniform that Irene had seen elsewhere on the airfield. It sported more braid and buttons than were strictly necessary to inspire confidence. 'May I help you, gentlemen?' she enquired in French.

Out of the corner of her eye she caught sight of Vale, still disguised, heading for their target zeppelin at a brisk jog. Good.

'Madame,' said the man with the most braid and the heaviest moustache, 'you and your companions must come with us at once, to answer charges of murder in the high street. Your companions also—'

Irene held up a hand to interrupt him and shifted to the Language. This one rarely failed her. **'You all perceive that we are not the people you're looking for,'** she commanded.

She saw the belief take hold as the Language adjusted their perceptions, and she relaxed – just in time for the resulting headache to hit hard. She winced and was about to add something along the lines of *You perceive they're actually at the other end of the airfield.* Then a bullet whipped through the air inches from her skull.

Trained reflexes made her drop flat and roll. Another bullet cut through the air, missing her by a bigger margin this time. The guards also scattered, diving for cover. Irene rolled across the wet grass, cursing her long dress. She could tell the shots were coming from behind the airfield's fence, but she couldn't see the shooter or the gun clearly.

Fine. She'd just have to make do with what she had. **'Fence, fall on the shooter!'** she shouted.

Metal came crashing down. There were screams. She didn't stop to look – she dragged herself to her feet, gathering her wet, muddy skirts in her fists, and staggered towards the zeppelin. Through the thickening rain she could see Vale waiting by the ladder. There was no sign of Kai and Catherine – hopefully they were already up and safe.

Vale caught her by the arm, hauling her onto the ladder. He shouted to the airship above, 'Take us up!'

The anchor detached, and with a stomach-churning swiftness the zeppelin rose into the sky. Vale and Irene clutched onto the rope ladder below, swinging like a lunatic pendulum with the impetus of their ascent. Irene wedged her feet around a rung and desperately clung to the ladder, trying not to panic as the airfield sank away beneath them. Her twisting stomach made a wonderful accompaniment to her aching head as the ladder was slowly winched into the belly of the zeppelin. Below her feet, she could see the airfield guards chasing the gunman – no, there were two gunmen, and they were running for it now, heading for a carriage . . .

'Witchcraft, smugglers, Lord Guantes, corruption, spies, and my sister's own agents subverted,' Vale noted, as they finally scrambled onto the decking. 'My files on Guernsey are sadly lacking. I really must return and update them.'

CHAPTER FIVE

The nuns looking after Kai and Catherine had the crisp manner and white aprons of nurses, but their robes were golden brown and white wimples covered their hair. They ignored Irene in the corner, leaving her alone with her valuable suitcase. Out of sheer boredom she'd resorted to reading a nursing textbook, and she was learning more than she ever wanted to know about the human digestive system.

Kai was the first to wake. His eyes flickered open and he stared at the ceiling. 'I feel awful,' he said.

'You've been given activated charcoal and you've had a stomach lavage – that's a washout. Your medical records show a list of the drugs that they injected you with, if you're interested.' Irene closed her textbook. 'On the positive side—'

'You love saying that,' Kai muttered.

'That's because I desperately cling to any optimism I can get.' She sat on the chair between his and Catherine's beds. 'There was more than ricin in that poison, but we caught it in time. If you hadn't made yourself vomit on the zeppelin, it would have been worse. Though the captain didn't look too happy about that. As it is, you should be up and about within twenty-four hours, though your guts may be a little tender.'

Kai sighed. 'I feel so stupid, being poisoned like that. My whole family would be disappointed in me.'

Irene knew dragons well enough to recognize the problem. It wasn't the poisoning that would disappoint his family, but the circumstances – he'd been dosed by a 'mere' witch in a cheap tearoom. Quite different from a respectable politically motivated assassination attempt. And so much more embarrassing. 'Your family would understand,' she said, looking around guardedly. 'Because there are bigger implications here. We've hit a serious problem.'

'What do you mean?' Kai tried to sit up, failed, and propped himself up on his elbow as if he'd meant to do that all along. 'And where are we? I don't recognize this place. The last thing I remember was the airship.'

Irene answered the second question, because she suspected that once she tackled the first, there wouldn't be space to discuss anything else. 'We're in the basement of St Henrietta's Hospital, under Whitehall. You and Catherine both passed out while we were over the Channel.' And she didn't want to remember just how terrified she'd been that they wouldn't make it to help in time.

Kai frowned. 'I don't remember a hospital by that name in London.'

'It's secret,' Irene explained, reaching over to check Catherine's pulse. Still asleep. Good. 'Excessively secret. As in founded by royalty and supported by a hidden order of nuns, secret. Vale says that only the top ranks of the civil service and London's criminal underworld know about it. Most importantly, it has some of the highest security in London – and some of the best treatment for poisons, too.'

'Hidden order of nuns?'

'The Order of St Anastasia. It's one of those situations where an order of nuns become experts at treating poisons, everyone suspects they're really poisoners, multiple cardinals die, the nuns have to flee for their lives . . . then they save a king's sister from dying and he builds them a secret nunnery. You know how it goes.'

'Oh, that happens all the time,' Kai agreed. 'My mother joined a few of those – only appearing in her human identity, of course. She says they're very convenient in an emergency. Almost as good as universal healthcare.'

Irene blinked. Kai rarely talked about his mother. It must be the effect of the poisons – or the antidotes. 'Do dragons support universal healthcare?' she asked curiously.

Kai shrugged. 'It leads to the general protection and well-being of humans. So my father's in favour of it, of course.'

Irene knew enough about dragons to recognize that *the general protection and well-being of humans* usually came secondary to *the general protection and well-being of dragons*. 'Sometimes I worry I'm too cynical,' she murmured.

'You're wandering off the subject,' Kai said, proving that even if he wasn't telepathic, he knew Irene very well by now. 'What is the "serious problem" and what have you discovered?'

It was amazing how the words *Lord Guantes is back* kept sticking in her throat, Irene thought, but she plunged in. 'Do you remember Lord and Lady Guantes?'

'Ah,' Kai said, jumping to the obvious conclusion. 'She's trying to murder us all because you killed her husband and destroyed their plans to start a Fae versus dragon war. Quite understandable.'

'She may be involved – she probably is, actually. But her husband is *definitely* involved.'

Kai hesitated, his confusion shading into worry. 'How so?'

It made Irene feel slightly better to see that Kai was as reluctant as she was to consider that Lord Guantes was somehow still alive. It didn't make sense. *And I'm not the only one who's still afraid of him . . .* 'Let me explain,' she said.

Ten minutes later she'd finished her account of events, with interruptions, and Kai was digging his fingers into his sheets. She suspected it was pure self-control which kept his nails from growing into claws and shredding them to pieces. Dragons were occasionally prone to letting a few of their natural traits show through their human form when strong emotions took hold – red eyes, claws, scales, local elemental effects . . .

'So,' she said, leaning back in her chair. 'What do we know so far?'

'Don't treat me like your pupil,' Kai snapped, proving he was more distressed than angry. Anger would never make him rude; it'd be more likely to provoke icy courtesy. 'We're past that.'

'All right,' Irene said equably. Better that he snarl at her than Catherine or the nuns. 'I apologize. I didn't want to prejudice your conclusions by giving my perspective first. What do you think of the whole affair?'

'Assuming you weren't somehow deceived, something very strange is going on.'

'That's not much of a conclusion.'

'We're lacking evidence. We can't be sure Lord Guantes – and Lady Guantes – are behind all the recent attacks on us. What if he was some kind of . . . illusion? Someone could have used his likeness to send us on the wrong track. Many others know about the Venice business.' Which was short-hand for *when I was kidnapped by Lord and Lady Guantes to start a war. You destroyed their power base while rescuing me, and killed him in the process.* She could see him shying away from the memory. He paused, thinking. 'It's undeniable *someone* was trying to kill us on Guernsey, though. Whether this is linked to the previous attempts is still up for debate.'

'True,' Irene agreed. 'But consider how it played out. It was . . . careless. It doesn't match his reputation as a master schemer. Why set up a complicated death trap in the submarine base, and then leave a back door open to his hideout?' She paused. 'I suppose the answer to that one is that he didn't expect me to be there and Vale couldn't have passed through that door. If Vale had been alone . . .' He would probably have died. And she'd never have known how or why. With an effort she continued her theorizing. 'Why get Julie Robilliard to give you a slow-acting poison, when he could have used his powers to persuade her to outright murder you? And then have people with guns waiting outside as well? It's all over the place. It's not like him.'

'He did almost get us killed, though,' Kai pointed out.

'You're not wrong,' she admitted. 'Let's go back to square one. We need to pool what we all know, what we can investigate, and what we should all do next for immediate self-preservation. Which means that Catherine needs to be awake – or rather, needs to admit she's awake.'

Catherine opened her eyes without bothering to argue. 'I find out a lot more by listening without you knowing I'm listening.'

Irene closed her eyes briefly. 'Aren't we supposed to be on the same side?' she asked.

'I don't care.' Catherine struggled to pull herself upright, bashing the pillows into submission. 'You're supposed to be making me a Librarian. So why don't you do it? Get me into the Library and you won't have to worry about anyone killing me anyway. You won't have to worry about *me* any longer.' The bitter undertone to her voice would have corroded crystal.

'Catherine . . .' Irene didn't count to ten, but she sorely wanted to. She could sense Kai vibrating like an offended high-voltage cable on her other side. 'I ask you as a rational adult: is this really the time for angst and venting your feelings?'

Catherine fumbled for her glasses on the bedside table and stared at Irene with malignant focus. 'I object to being a pawn in your games. I'm sure you already know the Guantes and my uncle had a thing, but that's over and done with.'

'When you say that they had a "thing" . . .' Kai said carefully.

Catherine winced. 'I didn't mean that sort of "thing". Though you know what he's like. I wouldn't be surprised.'

'If I might wrench this conversation back to its original topic,' Irene suggested firmly. 'Someone has tried to kidnap or kill me, Kai and Vale. Catherine may have been deliberately included, or she might be collateral damage – "a pawn", to use her words. And the attempts on Guernsey involved in-depth knowledge of our schedule and penetration of the British Secret Service. Which is where Vale is now, incidentally. He's trying to find out where the leak came from, as well as pursuing his mysterious crime lord case.'

'Does this mean we can sue the British Secret Service?' Catherine asked.

'No,' Irene said. 'They get very unhappy about people trying to sue them. The last person who tried was jailed for indecency with public transport—'

'With or on?'

'With. It was complicated . . . Look, Catherine, please stop distracting me or we're never going to get anywhere. It seems that Lord Guantes was behind the attempts to kill us, but he was acting in a highly unusual manner and crumbled into dust afterwards. That's certainly unusual. And there's been no sign of Lady Guantes.'

'Is that a fact?' Kai asked. 'In the sense of a data item, that is.'

'It absolutely is. Absence of someone who *should* be there is a definite fact. Now, moving on to avenues of investigation.

Catherine, I assume your uncle didn't mention anything about Lord Guantes returning from the dead to seek vengeance?'

'Not a word,' Catherine said. 'He did mention Lady Guantes might try and kill you at some point. But he didn't think she'd try to kill *me*, so he wasn't too worried about it.'

'Yes, that sounds like him,' Irene said with resignation. 'But if Lord Guantes *is* back, we should talk to Lord Silver. Maybe he'll remember something useful, if he's likely to be a target as well.'

'The problem *I* see is how we're going to split up to investigate,' Kai said. 'Or maybe we shouldn't split up at all. Separated, we're more vulnerable as targets. I'm not happy that Vale's gone off on his own.'

For a moment the light caught his eyes and made them flicker red. Dragons might not hoard gold, whatever legend said, but they could be remarkably possessive of things – or people – they considered they owned.

Irene shrugged. 'I'm not happy about it either. But if anyone's safe on his own in London, it's Vale.'

'Well, true,' Kai admitted. 'I suggest we bring in additional staff. My father would be happy to assign us some servants. Technically they'd be assigned to me, but in practice we can use them for all us treaty representatives.'

'That's actually a good idea,' Catherine agreed. 'Uncle has plenty of dangerous people on his private register too. Should we go primarily for bodyguards, poison-tasters or getaway specialists?'

Irene was loath to disrupt this positive interaction between the two of them. However, she was conjuring up a mental image of two separate groups of protective servants who – knowing dragons and Fae – would suspect the worst of each other. It could be almost as dangerous as having an active assassin on their trail. Possibly worse. 'Let's consider leads so far first,' she suggested, ticking them off on her fingers.

'Lord Silver, in case he knows something about Lord and Lady Guantes. The laptop I took. Whatever Vale finds out regarding the leak. And Sterrington, in case we need Fae intel. There may be relevant conspiracies in Fae circles which we haven't heard about.'

Kai frowned. 'Sterrington worked for Lord Guantes once.'

'She formally broke off their relationship when their plot to kidnap you and spark a war failed. Also, Sterrington serves the Cardinal now, and the Cardinal wants the peace treaty to succeed to benefit the Fae. It wouldn't be in Sterrington's interests to kill us.'

'Unless someone made her a better offer,' Kai said darkly.

'I doubt she'd want to get on the wrong side of the Cardinal.' And speaking of the Fae . . . 'Catherine,' she said, 'it might be best for you to stay with your uncle until all this blows over.'

Catherine hesitated. 'Irene, can I talk to you in private?'

'Of course,' Irene said. She glanced down; the beds were on wheels. 'If I push your bed out of the room . . .'

'Not necessary.' Kai levered himself to his feet with a grunt, legs showing under his nightshirt. 'I need to go next door in any case – I take it there is a next door?'

'It's just on your right,' Irene said with gratitude.

When they were alone in the room, Irene turned back to Catherine. 'What is it?'

Catherine grabbed her hands and clung to her like a limpet, her grip tight enough to hurt. 'Don't send me back to my uncle,' she said. 'Just get me into the Library and I'll do whatever you want, say whatever you want.'

'I don't want a puppet!' Irene exclaimed. 'Surely living with him can't be that bad?'

'I just can't stand him,' Catherine said. 'All he thinks about is one thing, and all I want is books. We don't have any common ground at all. He knew I'd be happy in your Library – much happier than living with him as his ward. Part of this whole thing is propaganda anyway, right? Having a Fae work with you to counterbalance your relationship with *him*.' Her eyes flicked to the door, indicating the absent Kai. 'I don't care about politics or the greater good or universal peace or whatever. I just want to be left in peace with books. The Library contains all the books I could ever need. Give me that and I'll do whatever you want.'

Her voice had been slowly rising as she spoke, and her eyes begged Irene to believe her. And Irene wanted to. It was so close to what Irene herself once wanted from life. But the colder, more cynical part of her said: *This is what she would tell you – if she wanted you to believe her. This is what she would say if she wanted to convince you she was just like you, to make you see yourself in her. You can trust Kai, and you can trust Vale, but can you really trust this woman? Are you really willing to let her into the Library?*

Irene took a deep breath. 'Catherine, I hear what you're saying. I understand how you feel. Any Librarian would.' She smiled ruefully. 'But we've already been through this. I've tried to get you through this world's permanent entrance to the Library. I've tried to get you through temporary ones. I've tried using the Language out loud. I've tried writing it down. I've even tried writing it in blood. The only time I've managed to get someone into the Library who was chaos-contaminated was by cleansing his system of the chaos first. And he was human.' That had been Vale, under desperate circumstances. 'I don't think I should try that on you.'

Catherine gave her a mutinous glare. 'They don't train you in original thinking much, do they?'

'I *beg* your pardon?' Irene said.

'Why don't you take a gateway to pieces or something,

so you can work out its basic principles and then get me in?'

Irene took a breath, let it out. 'Because there's only one gateway to the Library in any given world. Nobody's entirely sure how they come into existence, and I'm not going to destroy one. I sympathize with the scientific approach, but there aren't enough of them to risk it. Coppelia's collating all the research she can find to help.' Though a worm of doubt at the back of her mind wondered if Coppelia was trying hard enough.

After all, one of the Library's key safeguards was that Fae couldn't enter. If Irene proved they could, then who – or what – might follow?

No. That was paranoia. Coppelia herself had said that Irene *had* to succeed, for the sake of the Library's reputation and any future negotiations with the Fae. The problem with being too good at one's job was that one saw schemes everywhere.

She looked Catherine in the eye. 'I'm trying,' she said. 'I gave my word to your uncle – and to you – that I'd do my best to get you in there. Trust me.'

'How can I, when you don't trust *me*?'

Irene weighed that statement. Was it a teenage bleat of annoyance, or an accurate judgement? Or a mixture of the two? 'I understand you're impatient. So's Kai. So am I. For the moment, stay in bed and recover. I'll be back in a few hours.'

'This isn't *fair*!'

That was an inner teenager having a tantrum. 'How old are you, Catherine?' Irene asked pointedly.

'Mid-thirties,' Catherine muttered.

'Right,' Irene said. She rose to her feet and picked up the bundle with the laptop. 'Keep an eye on that suitcase – I'll return it to the Library later. Back soon.'

'I thought you said getting it to the Library was a priority?'

'It is,' Irene agreed, 'but staying alive is an even higher priority.'

Kai was waiting outside the door at a tactful distance, so if he had been listening it wasn't obvious. He drew Irene into an embrace, and for a moment she was able to forget their current worries and take comfort in his strength. 'So what now?' he asked.

'This is for you.' Irene passed him the laptop. 'You won't be able to do anything with it on this world, because of this world's magic – the moment you turn it on, a demon will attempt to possess it and it'll blow up.' She'd had that problem herself, last time she'd tried using a computer tablet from an alternate world in this one. 'Or something else equally unhelpful. And given who owned it, it's bound to be booby-trapped, password-protected, whatever. But can you take it elsewhere, get it analysed, and find out which world it came from?'

Kai's face lit up with enthusiasm. 'When we're done with it, can I trade it to one of my kin? I have cousins and friends who'd be delighted to go through a Fae's private files. I'm sure Lord Guantes isn't signed up to the truce, so we're well within the limits of the treaty.'

'Isn't it a lovely feeling to be operating within the law?' Irene said, barely able to suppress her own smirk. 'We'd better not get too used to it.'

Kai glanced towards the closed sickroom door, and raised an eyebrow. It said, *What are we going to do about her?*

Irene took him by the elbow and walked out of earshot. 'We're going to have to take her back to Lord Silver for the moment. It's too risky for her.'

'She's trained,' Kai said. 'She handled herself well on Guernsey.'

'She's also going to be a target if Lord Guantes *is* back, or if Lady Guantes is out for revenge. They can get to us through her, as she's my assistant. She could be used to get to Silver too. He'll probably want to take her and flee the city.'

Kai hesitated in the way he did when he was about to say something Irene wouldn't like. 'It's an apprentice's duty to share the master's work. And dangers.'

'I'm worried about her safety.'

'You never worried about mine like that. You never tried to send *me* home.'

Irene kept her voice down with an effort. She absolutely didn't want Catherine overhearing this conversation. 'We never had an assassin directly targeting us in the past—'

'What about Alberich? When he was trying to destroy the Library and was hunting you personally,' Kai said unhelpfully.

Irene generally tried *not* to think about that. Having the Library's most notorious traitor and enemy – now dead, she devoutly hoped – take an interest in her was the sort of thing that not only inspired nightmares, but fanned them to paranoia. Even if Alberich could somehow still be alive, though, this world had been warded against him. If there was a new crime lord in London, whoever it was, it wasn't *him*.

'Thank you for bringing that up,' she said drily. 'If we're looking for people with grudges against us, I agree Alberich has motive. I burned his headquarters, ruined his plans, et cetera. What he doesn't have is opportunity. But even when he was actively targeting me, we didn't act like sitting ducks, just waiting for him to make his move. That's why I want to get Catherine away . . .' Her voice trailed off thoughtfully as an idea half formed in her mind. *Obvious targets*. She filed it for later consideration.

'Well, we aren't doing that now,' Kai said. 'We're staying under cover till we have more information. Catherine is as safe here as she would be anywhere else.'

'She'd be even safer with Lord Silver,' Irene said firmly. 'And since I'm going to speak to him anyway, I can ask him about it.'

'I think you're making a mistake. She should be here.'

'She's my apprentice. If I have rights over her, then I have the right to put her somewhere safe.'

Kai frowned. 'Irene . . .' He trailed off.

'I should be moving,' she said, changing the subject. 'I'll be back as soon as I can. If you feel well enough to travel before I return, for pity's sake leave me a note saying where you've gone.'

'What's your own itinerary?' Kai asked.

Irene had to smile at that. Sauce for the gander was sauce for the goose. 'Visit Lord Silver at his embassy, then Sterrington, then our lodgings for messages, then Vale's lodgings, then back here. See – I'm completely transparent. It's just past ten o'clock in the morning, so Sterrington should be at her office.'

'If it's ten o'clock in the morning, then Silver will be in bed and hungover.'

'Yes,' Irene said cheerfully. 'I'm rather counting on that.'

CHAPTER SIX

It took repeated knocking at the Liechtenstein Embassy to raise any response, and the elderly woman who finally answered the back door glared at Irene. 'No hawkers welcome,' she said. 'No flowers, no love notes and no policemen. The Ambassador's out.'

'He's what?' Irene said, stunned. Lord Silver had scheduled a party for last night, and most of the day before it.

The woman sniffed and tugged her shawl tighter round her shoulders, apparently about to slam the door in her face.

'I beg your pardon,' Irene said quickly. 'I was just surprised. Do you know where Lord Silver has gone?'

The elderly woman leaned closer, breathing halitosis in Irene's direction. 'Fact is, he didn't rightly tell me. He left me to tidy up. And what I'm going to do with the food that's ordered for today I don't rightly know.'

'Can you get him a message? It's urgent . . .' Irene started, her irritation growing.

Then she looked more carefully at the woman. That nose was just a little too pronounced, the stoop overdone. The bad breath wafted in her face was the product of onions and garlic. The whole effect was staged. 'You know who I am,' she said quietly. 'Let me in.'

There was a flash of clarity in the woman's rheumy eyes. Then she stepped back to let Irene inside.

Irene lowered her umbrella and unwound her veil once the door was safely shut. She'd changed her hat, coat and veil from her usual subdued colours for something a bit brighter and cheaper. She'd change them again before going on to Sterrington. Standard protocols for when a spy – or a Librarian – suspected they were being followed. 'All right,' she said. 'For the record, I identify myself as Irene Winters. What's going on?'

The woman straightened up, rubbing her back. 'You have to tell me how you spotted that,' she said ruefully, her voice abruptly clearer and less dialect-ridden. 'I thought this persona would put off Peregrine Vale himself, if he came round asking nosy questions.'

'It was partly the shawl,' Irene said apologetically. 'It was far too clean. And something about the accent . . . but it was an excellent effort.'

The woman nodded appreciatively. 'So you were asking after Lord Silver. He's gone to Hawaii.'

'Hawaii?' Irene could hear her voice rising. 'Why?'

Silver's retainer shrugged. 'They were drinking rum and coconut milk cocktails last night and someone said, We should be drinking these in Hawaii. Lord Silver agreed. Then he loaded up the household and half the guests in ether-cabs and headed for the zeppelin port.'

Irene groaned. 'No . . . ulterior motives? An urgent need to get away?'

'Not unless you count the weather, miss. Lord Silver's not too fond of rain – unless he's bathing naked on the roof. In company.'

'Can you contact him?'

'I can send a message, miss, but I can't promise when he'll read it.'

Irene was silent for a moment. Was Silver really on holiday, or had something or someone scared him off? Maybe she was just being paranoid – but he rarely left London. In any case, she clearly couldn't leave Catherine here.

At least Lord Silver was probably safe from planned assassinations – if he *was* in Hawaii.

'I'll leave you a note to pass on,' she said. 'I'd also appreciate it if you could let me know of any attacks on the embassy. Lord Silver and I may have a mutual problem.'

'Can do, miss,' the woman said. 'Send your message, that is. The rest of it's at his lordship's discretion.'

Irene repressed a sigh. 'That'll have to do.'

Her next stop was across London Bridge, on the other side of the Thames. She was aiming for a tangle of 'modern' architecture – designed for bankers, lawyers and similar types. These offices sat cheek by jowl with classical Regency buildings, converted for the same aforesaid business types. She'd picked up an ether-cab shortly after leaving the Liechtenstein Embassy. No person of quality would be walking around this bustling neighbourhood for more than five minutes, even if the packed streets meant journeys took twice as long.

This also meant twice as long sitting in the back of a cab, wondering if a bullet would shatter the window at any moment. Twice as long worrying about Kai, and Vale, and Catherine, and all the things that could go wrong.

Kai didn't seem to realize quite how much danger he'd been in. He'd just shrugged it away: he'd been poisoned, received medical care, recovered. Catherine at least seemed to have a more sensible appreciation of the situation. Irene wished she knew more about her student's history. She kept on thinking of her as *the girl*, as she seemed so young. She claimed to be in her thirties – but really, how could a human tell a Fae's real age? Either way, she remained an unknown quantity at an uncertain time.

Sterrington's office was in one of the new buildings. It reared up ominously among the surrounding establishments, a structure in dark iron with windows as black as obsidian. Two small zeppelins floated above, tethered to the roof in permanent readiness to rush off on urgent business – a display of ostentatious wealth declaring *We have money to waste*. A constant stream of visitors flowed through the rotating doors, and Irene was glad to lose herself among them. Inside, her progress was further slowed by a group of workmen repainting the lobby. It was oddly reassuring to find this dark monolith of business wasn't as perfect as it looked.

To Irene's surprise she was shown to Sterrington's office immediately. She was whisked past two secretaries and a roomful of clerks, and Sterrington actually rose from her desk to greet her. 'Thank you so much for coming at once,' she said. 'I do appreciate it.'

Irene shook Sterrington's mechanical hand, feeling the workings of metal and plastic under the woman's silk glove, and wondered what she'd missed. 'I'm glad if this is timely,' she said, 'but I have to admit I came about my own problems. If you sent a message to my lodgings, I haven't been there since yesterday.'

'The important thing is that we can have a face-to-face, high priority.' Sterrington gestured Irene to a chair opposite. Her dark hair was restrained in a tight bun, and her face had the sort of smooth gloss that went with a perfect cleansing regimen. Her watered silk grey jacket and skirt radiated 'high-status businesswoman', topped off with a single ruffle of white silk at her throat. She came straight to the point. 'Yesterday I received an urgent message from Lord Silver. One of his spies warned him someone was plotting to assassinate him. So he was planning to leave London, without alerting any watchers that he knew of the plot. He thought I was involved too.'

'As additional target or as an assassin?' Irene asked innocently.

'Target,' Sterrington said. The Fae didn't seem insulted, which said something about her professional relationship with Lord Silver. 'His contacts told him you were at risk as well, and he asked me to tell you for the sake of the treaty. I expect he left a message for you too.'

'More than likely,' Irene agreed. 'I need to check my lodgings; the problem is doing it safely . . . we experienced an assassination attempt ourselves, in Guernsey. It was almost a success.'

'"We" being?'

'Myself, Prince Kai, Peregrine Vale and Catherine. It's the identity of the assassin that's relevant here. You see . . . Lord Guantes came back from the dead.'

'I find it alarming that you believe this.'

'So you think I've been fooled?' Irene asked.

'Let's say I think you should reconsider,' Sterrington said. 'Firstly, necromancy may be practised in some worlds, but it doesn't work on my kind. Secondly, you *definitely* killed Lord Guantes. I should know. I spent over an hour sitting in the same train carriage as his dead body. Thirdly, I believe you think you're speaking the truth. Therefore – lastly – you've been deceived in some way. Perfectly understandable, of course. But you haven't told anyone else . . . have you?'

Irene clicked her tongue. 'Really, Sterrington, give me credit for not being *entirely* lacking in sense.'

Sterrington flushed. 'I should have known better,' she said, neatly avoiding an actual apology. Fae didn't like admitting error any more than humans. 'It's just the Cardinal wouldn't like such rumours. It upsets the political balance. I don't suppose you have any evidence to back up your wild claim?'

'I do, actually, but it's with Kai for analysis.' Trusting anyone was a gamble, and Sterrington *had* worked for Lord Guantes before. But Sterrington's current patron, the Cardinal, was in favour of the peace treaty. As such, they might even count on his and Sterrington's aid. She ran through the details and saw doubt drift across Sterrington's face like a shadow crossing the moon. 'So you see,' she finished, 'I have valid evidence—'

'Of something, certainly,' Sterrington cut in. 'I wish you'd given *me* that laptop. We have our own expert analysts, you know.'

'Did the world I described sound familiar to you?' Irene asked, dodging the subject.

Sterrington looked thoughtful, turning her pen over and over between gloved fingers. 'Not specifically. It sounds like a world with a high degree of technology, and chaos, but there are so many of those. However, I find your description of that door into it rather worrying.'

'Why *worrying*?'

'Because of what it implies.'

'Sterrington, I've seen Fae travel between worlds on their own, or through the agency of a more powerful Fae. That wasn't treated as in any way unusual. And dragons can move between realms too . . . Is a permanent door between two worlds something new?'

Sterrington took several seconds to answer. Finally she said, 'It's new in my experience, and yes, troubling. There are legends that it is possible, but . . . different spheres,' she used the Fae term for alternate worlds, 'aren't meant to be tied so closely together. It's very bad for both realms.'

'That's not encouraging.'

'No, it isn't. I may need to report this.' Sterrington pulled herself together. 'I still don't think you saw Lord Guantes, though. Whoever threatened you is an impostor, or a clone, or a brainwashed minion . . . or something else set up to confuse you. You want to be looking for the person you *didn't* see.'

'And who is that?'

'Lady Guantes,' Sterrington said. 'She's trying to taunt you, using her dead husband. It makes perfect sense that she's behind the recent attacks upon you and your friends. And she's trying to kill me because I failed them, then took a new patron.'

'But how could they predict that I'd even be there with Vale, never mind that I'd find – and open – that door? Then see Lord Guantes waiting there . . .'

'May I be frank?' Sterrington asked.

Irene sighed. This was always the sign of a fast-approaching insult. 'Do go on,' she said drily.

'With the utmost respect, anyone who knows you would expect you to investigate a potentially dangerous door while already facing a life-or-death situation.'

Irene liked to think of herself as sensible, but she couldn't deny she'd gone through the door. 'I viewed it as a rational step in an urgent investigation,' she said with dignity.

There was a nagging feeling at the back of Irene's mind, however. It suggested that any hypothesis which fitted the data so conveniently was by nature unreliable. 'But why?' she said. 'What good does it do Lady Guantes to kill us? And why now, after all this time?'

'Vengeance. What else?' Sterrington said.

'Still . . .' Irene picked her words carefully. 'She's a prag-matic woman, from what I remember of her. Pursuing personal vengeance for its own sake doesn't feel like her style.'

'Just because we don't know *why* she's doing it, doesn't invalidate the hypothesis that it's her,' Sterrington persisted.

Irene hadn't finished. 'Could Lady Guantes be targeting

the peace treaty instead, with a sweetener of personal vengeance on the side? Killing all three representatives would cause havoc. She and her husband did try to trigger a dragon–Fae war before, to benefit from the chaos that war brings. That was the whole *point* of kidnapping Kai.'

Sterrington nodded slowly. 'It makes sense.'

'I just wish we knew more about her,' Irene said in frustration. 'Lord Guantes was always the more flamboyant one. Or do you know something that I don't?'

Sterrington shook her head. 'It seems she liked operating in the shadows. The very opposite to her husband's archetype. I don't even know her original name.'

Irene nodded, a thought occurring. 'Doesn't the Cardinal have files on everyone?'

'He certainly has files on *Lord* Guantes . . . Although, as we said, the lady is secretive,' Sterrington added.

'Could you share them?'

'I suppose I could put in a request,' she said grudgingly.

'Thank you.'

'In the meantime, there's the question of Silver's niece,' Sterrington said, her tone a little too casual. 'Now you're a target, you could leave her with me. I'll guarantee her safety. Then you can hunt down Lady Guantes – you and Prince Kai – without worrying about her.' Sterrington's barely hidden enthusiasm was disconcerting.

And give you full access to a Fae who might become a Librarian, a girl who is currently nervous, impressionable and off-balance, Irene thought. *I really don't think so.*

Irene knew Sterrington could see the denial in her eyes. However, the Fae just shrugged. 'The offer's open. I'd keep her safe. It might be safer for you, too.'

'In what way?'

'Catherine has come out of nowhere: no references but Lord Silver, no backing, no personal recommendations, no previous employment records.' Sterrington paused. 'Who can be sure about her background? And who might she be talking to behind your back? People have been trying to shoot all of us, but not *her*.'

Irene wanted to write all this off as spite on Sterrington's part because she wouldn't hand the girl over . . . but it did mirror some of her own earlier suspicions about Catherine. 'Given the savagery of Fae politics, I can see why Silver would keep young family members hidden,' she said. 'And so far she's proven herself trustworthy. Also, they did try to poison her too in Guernsey.'

'Oh, quite, quite.' Sterrington leaned forward. 'But I hope you're maintaining proper objectivity. Sometimes I think you have a tendency to become . . . *emotionally attached* to your junior co-workers.'

Irene met Sterrington's stare with her own best blank face. 'I'm only interested in books,' she said, and wished it was true.

There was a rap at the office door, then a young man burst in. The room must have been soundproofed, as Irene could only now hear screams and running in the corridors.

'Madame,' the man said, flinching at Sterrington's glare, 'forgive me, we need to evacuate. The building's on fire.'

CHAPTER SEVEN

'An accident or deliberate?' Sterrington demanded. The screams were getting louder and Irene could smell smoke.

'I don't know, madam . . . But the fire alarms didn't go off.'

'Where's the nearest fire escape?' Irene asked.

The man looked apologetic. 'I'm sorry, madam, but we discovered it was badly damaged. The lifts are down for maintenance and the fire has made the stairs impassable. We'll need to get to the roof and take one of the zeppelins instead.' He looked pale and his jacket was singed.

Sterrington quickly retrieved a few small objects from a desk drawer. 'Come on, let's move. No fire alarms, and the fire escape damaged? Clearly arson. Lead the way, Wickson.'

'Where is everyone?' Irene asked, following her into the now noticeably empty corridor. It had been bustling when she was ushered in but now just a few people were visible, disappearing at some speed down a corridor.

'It's lunchtime,' said Wickson, as if that explained everything. Maybe it did. Lunchbreak was a sacred institution in these times.

Sterrington refused to catch Irene's eye. 'My personal assistant doesn't need a lunch hour,' she said, in an almost defensive tone.

They turned a corner. The fire escape door swung open, offering a view of a black iron staircase, a few stragglers climbing to safety and the opposite city block twenty yards away. Thick smoke curled between them and distant safety.

'Isn't the fire escape damaged?' snapped Sterrington.

Flinching, Wickson said, 'Yes madam, but only that section below. We can still get to the roof.' It seemed the rickety rungs were their only hope.

'To the zeppelins, then,' Sterrington proclaimed, flinging herself out of the door and onto the stairs.

Of course Irene looked down, just for a moment. Ten storeys below, fire wreathed the building – and the blaze was at least three storeys high. Smoke billowed upwards, increasing with every passing moment, and the air was hot as she breathed it in. Through the windows of the building opposite she saw horrified faces. If only it were close enough to jump.

The metal steps rang beneath her feet as she hurried to the roof, following the fire escape in its zig-zag up the side of the building. She could hear people panicking above her.

Then there was a crash from above that shook the whole building. The stairs shuddered against the wall as though they were about to rip free, tossing them against the flimsy rail. Irene fell to her knees, clinging to the bare metal steps as they shivered under her. When she looked up, she could see that Wickson and Sterrington were braced against the wall.

Irene clawed herself to her feet again, and they all scrambled up the final section to the roof. There Irene paused, taking in the scope of the disaster.

One of the zeppelins had crashed in the middle of the landing space. The other, still anchored to the roof by a tether, was tilting in mid-air, the fans on one side working double-time while the other side faltered. The glass window at the front was shattered – and Irene caught a glimpse of a prone body inside. It began to lose height, also careening down to the landing area. The people on the roof screamed, scattering towards the edge.

No fire alarms, and the fire escape damaged? Clearly arson, Sterrington had said. And now the zeppelins were down too.

Irene pulled herself to her feet, assessing the possibilities. The building nearest to the fire escape was impossible to reach. The remains of the zeppelins were now piled up like a child's discarded toys, gasbags deflated and girders bent, ropes flapping loose and their canvas torn. The zeppelins' mooring gear lay uselessly beside them, cables still neatly coiled.

Cables.

The closest building was to the west. Irene ran in that direction, shouldering her way through the crowd to see if there was a chance of achieving what she had in mind. The neighbouring offices' roof also featured a flat platform surrounded by railings, in exactly the same style as Sterrington's office block. *Perfect.*

In the street below, the fire engines had finally turned up and were pumping water into the flames. It wasn't going to be enough. Smoke was already beginning to rise through the higher windows in the block, making the trapped mob around her cough and choke.

Sterrington's expression lightened as she saw Irene approaching. 'Have you found a way out of here?' she asked.

'I have, but I'll need your help,' Irene said, saving a snippy, *Do you think I can work miracles?* for another day. She lowered her voice. 'I need rope – the mooring cables from those zeppelins will do. We need to drag them over to the west side there. I'm going to make a bridge to the next building.'

Wickson coughed – admonitory, rather than smoke-induced. 'Madam, we can't throw ropes of that weight with any accuracy across that distance. And how would we tie them at the other end?'

Sterrington silenced him with a gesture. 'If she says she can do it, she can. Get her the ropes. Irene, do you seriously plan to have us tightrope-walk across?'

Wickson didn't give up his lack of hope easily. 'The mooring cables will be attached to the centre of the platform, madam.'

'Don't worry,' Irene said. 'I'll detach them. Be ready to carry them.'

After a bit of applied Language to detach the four cables from their mooring points, she was in position on the west side. Two of Sterrington's men had dragged the heavy cables over, while others kept the panicking crowd back while she worked. Everyone seemed to assume that ropes somehow equalled safety, rather than realizing that thirty yards of rope wouldn't get them to the ground. She had to work fast, before she was overrun.

She touched one of the cables and put her hand on one of the vertical railings. **'Rope which I'm touching, bind one end around the base of the railing I'm holding.'**

She repeated the process with the next mooring line, setting it a couple of feet above the first. The cables coiled like pythons, knotting themselves firmly in place. Good. This would work. This *had* to work.

She took a deep breath, ignoring the hot air that rippled her skirts, the sweat that ran down her back, the shouting behind her and the rising smoke. Then she touched the knotted cable before her and pointed to the adjacent building. **'Rope which I'm touching, bind your free end around the railing directly opposite belonging to the building I'm indicating with my finger.'**

Nobody ever said the Language was elegant. Especially when its wielder was almost on fire. She did the same with the next rope, again commanding it to fasten above the first. The cables were several inches thick, strong enough to hold an airship, but far too heavy to throw. Yet under the force of the Language each rose in turn, spearing across the twenty-yard gap and grappling around the railings on the far side.

It wasn't much of a bridge. One line was strung above the other, so an escapee could shuffle sideways along one while holding a guide rope at waist height to avoid plunging to their death. The hawsers were each about six inches in diameter, but it would still have required an acrobat to walk across them without something to hold. It would be terrifying. But it was a way off the top of this burning edifice.

'Right,' Irene said, leaning on the rail to catch her breath. The smoke made her cough. 'Sterrington, have your people keep this orderly . . .'

'On it already,' Sterrington said, passing her a hip flask which proved to contain brandy.

Irene took a reviving swallow, ignoring her growing headache, and repeated her words in the Language with the other two cables, setting up a second bridge. Sterrington was scanning the nearby buildings with a careful eye.

'Something I missed?' Irene asked.

'Those zeppelins were *shot down*,' Sterrington said quietly. People were being shepherded – or shoved – onto the cable 'bridges', and struggling across to the next building with varying degrees of grace. Nobody had fallen off. So far, anyway. 'Snipers. They must be nearby.' She jerked her chin towards the higher buildings, unwilling to point obviously. 'The question is whether they've gone, or whether they're waiting to make sure their targets don't get away. Whoever they may be.' She flicked a glance to Irene, then the remaining roof-dwellers.

Irene followed her gaze. 'Just how many people in this

building *are* there who might have assassins coming after them?'

Sterrington shrugged. 'We have the Mafia, or a holding company representing the Mumbai underworld. Also some dubious businessmen from Germany, plus shell companies for the Seventh Hell Brotherhood and the Cathedral of Reason. Both of the latter are secret societies, so you didn't hear that from me, by the way. I didn't pick this place by accident, you know. I wanted somewhere where the highly elite – and enormously wealthy – based their offices.'

'And the highly illegal,' Irene muttered.

Sterrington shrugged again. 'The highly effective.'

Irene coughed, and held her sleeve to her mouth to block the smoke. 'So if the snipers *are* still here . . . are you waiting to see if they shoot people as well as zeppelins?'

'Why else do you think I'm standing here, rather than escaping?'

'Yes, that did seem rather unusual,' Irene admitted. 'So you *do* think this is aimed at you.'

'Why say that?'

'Because otherwise you'd be out of here and to hell with the snipers.'

Sterrington looked as if she was about to object, then gave up. 'The Guantes duo were famous for the well-laid trap. They could be very useful, in fact. Sometimes I really regret they went out of business.'

Irene sighed. 'Come on,' she said. 'Snipers or no snipers, we need to get off the roof – now. The smoke's getting too thick for safety.'

Most people had fled to safety over her bridges, but Sterrington's men were still waiting. Irene ignored the itch on the back of her neck at the thought of a sniper taking aim, and concentrated. She tucked up her skirt and clambered over the railings, trying not to look down. Her feet found the lower rope and she began to inch sideways across the drop, clutching the guide rope with sweating hands.

The street below was dizzyingly far away – and busy. Through the smoke she could make out the uniforms of police and firemen, the black and grey of other office workers, and the more colourful clothing of ordinary people drawn by the excitement. Some of them seemed to be shouting and waving at her. She felt no urge to wave back. The flames were at the sixth or seventh floor now, and still rising, roaring, unstoppable. She could feel the incredible heat. Black smoke streamed upwards, building a pillar in the sky higher than any of the surrounding office blocks.

The heavy fibres of the cable were rough under her hands, and the narrow bridge was harder to manage than she'd expected. She forced herself to focus on the cable in front of her rather than the drop below.

A bullet whistled past her.

Irene relaxed her death grip on the cable and slid herself forward as fast as she could, letting the guide rope glide through her fingers as she forced herself along the bridge. Then she was tumbling over the railing and onto the roof in an ungainly sprawl.

But she wasn't safe. Not yet. Not so long as she was standing here in plain view. She stumbled through the crowd, trying to find cover. The yawning flight of stairs that led inside beckoned her, and she ran for it.

Sterrington joined her moments later, wiping smears of ash from her face, and they drew aside from the people streaming downstairs. 'You've brought trouble to my door,' she said sourly.

'I thought you'd decided *you* were the target.'

'Maybe. But nothing happened until you arrived.'

Irene worked on staying calm. She couldn't afford to alienate her fellow treaty representative. Her day was bad enough already. 'I arrived less than an hour ago. Nobody could have predicted my movements to set *this* up.' She paused, thinking. 'How long have workmen been painting downstairs?'

'Several days. Why do you ask – oh.' Sterrington frowned. 'I see. It would be the perfect cover for arranging the arson, wouldn't it? Flammable material, access to take the lifts out of service . . . I'll have someone look into it.'

Irene thought privately that it was a little late for that. She decided not to mention the bullet, either – it would only encourage Sterrington to blame her again. Instead she said, 'There was a murder attempt on you a couple of weeks ago, so after today, you're definitely on the hit list. It seems they *are* aiming for all the treaty representatives.' Though that left the question of why Vale had been targeted. Because he was an associate of Irene's? Or simply as a gesture of revenge from Lord Guantes? After all, he'd helped rescue Kai from the Guantes' kidnap plot. 'Assuming someone else here wasn't the target?' She glanced at the flames roaring from the neighbouring building. They really needed to move.

'I doubt it, but that's what I'll be telling the police,' Sterrington said briskly. 'I can do without the attention. Listen, Irene, I have to assume my apartment's been compromised, and you should presume the same for your lodgings. I'll take a room at Claridge's. Leave any messages for me there, or with my solicitor Sallers at the Middle Temple. We can use him as a dead drop – I've kept my link with him secret. Let me know when you have more on that laptop.'

For once, Irene was grateful the Fae was a professional schemer. She could also spot an opportunity. 'And on your side, can you check up on Lady Guantes – and see if any Guantes enemies have been murdered recently? I'm assuming the Cardinal will know.'

'He's extremely busy,' Sterrington hedged. 'You don't want the details.'

'Much as I sympathize with keeping a mess from one's boss until it's sorted out, he might be a target as well. Do you want to be the one who didn't warn him?'

'Now you're exaggerating. Nobody on *their* level has even the *slightest* chance of assassinating the Cardinal.'

The roof was nearly empty now and firemen were escorting stragglers downstairs. They needed to hurry if they wanted to lose themselves in the crowd. 'Look,' Irene said, 'whether we're facing Lord Guantes, Lady Guantes, or both – and whether they want personal revenge or to trigger another war – they've tried to assassinate all three peace treaty representatives. The Cardinal needs to know.'

'Oh, very well. I suppose some sort of memorandum might be in order. But I don't expect this plot to stay hidden for much longer. This London isn't the Guantes' home ground. With your Vale and the police after her, him or them, they'll have to retreat – and we'll be ready next time.'

Behind Sterrington, the whole building was aflame now. It was a warning that it could have been so much worse. Sterrington didn't seem to realize just how *close* they'd both come to death.

'All right,' Irene said, moving towards the stairs. 'I'll be in touch. Just . . . be careful. We've been lucky so far.'

They needed to resolve this – or their enemies would destroy even more of London in their desire for vengeance. When it came to Fae feuds, human lives were incidental damage.

The air was thick with smoke as Irene emerged from the building that had been their salvation. The street was packed so full of observers, bystanders, coffee vendors and book-makers that she had to shove her way through the crowd.

Fire engines were spraying thick gouts of water into the lower parts of the blazing building, but it didn't seem to be doing much good. Though Irene admitted she knew more about fires from the *running away from them* perspective than putting them out. At any rate, it wasn't her problem any more.

'Hold it!' Several people stopped in their tracks, Irene included, and there was a general turning of heads to see Inspector Singh approaching, trailed by policemen. His gaze fixed on Irene. 'Mrs Parker? I'd like a word with you.'

That was interesting – and worrying. Inspector Singh knew perfectly well that Irene's identity in this world was *Miss Winters* and not *Mrs Parker*. He also knew more about the Library, the dragons and Fae than Irene would have liked. If he was trying to have a private word, without identifying her publicly as Irene Winters, then Irene Winters was in trouble.

Irene let herself be escorted into a waiting police van. One of the policemen – a sturdy fellow with a moustache – climbed in, along with Inspector Singh. The harsh electric light inside the closed cab brought out every smut and smear on Irene's clothing. In contrast, Inspector Singh, sitting on the opposite bench with his attendant policeman, could have attended a public parade. From his polished boots to his turban and green sash – a token of his secondment from the Imperial Police in India – he looked pristine.

At that moment, Irene didn't even care why he'd brought her here. The fire was too fresh a terror. Even though she'd managed to control herself while they were escaping, now that she was out of danger her subconscious was sending messages. Apparently it would like to lie down and gibber for a few hours. 'You wanted to speak with me, inspector?' she asked curtly.

'Actually, Miss Winters, I wanted to thank you,' the

inspector said. 'I don't have all the details yet, but I understand you managed to organize the evacuation. Nice work.'

It made a pleasant change to have someone actually *congratulating* her for something. 'I'm glad I could help,' she answered. 'What I'm more worried about is why it happened.'

'Always to the point. Under normal circumstances I'd call the fire a terrible misfortune, but as things stand we were lucky that nothing worse happened.'

He glanced sideways to the other policeman, who somehow *relaxed*. His shoulders loosened and a new light came into in his eyes. 'Forgive me for not removing this disguise, Winters.' It was Vale's voice, unmistakable. 'We all need to be careful about showing ourselves in public right now. I have very little doubt that Sterrington – and possibly you as well – were meant to die in that fire. Though I have yet to determine whether your presence triggered the attack, or whether your involvement was accidental.'

Irene resigned herself to the fact that Vale's disguises really *were* that good. 'If I was an intended target, then someone must have waited until I visited to set the fire,' she said. 'If it was just meant for Sterrington, then my timing was indeed . . . unfortunate. The plan must have preceded our trip to Guernsey, though – the "painters" in the building had been there at least a couple of days.'

'Painters?' Singh asked.

Irene gave them a brief summary of events. 'So if this was the backup plan in case I survived Guernsey,' she finished, 'what's Plan C?'

'Precisely why I'm avoiding my lodgings,' Vale agreed. 'For the moment, our interests – and London's – are best served by us staying out of sight. You sent Strongrock to get that computer analysed?'

'I did. You know Lord Silver's left London?'

'Of course. What do you propose to do with his niece?'

'I'm still working on that,' Irene admitted. 'I have a set of rooms in Croydon, leased under an alias. I could leave her there with some good books.'

'Probably the best solution,' Vale agreed.

'So where will you go next, Miss Winters, if you're keeping a low profile?' Inspector Singh asked. 'I can have the cab drop you off somewhere.'

'Whitehall, please. I'll get Catherine to safety. Then I have another trail that might be worth following.'

'Really?' Vale asked.

'The books. I want to know if someone leaked information about that copy of *La Vie de Merlin*. Maybe it was bait to get us to Guernsey.'

'Probably an area that you're better qualified to investigate than I,' Vale said. Generous of him, Irene thought wryly. 'In the meantime, I will be investigating the presence of Lord or Lady Guantes in London – and whether or not this has anything to do with my criminal mastermind. I smell conspiracy and intrigue. I also intend to find this *Professor* that Lord Guantes mentioned.' Even beneath his disguise, the lines of his face were suddenly hawk-like – a hunter on the trail, a duellist looking for his opponent.

'Be careful,' Irene said.

Vale raised a brow. 'Surely I should be telling you that, and with far more cause. London is my home, Winters. I need no warnings to watch my step.'

But Irene wasn't afraid – well, wasn't *just* afraid – for his safety. She was afraid for his personality – his soul, if you cared to put it that way. Once he'd been infected by chaos, and it had come close to destroying him. It had tried to twist him into an archetype, rather than a human being, drawing on a strain of Fae blood in his family tree. The pull of this great detective archetype had tempted him to lose himself in the thrill of the chase, the lure of a puzzling crime. And what greater temptation than the presence of a 'master criminal' in London? There was a new gleam in Vale's eye, a controlled urgency in his posture.

Irene had realised how much she valued Vale as a friend, when she'd almost lost him. She didn't want to risk that again.

'I think we all need to be extremely careful,' she said. 'That may include you, Inspector Singh. Whether we are facing Lady Guantes, Lord Guantes, or some other malefactor entirely, if our aggressor knows you're a friend of ours, they could target you too.'

'I assure you I'm being prudent, Miss Winters,' Inspector Singh said. His sideways glance made it clear that he was more concerned about Vale. 'Whether criminal masterminds are present or not, I always watch my step. Besides, if anyone cares to take a shot at me, they'll need to be quick about it. My appointment book's a little overfull at the moment. The upcoming Hungarian state visit, the Grand Technological Exhibition—'

'Which reminds me, I need to look into Doctor Brabasmus and his work,' Vale interrupted. 'The cerebral controllers, you recall? Even if the doctor himself is dead, his inventions are clearly on the market, and it may be possible to find out who's been buying them.' The carriage rumbled to a halt. 'Your stop, I believe. Send any messages for me to my sister Columbine.'

'What if *you* need to contact *me*?' Irene asked.

'I'll find you,' Vale said, with a somewhat irritating certainty.

St Henrietta's Hospital was reassuringly quiet, clean and safe after the wilds of London. The layers of security which surrounded it were also a safeguard from any immediate attempts at assassination. Irene wondered briefly if she could leave Catherine *here* for the next few days. They probably didn't take lodgers, but maybe if she promised a sufficiently high donation . . .

Then she walked into the bedroom where she'd left Catherine. It was empty.

Panic rose, as she contemplated various horrific scenarios. She took a deep breath and forced herself to look around the room with clinical detachment, as Vale would have done. No bloodstains, no obvious signs of a struggle. But equally, no Catherine . . . and the suitcase containing the Merlin book was gone too.

The nun outside was happy to answer Irene's questions. 'Why yes, the young dear checked herself out. Since she was healthy and in her right mind, we didn't have any problem with that.'

'Did she say where she was going?' Irene asked desperately. 'Or leave a note?'

'No, nothing like that. But . . .'

'Yes?' Irene said hopefully.

Other nuns had quietly closed in. 'She did say that you'd be paying the bill,' the first nun said, with a flinty smile. 'We have the full accounting here. I do hope there won't be any problems.'

CHAPTER EIGHT

Fortunately the nuns took cheques.

But none of the others knew where Catherine had gone either. No, she hadn't said what she planned to do, but she'd only been gone for an hour at most – so she couldn't have ventured far.

Irene left with a polite smile pinned to her face, but behind it, she was furious. What did Catherine think she was *doing*? She'd been poisoned, just like Kai – the only thing stopping Irene from accusing her of betrayal. She must *know* the current situation was dangerous.

Outside, the city still stank of smoke, and drizzling rain made the air clammy and depressing. Irene drew her veil across her face and considered how best to hunt down an ungrateful, unthinking idiot apprentice.

Catherine had left an hour ago, but the convent's entrance was deliberately unobtrusive and unwatched. There wouldn't be any witnesses to her vanishing act.

Of course, it *was* always possible that Catherine had just gone back to their shared lodgings, without bothering to leave a message. Possible – though unlikely. Still, Irene reluctantly decided she should check first.

Fortunately she and Kai had taken a few 'simple' precautions when they moved house – such as renting the basement flat next door (doing so under another name) and installing a hidden entrance to their own cellar. After all, one never knew when one would have to sneak into one's own house. And if you had installed a secret entrance, for fear of assassination, so much the better.

Their house itself was quiet, with the slight patina of dust that came with several days' absence. The front doormat seemed untouched – but the back doormat revealed recent footprints. Small feet, narrow shoes, and a couple of traces where muddied skirts had brushed the skirting-boards. Catherine had indeed come in this way.

There were no bombs – no obvious ones, at least. No giant spiders. No assassins hiding behind curtains. Irene prowled silently through the house, looking for traces of someone trying to kill her. Her heart jumped into her throat at every noise from the street outside. Finally she had to admit that either the house wasn't primed to murder her, or the trap was so well prepared that she couldn't find any infernal devices.

Perhaps I'm looking at this the wrong way. If Lord Guantes is back, and given what a devious, gloating, overly intricate plotter he is, what would he do?

When she put it that way, the answer was obvious.

Her private study was as quiet and apparently undisturbed as the rest of the house. But, as she'd partly expected, there were two letters on the desk, in sealed envelopes. One was in Catherine's handwriting. The other . . . wasn't.

Gripped by a sense of urgency, she ripped open the letter from Catherine first. The peace treaty could be over if Catherine walked into a trap and ended up dead. But her first concern was for the safety of her apprentice. Catherine knew the situation was bad. She didn't know *how* bad.

The scrawled note inside – clearly written in haste, using

pen and ink from the study desk – was brief: *Irene, I'm going to check out Kenneth and Ruthcomb, the bookseller which helped arrange the Merlin sale. I'll meet you back at the hospital. Catherine.*

Irene suppressed her urge to tear up the missive and throw it in the bin. She forced herself to be fair. Catherine might be ridiculously careless of her own safety, but this was a reasonable line of investigation. The Fae had potential – if Irene could keep her alive long enough to realize it. Right now, Catherine couldn't be that far ahead of Irene.

But there was also the second envelope.

She drew on her gloves as an extra precaution and carefully eased it open with a paperknife.

The letter inside was written on expensive notepaper, in a distinguished hand. She glanced at the end and was rewarded by the signature – *Guantes*. Irene suppressed pleasure at this useful confirmation of her fears and continued reading.

> *My dear Miss Winters,*
>
> *You will have realized by now that I intend to bring down irretrievable ruin on you, your loved ones, your friends and associates, your workplace and anything else that comes to mind. Please don't feel obliged to thank me. It is my pleasure entirely.*

That was certainly Lord Guantes' style – as grandiose as ever. She read on.

> *You have always struck me as an understanding woman.*

Pure sarcasm. He hardly knew her. Besides, any discussion which began with how understanding she was, was likely to end with what she could do for them.

So I'm sure that you can appreciate quite how unpleasant it was for me when you foiled my plans and stabbed me. It also caused my wife a great deal of unhappiness. (She sends her regards.)

Irene felt the back of her neck crawl as she read, and suppressed the urge to check nobody had crept up behind her. These sentiments were usually expressed over the point of a dagger, or immediately after a target had drunk poison, or when the victim thought she was alone . . .

But as a reasonable man, I'm willing to propose a deal: if you hand yourself over, I will let the others live.

Just how stupid did he think she was? Even if the Fae had to keep their given word, a statement like that offered all sorts of opportunities for evasion. There were a great many things that could be done to someone while still 'letting them live'. Things that Irene didn't particularly want to consider.

I can hardly give you my address and expect you to turn up on my doorstep. However, we both know you'll think of some way to track me down. So my offer is this: if you find me and surrender yourself, I will call off the hunt. Otherwise . . . well, I won't go into details. It would be a waste of good paper.

If you don't find me, you will die in any case. But you will be taking your friends with you to an early grave. Their blood will be on your hands.

Consider that, before you make any rash decisions.
Guantes

She didn't think much of his attempt at emotional manipulation. Unfortunately, she was up against a melodramatic villain with no sense of proportion when it came to vengeance.

Irene pocketed the letter and left the house through the secret entrance. At the moment she felt like a juggler with too many balls in the air – Kai, Catherine, Sterrington, Vale, Singh – and the rest of London besides. She needed to at least catch Catherine before things became any worse.

The bottom of Irene's empty teacup stared up at her. After a very significant first stop, which had eased her mind a little, she was now staking out her target from an inexpensive teashop. It was the sort that served factory girls, underpaid secretaries and teachers. She'd changed her clothing to fit the location, and she was reasonably confident that she'd lost anyone trailing her. This London might be foggy and wet, but its prevailing fashion for scarves and veils was convenient for escaping followers. And now she had a plan – at least where Catherine was concerned.

She'd been looking at this from the wrong point of view. She didn't want to *follow* Catherine. She wanted to get ahead of her, but she needed to do it before the young woman threw herself neck-deep into trouble.

Catherine wanted to be useful, to show her worth to the Library. She'd been in on the hunt for the Malory book. Just as Irene had worked out their bookseller might have leaked information, so had Catherine. If only she'd broached this idea *before* Irene had left the hospital. Was it Irene's fault Catherine was so desperate to prove herself?

No. Irene wasn't going to take the blame for this. But clearly better communication was needed. Possibly from six inches away, while reading Catherine a lecture on common sense.

Irene would have to notify the Library of their findings so far, including Catherine's disappearance – but she needed to find Catherine *now*, and Lord Guantes would be watching likely Library access points anyway. It was so inconvenient having an opponent who knew one's capabilities. Although not quite as bad as going up against another Librarian. She thought of Alberich, and shivered.

The waitress was staring at Irene's empty cup meaningfully. In a moment she'd be coming over to ask if madam would like anything else, with the implication that if madam didn't want to order, then madam should be on her way.

But Irene wasn't going anywhere – because she was waiting.

Bookshops crowded along Charing Cross Road in vertical stacks and horizontal huddles, and spread down the side streets and back alleys on either side. The ones on the main street drew tourists and casual wanderers, but the hidden ones were far more interesting.

Irene's vantage point had an excellent view of the entrance – the only entrance – to one particular alley. This was why she'd picked it. A rapid change of clothing and a wig from her lodgings had left her looking plausibly dowdy, a visitor from the provinces without a sense of London fashion.

She was about to order more tea, when she glimpsed her target – a familiar gait and a glint of bronze hair underneath a cloak and heavy face-concealing hat. Irene made a mental note to go through basic principles of disguise with Catherine once this was all over. Voluminous clothing was *not* the best way to go unseen; it exposed you as someone who wanted to hide.

The Fae wasn't carrying anything more than a handbag; she must have left the Malory suitcase somewhere else. Somewhere safe, Irene devoutly hoped. While Catherine occasionally paused to look in shop windows as she drifted along Charing Cross Road, she wasn't taking any measures to shake off pursuit either . . .

. . . which was a mistake on her part, because two men were following her. They paused when she paused, and moved again when she moved. Both of them were burly types in bowler hats, with spotted kerchiefs wound round their necks – a flash of red against dark clothing. Both gave off an air of menace, the sort that made others get out of their way.

As Irene watched their progress, she realized where she'd seen them before. She knew who those two were – or rather, *what* they were. This could be useful.

Then Catherine turned into the side street Irene had been watching. The two men glanced at each other and quickened their pace.

Just as Irene had expected. One of the buildings in that alley housed Kenneth and Ruthcomb, a 'bookhound' agency. They tracked down rare books – whether for sale or not, by means fair and foul – and offered their services to anyone who could pay their rates. They'd been the first step in the chain that had taken Irene to Guernsey. As both she and Catherine had diagnosed, they were the logical source of that information leak – whether they'd done so maliciously or otherwise.

Pragmatism warred with concern as Irene paid for her tea, then followed Catherine in turn. She didn't *want* to use Catherine as bait, but these mysterious followers were the first real lead she'd found so far.

Catherine had wanted to make herself useful. Being a student was all about learning experiences.

She followed at a discreet distance. Fortunately there were enough people around for her to merge with the crowd, and the two men didn't notice her. As expected, Catherine headed directly towards the agency. Irene hung back long enough to watch the two men follow her apprentice before entering the building herself, using the Language to silence the doorbell. A narrow, musty hallway led to a flight of stairs that ran up to the first-floor landing.

Catherine paused there, about to knock on the book-hounds' office door, when she noticed the two men closing in. 'Is there some reason you two are following me?' she demanded. 'Because I have business here.'

'Your business is with us now,' the larger man said. 'You're Catherine, aren't you?'

'Of course not,' Catherine said quickly, failing to suppress a betraying start.

The office door opened, and a bespectacled man glanced round it. He saw the confrontation in progress and quickly shut the door again.

'Now we can do this the easy way,' the smaller man said, 'or we can do this the hard way. Either way, you're coming with us.'

'Don't be so silly,' Catherine said contemptuously. 'You can't just drag me through the streets in broad daylight like that. This is London. It's a civilized city.'

'There's lots of ways round that,' the larger man said, his right hand clenching.

Irene decided it was time to step in. 'Gentlemen, I'm sure there's no need for that,' she said, stepping out of the shadows and looking up the stairs.

'You don't want to get involved, miss,' the larger man said. 'Just turn around and walk away.'

'Young man, I'm a teacher back at home, and when I see some poor girl being lured into sin—'

'You've got it wrong, miss,' the smaller man said, hastily changing his approach. 'This young madam here's run away from her family. Took all the family money, she did. Broke her poor mother's heart.'

'I didn't!' Catherine said indignantly. Funnily enough, she didn't seem to have recognized Irene either. 'These men are lying!'

'Right, that's enough.' The bigger man grabbed her arm

and began hauling her towards the stairs, ignoring her attempts to pummel him. 'Stop that messing around, or I'll clout you one.'

The smaller man trotted down the stairs towards Irene, trying to smile in a friendly way. 'We've got this under control, miss, so you can leave her to us.' *Get out of the way or you'll get hurt*, was the unspoken message.

Irene plucked a heavy umbrella from the hatstand beside the door, swinging it to get a feel for its weight. 'On the contrary,' she said, her voice sharpening. 'You'll release the girl.'

Catherine gasped in belated recognition and Irene sighed. They'd definitely have words after this. But the two men didn't make the connection. 'Fred, deal with her,' the larger man ordered.

'Shoes, slip,' Irene said.

It was unfortunate for the smaller man that he was still heading down the stairs. His shoes lost their grip on the boards and slid out from under him, and he crashed headlong down the stairwell. Irene placed the metal tip of her umbrella in the hollow of his throat.

'I know what you are,' she said. She looked at the bigger man, who had a firm grip on the struggling Catherine. Like her, he'd been stationary when she'd used the Language, so he'd been unaffected. A pity. 'You're both werewolves. Are you in the London Underground pack? The one that follows Mr Dawkins?'

'How come you know the boss?' the one on the floor whimpered, trying to avoid the umbrella's cold tip. Silver might have a permanent effect on werewolves, but other physical objects could still do damage.

'Because we've met,' Irene said. She met the eyes of the larger man. 'I think he'll understand if I dispose of you two.'

There were too many teeth in the man's mouth as he grinned at her. 'I'm getting the feeling you're not a teacher.'

'I've had many jobs,' Irene said. 'Who sent you to grab the girl?'

The back of her mind was processing this information. If Mr Dawkins was knowingly involved in the assassination attempts, London's werewolves would be an active force in this fight. It wasn't just their lethality which worried Irene – it was their ability to track people. It'd be much harder to hide if the werewolves were on their tail.

'None of your business who sent us,' the larger man snarled. 'Now move. If you were going to stab Fred, you'd have done it already.'

Threats clearly wouldn't work here. Irene mentally sighed and went for her trusty second option. **'You perceive that I'm someone Mr Dawkins trusts,'** she said, before adding, 'I think we've been sent on the same errand. I'm here for the girl too.'

The man at her feet blinked. 'You are?'

'I am.' Irene removed the umbrella from his throat. 'They've changed the drop-off. I'm supposed to hand her over at the east entrance of King's Cross station. Or did you get told that too?'

The sharp teeth receded within the larger man's mouth, and his face looked normal again. 'Nah, we were told Flower and Dean Street in Spitalfields, at the Crown and Anchor pub. Why the change?'

Irene kept her face impassive, but inwardly she winced. Spitalfields was one of the nastier parts of London. It was where Jack the Ripper operated in some alternate worlds – though not this one, thank goodness – and was the sort of place where policemen went around in pairs because it wasn't safe alone. 'I think they want to get her out of London,' she invented. 'It's too risky to keep her here.'

Both men snorted with suppressed laughter. 'Even Peregrine Vale's not going to find her if the Professor puts her away,' Fred said.

The Professor – that name again. Lord Guantes had said, *The man behind the Professor knows you, and he wants you.* More confirmation that this was all tied in with the Guantes and the murder attempts on Guernsey. Irene desperately wanted more information, but she was on a timetable and the Language's influence might wear off at any moment. That was the problem with the *you perceive* trick. Once it stopped working, the people afflicted would remember exactly what they'd said and done – and chances were they wouldn't like it. 'Tell you what,' she suggested, starting to climb the stairs. 'You two go ahead to the drop-off point – we'll meet you there. It'll be too obvious if we travel together. But first I have some unfinished business to deal with here.'

'You want us to hold onto the girl for you?'

'No, I'll take her with me. I'm not letting her out of my sight.' Irene took hold of Catherine's arm, her ruthless tone backed by a very real urgency. She had to get Catherine away before this turned violent. She glared at Catherine in her most cold-blooded manner and felt a mean satisfaction when the other woman flinched.

The werewolf released Catherine. 'You could have said who you are *earlier*,' he complained.

Irene sniffed. 'It's not like anyone told me what you two looked like, any more than they told you about me,' she said. 'I'll meet you soon – I don't expect to be long.'

They both nodded and headed outside.

The werewolves dealt with, Irene banged on the office door with her umbrella. 'Kenneth and Ruthcomb? I'm here on business.'

There was a pause on the other side of the door, and then the noise of someone dragging away heavy furniture, before it creaked open. The bespectacled man from earlier peered out nervously. 'You are?'

Irene jammed her foot against the door before he could close it again. 'I am,' she said. 'Good business. Book business.'

His eyes widened as he recognized her. 'You'd better come in,' he said.

Irene suppressed a sigh of relief as she drew Catherine into the office and closed the door behind them.

CHAPTER NINE

Kai burst from the space between worlds, a rolling blueness of endless waves, and out into cold empty air. The mountain winds ripped at his wings, and he automatically curved his body to rise above them into calmer currents.

The Swiss Alps lay spread below him, untouched white snow on grey mountain ranges, with occasional markers of human habitation or flashes of colour from fields and lakes. The world itself felt calm with the settled flow of order, as reassuring to his draconic senses as the cadence of a marching army or the pulse of a lover. Beyond that, like a superimposed melody, he could sense the presence of other dragons. Much as he enjoyed Irene and Vale's company – and, though he might not admit it, the excitements of Vale's world – it was good to be away from the constant aftertaste of chaos, back where things were *right*. Orderly. As they should be.

And he knew the person he was searching for lay some-where below.

Cuifen had always been one of Kai's favourite cousins, but their connection was on his more low-born mother's side rather than his royal father's. As such, he didn't see her as much as he'd like. However, Cuifen still treated Kai with more generosity and affection than many of his siblings – and she was an expert in computers and data analysis.

She was one of several dragons who specialized in the field, working under Lord Zhang Yi, an undisputed expert. Zhang Yi was a dragon of such genius that it eclipsed his low birth and minor family. Kai certainly wouldn't be granted an audience with Zhang Yi – but Cuifen might be willing to do him a favour.

He drew his wings against his body and stooped towards a small cluster of buildings. Zhang Yi's headquarters were deceptively pastoral, with a central compound surrounded by lesser structures. But Kai knew power lines led here from the nearby waterfall, and the classically simplistic roofs housed solar panels. Lord Zhang Yi needed the electricity, even if style demanded that everything appear natural.

Half a dozen human servants hurried out to greet Kai, their footprints marring the untouched snow. They bowed as Kai settled to the ground and assumed human form, and one approached. 'Good afternoon, sir. My name is Hans Baumann, and this is the establishment of Lord Zhang Yi. May we know your name and family?'

'My name is Kai, son of his majesty Ao Guang, King of the Eastern Ocean,' Kai said. 'I am here to visit my cousin, the lady Cuifen, but I would be honoured to meet Lord Zhang Yi himself. I bear a small present which I hope may not displease him.' He offered one of two parcels he was holding – a Han Feizi text from Vale's world, which he'd been saving for such an occasion.

'Unfortunately Lord Zhang Yi is occupied,' Hans Baumann said, as Kai had expected. But custom demanded that both sides go through the motions. 'We will be glad to pass on your gift. If you follow my colleague Anna, she will escort you to lady Cuifen's quarters.'

Perfect. Kai followed Anna – a brisk young woman with

blonde braids curled into a bun – as she led him into one of the side compounds. 'This way, your highness,' she said.

The decor within was classically draconic in style, with bold red tiles, white walls and dark wood pillars. But the aesthetic had been subverted by personal tastes: sheepskin rugs were scattered on the floor like irregular islands, and paintings of vivid flowers and desert landscapes hung on the walls, gaudy and impossible to ignore.

The inner door swung open. 'I've *told* you, I'm still working on it,' a female dragon said as she emerged. 'I'll . . . heaven and earth, cousin Kai!'

Cuifen ignored propriety and gathered him into an embrace, her hug as strong as ever. She appeared almost human, but hadn't bothered to fully transform; she was as green as fresh grass, from her shoulder-length hair to the tiny scales that covered her flesh. Kai assumed a similar form in politeness, his skin and hair turning dark sapphire blue and small horns sprouting from his brow.

'You can go, Anna,' Cuifen said over Kai's shoulder. Humans were definitely lower in the hierarchy here. 'Well, cousin. I've been nagging you to visit me for a while now, but I have to tell you, this isn't the best moment. We're all busy, Uncle Zhang Yi in particular.'

'I was told he was too busy to receive me, but I'd assumed that was customary,' Kai said.

'Yes. Something happened – a month or so ago – which means we need to review much of the royal houses' security software.'

'I won't stay long – but I have a problem and would be very grateful for your advice,' Kai said. 'While I have no claim on your time or assistance—'

'Don't be ridiculous,' Cuifen said, clearly impatient with formalities. 'Sit down and tell me about it.' She dropped into one of the heavy chairs, folding her legs underneath her.

Despite her semi-draconic form, she was wearing a casual human wardrobe of heavy knitted jumper, jeans and striped woollen socks. Clearly humans had *some* influence here.

'All right,' he said, sitting opposite her. 'I have a laptop which I need analysed.'

'Can't you do it yourself? You've got access to worlds which have the technology – your lord uncle Ao Shun's hideout, for a start.'

'It shames me to admit it, but I'm not sure I have the level of skill needed. It's from a high-chaos world – and I can't risk mistakes.'

Cuifen's eyes widened in delight. 'You've brought me a computer from a high-chaos world? Cousin Kai, you are a darling!'

'More than that,' Kai said. 'The laptop belongs to a powerful Fae – someone who's trying to kill me. And Irene too.'

Cuifen rubbed her hands together. 'Better and better. How exquisite! I mean that in the nicest possible way, you understand. I don't usually get the chance to hack top-level Fae software.' She paused, remembering. 'But don't we have a truce with them? Why's a powerful Fae trying to kill *you*?'

'Personal matters,' Kai said. The less people knew about the individuals involved the better – especially while they were still investigating. He ran over the basic details of the last few days: the book-collecting mission, the poisoning attempt, the submarine base ambush, and how Irene had stolen the laptop as she fled. 'So you see,' he finished, 'I need an expert to take that thing apart and extract the data. Our lives might depend on it.' *We might even be lucky enough to find Lord Guantes' entire evil plan, with easy-to-follow presentations for his minions,* he thought. Fae were like that sometimes.

Cuifen's elegant brows drew together. 'I didn't realize your assignments were quite that *dangerous*,' she said. 'I thought you attended Fae cocktail parties and coaxed them into indiscretions over canapés.'

'Unfortunately not all Fae throw cocktail parties,' Kai said. 'Even those who do can be extremely dangerous. You should see their buffet selections – and I *never* touch the fugu livers. Or the absinthe.'

Cuifen frowned at his flippancy. 'There are risks, cousin, and then there are stupid risks . . . I'm not asking you to withdraw—'

'Thank you,' Kai said drily. 'It is my *job*, after all.'

'—but you need to consider your security from a more adult standpoint. Take a couple of bodyguards. You're putting yourself at risk.'

'*Life* is risk.'

Cuifen leaned forward, her eyes intense. 'Your life has *worth*, cousin. Don't throw it away.'

Between them, unspoken, lay the words, *because you care about a particular human being . . .*

'I doubt that *some* family members valued me before my new position,' Kai stated, his voice icy. There was a reason why he'd approached Cuifen rather than . . . a certain other computer expert here.

His cousin shrugged. 'You can sulk about your brother, or you can accept how things are and work with it. With the risks you're facing, perhaps you should relocate for a few years. If you move to a different world, your enemy will be inconvenienced. It's not as if you *have* to keep your embassy on that world, after all.'

She had a good point, but following her advice would mean deserting Vale's world – and Vale. *And would Irene follow me? If the Library told her to stay, which of us would she choose?* 'You're not wrong,' he said, desperately searching for a solid rebuttal. 'It's just that . . .'

The door clicked open, and Kai looked up with relief.

Coffee would be a welcome distraction. Then his heart sank to see his half-brother, the very person he'd hoped to avoid. He rose and bowed with a carefully judged level of courtesy. 'Elder brother,' he said, 'I did not expect to see you here.'

'Which explains why you didn't pay your respects to me first?' his brother said. Shan Yuan's scaled skin was the same clear ruby as his eyes, and he was gowned in heavy scarlet brocade. He acknowledged Cuifen's bow with a casual gesture. 'Still, it's good to see you. My letters appear to have been going astray.'

Kai had taken care to answer Shan Yuan's letters as politely as possible – but he'd had to meet all his brother's demands upon the embassy, or his attempts to restructure it, with variations on *No*. 'I apologize,' he said, rather than contradict his half-brother in company. 'I've had so much correspondence of late.' This was in fact true; a number of dragons had suddenly found him worthy of interest, after he'd gained his new position.

'So if you aren't here to see me, why are you actually here, little brother?'

'Someone's trying to kill me.'

For a moment Shan Yuan's brows rose in surprise – and what seemed to be genuine anger at *his* kin being targeted – but then he composed himself. 'I suppose that's an occupational hazard, given your current position.' Shan Yuan's tone suggested that if it *wasn't* for the treaty's importance to his people, he'd happily have sat back and watched with a bucket of popcorn. 'So did you come here to snivel on Cuifen's shoulder?'

Cuifen said pleasantly, 'Would you care for refreshments, Shan Yuan, even though you've barged into my territory, completely uninvited?'

Shan Yuan ignored her, his attention returning to Kai. 'What does Cuifen have to do with your little problem?'

'I'm here to get a laptop analysed. It may contain details of my adversary.'

'Fair enough.' Shan Yuan extended a long-fingered hand, claws gleaming like garnets. 'Hand it over.'

'Kai asked *me* to look at it!' Cuifen exclaimed.

'Yes. But my technical knowledge is superior to yours. I *am* Lord Zhang Yi's first student, after all.'

'You are indeed – since Indigo is no longer here,' Cuifen said, her smile icy. 'And, as you're always telling us, your skills are vital to Lord Zhang Yi's current project. You'll drop everything to help your brother? How touching.'

'I'll prioritize it . . . appropriately,' Shan Yuan said, a glint in his eyes.

Kai knew what *that* meant. He'd have to wait here until Shan Yuan 'found time', the very thing Kai didn't have to spare. He tried again. 'Elder brother, this matter may relate to the treaty. Those involved may be the ones who abducted me before.'

Cuifen snorted. 'Come on Kai, let's go visit the other students. *Some* people would be extremely interested to hear about your diplomatic work. Lord Zhang Yi might find time to talk too, over the next few days.'

Shan Yuan rounded on Kai. 'If you expect me to help you at *all*, I would suggest you don't remind me of your incompetence. Follow me. We'll look at the laptop in my quarters.'

Kai suppressed a smile. His cousin's comment had hit the mark. Clearly the last thing Shan Yuan wanted was Kai hanging about the compound, 'showing off' his work on the treaty and making Shan Yuan feel less important. He really hadn't realized Shan Yuan would feel so bitter about Kai's new role and higher status among their kind. With a nod of farewell to Cuifen, he followed his elder brother obediently.

Once they were outside, he said, 'The sooner I get that data, the sooner I can be gone.'

Snow melted on either side as Shan Yuan stalked along the path, revealing dead grass and bare earth. 'Oh?' he snarled.

'I didn't want to inconvenience you. I didn't even want you to know I was here.'

Shan Yuan's eyes narrowed, and the circle of melting snow around them expanded. The stone path beneath Kai's feet grew warm as Shan Yuan's ire rose. 'Are you telling me that you came here with the *deliberate intention* of avoiding me?'

Kai wasn't a great detective, but even he could deduce that *Yes* was the wrong answer here. Though he couldn't fathom why Shan Yuan would even care. He'd always treated Kai with dismissive contempt – and Kai had eventually duelled Shan Yuan over his refusal to acknowledge Kai's mother. He'd broken Kai's arm in that fight, which he won. He constantly criticized Kai's manners, skills, and conversation. Why *should* he want Kai to visit?

'I know how busy you are,' Kai offered hopefully. 'I know you're Lord Zhang Yi's senior student—'

'In Indigo's absence,' Shan Yuan interrupted. 'You don't need to say that.' He paused. 'Everyone else does.'

That surprised Kai. He'd never realized that his elder brother could feel any sort of inferiority. 'Well, it's not as if I'd know what goes on here, is it? *I* didn't get invited to study under Lord Zhang Yi.'

'You could have been,' Shan Yuan snapped, 'if you'd applied yourself. Instead you ran off to play around in high-chaos worlds and seduce Librarians. You are a *disappointment*.'

Fury ran through Kai like fire. He looked Shan Yuan in the eye. 'Our lord father is proud of what I have achieved.' Old grievance and current ire mingled in his heart and drove him to insult. 'I hope you can say as much.'

Shan Yuan's blow knocked him to the ground.

Kai clung to the laptop, shielding it from impact with his

body, but his cheek stung where his brother had struck him. He staggered to his feet, feeling his power call to the roaring waterfall nearby. 'Again, brother?' he snarled. 'You'll find I'm not as easily beaten as last time.'

'Cease this folly!' The voice was thin, but rang with authority. The brothers turned simultaneously, then bowed.

Lord Zhang Yi – for who else could it be? – showed his age, as did all dragons from less powerful families. He was in human form, wrapped in the same heavy brocade robes as Shan Yuan, though his were pale grey and far more ornate. His tufted white eyebrows shadowed his eyes like an eagle owl's, and his thinning hair was braided down his back.

He looked at them and sighed. 'Why must your father's children always come to blows beneath my roof? You will both attend on me at once. We have important matters to discuss.'

CHAPTER TEN

The bespectacled man – Mr Kenneth, the main face of the business – looked reproachful as Irene locked the door behind her. 'I thought you'd finished with us today, madam.'

'Wait, what?' Catherine said, surprised. 'You've already been here?'

Irene glanced around the rather basic office, checking for new threats and thankfully finding none. It was comparatively bare, if you were expecting a library of exotic tomes. The rare books were safely locked away elsewhere in the building.

'She has indeed,' Mr Kenneth said. 'One of our most valued customers, of course – always welcome, whatever the hour, whatever the circumstances . . .'

Werewolves certainly counted as 'circumstances'. 'We'll be leaving by the back way, if you don't mind.'

'What happens when those ruffians come back looking for you?' he asked.

'Tell them we paid you to let us out.'

'But you haven't . . . ah.' He swept up the coins that Irene was counting out on his desk. 'Always glad to oblige. Anything else before you go?'

'Yes. Get hold of that *Ivanhoe* we were discussing earlier, please. I'll pay the usual commission on delivery.' As he nodded, Irene added casually, 'Oh, one last thing – I didn't ask you this before, but does the name "the Professor" mean anything to you?'

Mr Kenneth's hand jerked, and a coin went spinning across the desk. When he looked up at Irene, she could see the fear in his eyes. 'I'm sure I don't know who you mean.'

'That bad, huh?' Irene said quietly. She'd avoided asking him during her first visit, as she'd suspected mentioning *that* name would be burning her boats with him. But since she had no plans to come back soon . . .

'You heard nothing from me. Now do me a favour and get out of here. You know where the back stairs are.'

Irene nodded. 'Come along, Catherine. I'll explain when we're out of here.'

To Irene's relief, there were no watchers – well, no obvious watchers – waiting at the back of the building. 'We'll walk towards Covent Garden,' she said quietly, 'and catch a cab on the way.'

'To stop any other werewolves following us by scent?' Catherine guessed.

'Correct. Well done.' She caught Catherine's hand as the Fae was about to signal an approaching cab. 'We won't take the first one. Never take the first cab.'

'But if everyone does that, won't the *second* cab always be a trap?'

'Unfortunately it's quite possible that the first half-dozen will all be traps,' Irene said. 'Sometimes devious plotters really irritate me.'

Irene had an ear cocked for distant screams and howls at their escape, as she flagged down a ride, but all seemed peaceful behind them – or as peaceful as could be expected for London. She helped Catherine in and took a seat opposite her.

'Where to, ma'am?' the driver asked.

'London Zoo,' Irene said firmly. With the current traffic, that should take at least half an hour too – hopefully long enough to find out what was going on with Catherine. 'First things first,' she said. 'Are you all right?'

'I think so,' Catherine answered. 'I wasn't hurt.' But she was clearly still on edge, glancing out of the window as though she expected to see werewolves running alongside them.

'Good. Now . . .' Should Irene immediately grill Catherine for information, or instead try to gain her confidence by explaining what she'd been up to? She decided to take the second route. 'I'd already spoken to Mr Kenneth before you arrived. He didn't want to admit it, but they had a break-in a week ago. And it wasn't to steal books – but information.'

'What sort of information?'

'Their shop records. Whom they sold to, their suppliers . . . They took a few obviously valuable books as well, but the information was the real prize.'

Catherine pursed her lips. 'And if their customers found out someone had stolen their data, it would mean losing those customers.'

'Exactly,' Irene agreed, glad she was so quick to understand. 'The thieves tried to conceal that they'd been into the records, but Mr Kenneth said that they disturbed some safeguards he and Mr Ruthcomb had in place. The records the thieves examined included the transaction Kenneth and Ruthcomb set up for us on Guernsey – including the date and time of the meeting with Madame Pipet.' The break-in had been several days ago, so their enemies could have arranged the ambush.

'So how come he admitted all that to *you*?'

'A carrot-and-stick approach,' Irene said. 'The carrot was me paying him a lot of money. The stick was threatening to tell his *other* regular customers about the data breach.'

'Would you have actually done that?'

Irene sighed. 'The bookhounds are even more unscrupulous than I am, in case you think that was unfair.' She wasn't sure whether Catherine wanted to be reassured that Irene was a fundamentally decent person – or a fundamentally ruthless one. 'Let's say I'm glad I wasn't forced to put it to the test. Mr Kenneth believed I would tell, which is the important thing.'

Catherine nodded, her eyes wary. 'So where are we going?'

'Ultimately? To a place I rent.' Irene wasn't going to give the address with the cab-driver listening. 'Now, what have you been up to?' She controlled her impulse to scold her apprentice for her disobedience. She wanted Catherine talking, not retreating into a sullen silence.

'I've been busy,' Catherine said, doing her best to make herself sound proactive, rather than werewolf bait. 'You read my note, didn't you? After securing the Malory book, I went on to investigate why our last assignment was jeopardized.'

'But I told you to stay where you were,' Irene said.

'I decided it was just too risky.' Catherine looked rather smug at her logic. 'And I bet the hospital's now been blown up or attacked by assassins, hasn't it?'

'Well, no. Not the last time I checked.'

'Oh.'

'You don't have to sound so depressed,' Irene said. 'Besides, our assassins were busy somewhere else. They set fire to Sterrington's office. While I was in it.'

Catherine frowned. 'That's rather reckless. Attacking *you* is one thing, but attacking the Cardinal's agent risks drawing *him* into this.'

'Thanks,' Irene said drily. 'But that's a good point. Perhaps that's why the attack was so sweeping in scope.'

Outside, London went about its business, the streets churning with afternoon traffic and the pavements crammed with pedestrians. Inside the cab, the two of them were as privately closeted as in a confessional. If one ignored the driver – which they did.

'What do you mean, "sweeping in scope"?' Catherine asked.

'There were other people in that building who might have been targets – assuming that the fire was even recognized as an assassination attempt, rather than an accident. If Sterrington had died, and if Kai, Vale and I were also mysteriously murdered, the Cardinal would have been left with no clear evidence as to who was responsible – even if all three treaty representatives dying accidentally might seem an unlikely coincidence.'

She could have made some gruesome predictions about the possible consequences of all three representatives dying, but she didn't want to unsettle Catherine – or at least, didn't want to unsettle her further. Being the target of a murderer left one in a natural state of unsettlement anyway. Instead, she said, 'So where *did* you secure our latest precious book?'

'It's in a left luggage locker,' Catherine said carefully.

'Oh?'

'At one of the railway stations.'

'I can't help noticing that you're not telling me which railway station.'

'Irene.' Catherine swallowed nervously. 'You know that I wouldn't want to consider blackmailing you.' Her shoulders were hunched, her hands tightened into fists; she was clearly already expecting opposition and punishment.

'I wish I *did* know that,' Irene said, 'because I have a nasty suspicion that what's coming next sounds a bit like "You don't get the Malory book back unless you do what I want."'
Be calm, she told herself. *Let her say her piece.*

'I don't *want* to blackmail you,' Catherine said, '. . . but I will if I have to!'

'A balanced and reasonable attitude,' Irene said drily. 'So what do you want?'

Catherine clenched her hands in her lap, her expression mulish. 'I don't want you dumping me with someone else. I want to learn how to be a Librarian. A *real* Librarian, even if that means joining some of your more . . . adventurous missions. I know you can work out a way to make this happen if you have to. I just need to motivate you properly.'

'Catherine . . .' Irene wanted to tear her hair out in frustration. 'You're behaving as if this is some sort of training exercise or comedy of errors. It isn't. People have *died*. Our enemies aren't afraid to blow up submarine bases or torch office buildings to get rid of us. We're currently on the run in a London that's been infiltrated by one of the most devious men I've ever known—'

'You have a monomania about Lord Guantes. And in any case, I don't think it's him.'

'I have a sensible and well-reasoned fear of Lord Guantes,' Irene said between her teeth, 'and there's only one other person who could pull off a plan of this scale – and would make me his primary target.'

'Who?'

'Alberich.' Whom Irene had left behind in a burning library, in a world deep in chaos, hoping that he was dead or permanently trapped there. She wasn't going to tempt fate by saying anything like *We'll never see him again*, but she did hope rather desperately that he was gone for good. But in any case, he definitely couldn't enter this world – so he couldn't have been responsible for the Guernsey ambush. That was something.

'Oh yes, Uncle told me about him.' Catherine sounded dismissive, as though *the greatest traitor in the Library's history* warranted no more than a footnote in some academic's research. 'You dealt with him before, though, didn't you? I don't see why you can't do it again. And he was a villain. Doesn't the Library have heroes to counter people like that?'

'No, we just have people who get the job done. A number of whom were killed by Alberich, in various unpleasant ways, so I advise you *not* to talk about him so casually. And speaking of your uncle, he's left town. Or did you already know that?'

Catherine clearly didn't. Her eyes widened in shock. 'He never leaves London if he can help it. Has something happened to him?'

'No. At least, I hope not. He's gone to Hawaii with his household. Ostensibly on holiday, but he was warned of an assassination attempt. Which is why I particularly want to make sure you're safe.'

'But I don't *want* to be safe!'

'You might feel a bit differently if *you'd* been trapped on the roof of a burning building earlier today.'

'I'm an adult.' Catherine folded her arms. 'And I'm your student. *Teach* me.'

'You seem to think that I'm your enemy, not your teacher,' Irene said, her voice a whipcrack. 'You've disobeyed me, you've endangered yourself and you've attempted to black-mail me. Why *should* I teach you?'

'I did what I did because I couldn't be sure you would teach me, otherwise.' Catherine glared at her, as if willing her to concede. 'You're not my kind. You aren't forced to keep your word if you give it. So I looked for other options.'

'No, I'm human,' Irene said slowly. 'Which means you're going to have to depend on my sense of honour instead.' And on her urgent need to get Catherine into the Library, so as not to disrupt Library–Fae relations. But it wasn't the moment for ulterior motives. 'Are you really asking me to pledge my name and power in the Language to teach you, in return for your Fae oath to obey me? Do you actually want to bind us in an unbreakable bond, unto death – as that's

119

what it would mean?' She leaned in closer. 'Do you think that you're actually going to be any happier or better off that way, Catherine?'

Catherine edged back in her seat a little, unease showing in her eyes. 'I . . . perhaps that might have some disadvantages I hadn't considered.'

'I'll do it if I must,' Irene went on, holding the Fae's gaze. 'I honestly thought we could trust each other. I've tried to be fair and honourable. But if a binding oath is the only thing you'll accept, then I'll do it, and God help us both. So make your choice, Catherine. Are you prepared to bind yourself to obey me as my loyal student? Or can we simply trust each other to keep the deal we've made, and do our best to behave like rational adults?'

'Perhaps I should consider apologizing instead?' Catherine suggested in a tiny voice.

'Perhaps you should. Just a moment.' The cab had slowed to a crawl. Irene rolled down the window and leaned out to call to the driver on the roof. 'Is something the matter?'

'Traffic jam, ma'am,' he said. 'We may be a bit late getting to the zoo.'

While Irene didn't *think* that Lord Guantes would tie up London's traffic, just to catch her, staying in one location was dangerous. 'We'll walk from here,' she said.

Two hours, three cabs and a fair amount of walking later, Irene finally sat down, feeling something approximating safety. The cheap rooms they were staying in were near Heathrow Aeroport, but within the zeppelin port's workers' district, rather than near the opulent hotels for incoming visitors. All her usual precautions were in place too, so she felt confident that Lord Guantes wouldn't have found *this* hideout yet.

'You said you wanted me to teach you,' she said to

Catherine, who was staring gloomily out of the window at the smoke-stained wall of the house opposite. 'This is a very important lesson. Always maintain a few alternate hideouts in case things go wrong. I rent this place and a few others, using different bank accounts under different names, and I drop by once or twice a month to check that things are in order.'

'All that for emergencies that might never happen?'

'Things *have* gone wrong,' Irene pointed out. 'This is not an academic exercise. You wanted to be a Librarian. You wanted me to teach you. So pay attention, because we're about to have a very thorough class on paranoia, why it's a good idea, and how to be motivated by it.'

Catherine pulled off her bonnet angrily and threw it down on the battered dresser. 'You're not listening! At least I've got you to myself now and I don't have to compete with Kai all the time. But I want to be a Librarian – a *real* one.'

Irene was about to say, *What do you think I am?* – but something made her pause. She had an unpleasant feeling that she and Catherine were operating on different wavelengths, and this had to be sorted out before matters became any more dangerous. 'So explain to me,' she said, keeping her voice mild as she sat down in the room's only chair. 'I'm listening now. Tell me what you mean.'

'Irene, you're a very nice person,' Catherine said, obviously slathering on the honey before she got to the vinegar stage of the conversation. 'I've nothing against you personally. I'm sure that you really believe in what you do.'

'But?' This didn't sound promising. Though it did sound patronizing.

'I don't want to be a librarian *spy*! I don't even want to be an archivist. I want to be a *proper librarian*. I want to be someone who shares books, who shares knowledge, who makes the library a better place!' Catherine was transfigured.

Her face was alight with eagerness, and her eyes were almost literally glowing with emotion. 'I want to be the sort of librarian who curates books, who loves them and cares for them and shares them with other people. I want to welcome little children into the library and hand them books which will make their imaginations blossom. I want to find the books people have spent their lives looking for, to help them achieve the things they were always meant to do. I want . . .' Catherine must have noticed Irene's horrified expression. 'You did ask,' she said resentfully.

Screaming would not help. 'How long have you felt this way?' Irene asked, as gently as she could manage.

'Years.' Catherine sat down on the edge of the bed. The springs creaked under her weight. 'I wasn't lying, you know. When I said I wanted to be a librarian I was telling the truth. If I have to go on a few adventures with you first, I don't mind doing that, as long as I end up where I want to be.'

'But your uncle negotiated your apprenticeship so you'd end up being a Librarian like *me*,' Irene said. That had been quite definite. 'Collecting rare stories, helping keep the many worlds stable, that sort of thing.' The *sort of thing* that was Irene's work and life. 'Not to become a glowing, romanticized librarian archetype.'

'I'm not responsible for what Uncle said to you,' Catherine said, hunching her shoulders again. 'Besides, he *knew* what I wanted, he must have deliberately chosen to ignore it. And it's not as if you have to do that much to help me. Just get me into the Library and I'll take care of the rest. If I can do that to keep them happy, they won't care what I do next. I want the books *and* I want to share them.'

How many other 'little details' had Lord Silver left out? Catherine's current over-emotional, brattish behaviour suggested one possibility. Irene tapped her finger on the arm of the chair. 'Catherine . . . your uncle assured me that you were "of age", and that you were experienced and reliable. That I shouldn't make any judgements based on your appearance. In retrospect, he was trying to make me think you were older than you look, wasn't he? Just how old *are* you?'

'Twenty-five,' Catherine said brazenly.

Irene met her gaze.

'. . . next year.'

Irene stayed silent.

'Okay, I'm twenty-three.'

Irene raised her eyebrows.

'Twenty-one?' Catherine said hopefully.

'Just tell me which side of eighteen you are,' Irene said wearily.

'I'm eighteen in five months' time,' Catherine muttered. 'And there are lots of cultures which consider me to be fully adult and capable of making my own decisions about my future.'

Dear merciful heavens. I have a teenage Fae on my hands. One who feels she has a vocation to be an archetypal librarian. Irene wished that she believed in prayer. It would have been nice to have someone to ask for help. Unfortunately she had committed herself to taking on Catherine as her apprentice – and neither Lord Silver nor the older Librarians were about to let her off the hook in a hurry.

'You're being very quiet,' Catherine said uncertainly.

Sighing won't help. Nor will screaming or throwing things. 'Perhaps you'd like to tell me a little bit more about your past employment,' Irene suggested. 'Previously you hinted you had a career in international intrigue. Should I assume that was a blatant lie too?'

Catherine stared at her hands. 'Well, I was Uncle's social secretary,' she mumbled. 'For three months. So you could call that international intrigue. Before that I grew up in the country, in a manor house in Liechtenstein with retainers. I didn't do much there besides read. That's why I want to be a librarian – a proper one – and spend all my time with books.'

'What about your parents?' Irene asked.

'They died when I was very young. Uncle Silver's my uncle on my mother's side. There was an accident while they were travelling and then Uncle did what he could for me. I chose my name because St Catherine is one of the patron saints of librarians . . .'

Irene had been wondering how her student had acquired her name. Powerful Fae hid their true names, choosing an appropriate pseudonym – like Silver, or Sterrington, or Lord Guantes – while the *really* powerful ones like the Cardinal or the Princess went by titles alone. She pulled herself away from speculation to reality. 'I wish you'd told me this before,' she said.

'Would you have taken me for an apprentice if I had?' Catherine asked.

'I don't know,' Irene admitted, 'but at least I'd have had a better idea of what was going on.'

Catherine chewed on her lower lip, trying and failing to look calm and unconcerned. 'So what are you going to do?'

'We're going to take this one day at a time,' Irene said finally. 'Our first objective is to stay alive. I'm not happy with you, Catherine – but I'm not going to abandon you.'

'Thank you,' Catherine whispered. 'I hoped you'd understand. Uncle said your parents had been Librarians too.'

Lord Silver had apparently been very free with his information about Irene's background. 'They were,' Irene said, deciding a bit of reciprocal honesty would be good for their relationship. 'They are. They adopted me as a baby, but yes – libraries are what I've known all my life. I've always loved books.'

She left out the fact that she'd only found out about the

adoption a few months ago. And that it had taken place under dubious circumstances, which her parents had been completely unwilling to discuss. Kai and Vale knew all about it, but she saw no reason to share those details with Catherine.

'How do you ever let go of them? To pass them to the Library?' Catherine asked. 'The books, that is?'

'Practice. And I do know I can visit them if I really want to . . . We'll collect the Malory in the morning. For now, get some sleep. You look tired.' And it would give Irene a chance to draft some letters – to Vale and to a certain Fae uncle. 'I'll wake you later so I can nap myself. We should probably take turns to keep watch.'

'I thought you said we were safe here!' Catherine protested.

'Relatively safe.' Irene looked out at the fog, dyed orange and red by the setting sun. 'I'd hate to find out I was wrong.'

CHAPTER ELEVEN

Kai glanced around the inner sanctum of Lord Zhang Yi's office. Zhang Yi favoured a calming palette of grey and white. The only notes of colour were framed slices of crystal and gemstone that hung on the walls – Kai spotted a deep green, a red and a purple. Even the chair was upholstered in bone-white cloth, the stools covered in dark grey silk. It was like being inside a frozen cloud. A single tablet rested on the low table.

'Sit,' Lord Zhang Yi said, lowering himself into the chair. His back was erect, but he moved with the slow care that Kai had seen in elderly humans with arthritis, like Irene's Librarian mentor Coppelia. 'Prince Kai, you have come at a convenient time.'

'I'm glad to be of service, sir, and hope that my present pleased you,' Kai answered. Even though Shan Yuan was a couple of feet away, he could sense tension emanating from his older brother. But Kai knew the proper forms of courtesy. He wasn't going to offend his revered senior – especially not when Zhang Yi was a dragon he truly respected.

'There was a present?' Lord Zhang Yi blinked. 'How kind. But that wasn't what I wanted to discuss.'

There were only two things that Kai could imagine Lord

Zhang Yi wanting to raise: treaty matters and Indigo. Of course, it would be nice to believe that Lord Zhang Yi had heard about his talent with computers and wanted personally to invite him to be his student . . . but that was about as likely as his brother deciding to forget their past rivalry. So he said, 'Of course, sir. How may I be of assistance?'

'Fae and computing.'

When it was clear that further detail wasn't forthcoming, Kai said tentatively, 'If you would explain, sir?'

'We do not have a *peace* with the Fae. We can never expect to be truly at peace. The best that we can hope for is this truce. However . . .' Lord Zhang Yi's eyes glittered beneath his thick eyebrows. 'While we *do have* the truce, we need to take advantage of it in every way possible.'

Wild images blossomed in Kai's mind. 'Are you considering a dragon–Fae student exchange, sir?'

'Of course not!' Shan Yuan snapped. 'Who in their right mind would agree to that?'

'The fact that you consider such a thing speaks well for your innocent warm-heartedness, boy,' Lord Zhang Yi said. 'No doubt this broad-minded attitude is what allows you to tolerate the Fae. Don't misunderstand me. I agree some of them have certain . . . qualities that would, in our own kind or humans, be worthwhile. Admirable, even. But that only makes them more dangerous. In the long run, we have to expect the worst and make preparations accordingly.'

'You speak as though you don't expect the truce to last, sir.'

Lord Zhang Yi briefly withdrew into himself, reduced to rigid weariness. 'Nothing lasts,' he said, his voice guttural with age and remembered pain. 'Neither knowledge, nor skill, nor family, nor the bond between master and student. In another thousand years I will be gone. In time you both will pass as well, and this place will be dust. For all that we pride ourselves on our power and our length of years, Prince Kai, ultimately dragons too are as fleeting as fireflies. There was a time when we never existed; there will also come a time when nobody will remember us. War changes to peace. But, ultimately, peace collapses into war and the cycle continues.'

'I've told you before, sir, you will be remembered as long as my father's kingdom lasts.' Shan Yuan spoke with affection, clearly repeating an old reassurance.

'That's not as reassuring as you might think.' Lord Zhang Yi was staring into emptiness. His eyes were on Kai, but his gaze passed through him. 'Not at all.'

Kai remembered a recently discovered painting which had suggested there was more to dragon history than the dragon monarchs ever wished to reveal. Could it be that a few of the very old dragons, like Lord Zhang Yi, knew something about this?

Lord Zhang Yi pulled himself together, his eyes refocusing. 'In the meantime, yes, we must take advantage. Nothing that would make us as vulnerable as exchanging students or sharing private research papers, of course, but we should certainly be *negotiating* with any Fae experts in the field who are willing to talk. Data on the latest technical advances in high-chaos worlds would be useful intelligence. As would anything on new developments, Fae open-source systems, their protocols, whether or not their worlds are using block-chain technology or bitcoin . . . Don't look so surprised, boy.'

Kai hadn't *thought* he'd looked surprised, but apparently he was an open book to his elders. 'But are they going to want to hand over that sort of information, sir?'

'Of course not. However, they're certainly going to want *us* to hand it over. So they'll have to approach us somehow. I imagine there will be some complicated dancing around in the middle before anyone on either side admits it.'

'So should I expect the Fae treaty representative to be approaching me?' This was actually sounding very intriguing. The Fae would have to make *some* concessions, after all, and the prospect of seeing how advanced some of the high-chaos worlds were . . . His lord father would be making the decisions, of course, but Kai would still be on the front lines for any bargaining. This would be *fun*.

'Yes. And you can pass all their queries directly to Shan Yuan here.'

Kai's heart sank at the thought of being cut out of the deals. Hand over everything *interesting* to Shan Yuan, of all people? *There has to be some way round this . . .* 'I'm sure my lord father will be sending you the information himself, sir.'

Lord Zhang Yi twitched one arthritic hand in disdain. 'His majesty Ao Guang has a great deal to oversee, and I am his technology adviser. You will be doing us all a favour by allowing us to triage any Fae advances directly. We'll then pass on just the relevant details for his majesty's attention. Naturally, closing any subsequent negotiations will remain with you.'

'Of course, sir,' Kai said, reassured. 'It will be my honour.'

Lord Zhang Yi stroked his beard. 'Good. Excellent. Your brother tells me that you've worked in our field yourself. You may be worth considering as a future student.'

Kai wasn't going to delude himself that this possibility was due to his talent alone. Apparently Lord Zhang Yi played politics and exchanged favours just as much as any other powerful figure. Still, that didn't mean it wasn't a genuine offer, and it was something he'd very much wanted . . . at one point. Right at this precise moment, with Irene as a lover, Vale as a friend, and his current position to enjoy, it was a choice that he'd rather postpone. He ducked his head and mumbled thanks.

'Do you underrate yourself? Remember that talent can set

its own terms.' Lord Zhang Yi gestured at the room around them. 'I may not be of royal blood, but I have the respect of my students. This world is my home, and if I feel like moving my establishment to the Alps, or Tibet, or Egypt, or Vietnam, then I simply give orders and it is done. In some respects I'm as well-informed as royalty, with their spymasters.'

He paused. 'There's actually something else I meant to discuss with you too. You must forgive an old man his lapses in memory, boy. It happens to all of us.'

Kai would believe that one of dragon-kind's most renowned geniuses had memory lapses when he believed his father was having an affair with a Fae. Or that Irene had gone to sleep without a book next to her bed. He made the appropriate polite noises and waited with interest.

'There's something going on out there.' Lord Zhang Yi delivered the statement as though it was earth-shattering news, then sat back, looking pleased with himself.

Kai bit back at least three variants of *There's always something going on out there*, and settled for, 'Would you please explain, sir?'

He stroked his beard again. 'Unfortunately I don't see the specifics. I only see indications. I am aware of equipment being sourced on various different worlds – superconductor technology, servers capable of handling yottabyte-level information – and then simply dropping off the radar. I hear about experts in artificial intelligence vanishing from those worlds. I am becoming aware of something perceptible only by its absence. It worries me.'

'How do you know all this, sir?' Kai asked.

'I know people,' Lord Zhang Yi said dismissively. 'High-level people. I read their emails.'

Kai wondered whether that meant *I read emails from them* or *I have access to their email accounts and they are blissfully ignorant of that fact*. The statement's ambiguity was rather frightening. 'I thought that worlds with a high technology level were more likely to be high-order, sir. Just as worlds with a high magic level are more likely to be high-chaos. There are anomalies, of course . . . but surely the Fae can't be *ahead* of us.'

'The only reason they could be is because they *cheat*,' Shan Yuan said flatly. 'Or sometimes, their environment does the cheating for them.'

Lord Zhang Yi gave Shan Yuan an approving look. 'Well put. A high-chaos environment favours impossible "rags-to-riches" success stories, as well as incredible failures. The bigger the rise or fall, the better the story. So it favours impossible computing – leaps of logic which no sane person would make, fortunate discoveries that go against all sensible principles of programming and engineering, and convenient . . . guesses.' He spoke the word *guesses* with a contempt worthy of Vale on such matters. 'The laws of science remain the same. But, given equal research opportunities in a high-chaos world versus a high-order world, Fae research may reach their goal sooner. This is simply because it's *appropriate to the story*. The hero makes their discovery at a crucial moment in time.'

'Of course they have twice as many destructive failures as we do, for the same reason but in reverse: the story demanded a tragic ending.' Shan Yuan clearly felt these were thoroughly well deserved. 'You see the problem, Kai? A Fae in a high-chaos world may hit upon a new one-chance-in-a-million discovery, because their personal fiction gives them that crucial stroke of luck or invention. But that one success story could be very dangerous for us.'

'I'd never thought of it that way,' Kai said soberly. He made a small bow to Lord Zhang Yi. 'Thank you for alerting me to the danger. How can we guard against this?'

'One of our advantages is that they do not cooperate as

we do. All dragons work as one, under the guidance and leadership of our monarchs.' *Was there just a shade of cynicism to Lord Zhang Yi's voice?* 'If the Fae have found a project to unite them, to share discoveries . . . well, then I am concerned. If these disappearances, this new technology, these advances in artificial intelligence are all somehow tied together, then we *need* to know more. Some Fae may believe in this truce, but others would break it without hesitation if they thought they had a superior weapon – and the opportunity to take us by surprise.'

'This may touch on the reason I'm here,' Kai said slowly. 'My lord—'

'You may address me as uncle,' Lord Zhang Yi said genially.

'Uncle, there have been several attempts to kidnap or assassinate me – and the Librarian treaty representative. The most recent one was just yesterday.'

'Yes, I've heard of the Librarian. Sensible, for a human. But how is this linked to the greater problem?'

'While she was investigating the assassination attempt, she encountered Lord Guantes, a Fae who kidnapped me in the past.' Kai felt himself flushing at the thought, from both rage and humiliation. 'She stole this laptop from him, on a high-technology world, which was why I came here. I wanted any useful data it contained. I'm not saying that the Fae assassination attempts are *necessarily* connected to the plot you suspect, but . . .' He shrugged and quoted an old maxim. 'Clamour in the east, then attack in the west.' A classic stratagem: cause a major distraction and then subtly pursue your goals. The treaty representatives dying, most likely killing the treaty too, would certainly be a major distraction.

'I will look at this laptop immediately,' Lord Zhang Yi declared.

Kai tried not to look too triumphant as he placed the laptop on the table. 'Thank you, Uncle.'

'It *may* all be part of a greater conspiracy,' Lord Zhang Yi said. He leaned forward like a predator about to strike. The room felt arid and sterile, offering no cover from his gaze, no protection from his attention. 'We must investigate everything. We can trust nothing. Remember that, boy. Nothing. We may be able to use Fae information, but we must never trust it. If the Fae are assembling some great creation, fuelled with their powers of narrative and story, then we must be ready to stand against it – or exploit it.'

'But you said yourself that some of them believed in the truce, Uncle,' Kai protested unwisely.

Lord Zhang Yi snorted and drew back – and again, Kai had the impression of a hunting owl, mantling wings and wide furious eyes. 'You must learn to recognize the difference between philosophy and practical reality. That will come with time. For the moment, you are dismissed – both of you. I should have the information for you tomorrow, Prince Kai.'

As Kai rose to complete the process of polite farewells, an icy thought nibbled at the edges of his mind. The future might demand that *both sides* changed, if the truce held and they were to build something permanent. How much would the older dragons, like Lord Zhang Yi – or like Kai's own father – be able to change?

He forced the thought away. The truce had only been in place for a few months. The future was still to be built.

'If the Fae are trying to develop new technology, do you think their magic will be a problem as well?' Kai asked. They were walking around the edge of the compound, taking the air together. Shan Yuan had been silent most of the way, brows drawn in thought.

'Magic? No.' Shan Yuan seemed relieved to have a question he could answer. 'That's too dependent on the structure of the particular world where it operates. It can be dangerous if used by someone skilled in local practices, but it shouldn't be an issue if this *is* a conspiracy across multiple worlds. If you're interested in that area, though, you should talk to one of our lord uncle Ao Qin's children or grandchildren – they're the family's experts.'

'I'll bear that in mind.' Shan Yuan seemed in a far better mood now than earlier. Quite possibly the most pleasant mood that Kai had ever known him to be in – which said a great deal about their relationship. 'Elder brother, some of what was said at that meeting concerned me.'

Shan Yuan eyed him sidelong, the sunset light burning in his eyes. 'You've impressed me favourably with your behaviour so far. Don't disappoint me now.'

'It's the possibility of technology exchange.' He decided some honesty might be a good idea. 'I'm not sure I have the background to fully assess the implications of Fae approaches on that front. Should I worry about this? Ask for additional staff or assistants, perhaps? What if I miss an important clue?'

'Be *worried* about the Fae, and chaos, and people trying to kill you,' Shan Yuan snapped. 'Don't get caught up in minor details.'

'But if any approaches concerning technology come through treaty channels, should I notify Lord Zhang Yi and our father about *everything* that seems relevant?'

'As Lord Zhang Yi said, I'll take care of them,' his brother said impatiently. 'Send them to me and I'll forward anything relevant to our lord father.'

Then Shan Yuan drew to a stop, lowering his voice and catching Kai's arm. 'Kai, I have studied here for over seventy years now, and Uncle Zhang Yi is my teacher and master. I have nothing but respect and affection for him. Current times are unstable, and this plot – this possible plot,' he corrected himself, 'has disturbed him. Is it any surprise if he wants tighter control over this sort of information? Things will return to normal again soon enough. Just behave yourself and do as you are told.'

If he *wants tighter control over this information – or if* you *do?* Kai thought. He trusted his brother absolutely in one respect: Shan Yuan was unfailingly loyal to their father. There was no way he'd betray Ao Guang – as their sister Indigo had done. But that didn't mean he lacked ambition. He had his own goals. But what if these conflicted with the things Kai cared about?

CHAPTER TWELVE

Night had fallen; the streets of London were full of shadows, and the rooftops even more so. The slates were wet and slippery under Vale's feet, inviting accidents. The street lamps which burned dimly below were suns, orbited by the night-dwelling citizens of London's underworld. Some stayed close to the comforting lights to display their wares, or to seek safety. Others kept their distance to avoid exposure.

Vale could feel the heat emanating from the attic window beside him, even though the room's owner had insulated it with dark cloth and layers of padding. This was confirmation that his information had been correct. He also wasn't surprised by the multiple locks or the hidden poison needle trap. Those too were entirely in keeping with the person who lived here. Silently, he opened the window and let himself drop through.

He landed with a faint thump – a squelch, even – on the well-watered soil that had been spread across the floor. He'd landed between two rows of hellebore, their five-petalled white flowers facing upwards like stars. The entire attic had been converted into a forcing-house for the owner's favourite varieties of plants. Ether-lamps blazed from the rafters, keeping the place well lit, and heaters stood along the walls.

Like the greenhouses at Kew Gardens, the air was scented with moist greenery – or perhaps tainted might be a more appropriate word, given the type of plants cultivated here.

Vale headed towards the door, taking care not to step on the plants. There was no point in aggravating their owner more than necessary, or destroying future evidence. But as he reached the door it swung open, and the house's owner faced him.

Her eyes widened in shock and one dainty hand went to her throat. She was in a comfortable-looking hyacinth-blue tea-gown, as might be expected for a woman of her class at home of an evening. A lacy shawl covered her shoulders. Ash-blonde ringlets were caught up in a deceptively simple style, and her round face was the picture of innocent vulnerability. 'Who are you?' she gasped. 'What are you doing here?'

'My name is Peregrine Vale, madam, as you are perfectly aware,' Vale said. 'I advise you against using the pistol under your shawl or the blade in your sleeve. It would be extremely difficult for you to explain my corpse's presence here – and fatal, if I may choose an appropriate word, to your line of work.'

She was an excellent actress. The flicker of calculation in her eyes was barely perceptible. 'I refuse to believe you're Peregrine Vale. The greatest detective in London wouldn't just show up in my attic like this. You're some sort of burglar. I insist that you leave right this minute, or I'll call the police!'

'Spare me the breathless histrionics,' Vale advised. 'Calling the police would be inconvenient for both of us. A few minutes of conversation would be a great deal more profitable, and then I will leave you in peace to start packing.'

This time the narrowing of her eyes was quite definite, however much she tried to hide it. 'Packing? Why should I do that?'

'Claribelle Houndston,' Vale said, turning away from her to stroll down a narrow path between the lines of herbs and flowers. 'Or should I call you Lucy Windermere? Or Ethel James? There's also Percival Felixton, John Brookes and several others – not to mention your foreign aliases. I will address you as madam out of courtesy, but I'm forced to admit that I am uncertain of your original gender or name.' A fact which galled him. He turned to face her. 'You are extremely efficient at covering your tracks. I must applaud the fact that you choose your aliases at random, rather than according to some personal theme or preference. Very few people can avoid that – however much they may consciously try.'

She cocked her head thoughtfully, like a bird trying to decide whether a worm would taste as good as it looked. 'Tell me, Mr Vale, does your sister know I'm living here?'

'Who do you think gave me your address?' He hoped his sister would never consider employing this woman, but his sister *did* work for the British government.

'Drat,' Claribelle Houndston said. 'Very well. Clearly there's something you want, or you wouldn't be here. Who's my new "client"?'

'I'm not hiring you to assassinate anyone,' Vale said curtly.

'No? I'm sure there are a few people in London whose removal would be convenient for you.'

'Madam, you seem to have misinterpreted my position. I am a detective, not some . . . Napoleon of crime.'

'In that case, I have *absolutely* no idea what you're doing here,' she said. 'Do close the window behind you. After all, as you've pointed out, I need to start packing if my location is known.'

Vale strolled towards her, ducking under some trailing fronds of wisteria. 'What I'm after, madam, is information.'

Her face went still, her expression deadly. 'That's not something I sell.'

'I'm quite aware. It's part of your reputation, after all. You are untraceable, unrecognizable, and you never betray your paymasters. The Secret Gardener, they call you. Morbid, but poetic.'

Claribelle Houndston sighed. 'If you know all that, then why are you bothering to ask me?'

'Because I hope I can persuade you otherwise. You are leaving town, after all. Our conversation will remain strictly confidential, with neither the police nor criminals knowing about it. I'm not asking you to provide *evidence*, madam – merely data for my own use.'

'I might be able to work with that,' she mused. 'But what sort of payment are we discussing here?'

'Come now,' Vale chided her, pausing a safe distance away from any unexpected knife thrust. 'I've made you aware that I and my sister know where to find you. Surely that's payment enough?'

She looked unconvinced, but didn't argue the point – probably already planning her departure to somewhere he and his sister *wouldn't* be able to find her. 'You're not making any new friends tonight, Mr Vale.'

'A fact of little or no significance to me,' Vale informed her. 'Let us be brief. My information suggests that you may have been hired for a contract on myself, and certain of my friends, rather than simply cultivating your garden.' He glanced across the range of flowers and herbs, identifying half a dozen as lethal and most of the rest as extremely dangerous. He spotted datura with its pale trumpet-flowers, black lotus in the tiny artificial pond, aconites and foxgloves along its banks and nightshade twining with the wisteria in an elegant purple backdrop. 'Is that correct?'

After a moment's consideration, she reluctantly nodded. 'I'll admit that a contract along those lines is currently under discussion. Not actually signed yet, though, so you needn't threaten to trample my flowers.'

'Thank you for confirming my suspicions. As it's not signed – yet – can you give me the details?'

She blinked. 'You're really taking this rather well. Are you sure you haven't been sampling my garden already?'

'Madam,' Vale said, 'I have grown used to attempts to murder me. I no longer view them with the concern that I once did. In some respects, I consider them a badge of honour – especially when undertaken by people such as yourself, or commissioned by the person I believe is behind this.'

'And who do you think *that* is?' she asked. She'd relaxed, and now employed the playful tone of someone trying to coax an indiscretion out of an indulgent uncle.

'Are you acquainted with the Professor?'

The winsomeness faded like a passing summer's day, and her mouth snapped shut. This time, she made no attempt to disguise her reaction. 'Right,' she said. 'Out. Now.'

'Thank you for confirming my hypothesis,' Vale needled her.

She glared at him as though he was an unexploded bomb just discovered on her premises. 'Why did you bother coming and asking me, if you already knew my employer?'

'Suspicion is one thing; confirmation is quite another. Such a beautiful specimen of oleander.' Vale put out a hand as if to touch it, before having second thoughts. 'I haven't seen that shade of crimson before. I don't suppose you would consider selling cuttings? No, perhaps not. Now why are you so averse to the Professor?'

She folded her arms and appeared to be counting silently to ten, or praying for patience. He often inspired this reaction in women – Vale had even seen it in Winters once or twice, however much she denied it. 'Having a criminal mastermind taking over the local underworld is bad news for independent specialists,' she said. 'Sooner or later one is faced with a choice between permanent employment or permanent relocation – either out of the country, or into a grave. I was prepared to consider taking a contract or two before leaving, so as not to end things on bad terms with the Professor. But I'm not in the habit of wasting my breath – and you seem to know all about these developments already.'

'The flattery is appreciated but unnecessary.' Vale stepped closer. 'What else do you know about him?'

She rolled her eyes. 'I might as well be hanged for a sheep as a lamb, I suppose . . . He's new to London, and he's very secretive. He's been taking over other organizations from the top down and keeping his own name out of it. Not that I know what his real name is, anyhow. Why bother with a name when you have an alias as good as *the Professor*?' She shrugged. 'And from what I've heard, he's *Fae*. I'm not interested in working for someone who thinks I should be able to achieve the impossible because it makes for a better story. Sometimes summer plants aren't supposed to flower in winter.'

Vale gestured to the many out-of-season flowers which crowded her attic greenhouse. 'But you do make summer flowers grow in winter.'

'That's down to good gardening,' Claribelle Houndston said firmly. 'Not supernatural powers.'

'Have you met him in person?'

She shook her head. 'All our communication's been through the post. I burned the letters after reading.'

Vale would expect no less from someone with her reputation. 'The details of the contract, please.'

She pursed her lips, and he could tell she was rethinking her decision to cooperate. 'Miss Houndston, bear in mind you are already heavily compromised. If the Professor finds out that I was here . . .'

'I could present him with your corpse,' she said speculatively. 'That might go a long way towards convincing him of my good faith.'

'You could certainly *try*,' Vale said.

For a moment she weighed up her options, and then accepted defeat. 'Very well. I was given two targets – you and a man named Kai Strongrock, a frequent visitor to your lodgings. That's all.'

Vale frowned. 'Nobody else?'

'No, just the two of you. In fact, there was a clause in the contract that nobody else in your vicinity – or among your friends – was to be injured or damaged in any way.'

'Is that sort of clause unusual?'

'Not really. It can be relevant when an inheritance is at stake, for instance, and a precise order of deaths is necessary. But I admit I couldn't see the point of it in this case. The Professor doesn't have a reputation for sparing the innocent.'

'Indeed.' Vale kept his guard up, but inwardly he found himself confused. This made little sense. Why hadn't this woman been ordered to murder Winters as well? More precisely, why were her orders almost specifically designed to ensure Winters remained safe and unharmed? 'You will be abandoning the contract, I trust?'

'Yes. It seems rather pointless, now I've alerted the primary target. I wasn't seriously planning to go up against you, in any case. I'm abandoning the contract and London for the foreseeable future. To be frank, you and the Professor are welcome to kill one another.' She glided past him, indicating the open window, steps confident as she wove between the rows of deadly flowers. 'Now get out of here, before you end up dying in my attic and I turn you into compost.'

'No doubt I'll see you again at some point,' he said affably.

For a moment, her expression was as lethal as her favourite poisons.

* * *

A couple of hours later – following two changes of clothing, an attempted mugging and some inconveniently persistent followers – Vale was sitting in a corner booth of a pub near the docks, nursing a pint of dubious beer. The fog outside lapped against the windows in a dank grey mass, as though the taproom had sunk beneath the Thames. Its ominous presence seemed to quiet conversation. So although the pub was busy, no one laughed, shouted or argued, and the customers hunched over their drinks, their voices muted to a background murmur.

The door creaked open and a man in battered sailor's gear shouldered in, his dark hair and beard glistening with raindrops. Singh's disguise wasn't on Vale's level, of course, but it was adequate – no one would recognize the Scotland Yard inspector. He glanced across the room, and Vale raised his tankard as a signal. Singh collected a beer of his own and joined him. As a practising Sikh he wouldn't actually drink the stuff, but a man ordering a non-alcoholic beverage here would've been more noticeable than a policeman in full uniform.

Singh and Vale sipped their drinks – or feigned to – until any casual interest had died away. Then Vale opened a cheap newspaper to the racing pages, and the two men bent their heads over it.

'Bad news, I'm afraid,' Singh said quietly. 'We're being pressured to find the culprit behind the arson attack as fast as possible. Madame Sterrington's being put forward as one of the possible suspects. Not the only one, of course – my superiors aren't *that* obvious – but her name's on the list.'

'Inconvenient, though also informative. I learn as much from what you're ordered to hush up as I do from what you're allowed to pass on to me.'

'And as long as they believe I *am* hushing it up, it keeps them trusting me,' Singh agreed. 'Otherwise I wouldn't have been given a sniff at the records you wanted today.'

Vale nodded. He understood that the police force, like any large institution, had ways of ensuring that certain information was kept secret. Sometimes word came down that a matter had to be 'solved' – by whatever means necessary – to keep it out of the papers. That was when the powers-that-be found people like him useful.

Of course, word didn't always come *down from above*. Sometimes it came from a distinctly lateral route. If he'd had more leisure, he would have investigated how pressure was being applied to Singh's superiors. But time was of the essence here. 'And *did* you get to see those records?' he asked.

'I had one of my runners pull them – together with a set of others to confuse the issue.' Singh feigned a swallow of beer. 'You were right that all the crimes in question show signs of a protection racket in operation, or blackmail. And all these cases were reported by concerned family members. The actual victims denied that any crime had occurred at all when the police came round to inquire. Denied it very vehemently, in some cases.'

Vale nodded. He would expect the Professor to be thorough when it came to controlling rumours of his activities. 'Was there any police follow-up?'

'Only in one case, and that only because the fellow committed suicide. Belson, the painter – the one who was implicated in the Flemish Primitives forgeries case, remember?' Singh waited for Vale's nod. 'He'd already lost all his money and a fair amount more at cards, so when he blew his brains out nobody was surprised. But his lady friend had gone to the police earlier, claiming that he was being blackmailed. It made his death look suspicious. She apparently left town the day after.'

'And I suspect that – conveniently – she hasn't been heard from since.'

'Not a word. So what do you have in mind?'

144

'I've told you I believe a new spider has entered London's web,' Vale said, allowing himself just a touch of metaphor. 'Previously, he's been acting through agents and catspaws. But his empire has now extended far enough that even the police begin to perceive it.'

'Miss Winters would tell you that such a spider can be female just as well as male,' Singh noted, tankard raised to conceal a smile.

Vale snorted. 'Very well. I concede the gender is uncon-firmed until we have further information. However, I am certain of this mastermind's presence – and I'm now sure that they're linked to the recent assassination attempts.'

Singh turned his tankard in his hand, watching the sway of liquid rather than meeting Vale's eyes. 'We've known each other for a while now. May I speak without prejudice?'

'Always,' Vale answered. He was not the sort of man to talk of 'friends' but he had known Singh for years – nearly a decade, all in all – and he trusted the man absolutely.

'I'm playing devil's advocate here,' Singh started cautiously. As ever, he was being tactful rather than refuting Vale's theory outright. 'But I ask you, what are the odds of someone taking control of London's underworld without the police hearing a single rumour of the fact? A smaller city, perhaps – but London?'

'I don't think this person controls all of London yet,' Vale replied. 'All the more reason for us to stop them before they take it entirely. The police may not have heard these rumours, but the criminal underworld certainly has. Earlier this after-noon I spoke with Claribelle Houndston. She confirmed that "the Professor" was negotiating a contract with her to assas-sinate myself and Strongrock. Before that I was visiting "friends" in the London Underground, and I found letters signed by *the Professor* in Mr Dawkins' own private desk.'

Singh pursed his lips in a whistle. 'If he's got Dawkins in

his pocket, then he has the rest of the werewolves too. They follow orders down there, or they get their throats ripped out.'

'Quite. As for the high finance sector, Wilkinson the banker – who's behind half the touts in Surrey – has been emptying his own bank accounts for two weeks now. He's been paying out to an unknown creditor, and he's not the only one. The Stepney counterfeiting ring, led by the Parr sisters, has recently doubled its output. Need I go on? Must I draw a diagram of all the threads which lead to this central antagonist?' The very thought invigorated him. A challenge at *this* level, a mind of his own quality to duel against, an enemy worthy of his steel . . .

'And you kept all these theories a secret until yesterday,' Singh said flatly.

'I wasn't certain,' Vale excused himself. 'The separate pieces were in my hands, but I lacked definite connections and proof. These last few weeks I have been gathering the strands of a veritable cobweb, and they have either broken under my fingers or melted into the morning dew. I prefer to spin my web and then let you take all the flies at once, if you'll excuse the metaphor. Besides, once we begin to move against our adversary, he or she will respond. For the moment our enemy thinks you are ignorant – and so you remain relatively safe.' Singh hadn't been included in Claribelle Houndston's contract. Yet if their foe realized how useful Singh was to Vale, or even that he was Vale's friend, then his life would be at risk.

Singh made a noise indicating his understanding, but also frustration. 'By not telling me or anyone else, you've put us *all* at risk. And we still know nothing about this Professor – this person's identity, hiding places, strengths and weaknesses . . .'

'Or there could be yet another person behind them,' Vale

said softly. He recalled what Winters had said about her meeting with Lord Guantes. He'd mentioned *the man behind the Professor* . . .

'One criminal mastermind at a time would be quite enough for me, thank you,' Singh said. 'Any thoughts about how we should take this forward?'

'From my investigations among the werewolves, I found a total lack of *personal* communication with the Professor. All orders came through the post, or via newspaper agony columns.'

Singh understood. 'Yes . . . any criminal might hide their identity in this way. But it could also mean he's someone they already know, whom they could identify in person.' Lord Guantes and his wife had been involved with London's werewolves before, using them as minions.

Maintaining their cover, Vale plucked out a coin and slid it across the table to Singh – as if he were settling a bet on the horses. 'Winters has gone to ground, together with her apprentice. Strongrock is absent. I intend to spend the rest of the night pursuing my investigations. I hope to have more information for you tomorrow. The more this Professor attempts to mobilize London against us, the more likely it is that a minion will become careless and can be arrested – and used against our antagonist.'

'You've yet to explain why the Professor wants you and Strongrock dead,' Singh said. 'If you alone were a target, then I'd understand it as part of controlling London. If Strongrock alone were the target, it could be down to some private dispute between Fae and dragons, or perhaps connected to this treaty of theirs. And if you, Strongrock and Irene Winters were named on Claribelle's contract, I could understand that too. It would make sense to dispose of all of you, for fear that surviving members of your group would come after the killer. But for it to be *just* you and Strongrock . . .'

'Yes. Most curious.' Winters had almost been caught in the submarine base attack with him – but she hadn't been expected to be there. Yet leaving her alive made no sense to him. 'Another loose end. I need *more data*. I have my sister looking into cerebral controllers and political intrigues, while you investigate the arson case – though be careful, Singh. If the Professor suspects that we know of our foe's existence, we can expect no mercy.'

'What I can give you is limited,' Singh said. 'If I were back home in Hyderabad – well, I have acquaintances there who could be of more assistance. But here – no. Your sister's likely to be more use than I am when it comes to the inner circles of power.'

Vale nodded. Singh was one of the few people who knew that Columbine, Vale's sister, was more than just a clerk in the Ministry offices. 'She dislikes involving herself in active investigations, but given the circumstances . . .'

'If this criminal mastermind of yours didn't want her attention, then he shouldn't have gone to these extremes.'

Vale frowned at the newspaper. For various reasons, he'd avoided bringing his sister into the side of his life that included Winters and Strongrock. His sister's primary concern was the safety of the British Empire. Although she preferred not to exert herself too much, or miss any meals, she still took her duties seriously. If Fae, dragons and the Library interfered with *her* Empire, London being its capital, she wouldn't spare any of them. Also, he couldn't protect her. She was well aware of these issues, as was Vale. So without either of them saying a single word, he'd known he should refrain from drawing his sister into certain exploits, for both of their sakes.

However, he no longer had a choice.

'What would you like me to do next?' Singh asked quietly.

'Keep a watchful eye for signs of the Professor's influence,'

Vale directed. 'If Madame Sterrington is apprehended, I'd appreciate it if she didn't suffer any mysterious accidents. Either in the cells or, as they say, while *trying to escape.*'

Singh would clearly have liked to refute that insinuation as a slander against the police, but he chewed his moustache and nodded. 'And you?'

'Send any messages to me via my sister. My lodgings are unsafe at present; I've already discovered some dynamite wired up in my cellar.'

'And did you trouble yourself to inform the police?' Singh asked rhetorically.

Vale shrugged. 'I couldn't be sure it was connected to this case. You know the company I keep, Singh. A fair number of my "acquaintances" would leave dynamite, if they thought they could get away with it.'

'We're working on a different scale entirely here, if you're right.' The *if* hung in the air between them. 'Get me some evidence, Vale. This can't go on.'

'Certainly it cannot,' Vale agreed. He tried to ignore the surge in his blood at the thought of the pursuit ahead and the thrill of challenging such an enemy. He would need all the cold logic at his command to track his adversary successfully.

Assuming that the Professor didn't find him first.

CHAPTER THIRTEEN

On the other side of London the air was also thick with fog. Morning might have broken, but there were no rays of sunshine to rouse sleepers. And Irene had it on good authority that London's starlings had long since given up on the dawn chorus. Instead they were hungry scavengers, as vicious as piranhas when they saw a chance at someone's breakfast.

She shook Catherine by the shoulder. 'Wake up,' she suggested.

Catherine grunted and tried to hide under the sheets.

While Irene sympathized, this was going to be a busy day and she had no time for other people's laziness. She pulled off the sheets and blankets, leaving Catherine shivering in her borrowed nightdress. 'Rise and shine, o would-be librarian. We've got a lot to do.'

Catherine was clearly about to complain. Then she took in Irene's expression and shut her mouth, setting about the business of washing and dressing instead. Irene rewarded her with a mug of coffee.

'All right,' she said, once Catherine was in a fit condition to listen. 'It's eight o'clock and we need to get moving. Given the many attempts to either kill or kidnap us, we have to assume we'll be in danger as soon as our enemies locate us.

Before we go any further, I want to be absolutely clear about this – if you continue to work with me, you're going to be in danger.' She was very grateful that Kai was out of London and that Vale was – well, Vale. 'You'd be much safer if you left London and stayed undercover until the current threat's blown over. I promise I'll still consider you as my apprentice and try to get you into the Library.'

Catherine glared at her. 'I'm not leaving you.'

'Don't you trust me?'

'I do, although I don't think you trust *me*. Besides, if something bad does happen, maybe it'll give you the crucial insight you need to get me into the Library.'

'You can't depend on the power of an ideal narrative,' Irene said wearily. 'Sometimes life gives you a dramatic tragedy instead. In fact, the more you depend on a storybook outcome . . .' She saw the look in Catherine's eyes, and gave up. 'Very well. You're sticking with me, then. In that case, we might as well retrieve the *Vie de Merlin* and get it to the Library. I have to report in on the current situation in any case. Where is it?'

Catherine visibly weighed up whether or not she wanted to give up her leverage, then said, 'Waterloo.'

'Good. Let me see. Thinking of nearby libraries . . . there's Methyll Street, St John the Beheaded, the Fosdyke Sanatorium and the Guest Collection. Also a couple of small ones that serve the local parishes.' She considered the likelihood that hostile forces might have staked them all out, and be waiting for them to show up. After all, their enemies – Lord Guantes or otherwise – knew Irene was a Librarian. They would be expecting her to make a run for the Library. But surely they couldn't watch *every* library in London. 'We'll try the Guest Collection. They own some valuable books, so they have better security measures than most; that should keep you safe while I access the Library.'

'Will you try to get me in while you're there?' Catherine asked eagerly.

'I haven't thought of anything new since last time,' Irene admitted. 'And we both know that nothing's worked yet. And I don't want to keep on hurting you until I *can* come up with a better idea. It does hurt, doesn't it?'

Catherine didn't respond, but the way that she looked aside was answer enough. 'Maybe if I really was an archetypal *proper* librarian, it would let me in,' she suggested.

'Have you considered settling down somewhere – somewhere *other* than here – and just working as a librarian for a few years? Somewhere safe?'

'My uncle won't let me do what I want, unless I do something useful for him – like finding out how a Fae can access the Library. This is my chance and you're my ticket in. I'm not letting go of you.'

'How nice to be valued for my true worth.' Irene took the coffee mug out of Catherine's hand. 'In that case, the next step is clothing and make-up. I know you don't *want* to train as a spy, but in the interests of keeping you alive today, you're going to be my co-researcher from France, and you need to look the part . . .'

The Guest Collection had originally displayed a gleaming white marble facade, but the London weather had taken it down a peg or two since. While its mock-baroque spires still towered above the neighbouring buildings, they were stained grey from the constant smog and acid rain. Any smears of white were due to visiting pigeons, rather than the underlying stone. The current owners had spent their money on security, not redecoration, and the elegant windows were firmly iron-barred. Stylized stone hawks still ornamented the building's columns, though, and brooded above the main door – retaining an air of classical menace.

Their hooded eyes seemed to watch Irene and Catherine as they entered.

Irene hadn't spotted any followers – but she wasn't about to take any risks. Posing as a French researcher whose application to visit the Collection had been lost in the post, she complained loudly (in French) before signing a one-day visiting application. She also handed over a large deposit for handling their books. Conveniently, the receptionists were more interested in making a profit from a visiting foreigner than looking too closely at her credentials. As the junior researcher, Catherine carried the small suitcase containing the *Vie de Merlin*. They'd had no problem collecting it from Waterloo station's left luggage department. Irene could only hope their luck would hold.

The building was devoted to the folklore of the British Isles. Irene had scoped it out once before and noted that the Scottish folklore rooms on the top floor were the most convenient for quiet working – and avoiding attention. She ignored Catherine's muttering as the younger woman hefted the case up the stairs, waiting until she was sure they were alone. Fortunately, the Collection tended to fill up later in the day. They should be undisturbed for a while – and an hour was all Irene wanted.

'Sit here and look as if you're studying,' she directed. 'If security shows up and asks where I am—'

'I know, you're in another room,' Catherine said. She wandered along the shelves pulling books down, her fingers lingering on their spines. 'Can I say I'm studying "redcaps" – they seem to be Scottish goblins?'

'As long as you can sound convincing about it.' Irene picked up the case. 'Now if anything goes wrong while I'm away, go back to our overnight lodgings. If that's impossible or if you're being followed, take a hotel room somewhere and *stay there*. Put a message for me in the agony column of the *Times* under the name Melodia Agnes.' A stupid name, but memorable – and no worse than the other pseudonyms there. 'And be careful.'

It was dangerous to leave Catherine alone – but Irene *had* to get into the Library. And without Kai to watch over Catherine, what else could she do?

She suppressed her growing unease. Kai should be the safest of them all. He was visiting family – well, other dragons, at least – and was well away from all this mess. If he was taking longer than expected, hopefully that was because there was plenty of information on that laptop. The fact that she personally missed him – very much – was beside the point.

Catherine already had her head in her selection of books. With an unnoticed wave, Irene went looking for a door.

The Collection was built in an old style, with a warren of rooms opening onto one another rather than being accessible from a central corridor, but they all encircled the central staircase. Inside the building the marble of the floors and walls was still white and luminous, and the shelved books were a finer decoration than any painting or panelling – in Irene's opinion, anyway. She passed deeper into the silent rooms of the Scottish folklore section until she found an unobtrusive cupboard. A quick look revealed cleaning supplies.

She closed the door and scribbled on it **This door opens to the Library** in the Language, using an anachronistic biro she carried for emergencies. She felt the drain of energy as the connection established itself. The portal would remain open for half an hour at most – hopefully long enough for her to report and ask for help.

Then she opened the door and stepped through.

Instead of revealing more pale marble and high windows, the room on the other side was low-ceilinged and timber-floored. The heavy door that led further into the Library was closed, and the single lamp that hung from the ceiling burned fitfully, making the whole room feel like an underground shelter. The shelves were packed with carefully organized and preserved scrolls; their ends seemed to lean towards Irene, as if tempting her to unroll one.

Fortunately this was one of the rooms containing computers, so Irene wouldn't have to waste time searching for one. She booted up a terminal and logged on, trying not to get too impatient at every second that slipped away.

Her first email was to Central Processing, before she'd even checked her own account, asking for someone to collect the Malory book from this room. She didn't have time to find a deposit point, so just this once she'd delegate. Then she looked at her messages.

And she swore.

The email at the very top was a bulletin to all Coppelia's students. Coppelia was an elder Librarian, Irene's own mentor and the very person she'd been going to ask for advice. It read: *The Librarian Coppelia is seriously ill with pneumonia and is not available for lessons or assistance. She is currently receiving the best possible medical care. Presents for her may be left with Musaka. No grapes.*

It wasn't just self-interest that made Irene blaspheme. Coppelia had been her teacher and friend for over a decade. Irene had known that the older woman was ill, ever since the last winter in Paris, but Coppelia had sworn she was getting over it. Irene should have pushed harder for her to have a check-up, she should have made her listen . . .

You're wasting time, the unwelcome voice of pragmatism said at the back of her mind. *Focus on what's important.*

But Coppelia *was* important. And the Library was important. All at once a rush of nostalgia came over Irene, a swell of despair at how everything kept on going *wrong*. She felt a desperate wish to just come back here, come back *home*, and let everything outside go to hell in its own way. What was the point of trying to support this damn truce, if the people she loved here were at risk? Why had she ever wanted anything outside the closed circle of stealing and reading books? What was it ultimately going to get her? Catherine had the right idea. Irene should be working with the books she loved, the people she loved, rather than playing politics.

Except that wasn't an option.

The Library wasn't *just* about collecting and preserving stories. It was also dedicated to protecting the worlds where those stories were written. And it wasn't a charity. Librarians *paid* for their use of the Language, their ability to travel between worlds via the Library, and their access to all its books. They paid with the coin of service. Once you were sealed to the Library and had its brand on your back, as Irene did, your life was no longer entirely your own. You followed orders – to collect books, or help maintain a peace treaty. Although you might have some discretion about *how* you followed those orders, refusal was not an option.

Irene could imagine Coppelia scolding her for the imprecision of that statement. *No, refusal is an option. It's just that refusal comes with consequences. If you make a choice, then you're responsible for the consequences of that choice.*

For a moment Irene allowed herself to look around the room, at the tantalizing shelves, the scrolls, the door that would lead deeper into the Library – where she could crawl into a corner and never come out again . . .

All right, now she was just being ridiculous.

She took a deep breath and scanned down the list of emails. Book request, book request, coffee request, nothing from her parents – but no news was good news, she didn't want to worry about them as well as everything else. Towards the bottom, she saw a system notification that had come in a couple of days ago. It was a routine mailing, giving details of ongoing hazards in alternate worlds. She skimmed it idly, skipping over references to civil wars, manhunts and volcanic eruptions, but came to an abrupt halt when she saw the designation of her own world – where she was Librarian-in-Residence – the one she'd just come from.

> *Warning to all concerned: the alternate world B-395 is suffering from an irregular and unstable level of chaos, cycling from moderate to high. We don't yet know the reason for this. As it's only been happening for the last week and a half, it may be only a temporary issue. Visitors to the world should be particularly vigilant.*

'This particular visitor has quite enough to worry about already,' Irene muttered to herself, and began to compose an urgent email to Melusine – the Library's head of Internal Security. In the absence of Coppelia and without any other formal superior, Melusine would have to do. Irene described the current situation, the new assassination attempts, the previous ones, the problem with Catherine's recently discovered ambitions, and added an urgent request that no other Librarians visit B-395 unless they were actually coming to *help*.

Then she sat back and thought. Was this fluctuating high chaos level in B-395 due to the interdimensional door she'd found – leading to the world where she'd encountered Lord Guantes? The creation of such a door was so far beyond her that she could only speculate about its metaphysics. Perhaps, when such a door was created, the two worlds tried to equalize their respective levels of chaos? That could explain sudden rises and subsequent falls.

But if so, that implied the door had been opened multiple times, or – worse still – that there were multiple doors . . .

She began to type another email.

Irene stepped back through the door into the Guest Collection. Melusine hadn't responded, and she couldn't afford to wait. If Irene *had* stayed, the link she'd created to the Guest Collection would have worn out and collapsed, and she'd have had to take a far longer route back.

This was clearly going to be one of those days when all possible choices were bad choices.

The back of her neck crawled. Though the room was empty, she felt that someone was watching her. Or more precisely . . . looking for her. It was like being in the path of a searchlight as it swept across a landscape by night. A glaring eye raking through the darkness – in search of a target it knew was there. Irene found herself holding her breath involuntarily, her shoulders hunching into a crouch as defensive as Catherine's own. As if that could somehow help her hide . . .

She'd only felt something like this once before, when Alberich had been searching for her; but this was different. It didn't have the same *flavour* of chaos and malignity to it, exactly, though she couldn't put her feeling into words which would have satisfied Vale.

Her nervousness kept her steps quiet and slow, which was why she heard noises from the ground floor. They didn't match the usual library whisper of rustling pages and hushed conversations.

She hurried to the central stairwell, dropping to her knees to peer through the banisters without risking observation. From that perspective she could see two receptionists and a security guard remonstrating with a group which must have just entered – a dozen men in dark overcoats. They didn't look like researchers. It was hard to catch what they were saying from three floors up, but she caught the odd word. 'Urgent . . . no warrant . . . immediate search . . .'

Right. Time to leave. She backed away and was straightening to her feet, when for some reason a small cloud of dust motes caught her eye. They'd glinted in the light from the overhead lamps as they fell. Some instinct for danger made her look upwards, and she caught sight of a shadowy figure on the other side of the stairwell. It was silently moving downwards towards her, and she didn't know if she'd been seen.

There was at least one other person up there too, their movements as stealthy as Irene's own. When Irene had signed in, she'd taken a glance at the visitors' book, and she and Catherine had been the only ones present at that point. Were the men in overcoats and these shadowy watchers unconnected . . . or this was a deliberate pincer movement? If so, Irene and Catherine might be caught in the middle.

She was sidling back towards where she'd left Catherine when she heard a familiar voice from below, raised to carry. It was Lord Guantes. 'Miss Winters? I suggest you come out, wherever you are. This library is now closed.'

CHAPTER FOURTEEN

There was a certain satisfaction to having one's worst expectations confirmed. Admittedly this meant that you had to deal with the results, but at least you could tell your colleagues later that you'd *told* them so.

However, these pleasures had to be deferred in favour of immediate escape. Irene had to assume the worst – that their enemies were waiting both above and below. She could use the Language to force a window open. But climbing out of a third-floor window, above a crowded London street, came with its own risks – such as the difficulty of adapting one's plan while halfway down the outside of a building.

Apparently Lord Guantes was giving Irene a few minutes to make up her mind. Catherine must also have realized something was wrong. She'd closed her books and was looking nervously from side to side. Irene put a finger to her lips as she approached, and beckoned her to follow.

The two of them made it to the book lift without being intercepted. It was an unobtrusive recent addition, and ran from the top to the bottom of the building. Irene swung the waist-high doors open. There was enough room inside for an athletic young woman, and Catherine certainly weighed less than a pile of some of this library's books.

'Wait here,' she said quietly. 'When you start hearing a commotion, climb inside and shut the door. That'll keep you hidden. Then I'll press the button on the ground floor to bring you down safely once the coast is clear. We'll get out together.'

'How?' Catherine hissed, panic showing in her eyes.

Irene wasn't sure which of her statements the *how* referred to, so she decided to leave explanations for later. Especially as her plans were better described as being in the formative, rather than the fully detailed, stage. 'If things go wrong and you hear me being dragged off screaming, remember our plans for meeting up,' she said.

'You'll scream?'

'I'll make sure I scream very loudly indeed.' Irene gave Catherine a comforting squeeze on the shoulder, to offset any panic her words might induce, and headed back to the stairwell.

'Miss Winters!' Apparently Lord Guantes had grown bored with waiting. 'I suggest you show yourself immediately, if you have any regard for the safety of this library's staff.'

Irene peered through the balustrade's pillars again. One of the receptionists, his glasses flashing in the light from the overhead lamps, was being shoved forward: two of the men in overcoats held his arms while a third put a gun to his head. The security guard and the other receptionist were watching in horror, oddly silent.

'Very well,' Irene called down, rising to her feet. 'Don't shoot. I'm coming down.'

She could hear footsteps above her now. She'd been right. They had been boxed in. She'd just have to hope she could find an advantage.

'Come on down then, and don't keep us waiting,' Lord Guantes ordered. He gestured to his minions; the one with the drawn gun lowered it, but the two holding the receptionist remained in place, a clear message that his safety was conditional on her obedience.

Irene began to descend the stairs, her mind whirring with possible plans. A pity that so many of them ended up in *And then he shoots me*. 'How has your day been so far, Lord Guantes?'

'Improving by the moment, my dear.' He stood looking up at her, all his attention on her. His followers copied his movements like hunting dogs, even the ones guarding the library staff. That could be useful. 'If only you were always this obliging.'

'Lord Guantes, I've had a stressful day. Under the circumstances I'm willing to grant you an interview, but please don't push me.'

'You're talking as if you're the one holding the balance of power here. Should I point out that I have three hostages, and this place is held by my men?'

A thrill of relief went through Irene. If he'd realized Catherine was here and that he could take her as a hostage too, he'd already be boasting about it. 'If I think I'm invulnerable, have you considered why I'm bothering to surrender to you?'

He snorted. 'A predictable concern for the lives and well-being of these useless pawns.'

'Excuse *me*!' one of the receptionists protested.

'Oh, not my opinion.' He faced the woman and smiled, and Irene knew that to her, he would be absolutely believable. Lord Guantes was a master manipulator – it was part of his archetype. 'I simply meant that Miss Winters has childish moral views on the sanctity of human life and so on, which makes *her* easily manipulated.'

'Oh, that's all right then,' the hostage said, and the other two nodded in agreement. Even the one who'd had a gun pointed at his head.

Fortunately Irene hadn't been counting on any help from

them. They would currently be rationalizing why they were fortunate to be Lord Guantes' prisoners and threatened with death. 'If I may just check something?' she asked.

'Yes?'

'Didn't I see you die just a couple of days ago?'

Lord Guantes looked sincerely confused. 'You must be mistaken. I've been delaying *any* meetings with you until I could trap you in an inescapable situation, with overwhelming resources. Plus a few hostages, just in case.'

'How flattering,' Irene replied coolly. Were there multiple Lord Guantes on the loose? And if so, which was the *real* one? 'And will your wife be joining us?'

'My dear wife is busy with . . . another project,' Lord Guantes said, far too much relish in his voice.

Irene had descended to the first floor by now. Far too close for comfort, and easily within gunshot range. One of the few reasons that she wasn't trying to run – which every instinct was screaming at her to do – was that Lord Guantes was having too much fun gloating. He was trapped in his criminal archetype. One couldn't gloat at a corpse. The corpse simply wouldn't appreciate it properly.

She suspected that his wife would have shot Irene as soon as she came into range, but then Lady Guantes had always been the more sensible of the pair. What a good thing she wasn't here. 'Might I ask what project?'

Lord Guantes stroked his beard. He was in a dark suit and overcoat, like the other men, but his were an order of magnitude more expensive and better-cut, and black gloves sheathed his hands. 'You may ask. But I think I'd prefer it if you asked while on your knees.'

She'd reached the ground floor now and was standing level with him. 'I confess I'm puzzled. You found me here – and I still don't know how you managed that. Did you pay library staff across London to watch out for me?'

'Come now, my dear. That would be rather too expensive for one little Librarian.' The fact that he knew something which she didn't visibly soothed him. 'My wife had a token which allowed her to locate you, that's all – and I borrowed it.'

'I didn't realize something like that could work on Librarians.' The Library brand on Irene's back blocked or defused magic specifically directed at her. It should have stopped anyone from scrying her location.

'I think we can say that this *specifically* works on Librarians.' His mouth curled in an unpleasant smirk. 'Now that you're safely down here – Reuben, anything to be found above?'

Irene followed his gaze upward. Half a dozen men were leaning over the balcony on different floors. 'No trace, sir,' one of them answered. 'She was the only one up here.'

'Yet you came with company.' Lord Guantes inspected Irene thoughtfully. 'Where is she?'

'Who?' Irene asked innocently.

He snapped his fingers. A couple of the men stepped forward to take her arms, pinioning her. 'The woman who entered here with you. I assume it was Lord Silver's niece. Where is she?'

Irene resigned herself to the inevitable. 'Safe.'

He backhanded her across the face. Irene's vision blurred, and she swallowed blood. 'Miss Winters,' he said, his voice all calm persuasion and reasonableness. 'That was to make a point about your current helplessness. I *could* have my men beat the answer out of you – but I think I'll get quicker results if I shoot these hostages. Now let's try again. Where is Lord Silver's niece?'

Irene tried to look desperate. 'If you're after her and I tell you, you'll have no reason to keep me alive.'

That smirk twitched across his face again – an expression that not only said, *I know something you don't know*, but also,

I know something which is really going to upset you when you find out. 'Oh, I have a very specific, very *definite* reason to keep you alive, Miss Winters. But it would spoil things if I told you too soon. So in the interests of saving these other library staff, where is Lord Silver's niece?'

The man with the gun raised it to the hostage's head.

Irene took a deep breath, and sagged, doing her best to look defeated. 'I took her into the Library.'

'You *what*?'

'That's not very grammatical,' Irene said, and earned another slap for it. *No*, she thought, waiting for the ringing in her ears to die down. *This isn't the 'real' Lord Guantes. The one I knew in Venice years ago, the one I killed, would have tried to overpower me by will alone. This physicality would have been completely beneath him. And the one I surprised recently, he seemed physically weak. It's as if they're all imperfect copies of the original, flawed in one way or another, physically or mentally . . .*

'What you've suggested is completely impossible,' Lord Guantes declared, breaking in on her speculations. 'Fae can't enter the Library.'

'Maybe not through force,' Irene said. She managed a smirk of her own. 'But with the willing cooperation of a Librarian, who knows what could be possible?'

Lord Guantes frowned, perhaps weighing the chance that Irene was lying against the fact that Catherine simply wasn't to be found.

'Which is why I'm here,' Irene said brightly. 'Waiting for you to catch up . . . I thought we should talk.'

Lord Guantes stared at her, then converted the blank look into a patrician sneer. 'How this goes, Miss Winters, is as follows: I will ask questions, and you will answer them.'

'As you wish,' Irene said with a shrug. 'I'd thought you *might* want to know more about how I granted a Fae access to the Library, to compensate for the fact that I killed you. Then we can forget this whole confrontation, no harm done.'

'You *thought* you'd killed me,' he corrected her. 'A serious wound, but as you can see, I'm perfectly alive.'

'So it seems,' Irene agreed. 'But the Lord Guantes I used to know – *he* would have been interested in the possibilities here. Admittedly we didn't have much of an acquaintance; our only real conversation was when you were trying to break my will and turn me into your slave . . .' She was gambling desperately, and her hand was weak. 'Even the Cardinal can't get Fae agents into the Library. What if *you could*?'

'Very well. Explain your methodology.'

'Reveal all my secrets – just like that?'

'Unless you want me to shoot the hostages, yes, *just* like that.'

'But if I tell you how it's done now, then my leverage is entirely gone,' Irene argued. 'And then you're free to do whatever you want with me. Kill me, sell me into slavery, shove me off a cliff . . .'

'Really, Miss Winters, are you *trying* to give me ideas?'

'I'm only making a point. I might leave something important out if I think you're just going to kill me – or your hostages – anyway. It makes revenge look like rather a short-sighted option. I thought you were a long-term thinker.'

She could see the calculation in his eyes. 'Is this a serious offer to negotiate, then?' he asked.

'My options are . . . being chased by you for the rest of my life, which will probably be short and messy, or coming to some sort of arrangement that will satisfy you. Or killing you, of course.' The more she could play to his archetype as schemer and manipulator, the more likely he'd be to believe what she was saying.

'Nicely put,' he agreed. 'Very well. I'm prepared to discuss the matter, in exchange for allowing you to live.'

Irene found it hard not to roll her eyes at that offer. *Allowing you to live* still left open so many unpleasant possibilities. 'In the interests of bargaining in good faith,' she said, 'I'd like you to let the hostages go.'

He considered a moment, then smiled. It wasn't reassuring. 'Of course. Joseph, Peter, release Miss Winters. And see these good people to the door and let them out. I'm sure they'll be happy to head home to relax.'

The two men who'd been holding Irene let her go. Irene rubbed her arms, frowning slightly. She hadn't expected Lord Guantes to give in so easily.

Lord Guantes waited until the library employees were safely out of the door, still bemused and smiling, before he turned back to Irene. 'It just struck me, my dear, that I have a whole *building* full of hostages here. If you don't cooperate, I'll start burning some of these books. Or should I cut them to pieces? Do tell me which would be more spiritually painful to you.'

Irene didn't need to feign her expression of chagrin at his words. 'You've made your point, Lord Guantes. I'll co-operate.' Still, she'd achieved a partial victory: the innocents were out of range. Now she just had to, somehow, deal with him and all his henchmen.

Something about that thought nagged at her. She glanced around as innocently as she could, getting a good look at her surroundings and the enemy forces. Yes, all the minions were of the same type: anonymous, muscular and male. Which meant that she and Catherine were now the only women in this library.

'If I may check one point before we begin,' she said. 'Am I correct in thinking that you're the mysterious Professor, London's new emperor of crime, puller of a thousand strings and master of its underworld?'

167

As she'd expected, his vanity made him preen under her praise. 'I'd ask how you found out, but I suspect I know. Your detective friend.'

'And you're behind the recent assassination attempts on us?'

'Define *us*.'

'Myself. Prince Kai. Vale. Sterrington.'

He smirked again, and her hand twitched at the urge to slap that expression off his face. 'Miss Winters, I assure you that I haven't attempted to assassinate *you*. Now let's get down to business. You will provide information – even if you don't reveal *everything* now – if you want to see these books left in one piece. I will judge if it is of sufficient quality to stay my hand.'

So if he hadn't attempted to assassinate *her*, 'just' the others, then what did he have in mind for her? That was useful information – if somewhat unsettling.

'I don't know how much you know about the Language,' Irene began, trying to sound as didactic as possible. 'You're aware that it's only usable by Librarians?'

'To an extent,' Lord Guantes said thoughtfully. 'After all, it's possible for you Librarians to write something down using the Language, and then give it to someone else to use.'

'How do you know that?'

His smile was positively edged. 'Now how do you think I tracked you?'

For a moment Irene froze, her blood turned to ice. That meant a *Librarian* had betrayed her. As she saw Lord Guantes' smirk widen at her reaction – visible, however much she tried to conceal it – she fought down her fear. He could just be lying, trying to break her morale. He hadn't sworn to tell the truth, after all.

But if it *was* true . . .

She swallowed and forced herself to continue. 'Very well, then. This is why I'm here – and it concerns the Language.

I've found a way to use it to modify an existing door to the Library, to allow Fae passage.' She chose her words carefully, to imply there was a permanent door to the Library inside this very building.

'And you did that today?'

Irene simply nodded. He seemed to be buying it.

'Is *this* why you think you're bargaining from a position of power? Are you going to threaten to bring Librarian reinforcements out through this door, to attack me?' He looked quite serious, to her surprise – and relief.

Irene didn't need to feign her snort of laughter. 'Oh, come on, Lord Guantes. You must know Librarians by now. Can you really see us doing that? I'm not in any sort of position of strength. I'm surrounded by armed men and you're in front of me.' Yet so long as he believed in her lie, so long as he thought she had something he wanted, she might not have strength but she had *control*.

'One point in your story puzzles me,' he said slowly, and Irene's throat tightened. She'd thought he'd accepted her story. 'If you took Catherine into the Library, why did you bother to come back here? You knew that I was hunting you. Why put yourself at risk?'

Irene sought frantically for a good answer. Then it came to her. 'It's Kai,' she said, feigning reluctance. 'Prince Kai. He went to get help. If he returns and I'm not here to get him into the Library too . . .'

'Ah, of course. You're quite right about the danger he faces – he's on my list. But it's just you and me now. And just think of how good it will feel to tell me everything. I expect you are tired of all this running . . .' He took a step towards her, meeting her eyes. She felt the swell of his power, like the shadow of a tidal wave massing above her.

Once before, he'd twisted her will and nearly broken it. But she was stronger now. She just had to keep this charade going a little longer, to find out which Librarian he'd subverted to track her, what was behind all this, and how much further its roots went . . .

A heavy book tumbled down from above, crashing into Lord Guantes. It struck him on the head, and he didn't stand a chance; he collapsed to the floor, out like a light. It wasn't just the weight, it was the impact as well – force equalling mass multiplied by acceleration, and all delivered without a whisper of warning.

Without his active guidance his men all reacted on instinct, turning towards this new threat. Irene saw them raising their guns towards the balcony and could only pray that Catherine – for who else could that have been? – had the sense to stay down.

Time for her own plan. **'Books, hit the men!'** she shouted at the top of her voice in tones intended to carry through the building. She dropped to the floor, covering her head with her arms.

She might not be able to see, but she could hear the crashing and shouts as every book within range of her voice threw itself at a man. The crossfire on the ground floor was particularly heavy, and several volumes ricocheted painfully off her. It was only when the noise stopped that she lowered her arms and looked around.

Nobody was moving. Well, nobody except for her. Good. Irene headed for Lord Guantes, who lay sprawled motionless, and rolled him over onto his front. She used his elegant silk scarf to tie his hands behind his back. 'Catherine, come on down!' she called.

She heard the girl's footsteps on the stairs as she went through Lord Guantes' pockets. He had a bulging wallet, which she tucked into her coat for later investigation. More interestingly, he also carried a highly ornate pocket watch which made her fingers tingle when she touched it.

'I know you said I was supposed to hide,' Catherine said, her steps slowing as she approached, 'but I couldn't just . . . keep my head down.'

'Well done – you did a good job,' Irene answered. It would have been totally unfair to complain that Lord Guantes had fallen for her string of lies and Catherine had messed it all up.

'I saw he was trying to do the *thing* to you.' Catherine waved her fingers dramatically, suggesting magical influence. 'I had to help.'

'I appreciate it. You provided the perfect distraction. Even though I'm not sure whether your archetypal librarian would have done the same. . .'

'I think there may be lots of different types of librarian,' Catherine said thoughtfully. She had the air of someone who's seen a whole new range of possibilities and found she liked them more than she expected. 'There's the sharing librarian, and the motherly librarian, and the spinster librarian, and the archivist librarian, and the adventurous librarian like you – there's nothing that says I can't be a *murderous* librarian.'

'True enough,' Irene had to admit.

'And *I* only dropped one book. Not every single book within earshot.'

Irene didn't need the reminder. She was feeling guilty enough about what she'd done to those books. 'Point taken,' she said shortly. 'Let's just agree that you hit him where it hurts and leave it at that.'

'Er . . . *is* he dead?'

'He's breathing but unconscious. There may be a skull fracture – I can't tell. At any rate, he's not a threat for the moment.'

Irene steeled herself and flipped open the pocket watch, half expecting some backlash. Instead of the usual mechanisms, it contained a needle, rather like that of a compass.

171

This was centred above a circular piece of paper, inscribed with Irene's own name in the Language. There were much smaller markings all around the rim – she couldn't guess their purpose. The needle pointed directly at Irene.

'Let's test this,' she said, passing it to Catherine and rubbing her fingers against her skirt to banish that odd tingling. She took a few steps to the right, circling the Fae, and could see the needle swivelling to track her.

'This looks useful,' Catherine said, with unwanted enthusiasm. 'Can I keep it?'

'No,' Irene said, hastily taking it back. That was her name in the Language. Which meant – another Librarian must have supplied it. But who? And how? Her fears mocked her. Did she honestly expect the person who wrote this to sign their name on the back?

Of course, it never hurt to *check*.

She worked a fingernail under the piece of paper, easing it away from its metal backing and up towards the needle until she could see its back. There *was* something scribbled on the other side – in English, not the Language. She tilted it for a better view.

Triumph abruptly turned to a cold terror that clamped around her heart and dried up her throat. *Ray*, the writing read.

'Irene?' Catherine was right next to her, grabbing at her elbow. 'Are you okay? Did it do something to you?'

Breathe, Irene told herself. *Breathe and get through this one moment at a time*. 'It says "Ray",' she told Catherine, her voice the only sound in the silent Collection. 'That was the name my parents gave me. A nickname. A private name. There's only one person, besides them, who'd know it.'

Alberich.

Now Lord Guantes' words from their previous encounter made sense – he'd mentioned the 'man behind the Professor' who wanted her personally. An enemy she'd thwarted twice now, both times nearly at the cost of hers and her friends' lives. And now she was holding this token of his malice, a way for Lord Guantes to track her down . . .

Irene bit her lip hard. Panic could come later. She had to get a grip on herself – and on the situation. 'We'll hand Lord Guantes over to Vale and the police,' she said, tucking the compass into an inner pocket, 'and then—'

Someone outside knocked firmly on the library's exterior door.

Irene realized that the building's interior, strewn with books and bodies, might attract undue attention. 'I'll get that,' she ordered. 'Stay back for the moment.'

The short vestibule leading to the main doors would appear comparatively normal: there had been no men in the vicinity, so no one for the books there to target. She carefully slid open the small Judas window to look onto the street.

Lady Guantes was standing there, backed by a dozen more men. 'Miss Winters,' she said briskly. 'My husband is in there. Will you bring him out to me, or shall I come in and get him?'

CHAPTER FIFTEEN

'An endless stream of borrowers today,' Irene muttered. The danger helped her to focus. Alberich was a *huge* – and terrifying – problem. But Lady Guantes was right in front of her, and suddenly seemed an almost welcome distraction.

'I beg your pardon?'

'Sorry – I didn't think of you or your husband as regular library patrons, and yet here you both are.' Irene was deeply grateful for the solid door between them. Lady Guantes was not one to waste time gloating. She was a practical woman who believed in disposing of enemies on the spot with overwhelming force.

Irene peered out of the corner of the Judas window, wanting to present as small a target as possible. Lady Guantes was dressed in the height of this London's fashion. Her finery included hat and veil, midnight-blue velvet cape and a matching silk dress. Her signature gloves were of exactly the same pattern as her husband's. *How sweet*, Irene thought caustically. Her dark hair was coiled into a bun, and although she was smiling pleasantly, her eyes were cold. The men behind her were more varied than Lord Guantes' strangely synchronized minions. One hefted a mysterious crate, and all of them seemed to be carrying potentially lethal weapons under their bulky overcoats. (Irene was guessing about the weapons' lethal qualities, but given how the day was going, it seemed wildly optimistic to assume anything else.)

Lady Guantes spread her hands self-deprecatingly. 'Miss Winters, I'm unarmed. May I come in?'

'Come *on*,' Irene said wearily. 'That wouldn't have worked the first time I met you. It's certainly not going to work now.'

'You're sounding rather hostile,' Lady Guantes noted. 'Have you been overstressed lately?'

'Your husband's assassination attempts have been quite stressful, yes. So the door remains *closed*.'

'I do understand. But I have fresh intelligence, which might just change your mind . . .' Lady Guantes seemed to come into focus suddenly, as though a camera lens had tightened its perspective around her, or a sunbeam had haloed her in light. 'I'm prepared to declare a temporary truce, Miss Winters: I'll even give you my word.'

Now that *was* interesting. Lady Guantes would phrase any promise to her advantage, of course, but Irene had played that game before. And Fae promises were binding.

'What's going on?' Catherine called nervously.

'Negotiations,' Irene answered. She turned back to the window. 'All right. What are your terms?'

'I'll enter,' Lady Guantes said. 'You'll refrain from taking action against me. My men and I will refrain from action against you and your allies. After we've talked, you'll return my husband, and my men and I will leave – rather than launching the attack we have planned. Then I will leave you and yours unmolested for the rest of the day. I swear this by my name and power.'

Irene considered. It *sounded* reasonable – but then, Fae bargains always did. 'What if you've *already* ordered your men to take action?'

Lady Guantes sighed. 'I suppose I should expect a linguist

to be pedantic. I give you my word that, if you agree to this truce, my men will not be a threat to you or yours for the rest of today.' She paused. 'Calling for the police to save you won't work either. We've planned for that.'

Irene's brain whirled with options. But she and Catherine were completely outnumbered here. She took a deep breath. 'I agree to your terms,' she said, 'but give me a moment to disable the door alarm.'

'One minute,' Lady Guantes said, tapping her watch.

Irene slid the window shut and ran to where Catherine stood over the bound Lord Guantes – fortunately out of Lady Guantes' line of sight. 'Get behind the counter,' she said briefly, indicating the receptionists' barrier along one wall. Irene scooped up one of the minions' dropped guns as Catherine concealed herself, and then she hurried back. 'I'm about to open the door,' she called.

'I'm waiting,' Lady Guantes answered composedly.

When she entered, she glanced at Irene's gun with an air of mild disdain. 'I thought you were above the need for such things.'

'Needs must.' Irene frowned as the men began to follow Lady Guantes inside. 'Wait. I'm not sure I want them in here too.'

'Well, they can't stand around on the street. People will talk. Either you trust me to be bound by my word and not attack you, or you don't. Make up your mind.'

Irene had a horrible feeling that she'd overlooked something crucial. But Lady Guantes was right – either she trusted the Fae, or she should have kept the door shut. 'Very well,' she said, leading the way and feeling the back of her neck itch with every step.

Irene came to a stop next to the unconscious Lord Guantes. 'Do you want to check his condition?' she asked.

'I can see that he's breathing,' Lady Guantes replied.

'Anything else can be handled by a doctor. Now, let's talk like reasonable women.'

'I'll come to the point straight off, then,' Irene began. 'These attacks against me and my allies are inconvenient. What would it take for you to call them off?'

Lady Guantes smiled. 'Your surrender to me. I would also require the surrender of the young dragon and the detective.'

'So, death or . . . slavery?' Irene said. 'That's not much of a choice.' Lady Guantes' choice of words had been very specific too. She'd only referred to herself in this bargain. There was no mention of Lord Guantes – or Alberich – neither of whom would be covered by any bargain made by Lady Guantes.

'If you don't surrender, a great many people could die.' The two of them faced each other over the body at their feet. 'Even if *you* don't care for the inhabitants of this world, your detective friend does. Perhaps I should make my offer to him? He's the sort who would sacrifice himself for the things he cares about.'

Irene raised an eyebrow. 'And we wouldn't, madam?'

'Oh, we're both too practical. We'd far rather sacrifice others instead.' There was something dreadfully casual about her manner. For her, it wasn't a question of whom she'd sacrifice or how many, but simply a case of organizing the logistics.

'There will be extremely serious consequences – for *you* – if you pursue this vendetta. Kai and I have been nominated to oversee the dragon—Fae treaty. If you attack us, you'll make very powerful enemies.'

'You're assuming I care about your patrons,' Lady Guantes said. 'There are others out there who'd reward me hand-somely for disrupting your treaty. On both sides.'

Unfortunately true, Irene knew. 'But are these risks really

worth taking? When you could just as easily work with us, rather than against?'

Lady Guantes looked briefly dumbfounded – and then she actually laughed. 'Miss Winters, are you seriously trying to recruit me? To *employ* me?'

'Look on it as a compliment,' Irene said. 'It means I recognize your abilities.' She didn't hold out much hope of Lady Guantes accepting, though – not if Alberich really was the Guantes' secretive patron.

'I'm genuinely flattered. It doesn't change anything – but I *am* flattered.'

'But no?'

'But no.'

'Where *do* we go from here, then?' Irene pressed. 'If you keep on doing this much damage, you'll have the authorities after you.' A thought struck Irene. 'I'd assumed Lord Guantes was the Professor. Should I be pointing the police towards you, instead?'

Lady Guantes ignored Irene's conjecture. 'I can avoid the authorities for longer than you can avoid me. But maybe there is something else you could offer me, to avoid this . . . impasse.'

'I'm listening.'

'Another Librarian. Alive, of course, and not in a condition to fight back.'

Irene's eyes widened. As if she'd hand over another Librarian – one of her own brothers and sisters – to whatever fate Lady Guantes might have in mind. And if Alberich was the Fae's evil genius, why would he want a Librarian? She didn't want to speculate about that. 'No. Non-negotiable,' she said, and heard the ice in her voice.

'Such a pity. It would have kept *you* safe.'

'The answer, madam, is still no.'

'Very well. Then our conversation is over.'

'Aren't you going to threaten me?' Irene asked.

'Miss Winters, if you don't already feel threatened, I'm not doing my job properly.'

'Oh, I absolutely do,' Irene assured her. 'Ultimately, though, is it worth all this effort to get revenge for me killing your husband? After all, he seems to have – survived somehow?'

Lady Guantes considered, a pensive look on her face. 'Some people would say it was worth it.'

'Would you?'

'No. No, I wouldn't. You're correct about that, Miss Winters. You may congratulate yourself.'

'Then what *do* you get out of all this?'

Lady Guantes looked down at her unconscious husband. 'I could say we'll gain power if we destabilize your precious treaty. And rewards from our patron, but ultimately . . . Would you believe that I'm doing all this for my husband's sake?'

Irene tried to parse that statement. 'You're pursuing revenge because Lord Guantes wants you to?' No, Lady Guantes made her own decisions. 'Or pursuing power to help him somehow?'

Lady Guantes clicked her tongue. 'Now that's what I get for rattling on. My dear husband always said that was *his* speciality, and he was absolutely right.'

A breath of ice crawled up Irene's spine. 'You used the past tense.'

'You're an observant woman, Miss Winters.' Lady Guantes slid a hand beneath her coat and brought out a small sleek pistol. 'You may wish to observe this.'

Irene had seen a Fae try to break his word once before, with disastrous results. Lady Guantes was far too savvy to risk the same, so Irene refrained from fleeing for cover. 'We have a sworn truce,' she said. And only she would have spotted the catch in her voice.

'Indeed we do.' Lady Guantes levelled the pistol instead

at her husband's unconscious body, and fired. It was a neat, precise shot. He jerked, then went still again, and a pool of blood began to spread around him. His breath rattled in his throat, then stopped.

Irene should have reacted – she *knew* she should be reacting – but sheer astonishment held her frozen. 'You just killed . . . your husband,' she said. That was the last thing she'd thought Lady Guantes would ever do. *Could* ever do.

'Which means he's no longer your hostage, you can't return him to me and our truce is over. Now.'

Her tone didn't change, but her men took her order for the signal it was. The two at the front ran forward, pulling masks over their faces and glass bottles from their coats. Irene was confused until they smashed them to the ground beside her, releasing a wave of gas. Lady Guantes had moved back and was now pulling on a mask of her own.

Irene couldn't escape the fumes that came boiling up from the smashed glass, and the vapour moved faster than she could form the Language. Her whole body shook from coughing so violently that she couldn't speak, and tears streamed from her burning eyes, blinding her. Her skin itched where the gas had touched it – hands, face, neck – and her nose was running as if she'd been hit by pneumonia and hay fever together.

Half her mind was raging at her for getting so close to an enemy who she *knew* was trying to kill her. The more practical part was focused on survival. She still had a gun in her hand. And as Lady Guantes had confirmed, the truce was over.

Irene raised her weapon as she backed away, and fired. She couldn't see where she was shooting, but Lady Guantes had been in front of her. She heard at least one shot ricochet off stone – but maybe the others hit something. She tried to remember how many bullets the gun held, and wished there were more.

'Men – move to phase two,' Lady Guantes said, her voice annoyingly calm.

Damn. I didn't hit her.

'Madam!' That was one of her men. 'Incoming, outside, police!'

The pause that followed was brief, yet Irene could almost hear Lady Guantes mentally cursing. 'Cancel that,' Lady Guantes said. 'Retreat. Begin diversion protocol. Goodbye, Miss Winters – you won't enjoy it when I see you again.'

Wood crashed to the floor. Irene *still* couldn't open her eyes, or manage coherent words. She tried to analyse the noises. Feet retreating. Noises from the street, briefly, the outer door slamming shut, then nothing. Followed by a sort of slithering, scraping sound.

She retreated, hoping that she was going in the right direction. Her back bumped against the reception desk, and if she had the breath, she would have sighed in relief.

It sounded as if Lady Guantes' party had left by the main door. But if so, what was making those noises? Her eyes were still streaming too much for her to see, and she felt trapped and helpless. Maybe the police would get here in time. Or maybe not.

'Irene?' Catherine sounded very unhappy, and Irene could sympathize with that. 'Irene, we have a problem.'

Irene tried to speak, but it only set off more coughing.

'They're moving!' Catherine's hand closed on Irene's shoulder, and Irene hoped she'd had the sense to cover her face against the gas. 'Lord Guantes' men – the ones you'd disabled – are getting up. *Do* something!'

Irene managed to get out the word, 'Water . . .' in between coughs. This wasn't good. She'd just identified that particular slithering, scraping noise. Those cerebral controller things in the submarine base had made precisely that sound when scrabbling across the floor. And thanks to Irene's earlier use of the Language, there were a dozen or so unconscious host bodies lying around. She and Catherine would never reach the door to the street in time.

'Here.' Catherine caught Irene's hand and guided it to what felt like the handle of a jug. 'I think it's for watering the plants.'

Irene upended the jug over her face, letting water sluice over her until it was empty. She didn't bother drinking any – it would only aggravate the coughing that still wracked her body.

When it was done, she could finally see again. Lord Guantes' minions were moving like puppets, first sluggish and hesitant – then jerking into uncoordinated bursts of speed. During these phases, their arms began flailing, their heads whipping round in what seemed to be attempts to orientate themselves. A few unattached mechanical serpents crawled round the wreckage of a wooden crate, seeking convenient hosts.

Irene was still coughing, her throat raw, and she felt sick; she'd never be able to choke out a sentence in the Language. She rounded the end of the reception desk and ducked down, joining Catherine. There had to be writing implements here – ah yes, just there, fountain pen and ink. That would work. She caught Catherine by the arm and pointed at one of the chairs, gesturing for the Fae to get up onto it.

Catherine looked confused but followed Irene's directions. Her eyes widened as she looked over at the men. 'They're coming towards us,' she said very quietly.

Irene dragged a heavy ledger off the desk, letting it crash to the floor, then knelt on it. With a huge effort she steadied herself; her nose still streamed and her upper body trembled, but her hands were deft enough for the task. She unscrewed the ink bottle and dipped in her finger, then scrawled on the white marble floor in the Language: **Floor, hold everything that touches you.**

She barely managed to finish the final word and yank her finger back before coughing overcame her again. Then she looked up, her head aching with the after-effects of using the Language.

It had *worked*. The men swayed where they stood, trying to approach them and failing, then trying again. They were unable to understand why they couldn't move forward, their eyes blank and mindless. The marble floor had swallowed their feet to the ankle and held them in a grip of stone. The mechanical serpents had been completely sucked under and now formed lines of silver, barely visible through the white stone, like veins of precious metal.

For the moment, their attackers were prisoners. However, enough wriggling – or even enough brute-force yanking with no concern for human bones or tendons – might be enough to get a foot free . . .

Catherine grabbed her hand. 'Let's get out of here – now!'

Irene decided that, if Catherine ever had an appraisal, this would merit bonus points. She'd grasped the basic principle of when to evacuate the scene – or more precisely, when to run for it.

The two of them circled the room towards the door, giving the trapped men and mechanical serpents a wide berth. Irene almost expected an ambush when she tugged open the door, but there was nothing unusual outside. No explosions, no kidnappers – nothing but a normal London street. And, wonder of wonders, a couple of police vans turning the corner. *Now where were you ten minutes ago?* Irene thought ungratefully.

Catherine led her to a bench, helping her to sit down in a rare patch of sunlight. Irene allowed herself to relax for a moment, focusing her sore eyes on the clouds above. For a moment sheer surprise stopped her coughing.

Catherine followed her gaze, and blinked. 'Why are there *two* of them?' she asked.

Coiling in the sky above, a blue dragon and a red dragon moved together in slow interlacing patterns. Against the grey mosaic of the clouds their wings shone as bright as gemstones, sparkling as they caught the sun's rays.

CHAPTER SIXTEEN

Irene had been introduced to Kai's brother Shan Yuan – fortunately not till *after* she'd stopped coughing and being sick, which always put a damper on introductions. He hadn't actually been *rude*. However, it was quite obvious that any courtesy he was giving her was due to her rank as a Library representative, rather than actual respect for her as a person.

But she couldn't bring herself to care. Being pursued by assassins, while Alberich wanted her as his prisoner, seemed a rather higher priority.

Irene felt far safer now she was practically on government territory. Vale's sister Columbine had invited him and his circle to her private rooms at the Dashwood Club, though she herself was absent. Busy looking for more information, Vale had told them. Irene had just finished her account of recent events. Catherine was carrying round cups of tea and coffee with a quiet subservience which had drawn looks of approval from Shan Yuan and badly hidden astonishment from Kai. Irene had quietly pointed out to her that menial service of this kind meant you could listen in to high-level discussions without being noticed. Otherwise, you'd likely be thrown out due to age or lack of experience.

Given the dragons in the room, it seemed a good idea for

Catherine to keep a low profile. Kai and Shan Yuan (Irene still didn't know why he was there) occupied the sofa, while Irene had commandeered the best armchair. She'd also ordered more tea, feeling the British government would understand their need. It had been quite a day. Inspector Singh was using the table to arrange his notes, and Vale was standing by the fireplace. Sterrington was on her way.

The ambience was very civilized. But while the club might outwardly look like a place for nobility and high-ranked civil servants to eat expensive meals and then nap, the walls were thick, the door guards – sorry, *receptionists* – were trained military in civilian clothing, and the windows were of reinforced glass. And those were only the things Irene had noticed so far.

It would take a zeppelin loaded with high explosives to make a dent in this place.

Irene really hoped that Lady Guantes didn't have access to any zeppelins loaded with high explosives.

'So,' she said, summing up, 'we face Lord and Lady Guantes, though something is very wrong with Lord Guantes – and he seems to be able to return from the dead. Both appear to be behind "the Professor" whose criminal activities Vale has described.'

Vale nodded in agreement.

'And behind *them*, we have Alberich.' She restrained herself from fidgeting with the compass in her pocket. 'After our last encounter, he can't enter this world in person – but his agents can.'

'I would appreciate more information on this Alberich,' Shan Yuan said. He had black hair and pale skin like Kai. Their resemblance was startling, but Shan Yuan's hair had a ruby undertone to it, and he accented his suit with a red tie rather than Kai's preferred blue. His irritated frown seemed a habitual expression and his manner was condescending.

'I have heard the name before – a Librarian who turned traitor?'

'That's correct, your highness,' Irene said. 'It was several centuries ago, but he's somehow survived outside the Library by contaminating himself with chaos – something no true Librarian could achieve, or would want to. He's also killed a large number of Librarians and attempted to destroy the Library itself.' *And he terrifies me.* 'He seems to have a grudge against me because I've ruined his plans twice. To be honest, I'm extremely disturbed that he wants me captured alive.'

'You're being economical with the details, Winters,' Vale put in. 'Alberich has a number of allies among the Fae – he provides them with information, creates wards for them using the Language, and so on. He's even worked with Lord and Lady Guantes before. He's demonstrated the ability to use the Language in ways that are unfamiliar to sanctioned Librarians, such as Winters here. And he may have a long-lost son out there somewhere – though we haven't yet seen any firm evidence of this.'

'Is it possible that this Lord Guantes is his long-lost son?' Singh asked.

'I don't think so,' Irene said. She thought about it some more. 'I really don't think so. I certainly hope not.'

'Why hasn't the Library executed this Alberich yet?' Shan Yuan demanded – somewhat unfairly, Irene felt. 'Having someone like this running around in league with chaos does nothing for its reputation.'

'Believe me, we've tried. He's difficult to locate and dangerous when he shows himself. And he's able to use the Language in combination with chaos . . . again, in ways that no regular Librarian could. I now believe *he* must have created the door which Vale and I saw in Guernsey. There may be other doors, as well.' Irene couldn't help wondering rather wistfully just how he'd done it.

187

'Alberich aside, how do you intend to arrest these Guantes murderers?'

'We've strong cases against them for multiple crimes, sir,' Inspector Singh said calmly. Presumably he was used to visiting officials making impossible demands. 'Arson, murder, attempted murder, theft and a few others I won't bore you with. The question is how we locate them and keep them in one place. It makes a policeman's life difficult when the criminals he's after can just go skipping off to some other world, evidence and all.'

'This place is inefficiently run,' Shan Yuan muttered. 'I'm disappointed in you, little brother. I thought you had things under better control here.'

Perhaps I should be grateful for a lack of older siblings, Irene reflected as Kai murmured an apology. She'd seen Kai interact with his elder half-sister Indigo on another occasion, but Indigo had been a rebel and a disgrace to the family. Kai had therefore felt himself free – no, *encouraged* – to be as rude to her as possible.

'I should note that Prince Kai doesn't hold any authority here, sir,' Inspector Singh said. 'While naturally we have the greatest respect for your brother's position, neither he nor Miss Winters here have any standing or status within this country's governance.' His words were carefully chosen, but they were also a formal declaration of independence from dragons, Fae and the Library.

'Of course,' Irene said. 'That's absolutely understood. We deeply regret that the Guantes – and their feud with us – have caused trouble to London.' She meant every word. It wasn't just that she was Librarian-in-Residence here. She *liked* this world, this London – its people, its locations, its books. But how could she and Kai stay here, if the Guantes were going to tear the city apart to get at them?

'You're thinking of offering to leave, Winters,' Vale said

flatly. 'I don't need to be a detective to see the thought crossing your mind. But don't blame yourself. It isn't *your* fault that these people have no morals.'

'No,' Irene argued, 'but now that I know their intentions, it is my responsibility.'

'So you do propose to leave here?' Shan Yuan demanded sharply.

'We don't have any other choice. If Kai and I go elsewhere and they follow us, we can at least draw them into an ambush on ground of *our* choosing—'

'Unlikely,' Vale cut her off. 'You must still be suffering from the effects of that gas. Do you seriously think they'll follow you into a trap?'

'I can set a perfectly good trap, thank you very much,' Irene said haughtily. 'So far they've been able to choose their ground, so we've been at their mercy. This is why we have to leave. Don't you agree, Inspector Singh?'

She'd expected him, as a Londoner and a police officer, to agree with her. So it was rather to her surprise that Inspector Singh said, 'Perhaps you haven't fully thought the matter through, Miss Winters.'

'What do you mean?'

He set down his pen, giving her his full attention. 'I mean, Miss Winters, that if you are seen to leave to protect our good city, Lord and Lady Guantes will use this against you. The more you try to lure them away, the more they'll threaten us to force your compliance. Which is why I think a different solution's needed here. You pay your taxes, Miss Winters, don't you?'

'Of course,' Irene said, leaving out *on my legal earnings, at least*.

'Very well: think of this help as a state benefit.' Leaving Irene feeling rather as if she'd been stampeded by a previously helpful sheep, he turned to Shan Yuan. 'Your attention in this matter is greatly appreciated, sir. May we ask you to share the information you've brought?'

'The data on the laptop was very informative,' Shan Yuan said, with a sudden keen enthusiasm which reminded Irene of Kai. 'Much of it was a high-level discussion of artificial intelligence. I also found the blueprints of a project which seems directly linked to your current problems.'

'What project?' Irene asked.

'To summarize,' Shan Yuan said, his tone shifting easily to a lecturer's didactic manner, 'its aim is to recreate the personality of a dead person.' He let that sink in as those in the room murmured in astonishment. 'This is achieved, firstly, by creating an artificial simulation of the deceased. Secondly, this is implanted into a living person under certain specific conditions. Apparently "an extreme plasticity of environment" is also required. This refers to a high-chaos world – to use a lay-person's terminology.' Irene could almost hear Shan Yuan sniff condescendingly at this. 'Under the right conditions, the living person would be transformed *into* the dead one – the original mind extinguished, the body even taking on the physical characteristics of the new host. This could be repeated as many times as necessary, superimposing the stored artificial simulation on a living victim.'

A horrified silence filled the room. 'Lord Guantes,' Irene finally said. 'That's what happened to him.'

'What you've told me fits with the project description,' Shan Yuan agreed. 'And as well as the process taking place in a high-chaos world, the imprinted subject needs to be a Fae. However, the documents suggest that the imprinted body doesn't last long. Physical or mental breakdown ensues within just a couple of weeks – a month at the most. Unfortunately, it was a high-level overview, so the granular details of processes involved were lacking. But Alberich was mentioned as a contributor – and it appears that he's retained information essential to the process.'

Irene frowned. As with any jigsaw, once one had the border assembled, it was easier to see how the other pieces related to one another. 'Perhaps the key to the process *isn't* chaotic power – or not chaos alone. Perhaps the Language is important somehow. If Alberich is contributing something only he could offer, it would interest many Fae – not only the Guantes.' This wasn't just personal any more. If Alberich possessed this sort of bargaining tool, he'd be able to find countless unscrupulous allies and turn them against the Library – always his ultimate goal.

Shan Yuan shrugged. 'You know the potential of your Language better than I do. But it does explain why only Alberich could provide the missing details. Perhaps if you had a closer look at the full process, you could hazard a guess at how the Language is used.'

'No, thank you,' Irene said with a shudder. 'Do you know if the dead person, the one who is imprinted upon a new body, realizes what's been done to them afterwards?'

'I don't believe it would be obvious to them – unless they were told, of course.'

Irene remembered Lord Guantes' words, during her Guernsey mission. He'd said he'd cooperated with her enemies but also said, *'I have been betrayed. I have been used.'* 'I think the first Lord Guantes I met must have known what had happened to him. Either he was told, or somehow he found out. Maybe someone gave him the project documentation to explain the process, or he found it for himself. It would have made him understand that he was a . . . I don't know what the right term is for it. A simulated personality? A recreation of one?'

'It's as close to necromancy as anything else I've come across, Winters,' Vale said. 'Not the least because it requires the sacrifice of another intelligent being. Was there anything else useful on the laptop?'

'There was also a set of news articles on the Sagrada Familia cathedral in Barcelona – in Spain. These covered strange events witnessed there recently. I'm not sure why these are relevant, but they must be there for a reason. But it's unclear within which world this Sagrada Familia is located.' Shan Yuan shrugged. 'A high-chaos world, presumably.'

'Under the cathedral,' Irene quoted to herself, remembering Lord Guantes' words. 'The dark archive . . .'

'Were any email addresses or other contact details supplied, connected to the project?' Singh asked, frowning. Irene hadn't expected him to be acquainted with such things, but maybe Vale had updated him on other worlds' developments. Or maybe there were technological advances going on here of which Irene simply wasn't aware.

'Unfortunately not,' Shan Yuan said. 'I specifically looked for a way to trace Alberich too, and there was nothing.'

Kai had remained silent, somehow more formal in his brother's presence. Now he spoke. 'Possibly Madame Sterrington can identify the Barcelona mentioned in those articles, when she arrives. Or her Fae contacts may have heard of this artificial intelligence research.'

'We can't share this with *her*,' Shan Yuan snapped. 'Don't be foolish, Kai. Do you want to see this information spread to *more* Fae?'

'She's extremely well connected, and the most likely person on this world to give us useful information,' Vale said. 'Are you here to help us save your brother's life, your highness, or is this merely your idea of entertainment?'

Shan Yuan's eyes flared red, and the flames in the fireplace leapt up in response. 'I am not amused by your words, detective. My brother may treat you as a favourite, but I have no such inclination.'

'Then kindly let us *use* the information you've brought us,' Vale demanded. 'I'd hoped you'd display the same broadmindedness as your brother in putting aside prejudice against the Fae.'

'I've had enough of your insolence.' Shan Yuan rose to his feet. The room became claustrophobic as the temperature rose. 'My brother will be safer elsewhere. Kai, we will—'

At that moment, the door opened as the tea Irene had ordered finally arrived. She'd never been more thankful to see a hot beverage. As the servant bustled about, Shan Yuan was forced to sit, his royal upbringing demanding that shows of emotion be kept strictly private. When they were alone again, the wind had been taken out of his sails enough for Irene to interject.

'If I might ask you something, your highness . . .' Irene began, hoping her tone would soothe his ego.

'Of course,' Shan Yuan said. Now that his temper had cooled, he seemed glad of the excuse to back down.

'Could we have more detail on those Sagrada Familia articles?' Irene had recognized the name of the cathedral – designed by Gaudi, the great Spanish architect. In most worlds where the cathedral appeared, it had taken over a century to construct. 'The Lord Guantes I met in Guernsey mentioned a cathedral.'

'It was a collection of media reports, covering a period of two months,' Shan Yuan explained. 'At first they simply recorded odd events – strange noises, computer systems in the crypts malfunctioning, lights appearing at unusual times. But the strangeness escalated and the cathedral gained a reputation as a nexus of – well, weirdness. Projections of a hooded monk were seen, loudspeakers ordered visitors to leave at unexpected times, bells were also rung at irregular hours and strange voices were heard in the archive below the main structure . . . Explanations ranged from hackers to demonic interference to a suggestion that the cathedral's computer system had become sentient. The final article revealed that the cathedral had been evacuated and placed under guard.'

'The dark archive,' Irene said softly, to the room this time. 'Under the cathedral. Those were his words.'

'So the cathedral *must* be connected,' Kai said. 'But *how*? And why?'

Vale frowned, his expression intent. 'Alberich must need somewhere safe to conduct his artificial intelligence experiments. Perhaps Lord Guantes caused the odd goings-on, to claim the Sagrada Familia as a private base of operations for Alberich – his patron? I believe it would fit Lord Guantes' pattern of behaviour to keep these media reports for his personal amusement.'

'The archive beneath the cathedral contains physical books and computer data, according to some reports.' Shan Yuan said thoughtfully. 'That would make it attractive to Alberich, if his power is also connected to books and libraries, as with Librarians such as Miss Winters. And the world in the reports is both highly computerized and presumably highly chaotic, as needed for his experiments.'

'Did you discover anything further about the archive – either on the laptop or through your research?' Irene asked.

'Something, although not as much as I'd like. It actually *pre-dates* the Sagrada Familia in that world. It was originally a storehouse for the Church – housing dubious materials such as heresies, apocrypha and the like. When the Sagrada Familia was updated with new technology, the archive was expanded to hold servers and data stores. The equipment there was even further upgraded recently. This coincides chronologically with black market transactions between worlds, on the dark web, trading in extremely rare technology. Perhaps that equipment was suitable for the work described in the project.'

A dark archive indeed, Irene reflected.

'That device Lord Guantes used to track you troubles me, Winters,' Vale said. 'What if they have more than one of those things? They may have pinpointed your location again.'

'I'm no more comfortable about it than you,' Irene agreed. 'But nobody attacked me last night, when I was hiding with Catherine. Maybe they did only have one – and we have it now. Or if they do have another . . . It's marked like a traditional compass – so maybe it can point in the right direction to locate me, but no more than that.'

'I think it only a matter of time before they can triangulate on your current location,' Vale responded. 'Your confrontation will make them even more determined. It is entirely possible that *another* Lord Guantes is on our trail already. Did you discover how long the process takes, your highness?'

'They had it down to a few hours,' Shan Yuan said. 'Although that doesn't include the revived personality coming to terms with their new body and reality, and reconciling any inconvenient memories.'

'Lady Guantes must be good at those explanations by now,' Irene said grimly. How many 'husbands' would she have used up, always seeking the perfect version? What must it be *like* to see a version of the person you loved degrade and die, multiple times? She thought of that happening to Kai – of losing him, regaining him in such a dreadful way then losing him again – and repressed a shudder.

'In that case—' Singh was interrupted by a knock at the door. 'Come in!'

A servant entered, suitably anonymous, with watchful eyes. 'Sir,' he said quickly, 'there's been a shooting on the doorstep. We brought the victim in and they're under guard downstairs.'

'Details?'

'A woman, madam – Miss Sterrington, of the Universal

Exports firm. She had just given her name at the door when someone shot her from a distance. Lung wound, critical condition. A medic is attending to her in the King Charles Room.'

Vale led the charge with Kai beside him, and the room emptied to follow them.

As Irene rose, Shan Yuan caught her arm and drew her to one side. 'I'd like a private word,' he said quietly.

'Why shouldn't your brother hear this?' Irene responded, freeing her arm.

'He is in danger.'

CHAPTER SEVENTEEN

Irene stopped in her tracks, her heart suddenly clenching in panic. 'Another danger . . . besides the assassination attempts?'

'Yes,' Shan Yuan said shortly. 'And I believe you genuinely care for him.'

'Of course I do.' Irene replied. She held back from commenting on his patronizing tone. Next he'd be describing her as *a credit to the Library* and mean it as a compliment.

'Good. In that case, leave your job.'

Irene stared at him blankly. 'Explain yourself, sir.'

Shan Yuan snorted and Irene had a sudden mental image of flame rolling from his nostrils, like a fictional dragon. He certainly expected people to do his bidding. 'Pass the role of treaty representative to some other Librarian. Go back to collecting books. Then Kai can resign *his* position to some older dragon who'll do a better job, and he can spend his time more usefully. You'll *both* be safer that way.'

Safer – and apart. 'Your lord father, his majesty Ao Guang, placed Kai in his current position,' Irene said, controlling her anger at his interference. 'Isn't the decision up to him?'

'If Kai himself requested assignment elsewhere, my lord father would consider it,' Shan Yuan replied. He now spoke with the patience of a man who'd already solved a problem to his own satisfaction. 'If you aren't the Library representative, I doubt Kai will be interested in the dragon representative position.'

Irene was silent, lost for words.

Shan Yuan nodded. 'Consider how much you care about his safety – and make the right decision.'

'And hide the fact that it was all your idea?' Irene demanded, her throat dry, bitter with murderous fury.

Shan Yuan shrugged. 'If you think it more likely that he'll resign that way, yes. How many times will you let him risk his life for you?'

'Kai is an adult and capable of making his own decisions,' Irene spat. 'I am *not* going to lie to him.'

'You're barely older than he is, and you are both children,' Shan Yuan snapped back. She could feel the heat radiating from him now, even without touching him. 'Do you want him to remain in danger? Don't you care about him?' He stepped closer, features so very like Kai's as he glared at her. 'Well? Will you do it?'

'What will you do if I say no?' Irene demanded. 'Will I have a tragic accident, removing me from my position that way? Will you simply deny everything if I mention it to Kai?'

'My little brother will certainly believe my word over yours.'

Irene twisted away from him. 'A word of advice, your highness. Don't make threats when your position is weak. My friends are within earshot and witnesses are plentiful. Intrigue is clearly not one of your talents.'

'That's your answer?' he growled.

Irene curved her lips in a smile. 'I will take your suggestion into account when making my future decisions. I thank you for your concern for our safety.' She turned to join the others.

His voice pursued her. 'You already have enough

enemies, Irene Winters. This is not a good time to be acquiring more.'

She was already walking away and didn't turn back. But his warning about Kai stayed with her, and she couldn't help wondering if some of what he'd said had been true.

The King Charles Room was notable, unsurprisingly given its name, for its huge portrait of Charles II. The monarch dominated the room, looking down cynically while spaniels played around his stockinged calves. Otherwise it was surprisingly bland for an expensive London club, with modern tables and chairs. The very latest ether-lamps ensured the room was brightly lit, despite its lack of windows.

Sterrington lay unconscious on one of the tables, her upper clothing cut away, and a doctor in the club's livery was bandaging her chest wound. Irene wondered if many clubs boasted a house medic, or just the government-sponsored ones. Vale was going through the contents of Sterrington's briefcase on another table, with Singh watching over his shoulder, while Kai and Catherine stood nearby looking strained.

Kai seized on Irene the moment she entered the room. 'Where's my brother?'

'He'll be along in a moment, I think,' Irene said, touching his shoulder. She didn't want to let go of him. 'Situation report, Kai, please.'

The familiar words visibly settled him. 'The bullet went right through Sterrington, so we don't need to worry about removing it. And some servants are cleaning the doorstep, in case anyone tries to use the blood for unholy purposes.'

Irene nodded. Every world had its own specific metaphysical inconveniences. 'Has Sterrington spoken yet?'

'No – she was conscious only briefly, and the doctor gave her a sedative.'

Irene bit back a curse. At least she'd recover. But now they couldn't ask her about the Sagrada Familia, and its possible location.

'Sterrington may not be able to speak, but her possessions are quite communicative,' Vale commented, not looking up from her papers. 'Can we have you over here, Winters?'

'Of course.' Irene inspected the briefcase. There were papers, handwritten and printed; three fountain pens; a purse, a powder compact and a copy of today's *Times*. 'What have you discovered?'

'Nothing here, except the type of cocaine she preferred.' He nodded to the powder compact. 'The papers concern her office's insurance – she's been checking her cover following the arson and has reached some interesting conclusions.'

'She's come to the same conclusion as our police investigation,' Singh said. 'That building was torched for profit. The assassination attempts might have been the primary goal, though; we can't know for certain. Additional cover was taken out in case of arson, deliberate or accidental, a fortnight ago. The insuring company is Weston Liability – a shell company with a large number of criminal investors.'

'Now we come to this letter here. It was in her inner pocket rather than the briefcase. Do you recognize the handwriting, Winters?'

Irene took the letter and stared at it. Then the writing snapped into focus and she remembered where she'd seen it before, only a few months ago. 'Oh dear,' she said.

'Ah good, you do. Give me your opinion on it.'

'Is it the Cardinal's handwriting?' Kai said eagerly. Sterrington's patron was incredibly powerful, but hugely mysterious.

'Yes,' Irene replied. '. . . and are you sure we should be

reading this, Vale?' She was in no doubt as to its author. Irene had seen multiple documents in the Fae's own hand during the Paris treaty business. His spies were everywhere.

He shrugged. 'If we don't pursue leads, we won't secure answers.'

She began to read the letter aloud, noting that Shan Yuan had just entered the room. *'My dear Sterrington, I am glad to hear that you have the situation under control. I wouldn't want to think I had favoured an incompetent.'*

'A mere two sentences and he's intimidating his subordinates,' Kai said. 'I see he hasn't changed.'

'He's very good at intimidation.' Irene remembered a darkened room and the Cardinal's dark presence. He'd given her an oh-so-calm description of exactly what would happen if she didn't solve a murder to his liking. She suppressed a shiver and continued reading. *'Your theory that Lady Guantes is plotting against us seems valid, given the arson attack and other indications. I cannot discover her current patron's identity, which is not a good sign.'*

'Why is *that* suspicious?' Shan Yuan interrupted. 'Is patronage now a matter of public record?'

'Of course not,' Vale answered. 'But nothing can be concealed from the Cardinal – supposedly. So keeping this patron hidden must seem highly unusual.'

'Ah.'

Irene continued. *'However, my network has unearthed some intelligence. The lady has been linked to a number of Fae groups involved in technology research and development. Their details are in the appendix.'* Irene caught the sharpening of Shan Yuan's interest. *'I've recently lost several agents, and am therefore concerned that a move against you may actually be a move against me. You're authorized to take whatever actions you consider necessary to preserve your life – and my interests – and I'll send assistance as soon as possible.'*

Irene folded the letter. 'His signature follows, then the appendix – though I don't know any of the names in it.'

'I'll check the Fae names,' Catherine said, taking the letter. 'I might recognize someone.'

'That's all. Unless there's spycraft involved – an encryption code, a cipher in the watermark, or something . . .'

Shan Yuan turned to his brother. 'Kai, your thoughts?'

'It is a positive that the Cardinal is on our side,' Kai began, then saw his brother's growing frown and added hastily, 'As much as any Fae ever is. And all clues seem to point towards artificial intelligence in some way. However, if the Cardinal is sending more agents here, this London could become increasingly . . . *dangerous*.'

The euphemism hung in the air. If the Cardinal considered Lady Guantes to be a serious threat, he'd want to kill her and tear up her organization root and branch. And God help poor London, caught in the middle.

'We *really* need a lead,' Irene said firmly. 'Inspector Singh, does the arson insurance fraud offer anything useful?'

'No,' Singh said with a sigh. 'I'm afraid not – in the short term, at least. My opinion on the situation, ma'am, is that you should let your enemies come to you. We know the city – so you'll have the advantage. And London's police will be on hand to shut them down.'

'I disagree.' Vale had a new look in his eyes; the hound on the scent, the hawk who'd spied a rabbit in the long grass. 'We have no idea what our adversaries might bring in from other worlds, through these doors that Winters has described. And we *do* have a lead, based on something most of the attacks have in common.'

Singh frowned. 'Yes, I remember you saying. So what exactly did you find in the Foreign Office reports? The ones your sister provided?'

'They covered the cerebral control devices, which were

present in several incidents. It seems possible that their inventor, Doctor Brabasmus, isn't even dead. When the local police checked his laboratory, after the explosions that destroyed it, they found a decapitated body. The evidence suggested multiple physical invasions via the cervical spinal canal, and exit wounds via various orifices. The head was thoroughly destroyed. Under the circumstances, at the time, everyone made the logical assumption that the doctor had perished.'

'You said . . . decapitated,' Irene murmured, trying to keep her visualizations to black and white rather than enthusiastic images in pink and red.

Vale shrugged. 'The skull was indeed thoroughly detached, and no firm identification could be made via the teeth. Dentures, alas. But given certain indications in the reports . . . I believe he *is* alive. What's more, I can guess at his location this very evening.'

'The report from Paris?' Singh frowned. 'I read that one. It wasn't what I'd call reliable. The writer said herself that the information was speculative and from a dubious source.'

'We can't be certain – but we *must* investigate.' Vale leaned forward, intent on his trail of thought, ignoring the rest of the room. 'Tonight Brabasmus has the perfect opportunity to attend an event – unrecognized and unnoticed – and meet a contact from the French government. Apparently, the contact wants the cerebral controllers, Brabasmus wants to sell them, and they will be meeting tonight at the People's Palace. This is a chance, Winters. If we can take Brabasmus, we can question him about the Guantes. They've made good use of his controllers – so why not his research on harnessing technology to alter the mind? And that avenue leads us to Alberich. Who knows . . . maybe the doctor has even visited his headquarters.'

The sudden burst of possible hope that seized Irene was

almost painful. 'What is the People's Palace, though, and why is it such good cover?'

'The "Grand Technological Exhibition" is taking place there tonight,' Singh explained. 'It's that place out by Wood Green – the one they might rename after the Princess of Wales.'

'Will technological advances actually be on display?' Shan Yuan demanded.

'That's the problem, sir. We don't know *what* will be there. It changes every year. You see, your highness, the Grand Technological Exhibition is an annual celebration for, shall we say, *over-enthusiastic* men and women of science. The police always attend as it could end with a bonfire, explosions or even a riot. I've seen giant robots bounce through the streets – and once half the drains in London ran pink and grew fluorite crystals. One year, a new underground bullet train destined for Paris went to Edinburgh instead. But a particular favourite of mine, if you can call it that, was the personal glider-suit driven by underarm flamethrowers. You might also see devices for communicating with dolphins, and usually at least half a dozen machines that are supposed to end world hunger and enforce world peace. Those are usually the worst.'

'Come now, Singh,' Vale said, 'your distress seems fresh, but they haven't held the event in London for five years now.'

'Maybe so. But after that last occasion, such a thing shouldn't be allowed anywhere south of the North Pole.'

'Inspector Singh, do you also think Doctor Brabasmus might be there?' Irene asked, trying to steer the conversation back.

'I'm not sure, ma'am,' Singh said slowly. 'Certainly it's where all London's leading scientists will be tonight. So it's *possible*. It's also possible that – based on the past record of some in this room, and naming no names – it's the very last place we should go. We could end up with London in flames, flooded and under attack, with an earthquake splitting the city from top to bottom.'

It was awkward when people started making judgements based on one's past record. Especially when they had a point. 'Are you sure this is worth our time, Vale?' Irene asked.

'Winters, I would hardly have mentioned it if I didn't think it was worth trying,' Vale said impatiently, practically vibrating with a febrile keenness. 'These cerebral controllers link several of the attacks upon us. We have few leads to follow, so I think we must pursue any and all that present themselves.' He gave a nod to Shan Yuan, who returned it. 'The French report tells us that the rendezvous between Doctor Brabasmus and his contact is scheduled for eleven o'clock, somewhere in the building. With the three of us to quarter the place in advance and find them –' his gesture took in Irene and Kai – 'we could apprehend Brabasmus and find out what he knows! And who is his contact, the person he's meeting there? This could also be of interest.'

'I dislike this option,' Singh muttered. 'We've known each other for years, and I'm telling you that I'm not convinced. I'm unwilling to hazard your lives, based on this one report. It could be a trap. It's certainly not safe.'

Irene looked at Kai, and he gave her a slight nod. It said that he'd abide by her choice, whatever it was. While Singh might not want to risk them . . . it wasn't his choice, or his responsibility, and they needed information.

'Can you arrange disguises and tickets for us?' she asked Singh. It was time to get practical, and stop procrastinating.

'I think I prefer your brother to your sister,' Irene said, staring into the mirror as she adjusted her glamorous blonde wig. She'd seen Kai's deference to his older brother; the direct approach wouldn't work. But after their recent clash, Irene needed to know a bit more about Shan Yuan. Did he genuinely care for Kai, or could he have other motives for wanting him to resign? Could he even want Kai's position for himself? The thought was unsettling.

'You have a very limited sample size to work from,' Kai muttered from where he was sprawled on the sofa, miraculously not mussing his evening suit. 'And that is faint praise, given that Indigo tried to kill us. *And* betrayed us.'

'I suppose I'm just glad one of your family wanted to help you out.' Though honestly, Irene wasn't sure if Shan Yuan was helping. He was quite obviously interested in the artificial intelligence developments. Beyond that, he'd been completely overriding Kai whenever he tried to speak for the last few hours. He'd even suggested going back to Kai and Irene's lodgings 'to review the evidence there'. Fortunately everyone had unanimously pointed out why this was a bad idea, as their lodgings were bound to be watched, and spared Kai from having to disagree with him publicly. But in that case, what *was* he after?

She watched Kai in the mirror – his familiar posture, his dark hair, his eagerness, his casual precision of movement, all the things that had become so familiar to her in the last year. As her heart softened, she tried not to think about how much Shan Yuan's suggestion had rattled her. She didn't want to lose him. She didn't *intend* to lose him. And if Shan Yuan thought that he could simply drop a word in her ear and she'd renounce Kai, like a handkerchief-clutching romantic heroine, then Shan Yuan was in for an unpleasant surprise.

'I didn't expect him to come here.' Kai had evidently misinterpreted her thoughtful expression. 'I thought he'd be content with just giving me the data analysis. I suppose he couldn't resist seeing the technological marvels it promised, if we can find them.'

'But they might not even be in this world,' Irene had to point out. 'If the process needs to be somewhere high-chaos, as we think, you and your brother couldn't use your dragon forms there. You'd have to be prepared for that.'

Kai's mouth twisted in disgust at the thought. 'Any news of Sterrington?' he asked, changing the subject.

'The surgeon said he didn't think she'd wake till tomorrow. She's lucky to have survived.'

'Do you find it irritating how our antagonists keep on cutting off our sources of information? Sterrington's contacts could have been helpful – but now, who knows when she'll be well enough to make use of them.'

'It's incredibly frustrating,' Irene agreed. 'Vale's dream is to cross blades with a master criminal, but I'd far rather deal with someone who couldn't out-think and outplan me. It makes me worry . . .'

'Worry about what?' He rose and came to stand behind her.

'That we're missing something. I'm concerned about unknown dangers, Kai, as well as the known ones.'

He stroked her shoulders, his hands warm and reassuring. 'Is it Alberich? I know that for a Librarian there's no threat quite like him.'

Irene tried to calm herself. 'Yes. Yes, it is him. I'm trying not to panic, Kai. But what am I supposed to feel, now we've found out that he wants me – and *alive* too?'

'I won't let him have you.' Kai's hands tightened on her shoulders, possessive and protective. 'Trust me. You've always come for me, through all perils and all obstacles. I'll do the same for you. I'd *never* leave you to him. Do you have faith in me?'

'More than I do in myself.' Irene put her hands on his, grateful for his touch, drawing comfort from having someone she could depend on without limits. She didn't always have to be the strong one. *We can be strong for each other.*

For a few moments they just shared the silence, feeling their closeness.

Then Kai released her shoulders, with one last fond squeeze, and adjusted her wig. 'Blonde really isn't your colour, though I like that purple dress. It's a good thing attendees to this exhibition are supposed to be masked.'

'I'm not trying to look beautiful – I'm trying to look unrecognizable. And if we weren't wearing masks, you'd be the one with the problem – given how easy it is to recognize a dragon, when you know how to spot one.'

'You could have taken me in there in heavy make-up, disguised as your latest biomechanical experiment,' he suggested lightly.

'That would have been interesting.' She appreciated his efforts to distract her, but she was too keyed up for the evening ahead. 'I realize that we're depending on luck to some extent, hoping this lead will pay off. But we're running out of time.'

'Vale's on the scent,' Kai reassured her. 'He's in the sort of mood where he'd spend a week in disguise, staking out an opium den, in the hope of spotting something relevant.'

'And I'm the sort of person who'd open a locked door, in the middle of a dangerous mission, just to find out what's on the other side,' Irene said ruefully.

'Well . . .' Kai looked amused. 'If I'd been there, I would have been at your shoulder egging you on, so I can't cast aspersions. And talking of missions, we should go.' He helped her into her coat.

Irene couldn't resist a bit of a dig at his brother, harking back to her previous worries. 'I'm glad Shan Yuan's not insisting on coming with us. I don't think he has your experience with subterfuge.'

'No, he hasn't,' Kai said, sounding distinctly smug at the idea that he might be superior to his older brother. 'Probably best we're not taking Catherine, for the same reason.' Then he added, thoughtfully, 'That does mean we have to leave them together . . . although I'm astonished that Shan Yuan's getting on so well with her.'

'She *is* on her best behaviour,' Irene said. The lure of getting a place in the Library was still working.

'I'm just surprised. Maybe it's because he's never actually encountered sensible, cooperative Fae before. If we can put Catherine in that category.'

'She's better than most,' Irene said. 'But let's get moving. It's nearly seven o'clock – and we have an exhibition to attend.'

CHAPTER EIGHTEEN

One could compare the road leading up the hillside to the People's Palace to a river of people. But if so, it was a river that had been dammed and was overflowing, while simultaneously trying to cope with an overdose of pollution. Police attempted to keep the flood moving ever upwards as night fell, while preventing it from spilling out onto the hillside, but people still seemed determined to demonstrate inventions and fight duels under the ether-lamps. Or, more prosaically, to escape to buy snacks from the vendors that had sprung up to serve the multitudes.

Irene was relieved to see that few in the crowded queue were solitary – she'd been worried that the three of them together might stand out. But whether they were associates, enemies, friends or a retinue of lab assistants, people clumped together in groups as they made their slow way forward. Occasional attempts to hasten the pace or bypass the queue altogether provided some amusement for those waiting – especially when these attempts went wrong. Irene had spotted chancers with nitrogen-powered rocket-boots, hang-glider wings, or extendable stilts. The most successful try so far had been an enterprising chap following his giant tunnelling badger. At least, Irene hoped the attempt had been successful. The huge creature's 'owner' certainly hadn't been seen since.

'And you are?' a black-haired woman ahead of them demanded, perhaps bored with her friends' conversation. She was ostentatiously dressed in a boiler suit and overcoat, as though to flaunt her practicality, but the overcoat was clearly new. Her otherwise utilitarian mask was trimmed with fancy copper filigree which glinted in the streetlights.

'Doctor Viltred,' Irene said. They'd discussed their cover identities beforehand. 'Anne Viltred. Timisoara University. I don't suppose you've read my work on preventing demonic interference in radio transmissions? And these are my colleagues, Doctors Balas and Waechter.' She gestured to Kai, then Vale, both of whom touched their hats politely.

'Sorry, I'm in bio-energetic amplification,' the woman said with a shrug. 'Ingrid Marie-Joseph, professor at the Sorbonne. You must have had quite a trip of it from Romania.'

'Forward planning helps,' Vale said. Even with his mask off, it would have been near-impossible to recognize him. His hair was grey and unruly, matching eyebrows curling over the edge of his mask. His slight Romanian accent was perfect and his back was hunched in the sort of stoop that could easily have stemmed from decades of bending over experiments. 'Though even forward planning couldn't help with this.' He gestured to the queue ahead of them.

'Oh, don't worry,' Ingrid said. She checked the watch hanging from her lapel. 'The programme isn't starting for an hour yet.'

Vale snorted, managing to sound about twenty years older than he was. 'And I am expected to wait out here, wasting my precious time—'

'Utterly abominable,' agreed a man from Ingrid's group, whose mask resembled a pair of binoculars, with different focusing levers on each lens. His drooping white moustache puffed out with every breath. 'I can see that you're a man with the right priorities, sir. Prudvark here – I'm from the Sorbonne too, for the moment at least, but I work in microphysics . . .'

His introduction was cut short by a shout, and some pointed as parachutists began to drift down from a zeppelin overhead. 'Trying *that* trick again,' Prudvark said with a sigh. 'One would have thought they'd know better.'

'Did we miss something?' Kai asked.

'No, dear, it was two years ago in Helsinki – didn't you get to that one?' Ingrid didn't wait for an answer. 'That year, the organizers used lasers to prevent queue jumpers – it's become quite a sport. But they *had* issued warnings beforehand, and I think at least one person made it to the ground without serious injuries.'

'And there they go,' Prudvark said, as the parachutists changed vector, blown off course as they descended. 'That hill was bound to interfere with wind patterns. What I want to know is what they've put in place to prevent intrusions via underground waterways.'

'But there isn't an underground river here,' Kai pointed out. As a dragon whose element was water, Irene reflected, he should know.

Prudvark merely smirked. 'That's what they said in Tokyo, and look what happened there . . .'

Irene reflected, as the queue shuffled forward, that Inspector Singh might be right to distrust the Grand Technological Exhibition.

The wide stone steps leading up to the building's entrance were flanked by uniformed police. They were kept busy monitoring attempts to avoid the checkpoint. The air was thick with the smell of ozone and flash-powder, as newspaper photographers took constant snapshots of anything interesting or disastrous. They had plenty of material.

Vale proffered their three highly sought-after tickets when they finally reached the guards, after what felt like years. His sister Columbine had supplied them, which guaranteed they were authentic. Even so, Irene couldn't help feeling the usual prickle of suspense that went with handing over documents under a false identity.

Of course, the guards here were probably far less dangerous than the guests inside . . .

'All in order,' said the official, barely looking at them after all that. 'Next.'

The entrance hall was thick with decorative palm trees. Groups of people were dissolving into furiously networking singletons, who then formed new groups. It would have made a splendid demonstration of molecules combining if anyone had been watching from above.

Irene looked around, orienting herself. 'Time to split up. See you in an hour at the theatre.'

Vale was already strolling away. The twitch of Kai's mouth indicated just how little he wanted to leave her on her own in this crowd, given the dangers they all faced. But they both knew that splitting up gave them a better chance of hearing something useful. 'In an hour,' he said, heading in a deliberately different direction.

Irene took in the main nave of the People's Palace where she stood, a room about three hundred yards long and already full of people. Three shorter corridors branched off from it like the three tines of an E, the middle one ending with a theatre where demonstrations would be held. An ornate dome reared high above, but the arabesque decorations were difficult to make out under the glare of artificial light, and its windows cast no light at this hour. The maze of cellars beneath the palace had been locked and barred for the occasion, which cut down on the area they needed to search.

The thickness of the crowd was reassuring, in a way. While it might be difficult for Irene to locate anyone in this mob, it would be just as hard for anyone to spot *her*. Even a werewolf would have problems following her scent here. To Irene's merely human nose, it already stank of too many people, too many perfumes and too much sulphuric acid.

'Try it!' Someone shoved a man-sized contraption in her face, and Irene backed away, blinking. The thing was a mechanical model of a human being, on wheels, costumed in heavy gold and red silks with a turban. It held a jar in one clawed hand. The man behind it was in singed evening wear and his coat pockets were heavy with spanners. 'You – madam. You'll do. Go on, give it a go.'

'Give what a go?' Irene asked nervously.

'My Automatic Fortune Teller. Put your hand on his forehead and think very hard about your question. It will then produce a paper giving the answer to your current problem!'

It was probably safe and the crowd *was* here to sample such curiosities. There weren't any electrocuted corpses in the device's wake. A good sign. Irene tentatively put her hand against the mechanism's porcelain forehead. *How do I find Alberich?* she wondered, unable to resist the urge to test it properly.

The device whirred into life, interior clockwork audibly ticking away. Then the automaton's jar flipped open and its free hand dived in, coming out with a piece of folded paper. It proffered this jerkily in Irene's general direction.

'Well?' its inventor demanded, practically bouncing up and down on his toes. An interested group was forming around the two of them.

Irene took the paper and unfolded it. '*The gulf will open beneath you,*' she read, '*and the Pit will swallow you.*'

Even the inventor could perceive this was a less than

cheerful message. 'Let me guess,' he said hopefully. 'You must work in submarines or bathyscaphes. I can see how this would be a really *useful* answer, right?'

'No,' Irene said flatly. Even if she absolutely didn't believe in fortune-telling, destiny or prophecies . . . it still wasn't a comforting message to receive this evening. 'I think your invention needs more fine-tuning.'

'The ferrets! The ferrets are loose!' someone screamed in tones of blind panic, and the circle of onlookers shattered in their desire to get away, see what was going on, or both. Irene took advantage of the distraction to return to circulating through the crowd, listening for comments relating to mind control, cerebral controllers or Doctor Brabasmus.

It was easy to drift from discussion to discussion. However, after half an hour of this she was beginning to think that the greatest invention of all would be an Automatic Listener, wound up and programmed to record conversation around key-words.

Then she heard the name *Brabasmus* over to her right, just a few feet away.

She nodded in agreement, as her latest cover complained about her funding – or lack thereof. Then she stole a glance to her right. Two men, both elderly, were chatting loudly. One had a German accent and both affected boiler suits and leather harnesses rather than evening dress. One wore a sleek black wig and a mask ornamented in amber and jet. The other was balding, sporting a plain mask and heavy canvas gauntlets. These were ill-considered, as they made it difficult for him to hold his wineglass.

'Of *course* they said it was an accident,' Black Wig was saying. 'No doubt it was also an accident that someone cornered the market in radium and quap, just a few days before that. Not to mention what happened to Quantrelle.'

'What about Quantrelle?' That was Gauntlets. 'I heard she

published something last October. Was she was working on programming theory?'

'Yes, that was the *official* story,' Black Wig shot back. 'But I had it from Pierre Gevenheim – you must know him, he's at the Sorbonne – that she was focusing on brain patterning. Not programming theory at all. She was basing her work on Brabasmus's theories. And she went missing last December. Or rather, they *said* she was hired by a private client.' His snort made it clear what he thought of that.

'I see you're admiring my perfectly cyborged Siamese,' someone directly in front of Irene said smugly.

Irene hastily refocused her attention on the man addressing her, while trying to keep up with the nearby conversation. The cat perched on his shoulder was a beautiful specimen of Siamese cat – or it had been, before someone inlaid wiring into its skull, added steel-tipped claws and replaced its eyes with gleaming red crystals. 'Good heavens,' she said diplomatically. 'I've never seen anything like it.'

'Exactly.' He offered her one of the glasses of wine he was carrying. 'My dear, I could feel your gaze across the room. You must tell me your name.'

'Whether or not Brabasmus was involved, you're wrong about Quantrelle,' Gauntlets said firmly. 'She's here tonight – I ran into her earlier, holding court by the ice rink.'

'Yes, but did you see her scars?' Black Wig demanded. 'And her left leg?'

'She didn't have a left leg.'

'Precisely!'

'Anne Viltred,' Irene said, taking the proffered glass of wine and trying to work out how to get rid of the man. 'Timisoara University.'

'Not *the* Professor Viltred?' he said in surprise. The light

216

glittered on the mica inlay of his mask. 'What a delightful surprise.'

Irene noted, with the sour recognition of one fake for another, the way that he'd skilfully managed to imply he knew about her and her work without having to say what it was, while also complimenting her with the title of professor. 'You're far too kind,' she parried. 'And you are?'

'Ruthven Davison.' He clinked his glass against her own, the cat perching comfortably on his shoulder glaring at her with those crystalline eyes. 'Bottoms up, my dear! Then you can tell me all about your work.'

Irene mentally scanned the list of famous scientists which Columbine had provided for tonight. The name didn't appear. And she had suspicions about the glass she'd been handed. A deliberate attack on her, or opportunistic predatory behaviour towards a young woman on her own? 'I'm so sorry,' she said. 'I never drink wine.'

Meanwhile Gauntlets had been thinking. 'Quantrelle isn't on the speakers' list for tonight,' he said, 'but Pieters is. And Pieters collaborated with Brabasmus on his cerebral work five years ago. If anyone knows about his work . . .'

'Now don't give me that,' Ruthven Davison said, leaning in close. It was like being accosted by Lord Silver, but without the charm. 'A woman as beautiful as you must be able to manage a glass of wine. And something more, perhaps.' His gaze dipped from her eyes to her bodice.

Irene's patience, already somewhat attenuated, snapped. She let herself smile sweetly. 'That's very kind of you,' she said, lowering her voice for his ears only. 'My field of research is geriatrics, you know, and I'm actually eighty years old. Would you like to go somewhere more private, so I can share some of my . . . secrets?'

He boggled at her, his uncertainty visible in spite of his mask. This was, after all, the sort of situation where she might well be speaking the truth. Irene stepped back as he hesitated, retreating with a faint smile towards the conversation she'd been monitoring.

Annoyingly the men were already moving away, still talking. She turned to pursue them, when a familiar posture caught her eye and she nearly spilled her drink.

That *couldn't* be . . .

He turned a little, so that Irene could see his profile despite the mask, and she cursed silently. What in the name of sanity was Shan Yuan doing here, stalking through the assembly like a leopard and doing a remarkably bad job of being inconspicuous?

She reluctantly gave up on her two targets – she'd already gleaned some useful names. Perhaps Vale could follow up on those later. Shan Yuan was now assessing the people around him with a cold and imperious eye and snubbing the few who tried to speak to him.

'Good evening,' she said, insinuating herself next to him and sliding her arm through his before he could back away. Her mouth was curved in a smile, but her voice was very nearly a snarl as she murmured, 'Your highness, what are you *doing* here?'

'Your job, it would seem.' He didn't try to distance himself – no doubt because it would have looked undignified to try and shrug her off – but there was clear annoyance in his eyes. 'This Brabasmus must be found and the technology investigated. I see no reason why I should not assist you. You may thank me later.'

If I don't kill you first. 'Have you worked undercover before?' Irene demanded. Somehow the *your highness* failed to materialize.

His eyes glinted dragon-red. 'You aren't showing an appropriate degree of gratitude.'

Irene abandoned courtesy for plain speaking – although

quietly, as anyone could be listening. 'If you'd honestly wanted to assist, you'd have told us rather than sneaking in like this. How did you get inside, anyway?' It wasn't as if he knew this London, after all.

For a moment he seemed about to refuse to answer, but then he smirked. 'Your apprentice assisted me.'

'Catherine?' Irene demanded, torn between fury, disbelief and horror. She'd been so relieved that the Fae girl was safe. If Shan Yuan had dragged her into trouble, being Kai's brother wouldn't save him.

Shan Yuan shrugged elegantly. 'She's here too, hunting for information. She wanted to prove herself to you – which, if you'll allow me to point out, is a highly laudable goal. You're doing her no favours by keeping her sheltered.'

Like you're trying to do with Kai? hovered on Irene's lips, but she bit the words back. This was not the time. 'You've made a mistake,' she said, her voice quiet and deadly. 'Catherine doesn't have the training or experience for a situation like this. If she told you she did, then she was mistaken. Where is she now?'

Something in her words or tone got through to Shan Yuan. He looked away, choosing not to meet her eyes. 'One learns by doing,' he protested. 'If you keep her out of work like this, how will she ever learn to do it properly?'

'*Where is she?*' Irene repeated, her voice deadly cold.

'She's only a—'

Irene's hand tightened on his arm. 'Your highness,' she said quietly, 'that had better not be "She's only a Fae". Not if you want me to have any respect for you at all.'

'I am the son of his majesty Ao Guang!' Shan Yuan snarled.

'Oh, I'll respect your *rank*,' Irene said. 'I just won't respect *you*.'

'Very well.' His words were nearly a hiss. 'We arrived here fifteen minutes ago. She said she was going to the theatre, then planned to check the cellars. That is all I know. *I* was far more concerned with investigating the artificial intelligence angle – seeing if I could overhear anything useful.'

'Thank you,' Irene said. She released his arm. 'For future reference . . . don't take advantage of those far younger than yourself. You've exposed Catherine to considerable danger.'

The air was perceptibly warmer around the two of them. Nearby discussion groups fanned themselves absently or complained about the heat. Shan Yuan showed no sign of caring. 'This makes me certain that you are no fit companion for my little brother,' he growled. 'You have no understanding of priorities. When I tell my father of your bad influence, he'll see to it that someone else is assigned as dragon treaty representative – someone who won't be distracted by your childish diversions.'

Someone like you? Irene wondered. *No wonder you want in on all this. Find the crucial new technology, demonstrate your ability, prove Kai's incompetent, get his position.* She could see the game plan. But trying to steal Kai's job was a petty offence compared to what he'd already managed to do tonight. Driven by fury, she jabbed a finger into his chest. 'That girl is *my apprentice*. She was entrusted to me by her only living relative. It is my *job* to keep her safe, whatever her birth, whatever her nature. If your father disapproves of that, then so be it, and I'll answer to him in person.' She met his eyes. 'But I'm not required to answer to *you*.'

'Excuse me, excuse me.' An attendant bustled by, ignoring their disagreement, just as he was ignoring all the other quarrels, arguments and outright duels. He thrust a paper into Irene's hand. 'Schedule for the evening's events, new additions marked in red . . .'

Irene looked at it automatically, and a name caught her eye. *Doctor Perchatki, Moscow University*. She translated from the Russian automatically. *Perchatki – gloves.*

Gloves. Guantes. Was this a coincidence? Irene wasn't sure she believed in coincidences any more – especially not in a high-chaos world like this one, where Fae abounded and narratives had an unfortunate habit of coming true. Perchatki's demonstration – it didn't say what – was due in fifteen minutes in the theatre.

'We will continue this later,' she said to Shan Yuan. 'I need to get to the theatre – now. If you see Kai or Vale, tell them where to find me.'

There was no time to waste. If Catherine was now in the theatre, she could be in very grave danger –if Irene's supposition that Perchatki was Lord Guantes was correct. And while she hoped against hope that she wasn't right, she had a strong feeling that she was . . .

CHAPTER NINETEEN

'I don't understand,' Shan Yuan complained, trailing behind her. He twitched the programme out of her fingers and scanned it. 'None of these names mean anything to me.'

'I'm interested in Doctor Perchatki. Excuse me.' Irene politely tilted a woman's arm as she ducked past, so her death ray was pointing at the ceiling and not at Irene. 'He's near the top of the list.'

'Why him?' Shan Yuan asked in bafflement. Either he didn't understand Russian, or he wasn't aware of Fae tendencies to pick appropriate and thematic pseudonyms.

Irene wasn't going to shout an explanation while shoving through the crowd – and they were close to the theatre's entrance now. However, as they neared, she could see it was blocked. A couple of security guards were doing gatekeeper duty, controlling the flow of people and policing the more dangerous pieces of equipment.

'Ah, Doctor Viltred,' Vale said, materializing at Irene's elbow. It took a moment for her to accept that it *was* Vale – despite recognizing his disguise. His make-up and the altered voice were simply that good. Her own attempts at changing her appearance were workmanlike and functional but couldn't match that level of artifice. 'I wasn't expecting *this* gentleman,' he said, his eyes shifting to Shan Yuan.

'Do I know you?' Shan Yuan asked, clearly not recognizing Vale, voice frosted with polite disdain.

'You do,' Irene confirmed shortly. She noticed that Vale was also carrying a programme. 'I take it you're here for Doctor Perchatki's demonstration?'

'Precisely. I had no doubt that you'd notice the name . . .'

'Wait, what?' Kai said, coming to a halt as he joined the group, his eyes widening at the sight of Shan Yuan. He glanced at Irene then back to his brother in confusion. 'I thought you'd said you weren't coming.'

'For all the thanks I've been getting, I shouldn't have bothered,' Shan Yuan muttered.

'Excuse me, coming through!' At the far end of the room, the crowd were being forcibly parted by a group of people carrying various pieces of experimental-looking apparatus – glass domes filled with circuitry, cables, a large console covered with levers and dials, and so on. Then towards the back of the procession . . .

Irene's hands tightened into fists and she felt the scars of old lacerations on her palms. Lord Guantes strode at the rear of the group, recognizable in spite of his mask. Beside him, a couple of men in lab coats were carrying the unconscious Catherine. If she'd been wearing a mask, they'd removed it. She was strapped into a stretcher, though the ties binding her had been mostly concealed.

This Lord Guantes showed no signs of having been shot, being about to crumble into dust or anything else untoward. He must be the latest personality imprint – and was probably thinking that he was the *real* Lord Guantes, just as the rest of them had. He was cloaked in an aura of firm determin-ation, every inch the noble scientist striving for the betterment of his fellows. In keeping with this persona, he gave his followers and the crowd the odd nod, wave or occasional word of encouragement. His eyes moved over the throng, and Irene was grateful for her mask and disguise.

Kai casually stepped behind Vale, using him for cover. But Kai's face – what Irene could see of it – had grown cold at the sight of Catherine being carried along helpless. 'How did they get hold of her?' he demanded under his breath. 'She was safe with Columbine.'

Fury knotted in Irene's stomach and she glared at Shan Yuan, locking her hand around his wrist as he began to inch away. 'Catherine is here because she wanted to *help*. Unwise, but she had good intentions. Vale, will claims of kidnapping be any use here?'

'This is almost certainly an attempt to draw us out, and that would expose us to whatever they have planned. So would any attempt to rescue Catherine.' Vale's expression was grim, and Kai was nodding.

'Agreed.' If sheer force of will could kill, Irene's thoughts would have bored a hole in the back of Lord Guantes' head. Unfortunately, she couldn't manage *that* – but there were other things she could try. 'But I can black the whole place out, which will give us a fighting chance at breaking her out. I can't turn the lights off from here, though – the Language would never be heard over the noise of that crowd. I'll get to the generators and turn the electricity off at source. If you wait in the theatre, you can grab Catherine in the chaos.'

'What about Lord Guantes?'

'At the moment, I'm more worried about Catherine.' How many times had Irene risked herself to get information? Of *course* Catherine would run off and do the very same thing. For the first time in a long while, she felt a degree of sympathy for her parents. 'If you can grab Lord Guantes as well, then by all means do so.'

'Am I to have no say in this operation?' Shan Yuan demanded.

'You are at perfect liberty to walk away,' Irene said through gritted teeth, 'but given that Catherine helped you get in here, I'd hope you'd feel *some* responsibility for her predicament.'

Shan Yuan opened his mouth, then shut it again. Perhaps he was considering the political optics. What would it do to his career if he was held responsible for losing an important Fae's niece – who also happened to be a Librarian's apprentice? Or perhaps he was considering Kai's opinion of him. After all, Kai was staring at him, wearing an expression of hope that his brother would do the right thing.

'Be careful, Winters,' Vale warned her. 'I cannot shake the feeling that we've missed something important.'

'There's one obvious thing we're missing. Lady Guantes isn't here.' She turned to view the throng of people around them – picturing them as a deck of cards, scattered face down on a table. Any one of them could turn out to be the deadly Queen of Spades. 'She may already be in the theatre. Watch out for her.'

'One of us should come with you—' Kai started.

'Three of you have a decent chance of getting Catherine to safety in the darkness, against Guantes' minions,' Irene said regretfully, 'but it would be harder for two of you. I'll take all precautions.' She touched Kai's hand for a moment, a reassurance to them both, then dived back into the crowd.

The architects had positioned the electrical generators on the top floor, away from the public areas. Fortunately Columbine had been able to provide plans of the building earlier, which meant that Irene knew roughly where she was going.

The upper levels of the building were formed of sturdy brick, rather than the elegant stone and tile of the areas beneath. The rooms here were oddly shaped, built to fit around the large glass dome which crowned the nave below. The building had only been open for a couple of weeks, so these rooms and corridors still looked new and sharp edged, without the distractions of the crowd. Under the harsh ether-lights which provided illumination, occasional numbers or words were scrawled on the whitewashed walls. These indicated which rooms were for storage or machinery – and which held the generators. But there was an obstacle, of course.

'Excuse me, ma'am.' Two men were guarding the generator room. Irene thought it was a sensible precaution, given the over-enthusiastic men and woman of science gathered below. Some would just *love* the chance to 'improve' the building's power supply. 'This area's out of bounds.'

Irene slipped a Secret Service identification card out of her handbag and displayed it. (Really, she was going to owe Columbine a *lot* of favours after tonight.) 'Government business,' she said. 'We're checking for saboteurs.'

He peered at it, frowning. 'Sorry, ma'am. It's been one of those nights. Will you need any assistance?'

'If you'll just unlock the door for me, please.'

He opened the door and switched on the light – and the sound hit her like a blow as she stepped inside. The room was huge, larger than it had seemed on the building's plans. Wheels twice her height spun in constant rotation, half-sunk into the floor. These were paired with and connected to smaller wheels on the same axles. Heavy cables led every-where – upwards to what looked like windmills which could be folded out onto the roof. They also led downwards through the floor and everywhere she tried to step, in a maze of connections. The air was harsh with the smells of oil, gasoline and iron – a sharp contrast to the perfumed guests and floral displays in the rooms below. The place seemed to pulse like a mechanical heart, and for a moment Irene was uncertain of her plan. She was staggered by the noise and complexity of the place.

But a moment of doubt was all she would allow herself. She took a deep breath and raised her voice above the ambient volume. **'Electrical generators, shut down safely and stop transmitting power!'**

The words hung in the air – and then it all went wrong.

It was as if her use of the Language had triggered some kind of paralysis. She couldn't move. She couldn't breathe. Dust motes glinted in the air as they spun downwards, and they fell slowly, so slowly, and the world itself shifted perspective around her. Her surroundings changed from a sharply lit room full of machinery, to a dimly lit twilight where silently turning wheels gently spun to a halt. Beneath her feet, a circle of light blinked into existence. Despite her frozen state, she could see it was edged with and ornamented by words in the Language that gleamed in the shadows.

And opposite her, barely a few yards away, a figure unfolded itself. It was as though it slipped sideways, through a line drawn in mid-air, to emerge into three dimensions. He was robed in black, like a Benedictine monk – or some other, darker order. But when he raised his hands to push his hood back, Irene recognized his face.

Irene could breathe again now, but horror and sheer terror made her throat dry. 'Alberich,' she whispered.

She'd seen this particular face once before, in a burning library. He could wear multiple faces and change his skin, so she wondered why he was attached to this one. Was it his true aspect, or had he left that far behind? There was nothing about his appearance to declare him a relentless traitor and the Library's greatest enemy. She noted the receding hairline, thin eyebrows, strong nose and jaw, deep-set eyes, lean shoulders and rope-sandalled feet – quite ordinary-looking, in fact. But she associated this face with unrelenting malice and eternal darkness. She quite simply could not look at him and see a normal man – not when she knew what he was.

'Ray,' he said, seeing straight through her mask and blonde wig. His eyes met hers in recognition.

'My name is Irene,' she corrected him. It was a small gesture of defiance, but one which gave her courage – and, more importantly, a moment to think.

'Ray is what your parents named you.' He smiled, his expression surprisingly rueful, surprisingly friendly. 'Though I have to approve of any step towards self-development. We talked about that once before, if you remember?'

'About evolution, and how both Fae and dragons were dead ends?' Irene remembered that far too well. They had been dancing in a Russian palace. But Kai had been there to save her that time. 'Yes, I remember. But why are you here now?'

'For you.'

Her guts cramped with panic. What did one say, when personal nightmares came strolling out of the darkness to tell you how pleased they were to see you? 'Surely you have more important things to do.'

He took a step towards her. She would have moved back, but the circle around her feet held her fast. 'On the contrary. You – and your friends – are extremely important.'

Irene ran through various conversational gambits in her head, and finally said, 'What's going on?'

Alberich blinked in surprise – another human gesture, but this time it seemed just a little affected, like an actor's projection for his audience. 'So blunt? We could play a game of riddles for answers instead. Or dance around the subject, gathering information without giving any away. Wouldn't that be more . . . fun? Or maybe—'

But she'd been gathering her nerve while he spoke. **'Floor, break under Alberich!'** she ordered with desperate speed, interrupting him mid-speech.

The circle around her flared, brightening as her voice was suddenly silenced. It was as if she stood inside a cone of perfect quiet. The Language had failed her, and the words she mouthed had no power.

'Yes, that would have been my next step too,' Alberich said. He took another step towards her. 'It's astonishing how much we think and plan alike. Librarians together, brothers and sisters in the same service . . .'

She'd shut down the generators – that part of her mission had been successful. She couldn't hear any noise of chaos downstairs as a result, but the floor and walls were thick enough to block that out. Hopefully Kai and Vale would get Catherine to safety, and then come looking for her. But for the moment, she was on her own. 'What do you *want* with me?' she demanded.

Alberich paused as a flicker of darkness ran through his body, like a glitch in a projection. 'Ah. I have less time than I'd thought. That gets your hopes up, doesn't it, Ray? You're thinking that if you keep me talking a bit longer, you may be able to save yourself.' His grin was pure malice. 'My scripts were set to react to your use of the Language. But you haven't worked out what that means.'

The day's uncertainty crystallized into raw panic. Irene had to work to keep her voice from shaking. 'You expected me to come here?'

Alberich nodded and made a *go on* gesture with a hand that seemed to be fraying at the edges, fuzzy with something resembling static.

'We came here because Doctor Brabasmus would be here tonight. So . . . did you have someone leak that information?' Singh had said that report was unreliable – and he'd been right. 'You expected me to use the Language.' She gestured at the shimmering circle around her feet. 'You set this up.'

Alberich nodded. 'The moment you used the Language . . .' He snapped his fingers. Shadows crackled between them. 'Activation. And now we really can't keep your friends waiting any longer, can we?'

Irene's eyes flicked to the door, but Alberich shook his head. 'No, it's simpler than that. Their names are also woven into the circuit I've created. They're coming with you. You're all useful to me, and I know just how dangerous it is to leave any of you on the loose while the others are prisoners.'

'Language, release me!' Irene ordered, putting the whole of her will into the words.

Pain splintered in her temples and she tasted her own blood in her mouth. For a moment the words seemed to hang in the air like an echo – struggling with the force that surrounded her, like desperate fingers scrabbling at a cliff's edge. The circle around her hummed as her will battled Alberich's scripted trap, Language against Language, Librarian against Librarian.

For a moment she thought she might succeed.

Then Alberich spoke in the Language, and his words had the strength of centuries behind them: **'My pattern, complete.'**

The circle of light around her feet started to turn, rotating like a whirlpool. A rising hum of power sang in the air, drowning out the echoes of Alberich's voice. The sound rose until it was louder than the generators had been before, until Irene had to press her hands against her ears to shut it out.

Flickers of fire ran through the darkness of Alberich's robe. He spread his arms wide, exultantly, and the flames leapt up to the ceiling. They veiled him in a swelling conflagration that flared too brightly for Irene's eyes to bear.

But Irene would not surrender. She could not let herself break if there was even the smallest chance of escape. She tugged against the circle, trying to pull free, and called out again and again in the Language. Yet she couldn't hear her own voice above the surrounding noise. Panic swelled in her, and her mind ran in circles – a trapped rat with no way out. If only she could find the right words to use, there *had* to be something . . . if Alberich could write it then she could rewrite it, she just needed *time*.

But then the floor dropped out beneath her, and she fell into fire and darkness.

CHAPTER TWENTY

It was a sad commentary on Irene's life that, on waking up in chains, her first thought was *Oh no, not again*.

At least she wasn't dangling from the ceiling. That was always hell on her shoulders.

She was lying on her back, hands outstretched to either side; metal cuffs circled her wrists. She was chained to a cold stone floor. The stillness and dead silence suggested she was in a large open space with nobody else nearby. She could taste the chaos in the air, and the Library brand on her back itched with it. Definitely a high-chaos alternate world, even nearer to the chaos end of the universe than Vale's world. Where *had* Alberich taken her?

At least she was still alive, Irene reminded herself firmly. Where there was life, there was hope. She'd escaped from difficult situations before. But, as she looked around, she decided this had to rate pretty highly on the *I'm really doomed this time* scale.

She was in a church . . . no, a cathedral, and the Sagrada Familia cathedral at that. She recognized it now. Not just from the reports found on Lord Guantes' laptop, but from images seen over the years. But this interior was far darker than versions of the place on other worlds. Black stone pillars rose like lithe young trees, twisting and branching out above her to support an intricately carved ceiling. Here patterns resembling open flowers bloomed across the stonework, petals spreading out to touch one other. Electrical cables wound around the pillars like vines, silver against their blackness. Some even passed *through* the pillars, as though the ancient structure had been designed to support them. Where she'd expected to find stained-glass windows were computer screens. They blazed high above, shining with colours that had nothing at all to do with natural daylight. The whole place was a forest of dark stone, its ornamental flowers outlined in bright but poisonous hues. This unnatural light illuminated the aisles and nave with a pale twilight glow. Irene herself lay roughly where the altar should be, if this were really a version of the Sagrada Familia. She didn't like the symbolism.

The cathedral was vast. She was so small compared with its immensity, a single human being in a huge silence that seemed to breathe. Strange lights behind the windows moved as though they were alive. They waxed and waned like distant moons, pulling up a tide of darkness to drown her. If she strained, she could just see doorways and stairwells leading to side chapels, crypts or who knew where – the shadows hid the details.

Her chains ran from the cuffs on her wrists to two bolts set into the stonework, far enough away from each other that she couldn't bring her hands together or rise to her feet. The most she could manage was to rise to her knees, to take stock of the situation. Her mask and wig were gone. Her hidden knife had been taken as well. And someone had hung a pendant around her neck on a leather cord – too short for her to see the object properly, she could only feel it against her skin. Whatever it was, though, it couldn't be good news.

But worst of all, surrounding her on the floor – a few feet

out from the bolts which held her chains – was a circle written in the Language. It formed a single line, word flowing into word like some form of ancient calligraphy, scrawled on the black stone in dull brown paint. The vocabulary was mostly unfamiliar to Irene, though she thought she could make out words referring to *binding, holding, chaining, repelling*. What she could *definitely* make out was her own name – forming part of the circle directly in front of her, as though to taunt her.

Irene sighed. *I might as well know the worst.*

'**Locks, open,**' she commanded, and was not particularly surprised when her words proved powerless.

The circle of Language was out of her reach, chained as she was. Even if she lay down and stretched to her limit, her feet still couldn't touch the writing. Her lock picks were gone, too. She forced down a growing sense of panic and tried to think. *The problem is that I'm fighting someone who knows full well what Librarians can do. And he's had plenty of practice at imprisoning our kind, which comes shortly before he skins his captive and sends a few spare organs back to the Library . . .*

Irene was out of good ideas and was seriously considering spitting on the circle, to see if her saliva did anything useful, when she heard the distant creak and boom of a door opening. She could identify two separate sets of footsteps. *I hope this is the start of visiting hours for prisoners – rather than someone here to do the dusting and change the flowers . . .*

Lord Guantes came into view first, a spring to his step and a smile curling his lips. Even at a distance, Irene could see his enthusiasm as he approached her. After all, gloating over a defeated enemy was a key part of his archetype as a Machiavellian villain. But that gave her a grain of hope. People who thought they'd already won made mistakes.

And then the second person came into view, and Irene stifled a gasp of horror. It was Catherine . . . but changed.

She walked with her head lowered, eyes cast down, taking small obedient steps. Her shapeless dress was grey and utilitarian, covering her from neck to toe, and her hair was pinned back into a tight bun. Black gloves like the ones the Guantes favoured sheathed her hands. Her habitual expressions – irritation, annoyance, determination and curiosity – had been wiped from her face. It was as though someone had erased her personality entirely. Now she looked calm and patient, placid and unconcerned . . . and utterly unlike herself. Lord Guantes had turned her into an obedient little acolyte, one that he could twist around his finger and have her thank him for it.

They advanced down the length of the cathedral, and the glowing windows were now flooding the aisles with crimson light so the pair seemed to trail blood in their wake.

Lord Guantes came to a stop five feet outside the circle, with Catherine a pace behind. He looked down at Irene. 'How pleasant, Miss Winters, to see you in a more suitable position – on your knees.'

'My faith is a constant comfort,' Irene said blandly. She could cope with this. He wasn't Alberich. She could even, on some level, feel sorry for Lord Guantes – now a mere puppet in someone else's show. But she really felt for whoever the original host had been, before 'Lord Guantes' was transplanted into his body.

He barked a short laugh at the obvious untruth, then beckoned Catherine forward. 'I thought I'd introduce my new student to you,' he said.

Catherine smiled in the sunlight of his attention. The expression seemed out of place on her features. Her face was made for fierce enthusiasms, not blind sheeplike adoration. 'What would you like me to do, sir?'

'I'd like you to tell Miss Winters here about your new position. And whether you like it or not, of course.'

Catherine looked down at Irene pityingly. 'I'm going to look after Lord Guantes' book collection,' she explained. 'I'm so grateful to Lord Guantes for giving me this opportunity, in spite of everything my uncle's done to him.'

Lord Guantes was practically preening himself. If he'd been a peacock, he would have been spreading his tail to be admired. 'I don't like to see talent wasted, my dear.' He patted her shoulder, but his eyes were on Irene, watching for her reaction.

'Aren't you grateful to Lady Guantes as well?' Irene asked innocently.

'I don't think she really understands my role yet,' Catherine said. She glanced uncertainly at Lord Guantes, clearly wanting to take her cue from him.

A shadow of discontent drifted across Lord Guantes' face. 'My beloved wife will come to appreciate you in time, Catherine. You simply need to be patient.'

Very interesting. 'I hope that I'll have the chance to see Lady Guantes again before I . . . well, before anything *happens*.'

'Why?' Lord Guantes asked curiously. 'Have the two of you formed some sort of secret bond while I wasn't around? Do you send each other letters in code and meet up to drink tea on alternate Fridays?'

'Absolutely not,' Irene said hastily. 'No, I just wanted to apologize. They do say that a person should try to apologize to everyone they've offended before they die . . . and I'm not going to survive this, am I?'

'Let's discuss *that* later,' Lord Guantes said, in tones that suggested he'd enjoy it rather more than Irene would. 'But why do you feel the need to apologize to her?'

'For killing you.'

His expression froze. There was a momentary blankness behind his eyes – normally so keen and dominating. It was as if a record player had jumped a notch, missing a note in the music. 'In case you haven't noticed, Miss Winters, I'm not dead.'

'*Lord Guantes* is dead,' Irene argued, watching his reaction like an angler playing a fish. If she could reawaken this body's previous personality, its true identity . . . 'Tell me, how good is your memory of yesterday? Or the day before?'

Lord Guantes flicked his gloved fingers in casual dismissal. 'You make no sense.'

'Did Lady Guantes tell you something to explain any discrepancies?' Irene asked. 'Do you ever catch her looking at you as though you were her latest specimen in a zoological breeding programme? Tell me—' She tried to put her will into the Language and make it *work*. **'Tell me who you really are!'**

But her words fell flat, drained by the circle which surrounded her. It was the sense of her words, rather than any power behind them, which made anger flare in his eyes. He stepped forward, raising his hand as though about to slap her, or something equally petty.

But then he stopped, his foot a few inches away from the circle. 'Your petty lies are no threat to me,' he declared.

'Can't you cross the circle?' Irene asked sympathetically. 'How *irritating* for you.'

Lord Guantes pulled himself together, but his voice lacked the perfect composure of a few minutes before. 'You're insulting me while *chained and on your knees*, in a pitiful attempt to assert your superiority. Are you trying to keep up your spirits in the face of impending doom, Miss Winters, or is this merely stupidity?'

Irene looked around at the shadowy cathedral, the glowing windows and the dark heights above her. 'I wouldn't want to judge based on appearances,' she said. 'And I'm certainly afraid of Alberich. But not of *you*.' A petty insult, but if he took the lure . . .

This time he nearly did cross the circle. His toe was on the very brink before he realized what he was doing and drew back, composing himself with icy fury. 'You, my dear, are going to be Alberich's new body. A grand fate indeed.'

'I'm aware of his habits of skinning people and donning their skin to masquerade as them,' Irene said, trying to sound as bored as possible, though her panic rose. She wouldn't give him the satisfaction of a reaction.

'Apparently you damaged his original body so much that it's unusable. So that option's no longer open to him. I don't suppose you'd care to explain how you did it?'

'Fire,' Irene said, 'carefully applied and in the highest possible quantity. That damages most things.'

'How tediously obvious. Well, the good news for you – dear me, that should probably be *bad* news – is that he is still very much *alive*.'

'I knew that already,' Irene said flatly. If she could just goad him one step further, one inch closer . . . 'I saw him at the People's Palace. He explained how he was using your wife – and you.'

'I think you'll find that we are using *him*.' Lord Guantes retorted smugly. 'He can project a hologram of himself to another world, but only once a direct link has been forged to that world. And he can't sustain it for very long. It's *much* easier if he can inhabit a host in that world. Previously he's been using this computer system.' He gestured at the Sagrada Familia around them. 'But what he really needs is a human nervous system. One that's stronger than normal flesh and bone. He needs a *Librarian*.'

'What fun,' Irene said, her throat dry as sand. It explained why he'd wanted her alive, at least. 'Tell me, will I be aware of this miraculous process, once it starts? Or will my own mind simply be wiped out, just like that?' She snapped her fingers.

'I wouldn't know.' Lord Guantes was enjoying himself now. 'Previous human subjects managed to scream, but they didn't last long. With you, we're hoping for something more permanent.'

'*He's* hoping, you mean,' Irene corrected him, feeling sick. Nightmarish images surged uncontrollably through her imagination – her mind being sponged away as Alberich took possession of her body. Or worse, her remaining conscious and screaming as he took up residence inside her, but unable to do anything about it. 'It's his project. You're . . . just following orders.'

His gloved hands curled into fists. 'Shall I tell you what's happened to your friends? They're prisoners, just like you. The dragon – no, make that *both* dragons – may be useful political hostages. I don't know where the second one came from. Do you go round collecting them?'

'They're like buses. You wait for one, and then half a dozen turn up at once.'

'I can only hope and trust that your ill-judged sense of humour is painfully scoured from your mind when Alberich takes possession of you,' Lord Guantes said.

Fae think in narrative patterns, Irene reminded herself. *For him, this is a story where he's the main protagonist and his enemies come to a satisfying end. This isn't a story which has a happy ending for me – unless I can change the plot. But I'm not sure that I can.*

'What about Vale?' she asked, trying to muster some hope. At least Kai was alive, and Shan Yuan was with him. Maybe they could find a way out of here, or at least be traded back to their father in return for some concession.

She tried not to think about Alberich confronting Kai while wearing her body: how it might feel, and what he might do. But the image wouldn't go away.

'My wife has some use for the detective,' Lord Guantes said. 'I haven't bothered to ask for details.'

Irene didn't like to think about Vale's fate either.

Lord Guantes must have seen the despair in her eyes. 'Yes,' he said. 'Precisely. All three of you are going to be used or destroyed. You most of all. Was it really worth it, Miss Winters? You could have been my valued servant – maybe even, in time, a friend. But now look at you.' His gesture took in the surroundings, her restraints, her helplessness. 'You chose to refuse me. You chose to *defy* me. Consider exactly how far you have fallen, Miss Winters, and—'

A mobile phone's buzz interrupted him. 'Excuse me one moment,' he said, and extracted it from a pocket.

His brows drew together in a frown. 'What? Of course not,' he said, in answer to some unheard question. 'I left strict instructions . . .'

He paused to glare suspiciously at Irene. She shrugged innocently.

The voice on the phone yammered something incoherent. The words might be inaudible, but the tone was very much one of rising panic.

'I'm coming,' Lord Guantes snapped. 'Hold off any direct action until I'm there.' He jammed the phone back into his pocket and turned to Catherine. 'Accompany me – no, wait. Stay here. Keep an eye on Miss Winters. Make sure she doesn't try anything.'

'You seem very certain that she'll obey you,' Irene noted.

Scarlet light reflected from the windows, adding a gleam to Lord Guantes' eyes. 'She's given me everything but her true name,' he said, 'and even that's only a matter of time. I hold her far more strongly than you ever could. Just try to persuade her. I look forward to seeing your face when I return, and you've failed . . . assuming that Alberich hasn't claimed you first.'

He swept out of the cathedral with an air of smug triumph,

and the door slammed shut behind him. It echoed with a distant boom, underscoring his words with an air of finality. Irene could have done without it.

She weighed her odds. High-chaos worlds made it likely that narratives would follow standard patterns and stories would come true. There were two main narratives here and unfortunately, depending on one's point of view, both were equally plausible. *Heroine persuades acolyte to break free from evil* versus *Villainess fails to lure devotee into disobeying orders*.

But she had to try something. Not just because her own life and soul were at stake, but because she'd promised to protect Catherine. And because Catherine didn't *deserve* this. Nobody deserved what Lord Guantes had done to her.

'Catherine, are you permitted to speak to me?' she asked experimentally.

'I haven't been told not to,' Catherine said sunnily. 'What would you like to talk about?'

'Do you realize that Lord Guantes has affected your mind?'

'He only did it because he cares about me – and he respects me,' Catherine said. 'He's just helping me see things more clearly.'

'But do you remember he and his wife were trying to kill both of us, before?'

Catherine shrugged. 'Everyone makes mistakes.'

'But what about the peace treaty, and their attempts to destroy it?' Irene tried. 'And just a few days ago, Lord Guantes had you poisoned?'

Catherine sighed. 'Like I said, everyone makes mistakes. If you'd done the sensible thing in the first place, they wouldn't have tried to kill you.'

'Just what would the "sensible thing" have been?'

'Obeying Lord Guantes' wishes, of course,' Catherine said,

in tones that suggested nothing could be simpler. 'It was very rude of you to try to kill him.'

'Catherine, *you* dropped a book on him. From a great height.'

'I've apologized for that, and he's forgiven me. I feel much better about my future now.'

'And how do you feel about our futures – where Kai, Vale and I are prisoners, or worse?'

'You never really cared about me anyhow,' Catherine said, still composed, still smiling. 'You were just using me.'

'What precisely was I using you for?'

'You wanted to seduce my uncle.'

Irene just looked at Catherine for a moment, speechless. Then she started laughing hysterically, the breath coming out of her in thick hiccupping gasps that she couldn't stop. '*I* wanted to seduce *him*?'

'Stop that!' Catherine stormed forward, nearly to the edge of the circle. 'How dare you laugh at me like that? I know perfectly well that he's *right*.'

Irene forced herself to stop laughing, sensing a tiny opportunity at last. It seemed Catherine was far more vulnerable to emotions than swayed by facts. 'I see Lord Guantes isn't bothering to tell you the truth. Perhaps he doesn't trust you as much as you think.'

Catherine jerked up her chin in a familiar stubborn gesture that gave Irene a surge of hope. 'I'm his loyal and faithful servant. I don't need him to tell me every little thing, just to make me feel more secure.'

'So tell me, what next?'

'What do you mean?'

'Well, after horrible things have happened to me and I'm out of the picture—' *Ah, sweet euphemisms, what would we do without you?* 'What then? Will you trot around behind Lord Guantes for the rest of your life? Or will you be locked away with his books, permanently, wherever they are? I thought you wanted to explore different librarian archetypes, to see which you wanted to be?'

'I'll do what he wants,' Catherine said stubbornly. 'He knows best.'

'And what about your uncle?' Irene left the question hanging, pregnant with possibility.

'I'll just leave him alone. Lord Guantes says that's the best thing to do. Lord Guantes says that he isn't going to be drawn into petty feuds. Lord Guantes says—'

'Lord Guantes will probably have you kill your uncle yourself,' Irene interrupted. 'He and your uncle hate each other, you know this – and you'd be the perfect assassin. Why would your uncle ever suspect you? A few more words dropped into your shell-like little ear, and you'll cut your uncle's throat with a smile.'

'That's not *true*.' Catherine was nearly shouting now. 'He wouldn't make me do *anything* like that.'

'Catherine, sweetheart, darling, if you stay with Lord Guantes for much longer you won't just do it, you'll thank him for the opportunity.' Irene saw that fragmentary uncertainty in Catherine's eyes again and pressed further. 'And what next? Lord Guantes isn't the sort of person who likes to share. You'll never leave his private book collection again. You'll spend the rest of your life fossilizing there with nothing new to read, nothing new to do. Is that really how you see your future?'

'He's giving me what I've always wanted,' Catherine answered, the words a little too automatic, too programmed. 'Of course I'm grateful.'

'Except that it isn't what you *want*, is it?' Irene pulled at her chains, leaning forward for emphasis as if that would help her words penetrate. 'You told me how you wanted to be a librarian, Catherine. But there's more to that than

243

just sitting on a pile of books in some private archive, isn't there?'

Catherine raised a gloved fist in protest. 'Shut up!'

'Come on, Catherine, listen to me.' Irene wished she could use the Language, but she had nothing but her own voice now and her understanding of the girl facing her. 'We both know what you told me, what you *confessed* to me, because you trusted me. You wanted to work in a library built to store and preserve books and knowledge. And you wanted to *share* that knowledge. You wanted to be right there at the heart of it, helping people find books they could love. Or information they really needed. And as part of all this, you'd go out to find new books, new stories, to make the library even better. You must have imagined what that would feel like. Finding a new book which nobody who visited had ever read before. Sharing it with new readers. You'd have felt the library itself accepting you, knowing you were a crucial part of how it worked.'

'SHUT UP!' Catherine screamed, anger and bitterness turning her face ugly.

'You're going to be something different now, though. Lord Guantes will *never* give you that. What he means by "librarian" isn't what *you* mean. He doesn't love books the way you and I do – he'll never understand. You'll grow old behind locked doors, never leaving his private collection, never reading anything *new*. But you'll be happy. He won't *let* you be anything else.'

'You'd do it too . . .' Tears were leaking from the corners of Catherine's eyes, trickling down her face. She brushed them away with one gloved hand. 'Don't . . . don't try and act as if you're somehow better than me—'

'I have absolutely no delusions about myself,' Irene said flatly. 'The Library steals books and keeps them for itself – but it does share them. Eventually. And by holding books for different worlds, it keeps those worlds stable. That way, their people can read stories and dream about them – without being forced into either living them or having to do without those stories. And I have free will. You won't. Your dreams are going to rot away, inch by inch and moment by moment. Then some day you won't even remember what you meant by "librarian" and everything that went with it. Maybe you'll be happier that way. I don't know. I'll be dead, after all. But what about you, Catherine? Some people would say that was worse than death.'

Catherine pushed both gloved hands against her face, rubbing at her eyes, her whole body trembling. 'I – I want – I don't want that – please, Irene, help me.'

'Catherine.' Irene lowered her voice, but the acoustics of the cathedral meant that it still carried down the long aisle and into the vaults. She could feel success or failure poised on a knife edge. There would be failure, utter failure, if this thin connection between her and the Fae girl snapped. *This is a church and I'm literally arguing to save her soul. If anyone's listening, help me . . .* 'Catherine, I'm here. I'm *here*. The Library's here. I'm not going to let you go. Just listen to me. You can say no.'

'But he won't *let me*.' Her voice rose in despair. 'I can't – can't – make him let go of me.'

Irene had to find some way to break the psychic control that Lord Guantes still exerted over Catherine. She didn't wear anything as obvious as Irene's chains, but there was indeed a controlling leash around the Fae's mind. Then a thought came to Irene like a gift, an image – a *symbol*. 'Catherine. Take off your gloves.'

Catherine shook her head repeatedly, a few tendrils of tightly bound hair fluttering around her face. But her hands were moving, fingers struggling as she began to claw at one glove's buttons.

'You can do it,' Irene encouraged her, heart in mouth. 'You're strong enough to say no to *me*. You can say no to Lord Guantes. Just keep on pushing . . .'

Catherine's eyes went worryingly blank. 'But he said I could be his librarian. He said he wanted me to be a librarian.' Her fingers fumbled, losing their grip on the buttons. 'I don't need to worry about anything . . .'

'Take off those gloves,' Irene said softly, 'or you'll never touch a book with your bare hands again. Do you remember holding the Malory? What it was like being able to touch those old pages, to open it and read it? What do you *want*, Catherine?'

'Stop nagging me,' Catherine snarled. Her eyes focused again, angry at Irene, but even more so at herself. She yanked at the glove, one last button ripping loose and bouncing to the floor. Then she dragged it off her hand, letting it drop as if it repulsed her. Fingers trembling, frowning at her own slowness, she pulled off the second glove. She was muttering to herself, her voice barely audible, as she dropped it in turn.

The two discarded gloves lay on the marble floor – uncannily lifelike, resembling some old sculpture of praying hands.

Catherine raked her arm across her face, wiping away tears, and looked at Irene. Finally her eyes showed true awareness. 'What do we do now?' she asked.

'We get out of here,' Irene said grimly. 'And we raise hell.'

CHAPTER TWENTY-ONE

'Is there nothing on except soap operas?' Shan Yuan demanded.

He'd taken possession of the apartment's sofa and reclined on it, in what should have been a commanding posture. However, it was more akin to an invalid's weariness. Kai sympathized. This world they'd been yanked into was towards the chaotic end of the universe – further than Vale's world, further than others he'd tolerated in the past. As a result, he and his brother were grossly inconvenienced. It felt like a particularly bad bout of influenza, or how he imagined radiation sickness might feel – or worse. They certainly couldn't take their natural forms here, and even if there was a large quantity of water nearby (which there wasn't), Kai wouldn't have been able to bend it to his will.

In fact, it was possible to imprison two dragon princes simply by locking the door – and that *really* galled Kai. Some things simply should not be allowed to happen.

They were in a rather nice apartment suite in a skyscraper. It was hard to be sure how high they were, but a glance out of the locked and barred window suggested the thirtieth floor at least. Outside, the city's lights glittered in the darkness. Kai could just make out tiny vehicles flashing between them like luminescent deep-sea fishes, both at ground level and in the air. In the far distance Kai could see the Sagrada Familia – a building he recognized at once. The cathedral was floodlit, revealing a facade as intricate and fascinating as coral. It was an impressive landmark in the surrounding darkness. The feel of chaos hung heavy in the air around him, but he could sense it lay even deeper there. Part of him wanted to flinch from the sight, but the more mature, combative side of his nature marked it as a target. Lord Guantes had been the last person Kai had seen, before they were snatched to this world. If that was the cathedral another Lord Guantes had mentioned to Irene with his last breath, then this was the centre of the conspiracy . . .

'I'm talking to you, Kai,' Shan Yuan amplified his complaint. 'Stop staring out of the window.'

'I'm analysing our surroundings from a military point of view,' Kai excused himself. He picked up the television remote control and skipped through channels, feeling lethargic. Everything was in Spanish. 'Do you suppose they're trying to brainwash us? With chaos?'

'It could explain why we've been kept alive,' his brother muttered.

Kai still didn't have an answer to that, other than wondering what came next. But he kept that to himself.

He did feel guilty about Shan Yuan's presence. When the lights had gone out, back in the People's Palace, some sort of chaos portal had formed under his feet. His brother had leapt to Kai's side without a moment's hesitation, trying to drag Kai free – and he had, as a result, been pulled through too. Kai was responsible for his brother being here, trapped at the wrong end of the universe, in peril of death, or worse . . .

'Kept alive to languish in this banal cell, forced into each other's society, deprived of liberty, with chaos sullying our bodies and spirits – you should have been able to handle your affairs better than this, Kai.'

. . . though he had to admit that Shan Yuan's attitude wasn't *helping*. And Shan Yuan hadn't been invited to join their mission anyway, so it was his own fault he was here.

'It could be a lot worse, elder brother,' he said. 'We could each be chained up in a windowless cell, on our own, with no idea whether the other is alive or dead.'

'Don't give them *ideas*, Kai,' Shan Yuan hissed. 'They might be listening for you to describe your worst nightmare, so that they can act on it.'

'Oh, I'm sure they're listening. We've seen this place is high-technology. Only someone really stupid wouldn't put hidden microphones in here.'

Kai sat down, giving in to the weariness that suffused his body and made his bones ache. He wished he could explain to Irene that he didn't loathe high-chaos worlds due to prejudice, but because they made him feel ill and utterly shattered. This brought his thoughts back to Irene again – and Vale, and Catherine – and he wondered where they were. In other rooms inside this skyscraper? Or somewhere far worse? The Sagrada Familia? His hand clenched on the remote as he brooded on his powerlessness.

He forced himself to loosen his fingers. Enough self-indulgence. Time to be proactive.

They – their mysterious captors – had removed his knife and lock picks. He prowled the apartment, assessing its furnishings and features with a view to mayhem. There were no sharp kitchen implements or razors, though the bottles in the drinks cupboard could be broken. There was no computer access. The window was possibly breakable, but given how high up they were, a human body wouldn't survive the fall – and jumping out, in the vague hope that he might take dragon form before he hit the ground, would probably end unhappily. However, Irene had shown him many useful applications for harmless household goods in the past . . .

'What are you doing?' Shan Yuan asked querulously.

'Reviewing the situation,' Kai answered. 'We have basic microwave meals in the kitchenette here. No sharp knives, though.'

'Microwave?' Shan Yuan pulled himself out of his despond and wandered over to inspect it. 'Probably not very useful,' he said, after a minute or two.

Kai construed that as *wouldn't cause significant damage if I rewired it to explode* and nodded. But something else had crossed his mind. 'Nice drinks cupboard,' he said, keeping his tone casual. 'At least we can get drunk while we're waiting for our possible doom.'

Shan Yuan made a noise of disgust. 'Is that your best idea? I thought you were keeping bad company, but now I know it for certain.'

'I might surprise you with my mixing skills,' Kai said. 'Let's see. I could make a dry martini, but that's boring. They don't have absinthe or blackberry liqueur, so an Aunt Roberta's out of the question, and I don't feel like a Death in the Afternoon or a Tropical Zombie . . . Do you? Or how about a Long Island Iced Tea?'

Shan Yuan glared at him and even here, in the depths of chaos, Kai could feel a brief surge of blazing heat from his brother's body. 'You embarrass yourself.'

Kai cursed silently. Apparently Shan Yuan didn't know his cocktails and hadn't grasped the salient factor here – all the drinks Kai had mentioned had an extremely high alcohol content. Since they were certainly being monitored, there was no way to be more direct. 'Older brother,' he said, 'we're both suffering due to the chaos level here. We won't be given any drugs – or if we are offered any, I wouldn't advise taking them. The most sensible option is to have a few drinks to dull the pain. Watch me and I'll show you.' He pulled a fork from the cutlery drawer and passed it to Shan Yuan, nodding meaningfully at the microwave.

Kai's control over water wouldn't extend to the liquids in this world – they were far too infested by chaos, too deeply infiltrated by its essence. And their captors would know this, assuming Kai would be just as helpless here as he'd been before, that time in Venice.

It was a rewarding experience to disprove one's enemies' expectations, and the more drastically the better.

Well, rewarding for *him*.

Shan Yuan took the fork and looked uncomprehendingly at it. Then he looked more closely at the spirits Kai was gathering. Gin, vodka, tequila, rum . . . 'Maybe you have a point,' he said, and pried off the microwave's control panel.

Kai suspected they'd only have a few moments to act, once his brother started mangling the microwave's electronic guts. He gave up on subtlety and started uncorking all the bottles.

From the lounge area, a gentle electronic voice intoned, 'Stand away from the kitchen equipment. This is an order.'

Shan Yuan hissed between his teeth and did something to the wiring.

'Stand away from the kitchen equipment, or we are authorized to use lethal force,' the voice continued, in the pleasant female tones of an electronic alarm system which had been designed to sound comforting and reassuring.

Shan Yuan nodded to Kai and jammed the fork into the wiring. Blue sparks jumped. Kai tipped the vodka onto the wiring; the sparks belched upwards, flaring into sudden alcohol-fuelled flames.

Fire wasn't like water. Fire existed only for a moment, remade with every passing second, constantly replaced by newly-created flames. While the burning materials might be of this world and contaminated by chaos, the actual tongues of fire were untouched. They were free from corruption as they winked in and out of existence. Which meant Shan Yuan could command the fire howsoever he wished.

The fire leapt up, wreathing the microwave and melting the plastic-topped counter it stood upon. Shan Yuan directed it downwards, so it could rush across the floor – then it flared across the room, charring the neutral beige carpeting and bland walls. It spread around Shan Yuan and Kai in a growing circle, blossoming outwards to shoot towards the apartment door.

Shan Yuan followed the flames, and Kai followed Shan Yuan, a bottle of vodka in his hand in case a top-up was required.

Guards had begun to assemble beyond the apartment door, but they weren't prepared for the rolling wall of flame that smashed the door down and came roaring towards them. A few had enough sense to shoot at the two dragons, but most sprayed their bullets blindly into the flames.

Kai knocked Shan Yuan to the floor and out of the line of fire, biting back a curse as a bullet seared his upper arm. Shan Yuan said nothing, but the heat of his body beneath Kai redoubled, and the flames burst forth with new fury, reaching out for the guards like living things.

The guards weren't being paid to face down an inferno. They broke and ran.

'Take one alive,' Kai murmured in Shan Yuan's ear. 'We need information.'

'Good idea. You do have more experience in these situations,' Shan Yuan admitted. He hooked his hand in a gesture and the flames leapt ahead of the rearmost guard, circling to cut him off.

The guard turned to face them. He was anonymous behind

his helmet, face mask and body armour, but his posture spoke eloquently of how much he feared the fire. 'Keep back!' he ordered them.

'Question this fool for me, Kai, before I incinerate him where he stands,' Shan Yuan said dismissively. The strain in his expression was only visible to Kai, and only because he knew his brother well.

As Kai glared at the guard, he was every inch the son of Ao Guang, Dragon King of the Eastern Ocean. Blood trickled down his arm from the bullet wound, merely adding to his anger. 'You,' he snapped at the man, and saw him flinch. 'We need information. You may assist us or you may die. The choice is yours.'

The guardroom nearby *did* have a computer terminal, and Shan Yuan bent over it with renewed energy. The flames had filled this floor of the building and were now rapidly spreading to other levels. This had apparently halted any attempts to find or recapture them, and the screaming mass of civilians being evacuated provided an additional distraction. Kai did feel guilty about their fright, and the damage. He reassured himself that once he and Shan Yuan were safely out of the building, the fire crews could put out the flames.

'How long will this take?' Kai asked, knotting a bandage of torn cloth over his wound. It would have seriously inconvenienced a human; as a dragon, he could endure it without too much difficulty.

Shan Yuan's fingers flickered across the keyboard. The guard had provided the password and his fingerprint to enter the system, and had therefore been allowed to keep his hand. 'I'm interfering with the building's security network – telling it to focus on the fire and evacuating the building. But we're bound to be discovered quickly . . . It'll take too long to reach the ground floor, but the system says there are aircars docked on the roof. Can you fly an aircar?'

'Yes.' Well, yes in other worlds. That would just have to do.

'But where shall we go?'

'The Sagrada Familia,' Kai replied, without hesitation. 'You can see it from the windows. It's guesswork, but Lord Guantes did talk about a cathedral, and there was the information on the laptop. It's too much of a coincidence to avoid. I'm assuming Irene will be in the most dangerous place and under the highest security.'

'Higher than us?' Shan Yuan didn't try to suppress the offended pride in his voice.

'Our enemy's folly is our good fortune. Can you sustain the flames until we reach the roof?'

'Of course,' Shan Yuan said disdainfully, ignoring the sweat that streaked his brow.

'*Without* burning down the entire building?'

'That might be more difficult,' Shan Yuan conceded. 'We should hurry.'

Bombarded by blaring sirens and warnings to evacuate immediately, and *without* using the lifts, they made for the roof. Shan Yuan's flames cleared their way, and roaming squads of guards and panicked civilians fled the walls of fire that surrounded them. Fortunately those same walls of fire hid the fact that Shan Yuan was leaning on Kai for support. The effort of moving the blaze ever onwards, against a background of chaos, drained him.

They staggered out onto the roof together – a landing zone marked into separate quadrants by artificial foliage and bordered by garages. Kai only saw a few parked aircars, and those were being fought over by panicked citizens. Multiple fire escapes offered safe routes to the roofs of other buildings – but it seemed that some refused to leave without their cars, or were taking advantage of the situation to do some looting.

'That one,' Kai said, pointing at the nearest – a sleek gold two-seater. Shan Yuan raised a hand. Flames blossomed from the halo that surrounded them, flowing across the tarmac like oil to circle the aircar. The fire forced back the pair who'd been about to seize it, and Kai grabbed the key card from one of the distracted opportunists. Another burst of flames caused them to flee, as Kai dragged Shan Yuan into the passenger's side before jumping into the driver's seat.

Kai stared at the rows of controls. A keyboard. A screen. Multiple buttons. Key-card reader. Close enough to aircars he'd flown before. He waved the key card at the reader hopefully, and was delighted as the controls all fired up. He spared just a moment to wonder if the card was a counterfeit or genuine, meaning they were stealing the aircar, then shrugged. Their need was great and the screen was glowing in readiness, showing what looked like a local map. He tapped a building, and the screen helpfully suggested various speeds and routes to reach it.

The fires were dying down without Shan Yuan to boost them. Emergency vehicles had now converged on the building, some pouring foam through open windows. Kai hit the choices for high speed and direct route, mentally urging the aircar to hurry. It rose, drifting into the air like an overweight pigeon trying to remember exactly how one went from pavement to airborne. It steadied a couple of yards up then rotated, before plunging into motion.

'Good job,' Kai said, relaxing for a moment. 'Well done, brother.'

'You were quite competent yourself,' Shan Yuan said, gracing him with a thin smile.

'Next stop the cathedral,' Kai said triumphantly, touching their *real* target this time – the Sagrada Familia – on the screen. Other aircars from the roof were heading in all directions, merging into what might be regular traffic flows. The emergency vehicles were fully occupied with the still-burning fire, darting around the building to squirt foam at the flames.

But the expected routing options failed to materialize. 'Unacceptable end point,' the aircar's voice unit said, sounding less friendly than earlier. 'Sagrada Familia is not a permitted destination. Please state new travel end point.'

Somehow, Kai wasn't too surprised. The reports on the stolen laptop had indicated the place was closed. He hunted for the manual override and turned it on. Luckily this was indeed like aircars he'd driven before. Two levers, a bit like joysticks, slid out from a concealed recess. 'Things may get a little bumpy from here on,' he warned his brother.

'Is that car approaching us?' Shan Yuan asked, pointing. The vehicle heading towards them was a sleek black with silver trim. It had red lights on its sides and looked worryingly official. Kai ignored it. Then the vehicle opened fire. The two dragons ducked in their seats as bullets came hammering through the roof, sides and windscreen; fragments of glass cascaded down upon them. Their pursuer slid sideways to draw level with them, matching their pace, and a rough amplified voice roared, 'Stop your car and maintain position or be shot down!'

'Right,' Kai said, a vicious smile curving his lips, and began to get creative. He urged the aircar into a rapid dive, dropping away from their pursuer. Then he curved to the right, ducking under a stream of traffic to slide between two skyscrapers.

'They're following us,' Shan Yuan shouted unhelpfully, as though this might assist Kai rather than distracting him. 'Do something!'

'This airborne business would be a great deal easier if we were in our proper forms,' Kai muttered between gritted teeth. He yanked on the vertical lever, pulling the aircar upwards. More glass came loose from the edges of the shattered windscreen, falling behind them in a glittering trail. 'This thing has no *style* . . .'

More bullets chattered through the air to their left. Kai swung to the right, wishing for a gun of his own. 'Do you think they're police, or the ones who were keeping us captive?'

'Does it matter?' Shan Yuan was huddled down as far as was possible in his seat, and clearly hating every second of this undignified crouching. 'Get us to that building and out of the air!'

Kai shared Shan Yuan's eagerness. They were weaponless and being shot to pieces up here. 'We're getting there,' he reassured his brother, putting the aircar through a couple of quick turns, then gliding under another traffic stream. He could see their target now. He just wished he had more idea of what they'd do once they arrived . . . besides the obvious *Rescue Irene and dispose of all enemies.*

'Halt or be shot down!' came the blast of another loudspeaker. Kai bit back a curse as a second vehicle came swooping in to join the chase. He yanked a joystick, forcing his aircar to climb, but he could feel the drag of air and wind.

The building ahead came into full view and for one moment, even mid-chase, he was distracted. It was *glorious*. He'd only seen images of the Sagrada Familia up close, and they were now perfectly positioned to admire it. Or would have been if they weren't under attack. The illuminated cathedral had the beauty of a living, organic creation – as fair and elegant as a coral reef, or a grove of trees, or one of his father's palaces. Dark stone curled upwards into glorious spires like singing poems, etched and patterned with designs that made him ache to see them properly in daylight. Ornate glass windows glowed with rich colours, lit from inside the building. The beauty of their burning hues ached against the darkness. He could have hung there in mid-air and stared at it for hours.

Their aircar shook with the impact of a bullet. 'Warning,' the pleasant female voice said from the console, 'fuel tank integrity is damaged. Please land and inspect your vehicle. Warning, fuel tank integrity is damaged . . .'

'Do all your escapades end up like this?' Shan Yuan demanded sourly.

'Make helpful suggestions, or stay quiet,' Kai replied, gauging their options. It was reassuring that Shan Yuan trusted him to handle this and hadn't just grabbed for the controls himself. He wasn't going to disappoint his brother now.

They could land outside the building, but their airborne pursuers could easily shoot them down. And he could see guard posts and security patrols down there. If they wanted to avoid being shot and get inside the building, he could think of only one way to do it. Kai felt an almost physical pain at the thought of what he was about to do. Any damage could be repaired, of course, but . . .

'Is it helpful to say we're on fire?' Shan Yuan pointed at the rear of the vehicle.

Kai didn't look round. Looking round wouldn't help, and it would just distract him from his plan. 'Don't worry,' he said, trying to sound soothing. 'Keep your head *down*. This will only take a moment.'

'Kai, what are you – no!'

Shan Yuan threw his arms across his face as Kai swept the aircar round in a curve, aiming for the great oval window ahead of them. They crashed through in an explosion of glass and light.

CHAPTER TWENTY-TWO

'Can you pass through the circle?' Irene said urgently. Normally she'd have given Catherine time to recover from such a traumatic experience, but Lord Guantes might return at any moment. Worse, Lady Guantes might show up. Not a talker, like her husband, she might go with a 'just shoot everyone' approach.

Catherine pulled herself together and took a careful step forward, hand extended. When her fingers touched the circle's boundary she came to a stop, jerking her hand back. 'No,' she said reluctantly. 'I don't think so.'

'Did it feel as if you touched an invisible surface, or did it evoke feelings of pain or disgust?' Might as well know the nature of her prison, Irene thought.

'It felt maybe more like . . . a force field, and I felt a sort of buzzing. It was more . . . achy than painful. I suppose I could try running at it and see if I get through?' Catherine was clearly doing her best, but the suggestion lacked enthusiasm.

'We'll save that for if we get desperate.' She didn't want to kill Catherine with a casual experiment. But what on earth *could* they try? 'All right, Catherine. Did Lord and Lady Guantes say anything that might be useful in front of you, when they thought you were under their control? Anything about what's going on?'

'I think that circle is drawn in Alberich's blood,' Catherine said, demonstrating that she was capable of identifying the most important facts in an emergency. Irene resolved to give her a commendation for that later. She was further impressed as Catherine continued. 'Lady Guantes has some sort of big set-up underneath this building, but I didn't get to see much of it. The vaults beneath here are pretty deep – and extensive – apparently. There are guards down there and guards outside, though I haven't been able to go outside. And I think we're in Spain – well, *a* Spain anyway. We're in the Sagrada Familia – I recognize the interior from those laptop reports. There are computers absolutely all over the place, which would also fit with this being the Guantes headquarters. Oh, and it's currently –' she checked her watch – 'half past eleven at night. And something is going to happen at midnight. Lord Guantes said *the ceremony*, but Lady Guantes called it *the overwrite*.'

'That gives us half an hour before that something happens,' Irene said, forcing herself to stay calm. 'Midnight. How very overdramatic. I suppose it matches the narrative of me being chained up in a cathedral.' She sighed. 'I think we should plan on leaving *at least* five minutes before that deadline.'

Catherine looked determined, but Irene noticed that her hands shook as she tried to master her fear. 'So we've only got twenty-five minutes, then.'

Irene nodded. 'All right. Now, walk round the circle – see if you can read any of the writing.' She was having difficulty seeing behind her, due to those awkward chains. It would be great if there were some convenient *To exit, break here* sections.

'It's in the Language, right? I know the Language is

supposed to read as if it's in my own native language, but this doesn't make sense.' Catherine was behind Irene now, her steps quick on the stone floor. 'It's like reading a really archaic form of English, mixed with higher mathematics. I can read that it's about binding and holding a prisoner – at least, I think that's what it is, it wouldn't make sense for it to be about tying knots. And . . . um.'

'"Um" what?' Irene demanded.

'This bit is rather dramatic . . . the circle can only be unmade by the blood of the person who wrote it. That's almost poetic.'

Irene took a deep breath. Her stomach was tight with panic again. She couldn't yank her wrists loose from those chains. And she'd been trying, desperately. Even if she managed to dislocate her thumbs – she'd read the theory, but had never done it in practice – she didn't think it would help. If only Alberich's blood could break the circle, and his arrival meant her death or worse . . . then there was no way out. Her mind flinched away from that conclusion.

As a Fae, Catherine *should* be able to travel between worlds on her own – if she was strong enough. But every other Fae whom Irene had seen do this had been older, and had already chosen their private archetype.

Yet if Catherine could travel . . . Irene could tell the girl to run while there was still time, to reach Vale's world and contact Sterrington – or even Silver. One of them would tell the Library what had happened. The Library could then safeguard itself against whatever might come knocking on its portals . . . dressed in Irene's own skin.

Of course, that wouldn't save Irene, but maybe it was time to make the least worst choice – how she hated that phrase – and accept the consequences.

'Irene, what are we going to do?' Catherine asked tentatively, clearly hoping for a positive reply. But even a Librarian couldn't conjure hope where there was none.

Irene bowed her head, trying to muster the will to tell Catherine to go. Her gaze fell on the crumpled gloves that Catherine had dragged off her hands. It had seemed like such a triumph to break her free of Lord Guantes' control. Now it just felt as if Irene had won a battle . . . but lost the war.

As she looked at the gloves, something clicked into place at the back of her mind. It wasn't quite a full idea; it was the beginning of a chain of logic. She found herself approaching it carefully and by degrees, as though it were a wild animal and she didn't want to frighten it away. The gloves had been symbolic. Here, deep within chaos, symbolism had power. Alberich was a Librarian, or at least had been, and Irene was also a Librarian. This made them metaphorical brother and sister, which meant that they were symbolically *of the same blood* . . .

'Catherine! Do you have anything sharp on you?'

Catherine dashed back to face Irene, galvanized by Irene's burst of energy. 'No – I don't think they trusted me that much.' She paused, and her bare hands went up to touch her hair, which had been carefully pinned back into a tight bun. 'Wait. Some of the hairpins she stuck in there felt sharp enough when they went in. Give me a moment.'

Irene watched impatiently as Catherine dismantled her hairstyle. A couple of dozen hair grips, a bun net, two lethal-looking silver-headed hairpins and two tortoiseshell combs. 'Right,' she said. 'Try rolling one of those hairpins across the circle. Let's see if it will let it through.'

The hairpin skittered across the stone, undeterred by the circle. Irene nodded in satisfaction. 'Good. Now move round to my right-hand side – that's right – and slide the other hairpin towards my right hand.'

'What are you going to do?' Catherine asked. 'You're not going to rip out your own intestines with a pin and arrange them to make words in the Language? Because if you are, I may throw up.'

'Have you considered a career as a horror novelist?'

'No – but if I had, being around you would give me *lots* of inspiration,' Catherine muttered. She followed Irene's instructions, and the hairpin rolled towards her. 'What are you going to do?'

'I'm going to get symbolic.' Irene tested the hairpin's point against her fingers. It was one of the brutally sharp variety, the sort which scraped the scalp. Good, that'd make what she was planning easier.

She deliberately avoided dwelling on what she was about to do, and shifted the hairpin around in her hand, bracing the point against the bare wrist below it. This would have been much easier if she'd been able to bring her hands together, but she'd just have to cope.

'Don't do it!'

Irene blinked. 'What?'

'Don't commit suicide!' Catherine dropped to her knees so they were both on a level, leaning forward urgently. 'Look, please, there has to be some way out of here, we can think of something, you're *good* at thinking of *something*—'

'Stop that.' Irene decided not to admit how she'd almost resigned herself to death just a few minutes before. 'I have a plan. And it involves me staying alive, you'll be glad to hear. I'm going to try to draw some blood and break the circle.'

'Oh,' Catherine said, looking rather embarrassed.

'We both need to stay calm.' *Which may be harder for you than me.* 'Keep talking to me while I work. Tell me something.'

'Tell you what?' The thought of making a meaningful contribution seemed to steady Catherine.

'Tell me about your family. Not Lord Silver. Who were your parents? Where were they from?' Irene began to push the hairpin into her wrist, bracing her hand against the floor.

'My mother was Lord Silver's great-great-niece, or something like that,' Catherine said, her hands clenching nervously as she watched Irene. 'Lord Silver is several generations older, but because he's powerful he hasn't aged the way humans would. She grew up in Liechtenstein, where he has a branch of the family who never really went *large* – if you know what I mean? They didn't try to make something of themselves or gain power. They were just . . . people. Nearly human. Father was from Brazil. They fell in love.'

'There was an accident while they were travelling, you said,' Irene prompted. She could see her flesh dimpling where the pin's point dug in. She could also feel the pressure of time ticking away as they talked, seconds hissing into oblivion like sand running through an hourglass. She visualized an imaginary sundial, a ray of dark light tracing its way towards midnight – the moment Alberich would arrive. She hadn't lied to Catherine, though; this casual conversation *was* keeping her steady, giving her a focus other than her own fate.

'Yes, that was what Uncle told me.'

'Why did he remove you from the rest of your family, after they died, to have you brought up in a lonely manor house?'

Silence. Irene looked up to see Catherine duck her head and hunch her shoulders stubbornly. Well, she knew of one reason why a Fae might hide a vulnerable young relation. 'Was your parents' death due to some feud?' she guessed. 'And *not* just an accident?'

Catherine sighed. 'That's what I think. He wouldn't tell me. And I wasn't old enough to protect myself, or walk between worlds. I'm *still* not powerful enough to travel between worlds on my own . . .'

Irene wouldn't normally expect Lord Silver to have any

interest in protecting innocents – or innocence. He was a libertine, a politician and a spymaster, and he lived up to all three archetypes with enthusiasm. To protect a young dependant and shield her from unpleasant realities was . . . out of character. If a Fae departed from their chosen narrative and archetype it weakened them. It reduced their power and longevity and drew them back towards the common mass of humanity. Silver's actions here seemed a flaw in his character, an off note in the perfect symphony of his immorality.

Then, between one heartbeat and the next, the hairpin bit in and drew blood. Irene's first reaction was a natural human response to pain – she wanted to snatch her hand back and get that point out of her flesh. Instead she set her teeth and forced it deeper, still bracing one end against the stone, dragging the pin sideways in an attempt to widen the wound. Blood trickled over her fingers.

'Ow,' she said, finding some relief in the word, a diversion from the fact she'd just torn her own wrist open. 'Ow, ow, ow, bloody ow. This had better work.'

'Why does Alberich hate you so much?' Catherine asked, apparently feeling that it was Irene's turn to do some sharing. 'Couldn't he just kidnap any Librarian, if he wanted to take one over, rather than going after one as difficult as you?'

'Thanks for the compliment.' More blood dribbled from her wrist. 'I think it's personal. Very personal. I've opposed him multiple times. I stopped him from securing a unique first edition which contained a secret about his Librarian background; I destroyed his plans to ruin or usurp the Library; I burned his private store of rare books—'

'You did *what*?'

Irene sighed. 'You know, that's pretty much the way he reacted too. I wasn't exactly happy about it either.' The hairpin dropped from her fingers, slippery with blood, but the wound was deep enough; it wasn't going to close of its own accord.

She shifted position again, wriggling so that her right arm was as near the edge of the circle as possible and cupped her hand to catch the trickle of blood running into it. 'Catherine, step back a bit – I'm not sure what effect this will have.'

'What about you? You're right next to it.'

'Your concern is noted and appreciated,' Irene said through gritted teeth. She'd already thought of that. 'Don't worry – if an explosion knocks me out, you can drag me to safety.'

Catherine took several steps back. Then, at Irene's glare, a few more.

Irene took a deep breath, readying herself, and shook the handful of blood in her palm towards the edge of the circle. As it fell, she spoke in the Language: **'Warding circle, break!'**

Where her blood hit the circle, it flowed over the writing like mercury or like oil in a hot pan. She watched in fascination as the droplets moved, keeping their coherence rather than soaking into the paving. The calligraphy dissolved as her blood rolled across it, draining her energy until she sagged forward in her chains – barely able to keep her head off the floor. Words blurred into incoherence, sentences snapped midway, and still her blood ran around the circle. It overlaid the dark brown lettering, leaving a brighter ring of colour which continued to seep towards the outer boundary of the warding.

The line of blood seemed to hesitate for a moment – and then it surged forward, breaking the final line of text. The circle's power ripped apart with an audible snap, and cold air rushed around Irene as though a door had been opened.

Irene's brain was spinning. She shook her head, trying to pull herself together, the blood still running down her arm and hand. 'Right,' she said weakly, 'let's have another go at this. **Manacles, unlock and open.**'

The cuffs around her wrists fell to the ground with a clatter, and Irene felt the almost-expected stab of a headache. She gratefully rolled her shoulders, then examined her right wrist. It didn't look good, but she wrapped a fold of her dress around it and staggered to her feet with an effort, aching from having been on her knees so long. She took one pace, then another, then finally crossed the broken circle.

The cathedral was still deathly silent. Where was everyone? Assuming this *was* the place described in Lord Guantes' reports, they must have put in considerable work to claim it as their headquarters.

She focused on immediate concerns. The first was to rip off the pendant around her neck. It was a single teardrop of cold black metal, inlaid with tiny lines of circuitry. She flung it into the shadows, unwilling to stay in contact with it a moment longer. But she kept the leather lace that held it – it was time to bind her wound. Leaving a trail of blood would be overdramatic, even for this world.

'Can you rip some of the flounces off this ridiculous petticoat under my dress?' she asked Catherine. 'Good. Use that bit as a pad and wrap that section around my wrist. You can bind the lot with this.' She proffered up the leather lace, feeling a hint of satisfaction as she put it to a better use. 'Now, we need to find Vale and Kai. And Shan Yuan.'

'At least one of them is being held prisoner down in the archive, but I don't know which one.'

'Okay. How do we get down there?'

'You can get in from a door in the cathedral's outer wall, but there are guards patrolling outside,' Catherine said, 'or we can use the stairs over there.' She nodded to a set of archways.

'Right,' Irene said. 'Stairs it is then. Next item on the adventurous librarian job-description, Catherine: rescuing prisoners. Workplace assessment time.'

The joke prompted a flicker of a smile from her apprentice,

but it didn't last. 'I'm afraid,' Catherine said, her voice barely audible. 'What if he tries to control me again – and I can't stop him?'

'The important thing is to focus on a plan,' Irene said. 'That way you have something to think about, besides what's the worst thing that could happen.'

'So has "mind control" ever happened to you? Do *you* have a plan?' Her tone was surly and challenging, but Irene could hear the very real need for reassurance behind it.

'It goes a bit like this,' Irene said, as they walked towards the stairs. 'The first step is, *I'll kill myself before I let him do that to me again.* The second step is to say, *Wait, it'd be much more practical to kill him rather than kill myself.* And there you have it. A sensible plan based on logical choices.'

Catherine frowned. 'But murdering my enemies won't work every time.'

'True,' Irene agreed. 'There's a whole spectrum of other choices in this case. I'm sure you can think of a few. Blocking your ears, distracting Lord Guantes, whatever . . . But it's important to hold onto at least one thing that you *can* do to save yourself. It's much better than thinking you can't do anything. Trust me on this one.'

'I'm not sure you're good for my moral development,' Catherine muttered.

'I said I'd teach you to be a Librarian,' Irene replied. 'Moral development is an optional extra – *get down!*'

The huge window at the far end of the cathedral shattered – coloured glass burst inwards like the petals of an exploding flower as a giant glowing object roared through. The almighty crash echoed through the building, and from high above she heard bells, shaken by the impact. Irene knocked Catherine to the floor and covered her body with her own. She ignored the girl's muffled cry of protest as she tried her best to shield her.

Glass fragments rained down, ricocheting off the stone paving to smash into ever smaller pieces. The projectile that had come crashing through the window shot downwards, air screaming around it as some sort of braking system tried desperately to reduce its speed. It skimmed along the floor with a long, horrendous shriek, scraping a deep gouge in the beautiful dark marble. It spun and then juddered to a halt, coming to rest only about ten yards from the circle where Irene had been trapped.

Now that it was still, Irene could see it was a flying car of some sort. And it was on fire.

Well, she could do something about *that* at least. **'Fires, extinguish!'** she called, getting to her feet.

The flames went out like blown candles, leaving only wisps of smoke. Something inside the sealed aircar beeped in a melancholy way. From outside, through the broken window, Irene could hear the whooping of sirens and the fierce ringing of alarms.

One of the aircar's doors swung open, and Kai came stumbling out. He brushed soot and broken glass from his face, coughing, then turned to drag Shan Yuan out of the car. The other dragon was staggering and looked on the verge of collapse, cradling his left arm across his chest. Kai himself had a bandaged arm and multiple scrapes, but he was alive. He was *here*.

Irene's heart turned over, and the sudden lightness inside her made her feel as if all enemies could be defeated, all ends achieved. 'I see you managed your own escape,' she said, giddy with happiness at the sight of him. 'Good job.'

Kai jerked as he heard her voice, turning to where she stood in the shadows. Dragging Shan Yuan along like an inconvenient doll, he strode towards her, his pace steadier with every step. When he was close enough he simply let Shan Yuan drop to the ground, lunging to take Irene in his arms. His grip was almost desperate, and for a moment they simply held each other – conscious of the other's presence, the other's *life*, knowing that in this moment the other was safe.

But mere moments, Irene remembered, were all that they had. She forced herself to let him go. 'We're on a deadline,' she said reluctantly. 'We think Alberich will turn up at midnight. And there's a prisoner below here – who must be Vale. We have to get him out of here before then.'

'He's here too?' Kai's hands lingered on her arms. Then he spotted the bandage on her wrist and snarled in anger. 'Who did this to you?'

'I did it to myself, to get out of that circle. It's not serious—'

'You always say that,' Kai sighed, subsiding.

'And you always fuss over me. We need to move. I'll explain as we go.' She saw Kai and Catherine exchange similar exasperated looks, and made a mental note to discuss justifiable risks with them later. Because there was going to be a later. Oh yes.

Catherine was helping Shan Yuan to his feet. 'I think you've sprained your shoulder,' she told him.

He looked down his nose at her and flexed his left arm with what looked like perfect equanimity. Irene identified this, with her practice at interpreting Kai's moods, as *hurting but unwilling to admit weakness*. 'Nothing serious,' he informed her. His words echoed Irene's own and she winced, but it was time to move on.

'Let's *go*,' she urged them. Before Lord Guantes returned, before the guards outside came breaking in, before Alberich arrived . . . Why was she the only one who ever kept track of time during this sort of crisis?

With the ease of practice she squashed the unhelpful thought that the problem wasn't *timekeeping*, it was getting repeatedly drawn into these crises in the first place.

The stairs were made of the same slick black marble as the floor, and red lights glowed ominously from the ceiling overhead. While the stairwell's stonework was unexceptional, the experience still felt somehow organic – as though they were making their way deeper into a living creature. Cables ran along the ceiling throughout, placed as unobtrusively as possible, but clearly added fairly recently. Irene gave Kai a quiet update as they moved ever downwards, alert for guards and other dangers.

Passages at the bottom branched off in three directions. Serpentine and reptilian figures were carved into the walls, emerging from the stonework like creatures from an ancient sea. In an unexpected yet extremely welcome development, there were actually *signs* on the walls – in Spanish – complete with pointing arrows. Irene found herself smiling for the first time that night.

Everyone else had seen them. 'It must be a trap,' Shan Yuan muttered.

'If this was a normal place of worship before the Guantes took it over, they might not have troubled to remove the signs,' Kai contradicted him. 'The question is, which way do we want?' He indicated the three marked directions: *Crypt, Relics* and *Archive*.

Irene waved Catherine forward. 'Does any of this look familiar to you?' she murmured, remembering how the first iteration of Lord Guantes had mentioned the '*archive*'.

'Yes. It's the *Archive* we want,' her student confirmed. She indicated the third direction, the one with dolphins arching sinuously within their carvings as if trying to break free from the wall.

The dolphin corridor took them through several bends, heading further and further down, and the stonework seemed older as they descended. The ornamentation must have been added later – it was in Gaudí's distinctive style, like the cathedral above, but these dark stones predated Gaudi by centuries. The air was cold enough down here to raise goose-bumps on her bare skin, but it also felt dead and dry. They could have been stepping into the past as they walked into the depths of the earth.

The corridor finally ended in a heavy iron-bound door – locked, as Irene found when she touched the handle. She gestured the others to stand back. **'Door, unlock and open,'** she told it.

Irene stared in delight as the door swung open and she saw what was on the other side. Common sense prodded at her to move, as she formed an easy target. But sheer relief held her in place, staring at what might be their way out of this nightmare.

She wasn't looking at a few worn books chained to lonely shelves. This archive was a full-scale, full-blooded and thoroughly packed floor-to-ceiling library.

CHAPTER TWENTY-THREE

'Right,' Irene murmured, stepping aside so the others could see too. The archive was a blend of ancient and modern. Leather-bound books shared shelves with modern ledgers, and computer screens could be found everywhere. Signage indicated some unusual categories – *Theology*, *Witchcraft*, *Artificial Intelligence*, *Goetia*, *History*, *Heresy*, *Lives of the Saints* . . . Some shelves were made of stone, some of wood. Others seemed to be constructed from modern plastics, metal, or some other artificial extruded substance – these shelves resembled crystallized oil. Distant fans kept the air moving, a faint whisper on the edge of hearing. There were no other sounds and no sign of guards, dark ceremonies or lurking nightmares.

She saw that the room was more than just a single space – it was a complex of spaces, separated by dark pillars like the ones in the cathedral's nave. These pillars rose to the ceiling, where they branched out to form organic abstract shapes. Looking at them, Irene was reminded of the way tree roots wove around clearings in a forest. Clear white lamps shaped like strange flowers hung from the ceiling; they dropped between clusters of cables which had been fastened up there, well out of the way of the books and the floor. Irene couldn't make out the far walls – but for all she could tell, this place extended the full length of the cathedral. Or even further. It might have been modified to echo the structure above, and had been filled with computers as well as books, but this place was old, very old indeed.

She felt wary, her instincts prickling uneasily. This felt like *home*. It was far too good to be true. Something had to be wrong.

Irene pulled herself together and turned to Shan Yuan. 'I'll get you out of here.' This wasn't his fight, and Kai would be relieved to have his brother out of danger. 'Stand back from the door a moment.'

Shan Yuan's eyes flared red and he made a furious motion of negation with his good hand. 'Don't be ridiculous! Do you expect me to leave you here like this?'

Irene bit back *Yes, actually, I do*, because she could see this would only serve to provoke him. Instead she said, 'Your highness, it would be invaluable if someone knows where we are and what happened to us. I can't send a Fae into the Library, Kai definitely wouldn't go –' Kai nodded emphatically – 'and Vale's still a prisoner and we need to find him.'

Though not all of that was *entirely* true. Lord Guantes had said something which had given her a half-formed idea about how to finally get Catherine into the Library. But she was still waiting for it to crystallize, hopefully into a full-formed stroke of genius.

'It makes no strategic sense to send away a quarter of your strength while still in danger,' Shan Yuan declared. 'I think you are more intelligent than that. Now, what are your plans?'

Irene glanced at Kai, but his face was troubled. Clearly he didn't want to put his brother in danger – but he could see his brother's point.

She was about to suggest they start their search for Vale, when a murmur came from deeper in the archive. It was a faint ripple of noise, perhaps speech. But it was modulated like conversation, rather than a yell for guards or worse. Irene pointed in the direction of the noise, then touched a finger to her lips to command silence. Kai nodded and gestured that he'd take the lead. Irene followed, with Catherine by her side, and Shan Yuan at the rear.

As they edged past shelves filled with books and computer screens resembling blank reflecting mirrors, Irene was struck again by how abandoned this place felt. Lights burned – all night, apparently – and yet nobody was here to open the books or consult the computers. The Guantes had cleared this place for their own purposes – and then left the books unread, the archive unused. If she hadn't already been so on edge and so terrified, she'd have found this depressing.

The distant voices echoed again, whispering past stone columns like tree trunks. They formed an irritated point and counterpoint – statement, question, pause and response. Kai's eyes narrowed as he listened with his superior dragon hearing, and he turned to mouth *Vale* at Irene.

The light had too cool a quality for comfort. It was certainly bright enough to see by, but didn't have the golden warmth of sunlight or lamplight. It illuminated their surroundings, picking out every individual book title, every angle of keyboard or screen, but it made Irene think of the light in a laboratory where infectious diseases lurked in sealed cabinets.

And then the voices came into focus.

'You are a distinct nuisance.' That was Lady Guantes. 'You've attempted to escape five times now.'

'And I assure you I will try again.' Irene's heart clenched with relief. That *was* Vale. 'But since you refuse to explain your plans or your motivations, I must find my entertainment in other ways.'

'You're supposed to be the great detective.' Metal clinked

against metal. Irene gathered her skirts tight in her hands to stop them rustling as the group drew closer. 'Why don't *you* tell *me*?'

'I must confess there is one thing I don't understand.'

'I'm sure there are quite a number of things you don't understand.'

'Let us not treat each other as fools. We have, after all, been playing against each other for several weeks now – Madam Professor. You may have allowed your husband to take this role in public, but *you* were the one doing the planning. If either of us had been lacking in ability, our game would have finished a great deal sooner.'

Kai had come to a stop. Irene peered over his shoulder. The conversation was being held in a large open area ahead of them – well lit, perhaps ten or fifteen yards across. There was no way to reach Vale and remain concealed.

'That's true,' Lady Guantes said slowly. 'So if we are so well matched, what is this one thing that remains obscure to the great detective Peregrine Vale?'

'Without wishing to insult you, madam, you have a talent for organization which you have chosen to use for crime. Your abilities surpass those of other criminals I've matched wits with before. I will admit that our game has been a challenge, and one I've enjoyed. It drove me to act hastily – even unwisely – while attempting to bring you down.'

'Flattery won't get me to free you,' Lady Guantes said.

'It was hardly meant as flattery,' Vale replied. 'But it does beg a question. You could be an empress of crime, a genius coordinating your network across multiple worlds. Yet you insist on elevating your husband to this role, reanimating him instead of letting him rest in peace. Why, in a situation where so many Fae would seize the moment, do *you* hesitate and draw back?'

Irene edged a little closer, enough to see more of the

tableau. Vale was strapped hand and foot to a large table. It looked uncomfortably laboratory-like in its stark cleanliness, with run-off drains – for blood? Irene suppressed a shudder. Lady Guantes stood at the head end of the table, bending over Vale like a confessor giving a man his last rites. But instead of robes, she wore an iron-grey business suit and gloves. For some reason, they were mismatched, black on the left hand and grey on the right. Five computer tablets rested on gilded lecterns around the table, as if they were open books. Banked servers stood in the background, forming a coordinated circle of processing power.

Behind the pair, on the far side of the space, a door was set between two stone pillars. It was out of step with the decor and made from pale wood. Irene could see it was marked with the Language, but she was too far away to make out the writing. But she didn't need to read it to recognize the threat it posed. Whatever it was, it was Alberich's work – and that couldn't be good.

Irene weighed their options. It was at least five yards from the nearest bookshelves to the table and Lady Guantes was almost certainly armed. That would make a direct assault highly risky for Vale and his rescuer. The Language might work – but had Alberich set up protective wards? And Irene would need to take out the Fae near-immediately.

'I *could* dominate a network of worlds myself,' Lady Guantes was saying. 'But my husband and I belong with one another, and we can achieve so much more together than apart. We nearly triggered a war between our kind and the dragons, after all . . . and I have learned much more since. So yes, I will pay any price to get him back, to beat death itself. To have him with me again – as he *should* be – will make it all worthwhile.'

'I suspected as much – and I appreciate your candour.' Vale took a deep breath. 'Reconsider. Come back to London and forge your own path to glory. Take control of London's underworld. Challenge me. Or if you truly want to test yourself, challenge my sister. But reconsider your current course of action.'

'What? For *you*? You're as vain as the stories say.'

'For yourself, madam. I know what you're about to do. You intend to transfer your husband's personality onto me – a new attempt to bring him back.'

'Your deduction is correct. The current version is growing unstable and his decisions are becoming unwise. Perhaps using you as a base will last longer – you have Fae blood, after all. You should be suitable.'

'For your own sake, madam, stop this.' Vale tilted his head to meet her eyes. 'You'll *never* be satisfied. You can try to bring your husband back as many times as you like, but—'

'We're wasting time,' Lady Guantes interrupted. She drew a small gun from her jacket and set it against Vale's temple. 'Miss Winters, and your companions, do come out and join us.'

Irene and Kai looked at each other. Was it a bluff?

'Believe me, I'll fire,' Lady Guantes said, a note of weary irritation in her voice. 'And I am addressing *all* of you. You, Prince Kai, the other dragon and the girl.'

Irene caught Catherine's attention, indicating she needed to see the time. Catherine showed her watch. Quarter of an hour till midnight. There was still time to negotiate. She mouthed *Stay here* to Kai, then stepped out of the shadows. 'I'm the one you want, aren't I? Let them go.'

'I suppose I can settle for you. For now.' Lady Guantes didn't move the muzzle of her gun from Vale's temple. 'After all, we both know perfectly well that they won't leave as long as you're here.'

Irene ignored that, asking instead, 'How did you know we were here?'

'Do you honestly think I haven't been following you on my screens?' Lady Guantes waved at the tablets which encircled her and Vale.

'I'm surprised you didn't send guards after us.'

Irene was burning to use the Language to jam Lady Guantes' gun, or heat it up, or *something* . . . But it would only take one touch of the Fae's finger on the trigger to kill Vale, and even a single word might not be fast enough. Then her heart leapt; while Lady Guantes had been speaking, Vale had half-slipped one hand free of its bindings.

She sought for ways to keep the other woman distracted. 'If you kill Vale, you can't use him to house your husband's personality.'

'I can find someone else.' Lady Guantes shrugged. 'Why so horrified, Miss Winters? Have you never loved anyone so much that you'd break all laws, natural and supernatural, to get them back?'

'I've never been in that position,' Irene said truthfully. *And I hope I never will.* But she didn't want to explore that route to keep Lady Guantes diverted. 'Let me guess what's going on here . . .' she said instead. 'Alberich is helping you get your husband back, by somehow twisting the Language. That's payback for the technology you've procured for him, and for helping him access other worlds through his doors. He also wanted you to kidnap *me*, which helped you to pursue my fellow treaty representatives at the same time. And by killing them, you can look forward to the treaty failing – making your Fae versus dragon war an option again. Or is the treaty failing a mutual bonus?'

Irene's speculation was keeping the Fae's attention on her; she hoped Vale would take full advantage of that. Perhaps Lady Guantes might even drop a few hints about Alberich's goal in all this – something that still wasn't entirely clear to Irene.

Lady Guantes' eyes narrowed as she considered Irene. 'We haven't hidden our motivations, so it's unsurprising that some of your conclusions are correct. Alberich and I *both* benefit if the treaty is destroyed. With two representatives dead, and the third one *changed* . . . Well, I'm sure you can imagine just how much damage Alberich could do, while wearing your face and your body. He isn't just seeking petty vengeance against *you*, you know. Once you've been "compromised" by him, he can have you betray *everyone*. Dragons, Fae and the Library alike.'

'You said earlier that Alberich could use any Librarian for his plans – so I could betray a colleague to save myself.'

Lady Guantes shrugged. 'I lied.'

'And you *trust* Alberich?'

'I'm not so foolish as to rely on trust—'

But Irene had done her part and Vale's wrist had finally slipped free. He locked his hand around the Fae's, gripping until his knuckles showed white, and tilted her gun away from his temple. Her finger tightened reflexively, and the gun fired: the bullet ricocheted off one of the pillars.

'Gun, heat up!' Irene ordered, running forward to grab Lady Guantes' other hand as she struggled in Vale's clasp. Kai and Shan Yuan were also rushing forward to seize and immobilize the Fae.

Lady Guantes screamed as the gun in her hand burned red hot, still locked in position by Vale's grip. Pain gave her the strength to drag herself free from Vale, but she couldn't keep hold of the gun. It clattered to the floor with a clang, leaving scorch marks on her glove.

Kai grabbed her left arm and twisted it behind her in a half-nelson. 'Don't try anything,' he advised her, voice cold. 'There are limits to what I can pardon for the sake of love.'

'The dragon's the one who has pity on me?' Hysteria cracked the polished tones of her voice for a moment before she suppressed it again. 'Very good, Miss Winters. Have your little triumph.'

'**Table restraints, open,**' Irene commanded, and watched with relief as the bindings holding Vale to the table snapped open. Vale swung himself off the table with a nod of thanks.

She glanced at the Language-decorated door. Now that she was close enough, she could read some of the words. One was **Alberich**, positioned right in the centre, in the same shade of dried blood as the circle upstairs. Running out from the centre to the edges were dense patterns of words speaking of openings, portals and secure passages. Perhaps it would slow Alberich down if she tried to destroy it – or perhaps it would just set off another trap. She couldn't risk it.

Shan Yuan, meanwhile, was poking at one of the tablets. 'As I thought,' he said, watching lines of code and diagrams flash across the screen. 'When a body used for the programme is present in this world, its personality matrix is supported and maintained by this AI infrastructure.'

'Can you sabotage it?'

He hesitated. 'We shouldn't be too quick to destroy this. It may have been put to evil uses, but this project has led to huge scientific advances; it would be a terrible waste to lose such significant discoveries—'

One of the cathedral bells began to ring, a single deep note which hummed in the throat and chest, counting out strokes that pulsed like dying breaths.

'It's not midnight yet!' Catherine shouted, as though her complaint could stop the tolling bell.

Lady Guantes began to laugh. 'Do you think I'm the only one who's been monitoring this cathedral? Alberich's been with us all this time. He's just . . . next door.'

Irene opened her mouth to tell the others to run, but the room blurred around her. It was as though she was standing in two places at once, where one location was real and the other was a watercolour overlay. But impressions from the second place were growing stronger with every moment. She suddenly found it impossible to coordinate her steps, and her brain was telling her opposing truths: that she was standing on smooth paving stones and upon a rough, fire-ravaged floor. She was breathing cool, book-scented air *and* air dirty with ash and foul with decay. She was in a low-ceilinged room and also in a vast chamber, surrounded by scorched ranks of bookshelves that reared up to impossible heights. And she couldn't move. Her brain wouldn't let her.

With the slowness of terror, as the bell counted out another stroke, she realized not everyone was with her. There was Catherine. Vale. Lady Guantes. The latter had staggered forward as she wrenched herself free from Kai. But Kai and Shan Yuan were fading, the two of them becoming shadows in this new post-holocaust landscape. Shadows that were growing fainter with every second.

The air is thick with chaos and they are dragons. Maybe they can't survive in this place, Irene thought, her mind racing. *Alberich has brought us here without needing a door, his link to this place is so strong. Is he overlaying his own world onto this one?* This wasn't like any story she'd ever read, any myth she'd ever been told. She couldn't even deduce; she could only guess.

Irene deliberately bit her tongue and tasted blood, wrenching her mind from the whirlpool of panic that was trying to claim it. The bell rang out one final shuddering time, and the second world came into full focus around them.

They were in a burned-out ruined library, with teetering shelves that loomed high above their heads. The ceiling was barely visible, so far above that it seemed to somehow blend with the sky. It was an impossible place – even more so now than the last time she'd invaded Alberich's realm. It appeared to be on the edge of collapse and final destruction, but

somehow it still held itself together through sheer determination and spite.

The only figure in the whole blasted landscape, besides
themselves, sat at a fire-scorched desk in a comfortable chair.
He was wrapped in a monk's robe, his face lean and near-
skeletal. And he was watching them. Irene was reminded of
a judge waiting to give a group of convicts his final ruling
– and their death sentence.

'Welcome to my kingdom,' Alberich said.

CHAPTER TWENTY-FOUR

'Lasciate ogne speranza, voi ch'intrate,' Irene quoted from Dante's *Inferno*. *All hope abandon, ye who enter here . . .* She had to say *something* to stem her horror, as her guts were knotting with fear. This was her very worst-case scenario – coming face to face with Alberich, on ground of his choosing and with her friends as hostages.

Out of the corner of her eye she could see Vale looking around speculatively, Catherine inching away from Alberich, and Lady Guantes distancing herself from her 'hostages'. But ninety per cent of her attention was on Alberich. 'Where are we?' she asked.

'Why, my kingdom, my library. You've been here before, Ray. You do remember that, don't you?' His tone was teasing. He knew perfectly well she'd never forget it as long as she lived.

But the question Irene was *most* curious about was, *If you're going to steal my body, why haven't you done it already?* Any information on *that* would be useful.

'Are we somehow in two locations at the same time?' she asked him. As long as he was talking, he wasn't killing anyone – and surely all villains loved to show off their plans? Even Alberich. 'Have you really managed to *superimpose* your kingdom over the Sagrada Familia archive? I've travelled between connected worlds, of course, but I've never heard of two worlds *coexisting* without one being displaced or destroyed. In fact, you were trying to replace the Library, using your realm, when we last met.'

Alberich gave her a look which chilled her to the bone. She suddenly realized that *she* was doing the talking, and she should never have mentioned that failure – seeing as she'd orchestrated it.

But Vale stepped in. 'Science tells us that two objects cannot exist in the same place at the same time,' he said. 'So logically we must now be in one place, not in the other.'

'Logic has its uses,' Alberich mused. 'However, you're not in full possession of the facts. Do you know who I am, Peregrine Vale?'

'You are the ex-Librarian known as Alberich,' Vale answered. 'I trust you will forgive me for not recognizing you instantly – the last time we met, you were inhabiting the skin of a young woman. Is this your original face and body?' There was a curious intensity in the way that he was staring at Alberich, as though he seemed to know the other man from somewhere.

'It is indeed. Well . . . a projection of the original, at least. I'm less *physical* than I used to be. You can blame your friend Irene for that.'

'So *you're* the famous Librarian traitor,' Catherine said, with an attempt at bravado. Irene realized with a sinking feeling that Catherine had an important lesson to learn. One didn't insult an enemy when one was in their power.

'I am,' Alberich replied, and he crooked a finger.

A book tumbled down from far above, slicing through the air spine-first. It hit the ground like a brick a mere foot away from Catherine, then fell open to reveal pages full of incoherent words. Many were written crosswise to each other and seemed to promise unwholesome secrets – if only one could decode them. Another book slammed into the floor just in front of Catherine, making her flinch. She looked up at the impossibly high burned shelves, with their tottering piles of decaying books, and wisely bit her lip. She didn't look inclined to say anything further.

Alberich nodded. 'Good decision,' he said. Then he turned to Irene. 'Don't let that give *you* ideas, either.'

Irene had just been pondering ways of toppling the nearest cliff-side of shelving onto Alberich. But his ability to control the landscape – or bookscape? – around them, with no apparent effort, gave her pause. And unlike their previous encounter, he now had hostages – Vale and Catherine – to use against her. 'I'd rather not start a fight,' she said carefully, 'but if you endanger me or my friends, I'll have no choice but to finish what I started last time.'

All above and around them the shelves creaked as though stretching themselves. It wasn't reassuring. The scent of ash and mould in the air strengthened until it was nearly a physical presence.

'Don't waste my time with your pointless threats. Last time you escaped by the skin of your teeth, and only because you set fire to my collection.' He waved a hand at his blackened shelves. 'And you have the *gall* to call yourself a librarian . . .'

'Much as I hate to disturb this conversation, aren't *we* wasting time?' Lady Guantes interrupted. '*We* have an agreement.'

'We do indeed,' Alberich said. 'We've sworn oaths that *you* can't break by your nature and *I* won't break because they're in the Language. And you've done a great deal to keep up your end of the pact.' His tone developed an edge. 'But a Fae who has failed in the most *important* part of the deal shouldn't push her luck . . . Don't take it as an insult.' He met her eyes. 'But do take it as a warning.'

Lady Guantes tilted her head, the picture of control. 'I brought her here, didn't I? She managed to escape from *your* circle, true. But I was still the one who brought her to the cathedral, then lured her to the archive – ensuring that you could bring her *here*. I've done my part, and I expect my payment.' Her eyes flicked to Vale.

Vale didn't even flinch. 'I must decline,' he said instead. 'My presence is required back in London.'

'I will, of course, consider your request,' Alberich said to Lady Guantes. He didn't bother answering Vale. 'But you must understand that my own affairs take priority.'

'Of course.' There was a momentary flash of poison – no, of murder – in Lady Guantes' eyes as she took a step back. 'I can wait.'

That was acceptance . . . but not obedience. Irene wondered if she might have found a weakness in their alliance. Lady Guantes was an experienced schemer and a meticulous planner, just as Vale had commented earlier. She might have made a deal with Alberich, but an old hand like her wouldn't have relied on trust. Surely she'd have made a backup plan, in case Alberich tried to double-cross her . . .

Irene tensed as Alberich turned his attention back to her. 'Why me?' she asked, her hands clenching nervously.

He understood her question without her needing to explain, and the light seemed to dim. 'Why you? Because, Ray, you've put yourself at the centre of this treaty – and have become invaluable to the Library itself. Possessing *you* will make it easy to bring them both down.' As he spoke, his fingers curled inwards, drawing into fists as tight as Irene's own. 'I don't deny that personal vengeance will be very sweet. But frankly, I might have forgotten about you if you hadn't become such a *perfect* tool. Possibly.'

Irene swallowed, her throat dry, as a thousand nightmare scenarios played out behind her eyes. She had no leverage.

If she argued that he had her now, so he could let her friends go, she'd just be inviting him to hurt them. She desperately tried to think of some way out of this, anything she could use to bargain with him . . .

Her mouth settled into a thin line. 'Very well,' she said. 'Let's talk.'

'Talk?' Alberich said lightly. 'I'm the one talking, Ray. You're the one listening. Or do I need to remind you who's in charge here?'

'I apologize.' Lady Guantes wasn't the only one who could bite her tongue and be polite. 'Please go on.'

'It really is a pity. You're cunning, duplicitous and capable of surprising feats with the Language. You would have made an excellent student.'

Irene shrugged. 'There's no point in insulting you while I try to find a way out of this. The fact that I can't find one is, well . . .'

'Horrifying, I hope.'

'Perhaps you have a better vocabulary than I do.' Irene cast a sidelong glance at Vale, as though weighing her options, before turning back to Alberich. 'Can we talk – in private?' she asked.

'Ah.' A narrow smirk crawled across his face. 'To convince me that you're ready to betray your friends? Lovely. Have you any comment to make, Peregrine Vale?'

'I'm merely watching with interest,' Vale answered. His gaze moved between Alberich and Irene again. 'Don't let me interrupt.'

Alberich raised his hand and the shelves shifted position, gliding across the floor as though on hidden tracks. Lady Guantes was herded to one side; Vale and Catherine to the other. Then he and Irene were facing each other, in a narrow corridor lined with burned and decaying books on either side. 'Well?' he said.

'I'm interested in staying alive. What can I offer you?'

He tilted his head like a vulture. 'What makes you think I have the slightest interest in your offers?'

You're standing here talking to me, Irene thought, *so there's that. If you really could just possess me, and it was that simple, surely you'd already have done it.* She took a deep breath. 'Alberich . . . I realize you hate me. And I know taking over my body, and using it to destroy everything I've ever worked for, would be extremely satisfying. But under the circumstances, I may be more use to you alive than dead.'

'So what's your offer?' His gaze was flat and gave nothing away. 'Are you going to go down on your knees and beg for mercy? Or are you going to say you'll be a willing host, if only I'll let your friends go?'

'Something a little different.' Irene made herself focus on her act. She had to *believe* what she was about to say to be perfectly convincing. She had to lie as she'd never lied before. 'I'd like to offer you an alternative host, and my assistance in securing it. They're right here. It'd be easy. I'll cooperate with you, doing whatever's necessary – we'd be two Librarians working together, using the Language in tandem.'

Alberich leaned forward, and she saw the flicker of eagerness in his face – not at her offer of a host, but at her betraying herself like this. He looked as if he was savouring her words, evidence of her willingness to debase herself to stay alive. He might claim his motivation in choosing *her* was pure pragmatism, but he clearly wanted to see her humbled. 'Go on. Which of your friends will you give up? Your student? Your detective? Your lover?'

'None of them.' Irene's throat was dry as bone. She forced the words out. 'There's a second dragon here – Shan Yuan, Kai's brother. He means nothing to me. You can have him. Just let us go.' She could hear the panicked, begging tone that entered her voice as she uttered those last few words – and the humiliation of it coloured her cheeks.

'It's true there are two dragons in the archive,' Alberich mused. 'Probably incapacitated, given the rising chaos levels . . . I haven't tried transferring into a dragon before. Do you really think I could do it, given that dragons are creatures of order?'

'How the hell should I know?' Irene forced herself to lower her voice, to walk closer and lean on his desk. 'You're the expert at transferring your essence into other people – or even into worlds like this one. Why *not* a dragon?'

Alberich leaned back in his chair. 'What will your lover say if you hand over his brother, so I can core out his personality like an apple and use his body?'

'You said it yourself. He's probably incapacitated, probably unconscious – so afterwards, I can convince him it wasn't my fault. I'll think of something to say.' She was talking faster now, desperate to convince him of her sincerity. He'd called her duplicitous – and it was true – but this was her biggest lie yet, against her most dangerous opponent. 'How often are you going to get the chance to use a dragon? Wouldn't the body be more resilient than a human one like mine?'

Now she could see the glint of satisfaction in his eyes. But it still wasn't the thought of a dragon host body that was pleasing him, if indeed he could use one – it was the sight of Irene abandoning all her principles. 'And if I let you live, and release you and your friends, you'll actively help me?'

Irene swallowed. 'Yes. Yes, I'll draw a new circle for you, I'll use the Language – whatever it takes. Just tell me what to do. Just don't . . . not to *me*.' She let herself show some of her genuine horror at the very thought of being possessed and used as his puppet.

'What if your lover *does* find out you cooperated? Will he still stay with you?'

That's exactly what you want, she thought. *You love the idea of Kai seeing me sell his brother out, then him rejecting me – before you dispose of me in turn. Come on, please, take the bait . . .*

'At least Kai will be *alive*,' she said. 'And I never asked his brother to get involved. He tried to get me to leave Kai, he dragged Catherine into danger – and his family doesn't even know he's here. He's an acceptable loss.'

'You're very convincing,' Alberich said slowly. 'Before I decide, tell me one last thing. How did you escape the circle? I set it so only my blood could break it.'

Irene raised her bandaged wrist. 'I used my own blood – and the fact that we're both Librarians, so metaphorically related.' A Kipling quote came to mind: *We be of one blood, thou and I.*

Alberich frowned. 'That shouldn't have worked.'

'But it did,' Irene said, a little smugly.

'No, really, it shouldn't. My work was far more precise than that – metaphors shouldn't have done the job.'

'Had you actually tested it before, though?' Irene couldn't quite believe she was discussing this with him, as though he was a colleague. 'On other Librarians, that is?'

His lips smirked, but his eyes were hollow. For a moment his face resembled a skull. 'Oh yes, Irene, I have most definitely tested it on other Librarians. Shall I tell you some stories about that?'

She flinched. She couldn't stop herself. The mental image of other Librarians trapped as she was, waiting for their final conversation with Alberich . . . She should never forget who he was. What he was.

'An improvement,' Alberich said, as though reading her thoughts. 'I shouldn't need to remind you of this again. Namely, that *I* am giving orders and *you* are obeying them. Otherwise, I will take your friends apart piece by piece, with you watching, before I deal with you. Do you understand?'

Irene nodded.

'Say yes,' he coaxed her. 'I want to hear you say, "Yes, Alberich," and sound as if you mean it.'

'Yes, Alberich,' Irene said through dry lips, watching him smile.

'Very well.' He stood up. 'I accept your deal . . . if we can make it work. You do understand that if we *can't*, then you are – back on the menu, I suppose we could say.'

More than anything else, this confirmed her suspicions. *If he truly meant to keep this bargain, he'd have made me swear in the Language. So no, there is no bargain.*

Irene didn't have to feign her nervousness; it was all too real. 'I get things done,' she said. 'You know that.'

'We shall see. Now come, Ray. Let's tell your friends where we're going.'

The bookcases slid back, letting Irene see the others. Vale and Lady Guantes had apparently been talking. Catherine was prodding at the bookshelves, frowning at the condition of the books.

'Winters, are you all right?' Vale demanded. 'You're as white as paper.'

'We will be returning to the cathedral for a little while,' Alberich informed them. 'I trust you will find something to read while you're waiting.'

'Wait,' Irene objected. 'I'd prefer it if Vale and Catherine came with us.'

'Overruled,' Alberich told her, with an air that suggested he'd been looking forward to saying that. 'For the moment they're *my* hostages.'

Which was exactly what Irene had expected. Now she had to pull off the second part of her manoeuvre and get the person she *really* wanted. 'I'm willing to cooperate,' she said stubbornly, 'but Vale's health and sanity are part of the deal. If *she* stays here with him,' and she nodded to Lady

Guantes, 'I'm not sure who I'll find in his body when I get back.'

A little smirk curved Lady Guantes' lips. 'You underrate my patience,' she informed Irene.

'Nevertheless, you may be useful.' Alberich turned to Irene. 'She'll return to the cathedral with us – and assist in the operation. Are you satisfied?' He was humouring her, indulging her like a child, as if he genuinely believed she was about to betray Shan Yuan.

Irene allowed herself to look faintly relieved. 'Yes. That'll do.' In the back of her mind she ticked off one more item on her threadbare checklist. 'So how do we get back? Or if we're already there as well as here, how do we get to be *more* there?'

Alberich smiled like a lecturer who'd been asked his favourite question. 'All those who have a certain level of chaos in their nature have been raised into my world. Basically, I pulled and you responded. The Fae, the human with more of a taint than he'd care to admit, the Librarian . . .'

'As a Librarian, I'm not chaos-contaminated,' Irene pointed out.

'How little you know.' He reached into the sleeve of his robe, and brought out a pendant, which he offered to Irene. It was the same as the one she'd removed earlier: a black metal teardrop on a leather thong, interlaced with circuitry almost too tiny to see. 'Take this. Put it on.'

Irene knew what a dangerous game she was playing, as she took the pendant hesitantly. *Perhaps this token signals my allegiance? Or is this the crucial element he needs to possess me . . .*

'I'm waiting,' Alberich said.

She could feel her pulse hammering as she met his eyes, knowing he'd see her reluctance. *He's enjoying this.* Jerkily she slid the thong over her head, feeling the pendant come to rest against her bare skin.

'I have one myself,' Lady Guantes said, touching her

bodice. 'A necessity, if Alberich is to move us between worlds or enable us to use his doors.'

'Ah yes, the doors.' Alberich gestured again – far too dramatically, Irene thought – and another bookshelf slid back. This revealed a door, standing by itself in its frame. It was marked with the Language, the words a perfect match to those on the one beneath the Sagrada Familia. Irene wondered if this was the other side of that door. 'Walk through. I'll meet you on the other side – in my virtual form.'

'We need to wait for the chaos levels to stabilize,' Lady Guantes volunteered sweetly, flaunting her superior knowledge.

'Correct,' Alberich said with a smile. 'It's something like a canal lock – the chaos levels on each side have to equalize for us to pass through. The Language creates a solid connection between the worlds, while the computing power sustains my manifestation. But we still have to wait until the chaos levels stop fluctuating before we can pass.'

Irene's heart sank. Kai and Shan Yuan were badly incapacitated within high-chaos worlds, and fluctuating levels of the stuff would make its effects even worse. This made it even less likely that they could help her with any plan she might have in mind – and Alberich knew it. He nodded her towards the door.

'Interesting,' Vale said, breaking the tense silence. 'So you require a link to move your projection to another world – and without that you're trapped here?'

'I'm a solitary and retiring man,' Alberich said smoothly. 'I don't like to go where I'm not invited.'

'Isn't that vampires?' Catherine asked. She set her jaw mutinously when Alberich turned to look at her with a vivisectionist's eye. 'Don't tell me. You're the origin of all vampire stories.'

'Oh, it's worse than that,' Alberich said. 'Much worse.

Now, Ray. Prove you mean what you say. Go through that door – and get things ready for me. I'll allow your friends through when I'm . . . satisfied.'

Irene didn't give herself time to hesitate, or to look at Vale and Catherine. She set her hand on the door and pushed.

It swung open into the room they'd left just a few minutes ago, though it felt like hours: the dark archive with its empty experimental table and shadowy pillars. Kai and Shan Yuan lay crumpled on the floor, shuddering as if stricken with an ague. The light itself seemed to have dimmed and become somehow less wholesome. Whether or not it was still midnight, the bell was still ringing far above.

Tablet screens glowed and then suddenly jumped to brilliant life as the door closed behind Irene and Lady Guantes. Irene caught images and lines of text flickering across their surfaces in columns and helixes. Other screens, deeper within the archive, lit up like distant polluted fires – flashing their own workings into the darkness. A singing hum rose in the background, as if some distant storm was coming ever closer.

Please, Irene thought, not sure who or what she was petitioning, or if this was an appeal to her own courage. *Let Alberich be distracted for one moment. Just half a moment, just long enough . . .*

Irene grabbed Lady Guantes by the arm and pulled her close. As the other woman blinked at her, taken aback by the sudden aggression, Irene leaned forward and breathed into her ear, **'You perceive that Alberich has utterly betrayed you and destroyed your husband, and that you must take immediate steps to stop him.'**

CHAPTER TWENTY-FIVE

Lady Guantes pulled away, her face tight with anger and horror, but she also looked far from surprised at this news of betrayal. Most importantly, she still looked in control – like a woman with a plan. A Fae couldn't *knowingly* break her given word. However, if Lady Guantes honestly believed her bargain with Alberich was already broken, she could do whatever she wanted. And if she thought he'd destroyed what was left of her husband . . .

The Fae woman plucked the pendant from her neck, dropping it and kicking it into the shadows. Then she withdrew an exquisite mobile phone from her jacket and began tapping in commands.

Irene desperately wished she could remove her own pendant – but that would alert Alberich. He'd be watching her more closely than his ally. Trying to ignore the pulsing lights, she moved towards Shan Yuan and looked for Alberich's projection. 'Alberich?' she called. 'Are you there?'

The screen lights settled to a regular glow and Alberich's shadow coalesced in the centre of the room. More shadows seeped into being around him, hinting at towering bookshelves and ruined flooring. It was as though the two worlds grew closer with every second. 'I'm most assuredly here,' he answered her.

The bell finally fell silent, no longer tolling out those deep notes that throbbed in her chest and throat. Instead, speakers formed Alberich's words; she could hear other computers echoing them in distant whispers throughout the room. She shivered at this, imagining a shadowy choir of lost souls. The air tasted ripe with chaos and the Library brand on Irene's back burned with it.

'This is Shan Yuan,' she said to him. She considered prodding the sprawling dragon with her foot, but decided that would be overdoing it. 'As I promised.'

Shan Yuan glared up at Irene. His eyes could barely focus in the rush of chaotic power that swelled around them. And she was about to make things worse for him, as her betrayal would – had to – seem genuine. Yet if she didn't distract Alberich, and he noticed Lady Guantes plotting, they were all dead.

'You did indeed promise,' Alberich replied. 'Very well. This confirms our bargain – this dragon's life for yours. Render him helpless for me.'

Kai lifted his head to look at Irene, trying to struggle to his knees but unable to raise himself from the floor. 'Irene?' he gasped, his voice uncertain as he tried to understand what was going on.

Lady Guantes was still typing, gloved fingers sliding across her phone's surface in a paroxysm of fury.

'Trust me,' Irene said, desperation seeping into her voice, 'trust me, Kai, everything's under control, just relax for a moment.' She could see Alberich smiling. *Yes, smile, enjoy it, gorge yourself on my despair, but don't look round. . .*

'I think I've changed my mind,' Alberich said.

'Oh?' Irene said without much hope. There were still two other possible hosts in the room, her – and Kai.

'Yes. I'll take your lover instead.' The pendant on her neck flared, hot enough to make her wince. 'Or you. Your choice, Ray.'

In the mix of emotions that followed, relief won. *Alberich could be distracted by his own sadism.* But how much time did she have? 'Fine!' she snapped, playing for even a few more seconds – she was relying on Lady Guantes to get them out of this. 'Take him, then. Better him than me. I'm like you, Alberich. I want to live – and I'll sacrifice whoever it takes to stay alive.'

Kai was still watching her, his eyes full of a trust she felt she didn't deserve. Her heart clenched. *He thinks I'm faking it, that I have a plan in mind. But if it doesn't work, this is the last thing he'll remember me saying . . .*

'Perfect,' Alberich said with amusement. 'I wondered how far you'd go for just a little bit of hope.' Distant computers continued to whisper his words. 'Humanity is so adaptable. Now how far can I push you, before you reach your limits? Perhaps you should dispose of this one's brother first, to get rid of witnesses? If I give you a knife, will you cut his throat with your own hands . . .'

Lady Guantes made a final, abrupt motion over her phone and slid it back into her jacket, vengeful satisfaction on her face. Then, almost in slow motion, a horrified realization took its place. The Language's effect had worn off. The Fae reached for her phone again.

Then the archive's lights flicked from dim to blinding, and the ambient whispering and humming of computers rose to a piercing shriek. It drilled into Irene's head and she pressed her hands against her ears. The books and papers lining the shelves shivered and trembled, stray pages floating out and down. Alberich's simulacrum froze, its colour draining to black and white like an old film.

Irene body-tackled Lady Guantes before she could reverse

whatever she'd just done. The two of them went rolling across the floor, Irene's long skirts tangling both their legs. Lady Guantes tried to struggle free at first, then attempted to incapacitate Irene by any means possible. She didn't waste her breath on cursing or calling for help. Instead she brought her knee up viciously, before elbowing Irene in the side of the head.

The blow wasn't enough to knock Irene out, but it made her dizzy. She clawed at Lady Guantes' eyes in desperation – and when the other woman pulled away, she thrust her forearm across the Fae's throat to pin her down. Lady Guantes slammed her right fist into Irene's side and, as she retaliated, Irene felt the bandage on her wrist give way and her wound start to bleed again.

Abruptly the floor rose in a long ridge between them, forcibly separating them and throwing them to either side. Irene tried to stagger to her feet, but her head was spinning too badly and she only managed to get to her knees. Lady Guantes straightened, coughing and clutching at her throat where Irene had hit her.

Lady Guantes was closer to the painted door than Irene – but she couldn't silence her. **'Door, open!'** Irene shouted, her voice cracking as she struggled to be heard over the scream of the computers.

Other doors within earshot flew open, booming as they wrenched themselves free of their locks and slammed into walls. But this one, the closest one, the most important one of all, tried to resist her. Even frozen by whatever Lady Guantes had done, Alberich's will was still set against hers.

And the pendant at her throat was burning into her skin.

She managed to stand and ran for the painted door, but Lady Guantes moved to intercept her – and fell with a crash, as Kai caught her ankle. As she passed, Irene kicked her in the ribs to keep her down and grabbed the door's handle with one bloody hand. **'Open!'** she screamed, yanking at it.

It swung open – and to Irene's vast relief, Vale and Catherine were just a few steps away on the other side. Beyond them, she could see the towering lines of bookshelves were shaking. The air was now full of dust, falling books and churning swarms of flies – but her friends were *there*. Alberich hadn't killed them or imprisoned them somewhere, miles away. She allowed herself a moment of hope that they might escape this nightmare after all.

Vale and Catherine had clearly been waiting for any opportunity to get out of there. They both surged for the door and stumbled into the archive together, while the door strained in Irene's hands.

She let it go, and it slammed back into position. The ambient chaos was beginning to ebb within the archive, now the door was closed. As the two worlds slid apart again, it was as if a tidal wave had started to recede, running back down the beach.

Throughout the archive, computers were shutting down, their blazing screens darkening to black and their whirring fans falling silent. The image of Alberich greyed out even further, blurring to static and then – finally – to nothingness.

'Are you all right?' Irene began to say to Catherine, drawing a deep breath, but then there was a clanging in her head. It was louder and more discordant even than the cathedral bells, and she found herself on her knees, clutching at the pendant around her neck. It wouldn't move. It was fixed to her flesh. She found herself unable to form words – for all languages, even the Language, were beyond her grasp. And she could sense *something*, something horrifying, settling into her head like a maggot. She wanted to scream as she felt it worming its way into position and making itself comfortable. Lady Guantes had broken Alberich's other links to this world by shutting down his computers. Now he was clinging to the only link he had left – the pendant – and through it, her.

She tried to fight back, but she had no idea how. She could only watch in terror as the horror spread. The thing inside her swept through her mind like decay, its spores corrupting every helpful thought or idea into colonies of itself.

But if I can still think, then perhaps I'm still here? she wondered stupidly, as those very thoughts blurred and slowed.

'Winters!' Vale had her by the shoulders and was shaking her, but she could hardly feel it. It was as though the sensations were being reported to her from a great distance. '*Fight back*, woman. You've fought worse. Remember – *you still have free will!*'

How amusing of him to think so. That wasn't even Irene's own reaction. That was Alberich's thought seeping through her mind. She felt it split for a moment into a whole layered set of thoughts about Victorian Christianity, English hypocrisy . . . and the cold certainty that anything and everything could be broken if one had the right tools. Then it coalesced into a thin stream of mockery which ran through Irene's thoughts like metal veins in rock.

Catherine tried to pry the pendant off Irene's chest, protecting her hand with a fold of her dress. But the pendant clung to Irene's skin as though melted in place. Irene heard herself manage to scream at last, but it was like hearing someone else's voice.

And soon it will be, Alberich said inside her mind. *It will be my voice and my body. With this body, I won't need Lady Guantes and her doors, and the Library itself will be mine for the taking . . .*

'Alberich!' Vale's fingers tightened on her shoulders, and

he looked squarely into her eyes. 'You're there. I know it. Release her, man, or you'll have killed *your own daughter!*'

Inside Irene's head there was a moment of sudden baffled shock but at the same time there was *comprehension*. A dozen faceted thoughts tumbled through Irene's head, and she was no longer certain if they were Alberich's or her own. *Daughter of two Librarians . . . didn't even know she was adopted . . . able to use my wards, able to break my wards . . . with her own blood . . . a good liar . . . cunning with the Language . . . looked me in the eyes, told me she was like me . . . should have known . . . could have guessed . . .*

But she had no time to study the fragmentary ideas that fell through her mind like broken glass. Instead she formed them into a single connected thought with a surface as smooth and reflective as obsidian, and slid it between Alberich's mind and her own. She took full advantage of his brief uncertainty and his belief in Vale's lie. *You. Me. Separate.*

The pendant suddenly came free of her chest; Catherine dragged it over her head, hurling it to one side. Irene's back arched as she screamed again, as the last vestiges of Alberich were stripped from her mind, leaving her – her *soul*, she supposed – feeling agonizingly raw.

The overhead lights dimmed to blood-red and thick shadows cloaked the shelves and columns, as the tide of chaos finally ebbed to a level more natural for this world.

Irene looked around, exhausted but taking stock. The inside of her head felt as if she'd had a particularly rotten molar extracted after a great deal of pain, but there was no time to rest. Vale and Catherine were nearby. Kai and Shan Yuan had both struggled to their feet, and now that the chaos levels were dropping, they were at least the equal of normal humans. Kai had Lady Guantes in an armlock, suitably restrained, with his other arm looped round her neck.

All the Fae's plans had come to nothing and Lord Guantes' stored personality would be lost, with their technology denied to them and no fresh host body to commandeer. Her expression was blank, as though some animating spirit had deserted her. Was this some side-effect of her broken oath, or simply the knowledge of defeat? 'I suppose you want a way out of here,' she said, her tone abstracted, flat, like a child repeating the rules of a game. 'We can make a deal, I'm sure.'

'Irene?' Kai asked, his tone grave, and she knew what he was asking.

She didn't want this, but she couldn't see any other choice. Lady Guantes had *defined* herself by her husband – and by her need for revenge. Any truce would be temporary, or a lie, after what had happened here.

Irene jerked her head in a nod, and Kai snapped the Fae's neck.

It was cold comfort to know that he'd taken Lady Guantes by surprise and it would have been over in a flash. This did nothing to ease the weight of what Irene had done. And it didn't help that neither Vale, Catherine nor the dragons uttered a word of blame. *They* hadn't made the decision. They'd left it to her.

Irene looked at Lady Guantes' body as Kai laid her down on the floor, feeling the bitter knowledge that she'd murdered the Fae turning over and over inside her. Kai could shrug it off easily enough, as a royal dragon with a feudal upbringing. But Irene knew that she'd relive this scene in her dreams. *This wasn't why I became a Librarian . . .*

The sound of running feet – multiple booted feet, coming in fast – broke the silence, and they all turned towards the noise. That was their only warning but it was enough, when the first bullet came singing out of the darkness, for Shan Yuan to push Kai out of the way. The bullet took him in the shoulder, knocking him to the floor. A barrage followed, and they all scrambled for cover.

'Guns, jam!' Irene screamed as she threw herself down and out of the direct firing line, and the bullets abruptly stopped. They were trapped in the middle of an open space, their only refuge being the experimental table and the painted door, and their aggressors stood between them and the nearest exit.

'Hold fire!' That was Lord Guantes' voice. He was concealed somewhere among the shadowy shelves. 'Your guns won't work – use the gas.'

The Language couldn't repel gas effectively. 'Retreat!' Irene called, scrambling to her feet and pulling Catherine with her.

Gas grenades were clattering into the area by the table as Irene and Catherine reached the shelves opposite Lord Guantes and his men. Kai and Vale were a few seconds behind, supporting Shan Yuan between them. 'Which way?' Kai demanded, most of his attention on his wounded brother.

'Straight ahead until we hit a wall, then sideways till we find a door—' Irene started.

'That's not necessary,' Catherine said, sudden certainty in her voice. 'I know the way out. Here.' She pointed with authority.

'We need to escape this world, not just the cathedral, and neither Shan Yuan nor I can take our true forms. If we can't fly, how can we leave?' Kai's eyes flicked to Catherine, and Irene heard what he wasn't saying. *We could all break out via the Library; she can't. We can't just leave her.*

Except – perhaps – was there a way she could get Catherine into the Library? 'Run first, I'll explain later,' Irene directed.

'Lord Guantes brought me down this way before and I remember it. *Follow me.*' Catherine led the way at a run, flitting between bookshelves and pillars without a moment's hesitation.

In the near-darkness the archive was harder to negotiate. Irene followed Catherine as closely as possible, unwilling to let the girl get out of her sight. Vale's lie to Alberich flashed through her mind. But it couldn't possibly be true, so she ignored it and focused on running. She could smell acrid gas on the air – not close enough to affect them, but close enough to remind her of the danger they faced. Lord Guantes could simply lock all the doors, turn off the ventilation and leave them to suffocate . . .

'Over here . . . there's a door!' Catherine had just reached the edge of the vast room. She pointed to her left, at something Irene couldn't yet see.

But as the group surged towards it, Catherine hesitated and caught Irene's wrist. 'I'll leave you here,' she said. Her chin was set, her face full of determination, but Irene could see the panic in her eyes as voices echoed in the shadows behind them. 'Lord Guantes might catch me, but he can't kill me, I don't think . . . My uncle would hunt him down. Or maybe I *can* walk out of here to another world on my own – after all, I've seen it done plenty of times.' But Irene knew her apprentice by now, and she knew wishful thinking when she saw it. 'I'll manage. You *go*,' Catherine insisted.

'Stay here a moment,' Irene ordered her apprentice – gripping her wrist, in case she decided to run off in a fit of heroism. Yes, Catherine had indeed found a door. It was labelled in various languages, *Fragmentary Texts: No Admission*. Well, a door was a door, and there were enough books in this archive for Irene to force a passage to the Library.

Irene set her free hand on the handle and focused her will. **'Door, unlock,'** she ordered. **'Open to the Library.'**

Slowly, all too slowly, the lock mechanism clicked open and the door shivered under Irene's hand. This close to chaos it was hard to make a door open to the Library. Hard, but not impossible, and she'd done it before from Alberich's own sanctum. With great reluctance it swung open into a well-lit, pale-walled room, its shelves neatly filled with black-bound books.

The light cast by the Library illuminated the darkness, a beacon for their pursuers. Irene cursed silently. 'Go through – now,' she ordered the men, then turned to Catherine. 'Give me your *name*,' she demanded.

'You know my name,' Catherine began, then she stopped. 'Oh.'

Yes. Irene required Catherine's true name, and for a Fae that was a huge demand. It was a request for the keys to Catherine's mind and soul. But Irene had an idea which she thought might just work. Vale had been contaminated by chaos once, and Irene had taken him to the Library to save him. She'd only managed this by using his real name. For the Fae, a true name – given at birth – had great power. No powerful Fae would reveal it, lest it be used against them – and none would ever pay that price to enter the Library. However, if Catherine trusted her . . .

'What if I don't want to give you my name?' Catherine said, looking into the darkness of the archive. 'I could run—'

'Then I'll shut this door and run with you,' Irene said. But she knew Catherine understood their chance of escape would be vanishingly slim. 'But if you can just trust me, I *promise* I won't use your name against you. And I think this might actually get you inside.'

Perhaps that was what tipped the balance, besides the alternative being capture and possible slavery at Lord Guantes' hands. Irene was offering the very thing that Catherine had wanted so much, for so long. She leaned in close, her voice barely audible as she whispered, 'Talita.'

Irene nodded, and stepped across the Library's threshold,

still holding Catherine by the hand. They'd run out of time for half-measures. **'Talita,'** she ordered, **'come into the Library.'**

As a sensation hummed through her body, Irene felt that something had fallen into place, like a key turning in a lock. And Catherine stumbled through the doorway, her eyes wide with shock.

Irene put one arm around her, holding her up. Or was Catherine holding her up, as her knees suddenly felt wobbly for some reason. Together, they looked back through the doorway into the dark archive. Their pursuers had found them, but were holding back, perhaps spooked by this door to nowhere they recognized.

Then Lord Guantes stalked into view, and there was murder in his eyes. 'You—' he started.

I'm doing you a favour, whoever you once were, Irene thought. *And now there's no Lady Guantes left to bring you back again and again. It's over.* Her voice was tired as she commanded, **'You perceive that you are not Lord Guantes.'**

The light streaming from the Library fell across Lord Guantes' face, and it revealed a sudden weariness. His features seemed to lack substance and reality now, as if Lord Guantes were a photograph fading out of focus. The shadow of another face appeared behind the one they knew, belonging to a different man. A man who now remembered who he was – but he was fading away, and knew it. That man inclined his head to Irene in a salute.

And then he fell to dust, leaving only his clothing behind.

CHAPTER TWENTY-SIX

Irene slammed the door to the archive shut. **'Close!'** she ordered.

She turned to the others, to check they were all there – as though Alberich could have sneaked in and stolen them away while she wasn't looking. Shan Yuan had collapsed to the polished wood floor, and Kai was tearing his shirt to shreds to bandage his brother's bullet wound. Vale was still upright, but looked shaken – understandably, given what he'd been through. Catherine (better to think of her by that name, in case of accidents) still supported Irene, but her eyes roved avidly around the room and she clearly longed to lose herself among the neat bookshelves.

Irene herself was still upright, alive and sane – relatively. It passed all belief.

'I'll find the nearest terminal and ask them to send help,' Irene said, with a glance at Shan Yuan. He was conscious, but the glare he shot her suggested he wasn't happy about the way events had played out. Really, some people were never satisfied. He might have been kidnapped, imprisoned, shot and threatened with possession – and the obliteration of his personality – but he was safe *now*, wasn't he?

She stopped for a moment to touch Kai's shoulder, then

headed into the corridor beyond. Vale was a step behind her, and Catherine followed Vale. *That* she'd been expecting, and she raised a hand towards the Fae girl. 'No. You stay here.'

'But . . .' Catherine protested, managing to pack whole volumes of protest into one syllable.

'I know you want to explore,' Irene said, striving for patience, 'but I need to report this – we've *never* had a Fae within our walls before. And I don't want to spend the next year hunting for you if you get lost.'

The look of enthusiasm in her apprentice's eyes made Irene realize she might have incited exploration, not curbed it. She sighed. 'Please, Catherine. Wait here.'

The *or else* in her voice must have got through, for Catherine slumped a little and nodded, rejoining the dragon brothers.

Relieved, Irene went to look for a computer. She didn't recognize the corridor that ran past the room. It was floored with distinctive mosaic tiles, arranged in a tessellated gold and brown pattern. Candles burned in sconces along the whitewashed stone walls, casting a gentle, forgiving light. She picked left at random, and two doors along she found what she was looking for – a computer terminal.

It only took her a moment to send a quick email demanding help, as a matter of urgency, and she could then turn and face Vale.

It had been a lie. What he'd said to Alberich *must* have been a lie.

But in his eyes she saw something far worse than complicity in a game, or guilt at an untruth. She saw a cold, compassionate pity. She managed to get out, 'Why did you say what you did, back there?'

'Be precise, Winters.' The candlelight emphasized the harsh lines of his face and body; a man of will and determination but little softness. 'Ask your real question. You will find it easier than your usual habit of avoiding awkward topics.'

'Why did you tell Alberich I was his daughter?' She'd meant to keep calm, but anger and disbelief made her voice shake. 'I know it confused him and that's how I escaped his control – but why would you say *something like that*?'

'Because all the evidence suggests that you are, Winters.' He sat down wearily in one of the chairs, resting an elbow on the table. 'You are the adopted child of two Librarians, and your parents have always been extremely reluctant to discuss this with you – they didn't even tell you that you were adopted until the information came out through other channels. Alberich had a child who was lost to him, whom the mother bore inside the Library. And you managed to break Alberich's warding circle using your own blood. You *thought* that you did it by exploiting a metaphorical loophole, relying on the metaphorical "family" of Librarians. But he himself said that should have been impossible. That only leaves a *genuine* blood connection with Alberich . . . which you could only have acquired through your parents – or parent.'

'How did you know that? About the warding circle?'

'Catherine told me.'

'Alberich could have been wrong about the warding circle,' she argued. 'Just because he managed to create something doesn't mean I *couldn't* subvert it.'

'To be frank, Winters, one of the most convincing pieces of evidence was seeing you both together when Alberich took the form of his original human body.'

'You mean I *look like him*?' The idea was not only ridiculous, it was repulsive.

'There is a . . . family resemblance.'

'This is all *complete supposition*.' Irene wanted to grab Vale by the shoulders and shake him. Her hands curled into fists, and she felt the scar tissue which laced her palms. A reminder of the first time she'd encountered Alberich. 'Vale, you pride yourself on your logical deductions, but what you've given me is no more than a hypothesis. Two negatives don't make a positive. Just because *I* may be an orphan and *he's* missing a child doesn't make us related. It was just a lie, a very *good* lie and one that staggered him enough for me to break his link—'

'But you may wish to ask yourself why *he* believed it.'

Irene remembered those moments when Alberich's thoughts were inside her mind, the way that they'd invaded her like the spores of fungus, like decay . . . and what his conclusion had been. Slowly, quietly, the foundations of her world began to fall away. She wanted to say that it wasn't fair, that it wasn't right, and that it *couldn't* have happened that way. But in front of her lay the clear and obvious possibility that it could be true.

That it was true.

Vale must have recognized her moment of acceptance. His shoulders sagged and she saw that he was as exhausted as she was. 'Sometimes Fate plays unkind tricks on us, Winters. Morally you are everything that he isn't – and yet, there is a resemblance.'

'Then why did nobody ever see it before?'

'Probably because very few have seen Alberich's original face.' Vale considered this, then added, 'And lived to describe him afterwards. Even fewer have seen him with you. Perhaps some of the older Librarians . . .'

'They'd know. They must know. Even if my parents don't know where I came from, the Librarians who organized the adoption *must* have known . . .' She turned away and began to pace the chamber. She was remembering every time a senior Librarian had looked at her strangely, every time she'd been reprimanded for doing something wrong . . . everything seemed to signal that the whole Library had known except for her. 'I don't *care* what my superiors want any more, what they think would be best for me. I'm going to demand the truth – whatever it costs. Even if I have to leave the Library. I have to *know*.'

She took a deep breath and made herself stop pacing. Then she turned and saw Kai in the doorway, and her self-control went out of the window. She couldn't meet his eyes. For the first time she actually understood the impulse that made fictional protagonists scream they were unclean, damned for life, just because of some little problem like being bitten by a vampire or blackmailed for a past love affair. She didn't want him to know this about her. She didn't want him to have *any reason* to connect her with Alberich.

And yet, she also wanted his comfort, his understanding. She felt her lip wobble and suddenly wanted to sit down, to curl in a ball and hide. She could talk to Vale about this rationally, or at least relatively rationally. But with Kai it was . . . different. He'd given her the gift of his trust. She didn't want to lose it. To lose him.

'It doesn't matter whether it's true or not,' Kai said softly. He crossed the room and took her hands in his. 'Even if it is, you're not your father.'

'You heard?' she faltered.

'I heard enough.' He wouldn't let go of her hands, but he did raise them so that he could inspect her wrist. 'That needs bandaging again. Sit down and I'll see what I can do.'

Vale rose and placed his hand on Irene's shoulder for a moment. 'I'll see to the others, Winters,' he said. 'You stay here until you've got your breath back.' He left the two of them together.

'But Kai, I need to report this . . . I must go back and help Catherine!' Irene's mind was spinning after Vale's revelations, and she needed the structure of her default position – taking charge, *doing something*.

'You're in shock.' Kai backed her towards one of the chairs and gave her a gentle push. The chair caught her behind the knees and she sat down involuntarily. He knelt in front of her and began unwinding the crude bandage round her wrist, inspecting the wound. 'As someone who loves you, it's my duty to make sure you don't do anything now that you'll regret later.'

Irene opened her mouth, then shut it again. They'd avoided the word *love*. It had been enough for them to know that they'd go into danger, risk their lives for each other . . . do whatever was necessary for each other's life, liberty and pursuit of happiness. They both knew their superiors could order them apart, and that they'd be expected to obey. Irene might be assigned elsewhere. Kai might be also be posted to a different world, or ordered into a mating contract by his father. And even if none of that happened – she was human, and he was a dragon. He would outlive her by centuries.

The fact that they *were* together, that they'd somehow managed to reach this point where they could share a bed, a house and each other's trust, was more than Irene had hoped or dreamed. She didn't need to add the word *love* to it as well. Wasn't that too dangerous? Wasn't it tempting fate?

She wanted to cry. She bit her lip instead and stayed silent, looking down at Kai's hands on hers as he rewrapped her wound with another strip torn from his shirt. Her wrist ached. Her whole body ached. And her mind ached – both from Alberich's attempted possession and from what she'd just discovered. Here in the silence of the Library, at *home*, she thought she'd be able to find peace. But instead her mind ran in circles and she couldn't find a way out.

'Kai,' she said very quietly, 'what am I going to do?'

'Stop. Think. We'll find a way.' He shrugged. His arms were bare: he'd torn off his shirtsleeves to make bandages. 'You've already dealt with the Guantes and checkmated Alberich. This revelation is just the next thing, one more problem to solve.' He looked up at her and smiled. And in spite of the smoke and blood that matted his hair, the grazes on his alabaster skin and the tiredness in his blue eyes – or perhaps because of them – he was utterly beautiful. 'I *know* you, Irene. So do your friends. And if anyone tries to make assumptions, on the basis of blood or family, they will be badly mistaken.'

But what – the thought crossed her mind belatedly – what about her mother?

'Is your brother all right?' she asked, trying to focus on something manageable.

Kai shrugged. 'He's unhappy. He really wanted that artificial intelligence research. He says he's going to apply to my father to have me removed from my post – for incompetence.'

Irene sat up straight. '*Incompetence*? He was the one who jumped in uninvited and almost . . .' She restrained herself from stronger language. '. . . made a big mess of things. You did an excellent job.'

'So did you.' He finished tying the bandages. '*And* you brought Catherine into the Library. An amazing job. No one else has ever managed such a thing—'

'Which means an even harder assignment next time,' Irene said with a sigh. But this was familiar territory.

Catherine chose that moment to poke her head around the door. 'Are you up for answering questions, Irene?'

'Possibly,' Irene said. 'Probably. What questions?'

'Mostly, what's next?'

'Right this minute? We wait for help to arrive. We have injured. Including me. On a wider scale – I'd say it's up to you.' Irene met the Fae's eyes. 'What do you actually want,

Catherine? Are you still prepared to give up everything to be a librarian – or do you want to be a Librarian?'

Catherine affected a look of deep consideration, but she'd clearly already come to a decision. 'I may have been a bit hasty before,' she said with the air of someone making a major concession. 'I can actually see a number of good points in being a Librarian spy, like you. As long as missions don't all end up like this. Of course, I need more lessons. More experience. Perhaps some more book-collecting expeditions . . .'

'We can definitely work on that.' Irene let Kai help her to her feet, leaning on him, and remembered why she'd become a Librarian in the first place. Whether or not Alberich was her father, her love of books, her pure enthusiasm for the job, had been all her own. It was healing to see it reflected in her apprentice's face. 'Yes,' she said, squeezing Kai's hand and feeling the pressure returned, 'we'll help you become a Librarian.' She looked around at the Library, her home. 'Whatever else may come – that journey starts here.'

EPILOGUE

The heavy books were crowded together on their stone shelves. A fanciful bibliophile might imagine them fossilized into strata, forming veins of precious literature running through the rock. There were no artificial lights down here, but glowing translucent forms flickered along the book-lined corridors and illuminated the place, allowing a hypothetical observer to at least read the titles of the volumes they passed. There had been no attempt at organization or classification; this was a black hole of tightly packed fiction.

Subterranean passages wound through the stacks. It was possible to lose oneself among books in multiple directions, up and down and in between, but the walkways finally led to an open space. This seemed incongruous when compared with its cramped surroundings – it was somehow larger than it should have been, with no discernible ceiling. The stone-work that supported its sides was ancient, yet well preserved. The river that ran through its centre, before plunging into the hidden depths below, supplied a constant background murmur of sound. Two figures lounged at a table by the river's side, and a third paced nearby.

'Well,' said one seated figure. Shadows trailed behind him

in a long serpentine sweep, and yet more shadows crowned his brow with horns. '*Finally.*'

'It took them long enough.' The second seated figure was swathed in darkness, its face changing from one moment to the next, as though constantly shifting between a selection of masks. 'But certain criteria had to be fulfilled for us to move forward. First, we needed peace and stability. Next, Fae needed to be able to get in here. If we'd given them a nudge, prompted someone earlier —'

'We've discussed this matter before.' A brief thunder echoed in the wake of the first speaker's voice, rumbling in the impossible sky above. 'We agreed no interference. They can't be allowed to suspect *anything* until we're ready to move. The traitor showed just how dangerous that could be to us.'

The masked figure made a dismissive gesture; thousands of actors would have died with envy at the sheer perfection of the movement. 'That was why we installed the failsafe in their brands, remember. Though I still think that "instant death" was overdoing it. Triggering deafness would have been just as effective.'

'But not as reliable,' the first said.

The third figure stopped pacing to approach the seated pair. Her robe was plain, her manner deferential, but she spoke with the ease of centuries of acquaintance. Her use of honorifics seemed more of a habit than a genuine courtesy. 'My lords, we've been through this so many times before. Does this mean we're ready to set things in motion at last?'

'We're ready to deploy our agents, on both sides,' the second figure said. 'But what about the traitor? When he finds out that a Fae's accessed the Library, he'll know we're ready for our endgame. He's been a danger throughout, but if he perceives we're about to move . . .'

'We could kill two birds with one stone?' the third

suggested. 'The other Librarian's uncomfortably well informed. I still don't know *why* she was directed to the Egyptian document, as it told her far too much. If we have her dispose of the traitor, neither might survive the encounter. But even if she makes it and he doesn't, we still come out ahead.'

'There's the risk of the traitor converting her,' the second said. 'If he can tell her his story . . .'

The first snorted. 'No risk now. He's put himself beyond forgiveness. Very well, I concur. And if we send her after him, she won't be investigating what we're doing with the treaty. She's the Library's official representative, so there's a good chance she'd be drawn into that otherwise. We need the treaty and the stability it brings – but we don't need *her*.'

The second slowly nodded. 'Agreed, then. But tell me – why was the Egyptian document marked for Library acquisition in the first place? We agreed centuries ago that nothing relating to *our* history should be brought here.'

The first turned his head to look at the third figure. 'You're the one with the closest relationship to the living mortals who work here. Why *was* it permitted?'

She spread her hands. 'I don't know, my lords. I regularly curate the acquisition lists to check these risks are managed – but somehow it slipped past. As to why *she* was given the assignment, I don't understand that either. I sometimes think . . .'

'Yes?' the second asked, when she was silent a little too long.

'I sometimes think, my lords, that the Library has a will of its own.'